Game

Game

BARRY LYGA

Ⓛ Ⓑ

Little, Brown and Company

New York   Boston

Copyright © 2013 by Barry Lyga

Little, Brown and Company

Hachette Book Group
237 Park Avenue, New York, NY 10017
Visit our website at www.lb-teens.com

Little, Brown and Company is a division of Hachette Book Group, Inc.
The Little, Brown name and logo are trademarks of Hachette Book Group, Inc.

The publisher is not responsible for websites (or their content) that are not owned by the publisher.

First Edition: April 2013

Library of Congress Cataloging-in-Publication Data

Lyga, Barry.
  Game / by Barry Lyga. — First edition.
    pages cm
  Sequel to: I hunt killers.
  Summary: After solving a deadly case in the small town of Lobo's Nod, seventeen-year-old Jazz, the son of history's most infamous serial murderer, travels to New York City to help the police track down the Hat-Dog Killer.
  ISBN 978-0-316-12587-1
  [1. Serial murderers—Fiction. 2. Murder—Fiction. 3. Psychopaths—Fiction. 4. New York (N.Y.)—Fiction. 5. Mystery and detective stories.]
  I. Title.
  PZ7.L97967Gam 2013
  [Fic]—dc23

                                                            2012040157

10 9 8 7 6 5 4 3 2 1

RRD-C

Book design by Alison Impey

Printed in the United States of America

For Kathy. Finally.

Part One

3 Players, 2 Sides

CHAPTER 1

She had screamed, but she had not cried.

That's what he would remember about this one, he thought. Not the color of her hair or her eyes. Not the tilt of her hips, the curve of her lips. None of those things. Not even her name.

She had screamed. Screamed to an uncaring, star-pocked sky. They all screamed. Everyone screamed.

But she had not cried.

Not that crying would have helped. He was going to kill her no matter what, so her behavior was moot. And yet it stuck with him: No tears. No weeping. Women always cried. It was their last, best weapon. It made boyfriends apologize and husbands fold them in their arms. It made Daddy spend the extra money on the prom dress.

She screamed. Her screaming was beautiful.

But, truth be told, he missed the crying.

Later, when he was finished, he looked down on her. The early morning—so early the sun had yet to rise—was warm and the air held the slight tang of motor oil. Now that she was silent and dead and still, he could no longer remember why he had killed her. For a brief moment, he wondered if that was strange, but dismissed the doubt immediately. She was one of what would be many. There had been others, and there would be more.

Kneeling next to her, he unsheathed a short, sharp knife. Ran his fingertips over her for a moment.

He decided on the left hip. He began to carve.

CHAPTER 2

The dying man's name was...

Well, it didn't matter. Not anymore. Not right now. Names were labels for *things*, the killer knew. Nouns. Person, place, thing, idea—just like you learned in school. See this thing I drink from? I give it the label of "cup," and so what? See this thing I cover my body with? I give it the label of "shirt," and so what? See this thing I have opened to the darkening sky, allowing beautiful moonlight to shine within? I give it the label of "Jerome Herrington," and so what?

The killer stood and stretched, arching his back. Carrying the thing labeled Jerome Herrington up five flights of stairs hadn't been easy; his muscles were sore. Fortunately, he wouldn't have to carry the thing labeled Jerome Herrington back down.

The thing's head twisted left and right, the eyes staring straight ahead, unblinking. Unblinking because they had no choice—the killer had removed the eyelids first. Always first. Very important.

The killer crouched down near the thing's head and whispered, "We're very close now. Very close. I've opened your gut, and I have to say—you're beautiful in the moonlight. So very beautiful."

The thing labeled Jerome Herrington said nothing, which the killer found rude. And yet the killer was not angry. The killer knew what anger was, but had never experienced it. Anger was a waste of time and energy. Anger was useless. "Anger" was the label given to an emotion that accomplished nothing.

Maybe the thing labeled Jerome Herrington simply did not and could not appreciate its own beauty. The killer pondered a moment, then reached down and lifted a blood-slippery mass of intestines from the thing's open cavity. Moonlight glinted on the shiny, gray-red loops.

The thing labeled Jerome Herrington groaned with deep and abiding agony. It raised its head, straining as though to escape, barely able to keep its head aloft.

The thing blubbered. Tears streamed down its cheeks and it tried to speak.

The killer beamed. The thing sounded happy. That was good.

"Almost done," the killer promised, dropping the guts. At the same moment, the thing's neck gave out and its head dropped. *Kunk!* went one. *Splet!* went the other.

The killer slid a small, sharp knife from his boot. "I think the forehead," he said, and began to carve.

CHAPTER 3

Billy Dent stared in the mirror. He didn't quite recognize himself, but that was nothing new. Billy had almost always seen a stranger in mirrors, ever since childhood. At first he had hated and feared the figure that seemed to pursue him everywhere, stalking him through mirrors and store windows. But eventually Billy came to understand that what he saw in the mirror was what other people saw when they looked at him.

Other people somehow did not see the real Billy. They saw something that looked like them. Something that looked human and mortal. Something that looked like a prospect.

From outside came the grinding, mechanical sound of a trash compactor. Billy parted the curtains and looked out. Three stories down, a trash truck was smashing recycled cans and bottles.

Billy grinned. "Oh, New York," he whispered. "We're gonna have so much fun."

Part Two

4 Players, 3 Sides

CHAPTER 4

It was a cold, clear January day when they gathered to bury Jazz's mother.

Bury was probably the wrong word; there was no body. Janice Dent had disappeared more than nine years ago, when Jazz was eight, and hadn't been seen since. The world knew she was dead; the courts had declared her dead after the requisite seven-year waiting period. Jazz just hadn't been able to bring himself to take the final step.

A funeral.

As the only child of the world's most notorious serial killer, he'd grown up with an intimate understanding of the mechanisms and the causes of death. But, strangely enough, he'd never attended a funeral until now.

This was poetic justice, in a way: Many of his father's victims had had funerals without bodies, too. They would have had more mourners, of course. For Janice Dent, wife of Billy, there were fewer than a dozen people. The press, fortunately, was held back at the cemetery gate.

No one would cry for Janice Dent. Not today. Her parents were long dead, and she'd been an only child. She had no friends left in Lobo's Nod that Jazz knew of, at least no one who had come forth when the funeral had been announced. Jazz figured this was fitting; she had vanished alone, and now she would be buried alone.

Next to him, his girlfriend, Connie, squeezed his hand tightly. On the other side of him stood G. William Tanner, the sheriff of Lobo's Nod and the man who had brought Billy Dent to justice more than four years ago. He was the closest thing Jazz had to a father figure, an irony that Billy would probably have laughed at. That was just Billy's sense of humor.

"Dear Lord," the priest said, "we ask that you continue to look over our beloved sister Janice in your kingdom. She has been gone from us for a while, O Lord, and we know you have watched over her in that time. Now we ask you to watch over us, as well, as we grieve for her."

Jazz found himself in the strange position of wanting this to be over as quickly as possible, for the priest to wrap things up and let them all go. Ever since Lobo's Nod's assault by the Impressionist—a Billy Dent wannabe—and then Billy's escape from prison into the wide world a couple of months ago, Jazz had felt a burning need to close off as much of his past as possible. He knew the future portended a brutal reckoning (Billy had been quiet, but that wouldn't last), so he wanted his past put to rest. Finally acknowledging his mother's death was the biggest step he'd taken so far.

Jazz hadn't cared which faith buried his mother; Father

McKane at the local church had been the most willing to perform the service, so Jazz had gone Catholic. Now, as the priest droned on and on, Jazz wondered if he should have held out for a less verbose brand of religion. He sighed and gripped Connie's hand and stared straight ahead at the casket. It contained a bunch of brand-new stuffed animals, similar to the ones Jazz remembered his mother buying him as a child. It also contained a batch of lemon-frosted cupcakes Jazz had baked. That was his strongest memory of his mother—the lemon-frosted cupcakes she used to bake. He could have just had a service and a stone, but he'd wanted the whole experience, the totality of the funeral ritual. He wanted to witness the literal expression of burying his past.

Sentimental? Probably. And what of it? Bury it all. Bury the memories and the sentiment and move on.

Arrayed around the cemetery, he knew, were more than a dozen police officers and federal agents. Once the authorities had gotten wind of Jazz's plan to hold a funeral service for his mother, they had insisted on staking it out, certain (or maybe just hopeful) that Billy wouldn't be able to resist this opportunity to emerge from hiding. It was a waste of time, Jazz had told them, his insistence as useless as a sledgehammer against a tidal wave.

Billy would never reveal himself for something as prosaic and predictable as a funeral. He had occasionally attended the funerals of his victims, but that was before cable news had splashed his face on HD screens all around the world. "Butcher Billy" was too smart to show that famous face here, of all places.

"We're going to make a go of it, anyway," an FBI agent had told Jazz, who had shrugged and said, "You want to waste tax dollars, I guess that's your prerogative."

Finally the priest finished up. He asked if anyone would like to say anything at the grave, looking pointedly at Jazz. But Jazz had nothing to say. Nothing to say in public, at least. He'd come to terms with his mother's death years ago. There was nothing *left* to say.

To his surprise, though, the priest nodded and pointed just over Jazz's shoulder. Jazz and Connie both turned—he caught the shock of her expression, too—and watched as Howie Gersten, Jazz's best friend, threaded carefully between G. William and Jazz, studiously avoiding meeting Jazz's eyes. Dressed in a black suit with a somber olive tie, six foot seven at the age of seventeen, Howie looked like a white-boy version of the images Jazz had seen of Baron Samedi, the skeletal voodoo god of the dead. The suit jacket was slightly too short for Howie's ridiculously long limbs, and a good two inches of white shirt cuff and pale wrist jutted out.

"My name is Howie Gersten," Howie said once he'd gotten to the gravestone. Jazz almost burst out laughing. Everyone here knew who Howie was already. "I didn't know Mrs. Dent. But I just really feel like when you bury someone, when you say good-bye, that someone should say something. And I figure that's my job as Jazz's best friend." Howie cleared his throat and glanced at Jazz for the first time. "Don't be pissed, dude," he stage-whispered.

A ripple of laughter washed over the attendees. Connie shook her head. "That boy..."

14

"Anyway," Howie went on, "here's the thing: When I was a kid, I used to get pushed around a lot. I'm a hemophiliac, so I have to be careful all the time, and when you combine that with being a gangly string bean, it's like you're just asking for trouble, you know? And I wish I could tell you that Mrs. Dent was nice to me and used to say kind and encouraging things to me when I was going through all of that, but like I said, I didn't know her. By the time I met Jazz, she was already, y'know, not around.

"But here's the thing. Here's the thing. And I think it's an obvious thing, but someone needs to say it. We all know that, uh, Jazz's dad wasn't, isn't, exactly a great role model. But there I was one day when I was like ten or something and these kids were having a fine old time poking bruises into my arms. And Jazz came along. He was smaller than them and outnumbered, and let's face it—I wasn't going to be much help—"

Another ripple of laughter.

"But Jazz just waded into those douchebags—um, sorry, Father. He just waded into them and kicked their, um, rears, which I know isn't terribly Christian or anything, but I'll tell you, it looked pretty good from where I was standing. And I guess the thing is—the obvious thing that I mentioned before is—that I never met Mrs. Dent, but I know she must have been a good person because I'm pretty sure Billy Dent didn't raise Jazz to rescue helpless hemophiliacs from bullies. And that's all I have to say. I'll miss you, Mrs. Dent, even though I never met you. I wish I had." He started to walk back to the group of mourners, then stopped and said, "Um, God bless you and amen and stuff," before hustling back to his spot.

15

And then they lowered the casket into the ground. The stone said JANICE DENT, MOTHER. No dates, because Jazz couldn't be sure exactly when Billy had killed her.

He took the small spade from the priest and shoveled some dirt into the grave. It rattled.

G. William and Connie and Howie followed suit. Then they backed away so that the cemetery workers could do the real shoveling.

Jazz became aware that he was staring at the shovels as they heaved dirt on top of the casket that did not hold his mother's body, snapping out of it only when Connie poked him to get his attention. She held a tissue out for him.

"What's this for?" he asked, taking it automatically.

"Your eyes," she said, and Jazz realized that—much to his surprise—he was crying.

CHAPTER 5

Jazz's grandmother was waiting for him when he got home, sitting on the porch in a rocking chair, a blanket thrown over her legs. From all appearances, she looked like just another old lady enjoying a crisp day in January.

"They're here," she whispered to Jazz as he mounted the front steps. "They've come for your daddy."

Jazz wasn't sure who she meant when she said "your daddy." Gramma was delusional enough that she sometimes thought Jazz was Billy, meaning that she could think "they" had come for Jazz's long-dead grandfather. Or she could be lucid enough to think that the "they" in question—actually Deputy Michael Erickson, who had volunteered to keep an eye on Gramma during the funeral—were here for Billy himself. Which meant that Gramma's thinking was roughly on par with the FBI's these days. Jazz wasn't sure if that was funny or sad.

He could see Erickson peering out at them from the corner of a window. Gramma had hated Mom, so there was no way in the world Jazz was going to have her at the funeral.

And even if Gramma had loved Janice, when given the choice between inviting his black girlfriend or his insane, racist grandmother, Jazz would choose Connie every time.

"They sent spies," Gramma went on, her voice a hush, "and they look like one man, but they can split into two, then four, and so on. I've seen it before. During the war. It's a Communist trick and they taught it to the Democrats so that they could take our guns. I would have fought them off, but they already made the shotgun disappear."

No, *Jazz* had made the shotgun disappear. It was Grampa's old hunting piece, and Jazz had plugged both barrels and removed the firing pins so that Gramma couldn't really hurt anyone with it. But when he was going to be gone for a long stretch—like today—he made sure to hide it from her. It was nice to know that she was blaming Washington politicians and not him.

Years of dealing with Gramma's progressively deteriorating mental state had rendered Jazz pretty much impervious to shock. "So, there's a commie spy in the house looking for Dad, huh?" he said. *There's a sentence I never thought I'd hear myself say.* "Don't worry. I'm gonna go in there and run him out. He won't dare come back by the time I'm done with him." He brandished the ceremonial spade the priest had given him at the end of the service as though it were a samurai sword.

Gramma's eyes widened, and she clapped her hands. "Gut him!" she yelled. "Gut him like that raccoon you gutted on Fourth of July that one year!" And she made vicious stabbing and hacking motions as Jazz went inside.

"How's it going?" he asked Erickson. "Other than the usual."

Erickson shrugged. "She started bugging out about an hour ago. I just decided to go with it. As long as I could keep an eye on her from in here, I figured it was better just to let her sit outside."

"Good call. She thinks you're some kind of Communist clone, by the way."

Erickson laughed. "That explains a lot."

"Anyway, I'd consider it a big personal favor if you could sort of run like hell on your way out of here."

"For you? Anything."

Jazz felt a pang of guilt. Erickson was a good cop, relatively new to the tiny town of Lobo's Nod, transferring in right as the Impressionist had begun his string of Billy Dent–inspired murders. To his eternal shame, Jazz had suspected Erickson in the crimes and hadn't been shy about letting the sheriff know it. After that, he figured he was the one who owed Erickson, but the deputy didn't see it that way. As far as Erickson was concerned, Jazz's deducing and rescuing the Impressionist's next victim made him a hero.

"Thanks again for watching her."

"Take care of yourself, Jasper." Erickson opened the door and then burst through as if chased by demons, screaming in a hilariously high voice all the way to his squad car.

Gramma minced into the house, peering around. "He didn't leave any little baby spiders, did he? They're tiny mind-controllers, and they crawl into your ears while you're

19

asleep and rewire your brain until you don't know who you are anymore."

Ah, so that's what had happened to Gramma....Jazz sighed. She was getting worse. He'd always known she was getting worse, but somehow he'd convinced himself that her madness was manageable and harmless. Once upon a time not long ago, a social worker named Melissa Hoover had moved heaven and earth to get Jazz removed from Gramma's house to a foster home. Jazz had resisted, and then Billy—after his escape from prison—had killed Melissa before she could submit her report, putting an end to that particular problem.

For now.

The fact of the matter was that soon enough Social Services would get around to assigning another caseworker to Jazz. He still had six months until his eighteenth birthday— they could still yank him from Gramma's house. And Jazz was beginning to think that maybe Melissa had been right after all. Maybe he needed to be out of this environment. Away from his grandmother. Away from Lobo's Nod, even. Away from all the memories of his childhood and of Billy.

Oh, who was he kidding? Billy was out there in the world somewhere. As long as Billy was free, Jazz could never escape his past. His father would, he knew, find him and contact him. Somehow. Some way. No matter how many cops and FBI agents were looking for him and surveilling Jazz, Billy would find a way.

Jazz settled Gramma in the parlor in front of the TV. The first channel he happened to see was local news. Doug

Weathers—sleazebag reporter par excellence—was speaking to the camera: "—funeral of Janice Dent, wife of the notorious William Cornelius Dent, also known as the Artist, Green Jack, Hand-in-Glove, and many other aliases. The press was not invited, but we can tell you that the service was brief and sparsely attended—"

Jazz quickly flipped over to a shopping channel. Gramma found them hilarious.

In the kitchen, he started washing the dishes Gramma had used while he was gone. Erickson had stacked them neatly in the sink for him, a far cry from Gramma's latest habit of sticking them in the broiler. As he soaped and sponged them, he gazed out the kitchen window at the backyard.

And the birdbath.

You know that old birdbath my momma's got in her backyard?

Billy. In the visitation room at Wammaket State Penitentiary.

She's got it oriented to a western exposure. See? It's not gettin' the morning light, and that's what them birds want. It needs to be moved to the opposite edge of the lawn.

They'd argued. Jazz had felt like an idiot, arguing with his sociopathic mass-murdering father about a *birdbath....*

Just move the damn thing. Go when she's asleep and just move it. You know, where that big ol' sycamore sits.

And this, Jazz had said with incredulity, *is the price of your help?*

And it had been. And so Jazz had done as Billy had commanded. Even now, months later, he wasn't sure exactly why.

Billy had no way of enforcing the favor he'd asked, after all. But Jazz had felt honor bound to do it. As though not moving that damn birdbath would have proven that he was an uncaring, unfeeling sociopath like Dear Old Dad, would have cemented his fate. So he'd moved it, and that very night Billy had broken out of prison.

Soon after the escape and its horrifying aftermath, Jazz had come clean to G. William, confessing to the sheriff that he'd done a favor for Billy. "I don't see how it could be connected," he'd said. "But I also don't see how it couldn't be."

The next day—much to Gramma's deluded consternation—a team made up of local cops and FBI analysts had descended on Jazz's backyard. They dug up the ground where the birdbath had rested for years. They dug up the ground under its current location. They took sightings with surveyors' tools along multiple angles, checking to see who or what might have a clear line of sight to the birdbath.

And they had also examined the birdbath itself, ultimately discovering the truth that destroyed Jazz.

Four screws held part of the fountain casing in place. Three of them were old and tarnished, but one was newer, still shiny. A bomb expert was called in—just in case—and when the screws were removed and the mechanism disassembled, they found...

"A GPS transmitter," G. William told Jazz later that night in the sheriff's office, where he'd summoned Jazz. "Pretty good one, too. Accurate to five meters."

"Or one backyard," Jazz muttered.

"Well..." G. William clearly didn't want to confirm it.

The big man's florid, misshapen nose—bashed out of normalcy after a lifetime of being a cop—went bright red as the rest of his face paled. "Well, yeah."

"So I move the birdbath and somewhere in the world, Billy's lunatic confederate sees the Bat-signal and realizes it's time to spring his Lord and Master from Wammaket. Next thing you know, there are dead guardo—"

"Corrections officers," G. William emended.

"Corrections officers, right, and Billy is in the wind."

Billy's escape gnawed at him with rat teeth. Obviously, he would rather Dear Old Dad stay behind bars, leaving Wammaket only when zipped up into a nice little body bag all his own. But Melissa...and the deaths of the COs...ah, now those chewed at him with saber-tooth fangs. Was *he* responsible for their deaths? In a manner of speaking, sure—he had set in motion the events leading to Billy's escape, and the COs and Melissa had died as a result of that escape. But Jazz himself hadn't killed them. The corrections officers had died during a mini-riot that covered Billy as he broke out of the infirmary and made his way outside. And Melissa had died ugly, at Billy's own hand. Even if Jazz had known that moving the birdbath would mean Billy's escape, could he reasonably have assumed people would die in the process?

He didn't know. That didn't stop him from feeling guilt, though.

Unless it wasn't really guilt.

They got all these emotions, Billy had told him once. *Things like love and fear and compassion and regret. They got 'em deep inside, all twisty and tight like a knot of living snakes. They think they're in control of themselves, but they really just do what the snakes tell them.*

"They," of course, were ordinary people. Sheep. Potential victims. *Prospects* was the word Billy used to describe them. And their emotions? Well, those things were useless for people like Billy, but it was important to know how to fake them.

Is that what I'm doing? Jazz wondered. *I know I should feel guilty for getting those people killed. And Billy spent my whole life teaching me how to pretend to feel things I wasn't really feeling. Am I just fooling myself? Am I just acting guilty because that's how I'm supposed to act? What is it really supposed to feel like?*

Maybe Connie would know. Maybe Connie could describe it to him. Help him understand.

Maybe.

Almost against his will, he had shared more with Connie than he'd ever intended. He'd told her about the dreams, for example, the dreams in which he held a knife and cut... something. Or someone. He didn't know for sure. He'd wondered for the longest time who he'd been cutting in the dream. Maybe it was his mother, he'd wondered. Maybe he had killed her....

But the last time he'd seen Billy, his father had seemed to deny that, saying that Jazz was a killer...just one who hadn't killed yet. It was typical Billy double-talk, the kind of stuff Billy had said all of Jazz's life, words defined and redefined and misdefined to break down Jazz's natural inhibitions. *People out there ain't real*, Billy would say. *They ain't really real, not real like you're real or I'm real. They're real in their own false way. They think they're real, but they only get to think it because we let them, you see?*

Classic brainwashing tactics. Cults used them. Heck, most established religions did, too. The human mind was a horribly fragile thing—breaking it and reassembling it in a new order was so easy it was depressing.

People are real, Jazz told himself, repeating his mantra. *People matter.*

In the dream, though, nothing mattered. Nothing, that is, except for bringing down the knife, his father's voice urgent, the knife meeting the flesh...then parting it...

That dream was bad enough. But the new one...the one that had started the very night Billy escaped, the night Jazz met and defeated the Impressionist...

—touch—
—his hand runs up—
Oh, yes, you know—
—touching—
—you know how to—
The doorbell rang. Thank God.

Jazz got to the door before Gramma could, calming her as he cut through the parlor. "It's just the doorbell," he told her.

"Air raid!" Gramma screamed. "Air raid! Commie missiles!"

"Doorbell," Jazz assured her. "Look—Bowflex on TV!"

Gramma swiveled and hitched in a breath at the sight of

an oiled bodybuilder doing bench presses. "Muscles!" she shouted, and clapped like a little girl.

Jazz peered through the small window next to the door and heaved a sigh of relief that Gramma hadn't made it to the door first—the man on the porch was black, and Gramma's notion of racial tolerance hadn't evolved past the late forties. The *eighteen*-forties.

The man was unfamiliar, but Jazz recognized the stance, the poise. Not a reporter, thank God. The guy was a cop of some variety. Maybe even an FBI agent. In any event, it was no one Jazz wanted to talk to. He would have to shoo the guy off—if he just ignored him, he would ring the bell again and set Gramma off.

So he opened the door a crack and focused his sternest gaze out onto the porch. "We gave at the office. I don't like Girl Scout cookies. No, I would not like a copy of *The Watchtower*—we're Buddhist. Thanks and bye."

Before he could get the door closed, though, the cop moved with practiced ease and jammed his toe in the gap. "You don't work at an office. You were raised Lutheran. And what on earth do you have against Thin Mints?"

Jazz pushed against the door. Nothing doing. The cop was wearing steel-toed boots; he could stand there all day. "You caught me. I just don't like cops."

"Neither do I," the man said with forced joviality. "Come on, kid." His voice became suddenly earnest, almost pleading. "Give me five minutes. I promise I'll leave you alone after that."

"Last person I opened this door for turned out to be doing

his best impersonation of my father. You understand why I'm hesitant."

The man flipped open a small leather folder to reveal his badge. "I came all the way from New York to see you. Should be, like, a two-hour flight, but the department's so damn cheap, would you believe I had to make *two* connections? Took more like five hours. Plus, I had to rent a car. And I *hate* driving like you hate your pops. Five minutes. I swear on my badge."

Jazz scrutinized the badge. Looked authentic, as best he could tell. He'd never seen an actual NYPD badge, but he knew the basics. The ID card next to it had a lousy photo of the man on the porch, along with his name and rank: LOUIS L. HUGHES, DET. 2ND/GRADE. NYPD. BROOKLYN SOUTH. HOMICIDE DIVISION.

Despite himself, he was intrigued. New York. A New York cop. What could he—

Ah. Ah, he got it.

"This is about Hat-Dog, isn't it?"

"Five minutes. That's all."

That toe wasn't going anywhere, and as long as it stayed, Hughes would stay, too. Jazz sighed and opened the door. Before Hughes could step in, Jazz pushed him back and joined him on the porch, closing the door behind.

"It's getting cold out here," Hughes complained.

"I would invite you in, but my grandmother is an insane racist."

A snort. "As opposed to all those nice, *sane* racists out there?"

Jazz folded his arms over his chest. "Your five minutes

27

started thirty seconds ago. We can talk about the historic injustices that continue to be visited upon the African American community to this day, or you can talk about Hat-Dog."

Hughes nodded. "What do you know already?"

Jazz shrugged. "Just what's been on the news. Which means probably less than anything real or relevant." They shared a grimace of disdain for the media. "First killing was about seven months ago. There've been a total of fourteen so far. Most in Brooklyn. All show signs of a mixed organization killer—he's good at covering his tracks, but he goes buck wild on the bodies. Lots of mutilation. Maiming. Details withheld by the police 'to weed out possible false leads.'" Jazz thought for a moment. "I bet he's started disemboweling them, right?"

Hughes did a good job covering his surprise, but not so good that Jazz couldn't tell. "Yeah. How did you know that? That's one of the things we kept out of the news."

"Reading between the lines. There was a quote in one news story from the medical examiner, talking about 'a real mess.' And in the background of one of the pictures in the paper, you can see a CSI with a covered bucket. I played the odds."

Hughes pressed his lips together. "Not bad. Yeah, he's started disemboweling them."

"And his deal is he marks them, right? Didn't I read that? Some of them with a hat, some with a dog? Cuts it into them."

"Yeah. There's no pattern to that. At first we thought he was alternating, or marking the women with hats and the men with dogs. That would fit a certain sort of pathology.

But then we got a dog on a woman. Then two hats in a row. And a hat on a man. And then another couple of hats in a row. There's no pattern to it."

"There's a pattern to it," Jazz said. "It's just not one that you can see."

"And you can?"

"I didn't say that. It makes sense to *him*, though."

"I know," Hughes said testily. "I'm not right out of the academy. In this guy's head, the most sensible thing in the world is to grab up people and torture them and kill them and carve hats and dogs on them. I get it."

Jazz looked at his watch. "There's your five. I hope it was worth it."

"Wait!" Hughes threw out a beefy arm, blocking the front door. "Look, I didn't come here to gab with you on your front porch. I need—we, that is. We need your help."

Jazz laughed. "My help? What, because I caught the Impressionist? That was sort of a special circumstance."

"Oh? How so?"

"He was imitating my father. He was practically killing people in my backyard."

"I get it—so you only take the easy ones. And the people of New York just don't count. They might as well not be real to you."

People are real. People matter.

Words to live by, for Jazz. He had no other choice—the moment he stopped believing that (and it would be depressingly easy to do so, he feared) would be the moment he turned into his father.

But, yeah, people were real and people mattered, but Jazz couldn't save them all. Flush off his success of capturing the Impressionist, he'd gone and tattooed I HUNT KILLERS in gigantic black Gothic letters on his chest. A new mantra, this one inked directly into flesh so that he couldn't forget.

But in the months since the Impressionist's arrest, Jazz had hunted nothing more than his own self-doubt. Sure, "I hunt killers" *sounded* great and made for a nice little slogan, but at the end of the day, he was still seventeen. Still dealing with his disintegrating grandmother and her dilapidated house. Still trying to get through school. To figure out what the hell he would do when he graduated. The million mundane details of everyday life had made him feel old before his time, as though the promise of that tattoo had begun to fade the instant the ink dried. Maybe even while it was still wet.

Jazz sighed and watched his breath drift off and dissipate. "Look, Detective Hughes. I got...I got lucky. Once. I'm sure you guys are doing the best you can. You have the FBI and all the resources of the NYPD. I'm not going to be much more help."

"I disagree." Hughes leaned in close, his eyes wide and insistent. "You understand these guys, don't you? You have a lifetime's experience with them, in a way even the best, most dedicated profiler can't understand. All we can do is ask them questions after the fact. And who knows if they tell us the truth, or how much of the truth they bother with?

"You're different. You grew up with him. While he was still hunting. And he told you everything, didn't he?"

"Prospecting..." Jazz whispered before he could stop himself.

"What's that?"

"Nothing."

"You said 'prospecting.' Is that what your dad called it?"

"I said it's nothing." Jazz shoved Hughes's arm away from the door. "I can't help you. I'm seventeen, man. I've got school starting up in a few days."

"So? I'll write you a note. I write good notes." Hughes grinned, his teeth huge and almost predatory. "Look, it'll just be a couple of days. You come up, you look at some of the case files. Go to some of the crime scenes and work your mojo." Hughes waved his hands like a magician. "You're back before Christmas break is over. Maybe you miss one day of school. I will seriously write you a note, on NYPD letterhead and everything. I'll get the commissioner to sign it. The mayor. You can eBay it when he runs for president someday."

"I'm really sorry," Jazz said, and even though he wasn't all that sorry, it was no big trick to make Hughes think he was. The word *sorry* had magical properties. Say it with the right intonation and downcast eyes, and people will always believe it.

"My card," Hughes said, believing. "In case you change your mind."

Jazz tucked the card into his pocket without looking at it. "I won't," he said, and went inside.

31

CHAPTER 6

Touch me
   says the voice
   like that
   it goes on
   And he does.
   He touches.
   His fingers glide over warm, supple flesh.
   Touch me like that
   His skin on hers.
   Move on
   says the voice
   like that
   And his legs, the friction of them—
   And so warm
   So warm
   like that

Jazz woke up, trembling, but not because of the cold. His grandmother's old house was drafty and leaked like a torpedoed tugboat, but the space heater next to the bed kept him plenty warm.

He trembled from the dream. From what it meant. Or didn't mean. Or could mean.

He didn't know. Days like this—*nights* like this, he checked himself—he felt like he didn't know anything. Not a single thing in the whole wide world.

The new dream...

It was sex.

Duh.

Obviously.

In the old dream—the dream which now seemed to be relegated to special guest appearances as the new one took over the starring role, yee-haw!—he had been hurting someone. Cutting someone with a knife. And the question for him then had been this: Unless I've actually cut someone with a knife before, how could I know what it feels like? How could I dream it so...so...*keenly*?

Jazz was a virgin. Despite what Billy chose to believe, Jazz had never had sex. He was terrified by the possibility and the probability of it.

He longed for it, too, of course. He was, after all, seventeen years old and in good health. He had hormones pumping through his bloodstream like any other seventeen-year-old. Sometimes he wanted sex so bad that he thought he would pass out from the strain of desire. He was dizzy with wanting it.

But he was afraid of what it could lead to. Yes, there were

serial killers out there who had no sexual component to their depredations, but they were few and far between, so rare as to be almost nonexistent. And none of them had been programmed since birth by William Cornelius "Billy" Dent.

Jazz couldn't remember much of his childhood. Who knew what time bombs Billy had planted deep down in his subconscious?

Yeah, it was better to avoid sex. No matter how much he wanted it. No matter how smoking-hot his girlfriend was.

Would that last forever? Or just until the raging flush of teen hormones abated in his bloodstream? He had no idea. Didn't even want to speculate. But priests managed to live lifetimes without sex, right?

Well, some of them managed.

Poor Connie. She pretended like she didn't mind missing out on sex, but especially in the last couple of months, it had become obvious to Jazz that she was ready—eager, even— to take things to the next level. And he just couldn't do it.

He had to be strong. For both of them.

Rolling out of bed, he crept down the stairs. There was a bathroom upstairs, but it shared a wall with Gramma's room, and flushing the toilet would wake her up.

Washing his hands in the sink, he caught his bare torso in the mirror, and there it was: I HUNT KILLERS, tattooed in a V along his collarbone in those tall, black Gothic letters. It was tattooed backward so that he could read it in the mirror.

That's what I thought I was. A stalker of stalkers. A predator preying on predators.

Sounded good. In theory. But the reality was this: He was

just a messed-up kid living in a little town called Lobo's Nod. What could he do? Hop on a plane to New York at a moment's notice? Right. Who would watch Gramma? Who would take care of her and keep her deteriorating mental state a secret if he went off gallivanting to the big city to...do what? Sit in a squad room somewhere and regale a bunch of cops with tales of growing up under Billy's thumb? Would that really accomplish anything?

He turned this way and that in the mirror. In addition to his own tattoo, he also had four others: a massive pistol-packin' Yosemite Sam on his back, a stylized CP3 (for basketballer Chris Paul) on one shoulder, a string of Korean characters around his right biceps, and the latest addition: a flaming basketball on the other shoulder. These weren't really his tats—they were just renting space on his body. Howie's hemophilia prohibited him from getting tattoos, so Jazz had volunteered his body as Howie's personal billboard. He had always felt that this gesture was a point in his favor, something a true sociopath would never do. Now he wasn't so sure. Offering up his body like that? Permanently marring it without even really thinking about it? Was that the height of friendship or the height of lunacy?

He dried his hands and sneaked back upstairs without waking Gramma.

He'd gotten lucky with the Impressionist. Simple as that. The man had been obsessed with Billy, and that obsession bled over to Jazz. It would have been nearly impossible *not* to catch the Impressionist. The man had literally come knocking at Jazz's front door.

I don't hunt killers. I couldn't save Ginny Davis. I couldn't save Melissa Hoover. I almost couldn't save myself. Who am I kidding?

The Impressionist had been taking pictures and video of Jazz while he'd been in Lobo's Nod. Where he'd found the time between murdering Helen Myerson and Jazz's drama teacher and the others, Jazz had no idea. But the cops had recovered the pictures and video from the killer's cell phone when they'd arrested him. As soon as Jazz found out about them, he'd insisted on seeing them.

G. William, of course, had resisted. But Jazz was very persuasive. Natural gift for the progeny of a sociopath.

We're the most convincing people in the world, Billy liked to say. *Everyone wants to do us favors. Everyone wants to make us happy. Until they know what it* really *takes to make us happy. Then they tend to put up a fight.* He grinned here. *By then, it's usually too late for the fighting. But I guess they think they gotta try.*

So it had been a fait accompli—Jazz saw what his stalker had seen. Jazz outside the police station. On his way to the Coff-E-Shop. Hanging out with Howie. Holding hands with Connie on the way to play practice. A shot of his bedroom window at night, the light dimming.

"This is what it feels like," Jazz had murmured, clicking through the photos on G. William's computer.

"What what feels like?" the sheriff asked.

Jazz had paused before answering, "To be stalked." But that was just the kind answer, the answer G. William could accept. And of course he accepted it because it came from

Jazz and Jazz was the most convincing person in the world when he needed to be.

The truth—the *real* answer—was what he wanted to say but didn't: This is what it feels like to be one of *you*. This is what it feels like to be vulnerable. And weak. And merely human.

This is what it feels like to be a prospect.

Now Jazz tossed and turned in bed. On his wall were photographs of the one hundred and twenty-three people Billy Dent had admitted to murdering. Plus a photo of his mother.

His own mother had been a prospect.

He drifted into that twilight space between wakefulness and sleep, that place where the world is plastic and malleable and unsure.

His own mother...

He groaned as sleep fled from him, and stretched to grab up his jeans from the floor where he'd left them. Pawed around until he found the pocket and the card within.

There was a gold embossed shield to the left, with the words CITY OF NEW YORK POLICE DETECTIVE. The name LOUIS L. HUGHES, with DETECTIVE beneath it, along with two phone numbers, a fax number, and an e-mail address.

Oh, hell. Jazz reached for the phone. If he was gonna do this, he might as well enjoy waking Hughes up in the middle of the night.

CHAPTER 7

"Well," Connie told Jazz, doing her best to sound both forceful and casual at the same time, "obviously I'm going with you."

Jazz's expression didn't change. Connie cursed inwardly. It was so difficult to tell whether she'd gotten to him or not. He could conceal his reactions or fake them so well that even for her—even for the person who had gotten closer to him than anyone else in the world—it was impossible more often than not to tell what was going on behind those sexy and enigmatic eyes. Better luck reading a reaction from a portrait of him than the real deal.

"You're not going with me," he said very calmly, with the slightest hint of a smile. That smile...was it to catch her off guard? Was it a slip on his part? Did he want her to think it was a slip? Or was it—

"You're such a pain sometimes," she announced. "Would it kill you just to tell me what you're thinking and maybe not try to manipulate me?"

"I'm not trying to manipulate you. But you can't come to New York with me. For one thing, your dad would go ballistic, and I don't need that noise in my life."

Connie's father made no secret of his deep and abiding loathing for Jazz. Between Jazz's racist grandmother and Connie's dad, she figured they had the makings of a modern-day Romeo and Juliet on their hands. Only with more blood and death than even Shakespeare's fertile imagination could conjure.

"I can handle my dad," she said confidently. They were at the Hideout, Jazz's secret sanctum in the woods outside Lobo's Nod. It was an old moonshining shack that he'd repaired and outfitted with the bare essentials as a getaway from the rest of the world. Connie was pretty sure she was the only person he'd shared it with. She tried not to let him know how much that meant to her—he was constitutionally leery of opening himself to other people, and she didn't want to frighten him away. Snuggled together on a beanbag chair, they were as entwined as two clothed people could be, warmed by a space heater he'd rescued from his grandmother's basement.

"No one can handle your dad. Besides, I don't know how long I'll be gone, and you shouldn't miss school. And *besides* besides, what are you going to do while I'm off with the cops?"

"Golly," she chirped in her very best sorority girl impression, "maybe I'll go shopping and buy shoes and kicky skirts and makeup! Dumbass," she said, punching him in the shoulder and dropping her voice. "I'll be *helping* you. You think I'm going to see the sights?"

"I hear they have really tall buildings."

"And subways."

"And museums."

"And more than a dozen black people, too. It's truly a land of wonder."

"A miracle of our modern age," Jazz agreed, and kissed the back of her neck.

"Oh, don't do that," she admonished in a tone of voice that didn't convince even herself. "You're trying to distract me."

He kissed where her neck met her shoulder. "Mea culpa."

Connie's head swam. She both hated and loved being so deliriously vulnerable to him. She'd never felt this way with another boy, and she knew Jazz had never felt this way with another girl. Her friends were fond of telling her that she was drawn to Jazz Dent because he was the ultimate bad boy—whereas some girls fell for selfish jerks, Connie was in love with a guy who was quite literally deadly.

But that wasn't it. Connie loved him despite his past, despite his darkness, not because of it. She saw in him a light, a light buried so deep that Jazz himself never saw it. But she did. Not always. There were hours and days and sometimes whole weeks that would go by where she lost track of it, but never had it failed to resurface. Connie believed in Jazz's humanity more than he did.

A sexy, brooding boyfriend who didn't realize exactly *how* sexy and brooding he was? God save her! It was all she could do sometimes not to jump him, but she knew that he wasn't ready for that, no matter how ready he acted and felt.

They'd never discussed it, but it was clear to her. And she understood. Just reading about Billy Dent's crimes had freaked her out; growing up with a dad whose version of "the talk" included binding techniques and torture tactics would be even worse.

"What are you thinking?" he asked.

"I'm thinking," she managed to say, "that if you keep doing that thing with your tongue on my shoulder, I'm going to force myself on you."

He nipped her shoulder playfully and then disentangled from her, rising to adjust the space heater. "We're running out of kerosene. It's gonna get really cold in here soon. We should get going."

Connie kicked at his shin with the point of her toe. "You jerk. I'm onto you. You think you can make the sexy time with me and get me to forget what we were talking about? Not a chance. I'm going to New York with you."

He sighed that very special sigh, the one that said he was exasperated that she couldn't just be manipulated and stay manipulated like his Dear Old Dad had promised him people would. "Hughes already has my ticket. We're flying out tonight."

"Believe it or not, there are other ways of flying out that don't rely on Detective Louis L. Hughes. If that's really who he is."

Jazz grunted. "The middle initial? Stands for Lincoln. How do I know? I called his precinct commander to make sure he was an actual cop. I'm not getting Fultoned again."

They both fell silent. The Impressionist had suckered Jazz

early and easily, claiming to be Jeff Fulton, the father of one of Billy Dent's victims. Jazz had taken the man at his word and never bothered to check up on him. No one would ever know for sure, but Jazz was convinced that if he'd done some background snooping on Jeff Fulton, Ginny Davis and Helen Myerson and Irene Heller would still be alive.

"You can't go on your own."

"Why not?" he asked with infuriating aplomb, as though the question had already occurred to him and he was just letting her get it out of her system.

"You've never been in a town bigger than the Nod in your life. I've been to New York three times and grew up near Charlotte before we moved here."

Jazz snorted and helped her up from the beanbag. "I'll be with an NYPD detective. Somehow I think I'll manage to avoid getting lost in the subway system. And even if I do get lost..." He dug into his pocket and proudly held up his new cell phone. After the disaster of the Impressionist, Connie, Howie, and even Sheriff Tanner had all chipped in to get Jazz his first cell.

"Shows what you know, smart guy: Cell phones don't work in the subway. Are you taking Howie with you instead of me? Is that it? Two guys out in the big city?"

"Ha! Yeah, right. Are you kidding? After he got stabbed, his mother won't let him outside of a ten-mile radius without a bodyguard and a Kevlar vest. I'd have to kidnap him to get him to New York...." Jazz drifted off, stroking his jaw. "Hmm...kidnap him..."

Coming from anyone else, it would be funny. A brief

moment of levity. But Jazz couldn't quite pull it off, and Connie told him so. "Yeah, I know what you're going for there, but I just got a chill down my spine."

"Really?" Jazz blinked. "That wasn't funny?"

"It's all in the delivery. And you don't have what it takes to pull off that kind of joke." She pecked him on the lips, not wanting to tell him that for a moment there she'd actually been in fear for Howie's life. "Come on, let's get going. It's already freezing in here."

"Does this mean you've given up trying to convince me you're coming with me?"

Connie thought for a moment and answered very carefully, very precisely. "Yes. It means I have given up trying to convince you."

But, she knew, that didn't mean that she wasn't going.

That night, Connie toyed with her dinner at the Hall house, her appetite somewhere on a future flight with Jazz and Detective Hughes.

"Something wrong, Conscience?" her father asked gently as she introduced her peas one by one to her untouched pile of mashed potatoes. Only her father ever used her full name. Everyone else, including her mother, called her Connie. Jerome Hall believed that names held power, and he wanted his children to have all the advantages such names conferred. And so Connie was Conscience and her younger brother—nicknamed Whiz—was Wisdom.

"I'm okay," Connie lied without even thinking about it. "Just not hungry, I guess."

"She was with her *boyfriend* today," Whiz said, almost singsonging it. "I saw the text on her phone. They have a hideout somewhere."

Connie bristled. Whiz was ten years old, and his favorite pastime these days, it seemed, was spying on his big sister. "You're a little sneak," she told him.

Ignoring Connie, Whiz shoveled a forkful of ham and potatoes into his mouth. "They text all the time," he went on, "now that *he* has a cell phone. Jasper Dent," Whiz added helpfully, in case anyone didn't already know.

"Whiz, I know your sister is still seeing that Dent boy. I don't need you tattling on her."

"But, Dad—"

"A butt is something you sit on and something I'm gonna kick if you don't mind me."

Connie held back a smirk. Her father was all talk. There had never been a spanking in the Hall house that she could remember. It was actually annoying that her father was the kindest, wisest man Connie knew...except for that special and pernicious blind spot he had toward her boyfriend.

Sure, she understood that Jazz wasn't the ideal boyfriend. At least, not from a parent's perspective. Raised by a serial killer—and not just *any* serial killer, really: *the* serial killer—Jazz had his share of issues, but she didn't think his father's sins should be held against him. In any event, Jazz could have been the son of the local saint and Connie's dad still would have been against the relationship. The black/

white thing. Racial memories that hadn't yet been purged. Jerome Hall just couldn't abide seeing his daughter like that.

For her part, Connie wished someone would invent a drug that would make the world forget the past and get on with the future. Her love life was seriously being messed with, and she couldn't take it any longer. And now she had before her a nearly impossible task: how to convince her parents to let her take the last few days of winter break and go to New York with Jazz. Jazz had said no way, but who was he to boss her around? She could make her own decisions, and this was the one she'd made. Jazz would have no choice but to deal with it. It's not like it was against the law for her to go to New York. He couldn't stop her.

Only her parents could do that.

"I know there's not much more I can do to stop you from seeing him," her dad was saying, "because you'll be eighteen soon and because I've always treated you like an adult. But I wish you would maybe cool it off a little."

"Dad has a point," Mom said, jumping in before Connie could speak. "I know you feel strongly about Jasper, but you're young. He's your first real boyfriend. Maybe you should play the field a little. See what else is out there."

Connie sighed. What her parents said made sense. *If* you assumed she wasn't in love with Jazz. Which she was. She didn't know what the future might hold—she hadn't given herself permission to think beyond the next couple of years—but she did know that she wanted to find out with him at her side.

So what would Jazz do in this situation? Easy: He would manipulate. Which, of course, was a polite word for lie.

And lying, she realized, *is really just acting. And I'm good at acting.*

Almost without realizing what she was doing, she started speaking, putting down her fork and focusing intently on her father, the tough one to persuade.

"Here's the problem," she said, the blanks in her plan filling themselves in as she spoke, her heart beating faster as she realized what she was doing. She was Billying her parents. *So this is what that feels like.* "Here's the problem. We only have a few more days of break left, and I really want to spend them with Jazz"—she marked the tightening of her father's expression, the deepening of the worry lines around her mother's eyes—"but there's a great orientation weekend at Columbia, too. I know it's sort of early for me, but Columbia's where I want to go and I could narrow down my application choices for the fall right now. But here's the thing: I would have to leave tomorrow." Before her parents could say anything, she rushed on. "Remember Larissa? She played Maria in that weird version of *West Side Story* I did that summer at drama camp in Charlotte? Well, she's already in college at Columbia, and she's the one who told me about it. It sounds *amazing,* and I could totally stay with her. But then"—she said it expertly, as though it were just occurring to her—"I wouldn't see Jazz until school started up again."

Her parents exchanged a glance.

"How much would this trip cost?" her father asked, and Connie knew she had them.

"I can stay with Larissa for free. And you'll always be able to reach me on my cell." With a couple of texts, she could easily get Larissa to cover for her. And she figured Jazz would have a hotel room. Just the two of them...in a hotel room...The thought made her head spin and did things to her body she couldn't enjoy right now. "I can probably fly standby since it's last minute, and I can help pay for it I have money from babysitting and Grampa's Christmas check."

Her father stroked his jaw and exchanged another look with her mother.

"She shouldn't get to go to New York all on her own!" Whiz complained. "That's not fair! I don't get to go anywhere!"

Dad rolled his eyes in exasperation, and Connie knew she had him.

So this was how Jazz felt. All the time. Every day.

Connie had to admit it was pretty spectacular.

CHAPTER 8

"Can't say as I like this idea," G. William told Jazz, settling with a sigh into the chair behind his desk. The chair wheezed and squeaked with complaint, and Jazz wondered—as he always did—if he would be there on that inevitable day when the chair gave up entirely and dumped its occupant to the floor. Today was not that day, apparently.

"Connie agrees with you," Jazz told him. "She thinks I shouldn't be going alone."

"Then this is one of the few times I disagree with your girlfriend. Because I don't think you should be going at all. You're seventeen. You—"

" '—should be thinking about college applications and getting into your girlfriend's pants, not gallivantin' all over God's creation,' " Jazz quoted, finishing the riot act G. William read to him on a regular basis. "I know. I've heard it all before."

"I'm not gonna deny you were a big help with Frederick Thurber"—the Impressionist's real name, finally dug up after some intense detective work on G. William's part—"but that was a special case. He was imitating your daddy. Someone whose methods and special blend of crazy you knew real well. What makes you think you got any special insight into this Hot Dog?"

"The Hat-Dog Killer," Jazz corrected him.

"All crazy people don't think the same," G. William went on. "It's hubris to think otherwise in your case."

"Hubris? Been hitting the word-a-day calendar, G. William?"

The sheriff cracked a smile for the first time since Jazz had walked into the office and told him of his intention to go to New York with Hughes. "That trick doesn't work on me. The one where you insult someone, try to get them off their game, rattled? File that away as one way you can't manipulate ol' G. William."

"Look," Jazz said, leaning forward urgently, as if he'd never even tried manipulating the sheriff, "you caught Billy, right? You figured out the connections between all of his victims and the ones here in Lobo's Nod, and then you went out and caught him when no one else in the world could have. But if someone else—someone other than the Impressionist, someone *not* copying Billy—started stacking up bodies in the Nod again, it's not like you would just throw your hands up in the air and say, 'Oh, well—all crazy people don't think the same. I guess I won't even try to catch this new guy.' Would you?"

The sheriff drew one of his impeccably laundered, monogrammed handkerchiefs from a pocket and snorted heartily into it. "Nah. All that tells me is that *I* oughtta be the one headed to New York, not you."

Was that a joke? Sometimes Jazz couldn't tell. The sheriff had sworn that catching Billy Dent had been one serial killer too many for him, but maybe G. William was jealous that Jazz was getting called up to the big leagues.

"I could put in a good word for you," he said lightly.

G. William waved the very idea out of the air like a bad smell. "If I wanted to go to the city, I'd've taken up the FBI on their offer when I was a much younger man and could still make the pretty girls swoon. You want to go to New York and try to help these folks, that's your business."

"Well, yeah."

"But"—and here G. William leaned across the desk, pointing a stubby finger—"you listen and listen good, Jasper Francis: No good will come of this. You think you're gonna find something there in New York."

"No kidding. A serial killer."

"No. More than that. You think you're gonna find your soul. Ever since I've known you, you've been thinkin' that someday you're gonna crack and end up like your daddy. And you've been looking for proof that you won't. What you don't realize is this: The looking *is* the proof. Trust me when I tell you that Billy Dent never had a moment's doubt in his life about what he was and what he was doing. Your doubt is your soul, kid."

It made all the sense in the world, and Jazz wished he could believe it. But he knew too much. He knew of too many serial killers who'd been horrified by their own actions, ones who'd acted on impulse and later didn't understand that impulse. And, of course, the ones who'd acted on impulse and then discovered—to their delight—that they loved it, that the blood and the torture and the other things fulfilled them and assuaged their longings in ways that nothing else could.

"I'm just looking for a killer in New York. And I hear they have good bagels."

G. William regarded him in silence for a moment, then sighed. "Bring me back a knish," he said at last. "Haven't had a decent one in ten years."

Going to New York should have been as easy as packing a suitcase and heading to the airport, but Jazz didn't even own a suitcase. The closest thing in the house was a dusty, mothball-reeking valise that Gramma had probably used on her honeymoon back in 1887. Or whenever she'd been young. The idea of accompanying an NYPD detective to New York with Gramma's beaten, smelly brick of a suitcase was a non-starter. So Jazz did what he always did when he needed help.

"This here," Howie said, hefting a sleek black roller bag as if it contained purloined diamonds from some fantasy kingdom, "is the latest and greatest in travel technology. Guaranteed not to tip over. Mesh pocket for water bottle. Separate exterior compartment for laptop—"

"I don't have a laptop."

"—single-post handle construction for pushing or pulling," Howie went on, undeterred. "Extra-lubricated ball bearings for smooth gliding action." Howie waggled his eyebrows. "That's what *she* said."

Jazz took the roller bag from Howie, unzipped it, and

peered inside. "Plenty of room, and I won't be embarrassed with it in the airport. That's all I care about."

" 'Who's going to watch your grandmother while you're gone?' he asked, knowing the answer already," Howie said drily.

"Yeah, about that..."

Jazz had thought long and hard and then longer and harder about what to do with his grandmother for the next couple of days. He had actually considered bringing her to New York with him, but the thought of being in a confined space with her for the duration of the flight was enough to make him want to bail out of the plane without a parachute. And then there was the idea of Gramma on her own in the biggest, craziest city in the world while Jazz was off prospecting the prospector for the NYPD. There was a slight chance that Gramma's crazy would complement New York's just fine, but he wasn't going to bank on it. Images of Gramma attacking tourists capered in before his mind's eye, and he could almost hear her shrieking, "Tell that bitch to stop staring at me!" while pointing at the Statue of Liberty.

No, Gramma would have to stay in Lobo's Nod. And he couldn't rely on the usual suspects to take care of her—it was one thing to let Erickson sit with her for a couple of hours, but if he had anyone on G. William's staff looking after her, it would take no time at all before the sheriff had Jazz's case with Social Services expedited right up the priority list...and bounced Jazz into a foster home and Gramma into an assisted-living facility. He'd already dodged that bullet once when Billy—in a fit of parental protection like no other—had horrifically tortured and slaughtered Melissa Hoover and conveniently deleted the files she'd accumulated on Jazz's situation. It would be months before the Social Services people reconstructed anything incriminating. Jazz hoped it would take until he turned eighteen, at which point it would become moot.

In the meantime, the cops—friendly to Jazz, but honor bound to report Gramma's attenuating connection to planet earth—were out as babysitters. And Howie was willing but too weak. Gramma could cause some serious damage if she went on one of her crazed slapping and punching benders.

Jazz had had no choice but to call his aunt Samantha.

It felt strange to think of her as "Aunt Samantha." He'd never met the woman in his life—Billy's older sister had moved away from Lobo's Nod right after graduating high school and never looked back. In the years since Billy's ravages had become nighttime news fodder, she had done her level best to stay out of the limelight, avoiding the press at every turn. Her only comment had come at the end of a long day of being hunted by the media, stalked with the same precision and tenacity Billy evinced when prospecting. A reporter with a camera crew had finally pinned her down in a mall parking garage, where she struggled with a recalcitrant door while trying to balance her purse, a shopping bag, a precarious cup of coffee, and a plastic hanger sheath with a red dress within. As the reporter pestered her for a comment, Samantha gamely and repeatedly said, "I have nothing to say," as though it were a protective mantra shielding her from a demon.

But then the door finally came open, jerking her back, and

53

the beautiful new dress slid off the hanger onto the grimy parking garage floor, with the coffee landing on top of it. To prove that the universe loves synchronicity—whether good or ill—this happened at the exact moment that the reporter asked, "What do you think should happen to your brother?"

And poor Samantha had had enough. Enough her brother. Enough of the reporters. Enough of the damn dress it had taken her all day to find. She'd kicked the car door and screamed, "There isn't a hell in the universe hot enough for my [bleep]damned brother! If they wanted to kill him, I'd flip the [bleep]ing switch myself!"

The bleeps, of course, were courtesy of network censors. Obviously, they found her justifiable "mature language" too offensive and shocking for the delicate sensibilities of the same viewers who regularly tuned in to hear details of Billy's extensive career of raping, torturing, and murdering mostly young women.

"I've got some coverage," Jazz told Howie, "but I need you to backstop."

"So that Social Services doesn't go medieval on you," Howie said, with what he thought was the air of some Far Eastern mystic. "You could solve all of this, you know, with some paperwork...."

Jazz groaned. He didn't want to have this conversation again. Howie had been bugging him recently about filing the paperwork to become an emancipated minor. It would mean no more looking over his shoulder for Social Services and would give him more latitude in taking care of his grandmother.

"No. We've been through this before—"

"You've *dismissed* it before. Not the same thing, bro."

"You sound like an idiot when you say 'bro.' And it's too complicated. The background checks and interviews alone would have them swooping down on the house. She'd end up in adult care somewhere, and I'd spend my last few months before I hit eighteen in a foster home while the freakin' emancipation paperwork was still being processed. No, Howie. Forget it. It's easier just to lay low until I'm eighteen."

"Well, first of all," Howie said, ticking off points on his fingers, "I totally sound like Ice-T when I say 'bro.' Second of all, it's still your best move. You can't keep this up forever." He gestured to the house, encompassing with that one motion the entire complexity of Jazz's life.

"I don't have to. I just have to hold on a little longer. And all you have to do is spell me for a couple of days. Gramma likes you."

"Usually she likes me," Howie said darkly. "Sometimes she thinks I'm some kind of giant skeleton come to eat her soul."

"Sometimes you *look* like a giant skeleton," Jazz reminded him.

"Yeah, but the soul-eating part is tough to get over. Very well, then. I will be your Sancho Panza once more."

"I don't think that exactly means what you—"

"But there is, of course, the small matter of my baby-sitting fee to discuss...."

"For God's sake, Howie! How many more tattoos can you put on me? I'm running out of space!"

55

"*Au contraire, mein freund.* You have your legs and your forearms, for example."

"I'm gonna look like a complete freak by the time you're done with me. Can you at least make it something cool?"

"A flaming basketball *is* cool!" Howie protested.

"No. It isn't. A flaming basketball is cool to a ten-year-old. And Yosemite Sam is only cool in comparison to SpongeBob SquarePants. So, please—think carefully. Something cool."

Howie folded his unending arms over his sunken chest. "Your words hurt, Jazz. They hurt like cotton balls thrown in my direction. But I'll consider your request, and by the time you get back from New York, I will be prepared with the kick-assingest of the kick-ass to adorn your form."

"I can hardly wait." Maybe, Jazz thought, he should just stay in New York. "Look, it won't all be on you. My aunt Samantha will be here."

Howie actually gasped, just like a character in one of those Victorian romance movies, hand to his chest and everything. All he needed to do was say, "Oh, my soul!" to complete the image.

"Samantha? The legendary un-crazy Dent, told of in myth and fables? The only teenage girl to see Billy Dent's tally-whacker and live to tell the tale? *That* Samantha?"

Jazz sighed. Not only had he never met her, he'd never *spoken* to her. He'd found her phone number in Gramma's address book. Actually, he'd found ten phone numbers, crossed out and written over. The only legible one seemed relatively recent, and the area code was in Indiana, where that reporter had waylaid her. Jazz took a gamble that Gramma had managed to get the phone number right and called.

"Hello?" a tentative female voice had said.

"Is this Samantha Dennis?" She hadn't married, but she'd changed her name legally years ago.

"Yes." A note of suspicion. "Who is this? How did you get this number?"

For Jazz, it was a moment of liquid reality, as though the world had begun to melt in places where it usually remained solid. He was speaking to the only flesh and blood he had on the entire planet that wasn't completely insane. He had no idea how to act. How did people talk to their relatives when their relatives weren't sociopaths or extreme-level seniles?

"My name is..." He stopped. It seemed too formal. "This is Jazz," he said. "Jasper, I mean. Your nephew."

The silence from the other end of the connection burrowed into his brain and seemed to hollow him out from within.

"Jasper," she said at last, her voice so carefully neutral that even Jazz's skilled ear couldn't tell what she was thinking or feeling.

"It took some persuading," Jazz told Howie, "but she's arriving tomorrow morning and she'll stay until school starts again. I just need you to come over and help her out in the afternoon and evening. That's Gramma's worst time. She's okay most of the morning."

"So I get to help out during the Bad Hours. Great. Should have let the Impressionist kill you," Howie grumbled.

"He wasn't going to kill me."

"That's just because he didn't really, *really* know you."

A few hours later, after Gramma was tucked safely in bed and Howie had wheedled permission to order dirty movies on pay-per-view while on duty, Jazz wheeled his borrowed suitcase down his driveway to Hughes's rental car. He had called Connie to say good-bye to her, but she hadn't answered. Maybe she was angry that he was going to New York without her. Well, he couldn't worry about that right now.

"Let's do this," he said, and climbed in.

They said nothing for most of the ride to the airport. Jazz had thought the fast-talking New York detective would start right in with information about the Hat-Dog Killer, but Hughes seemed content to focus on the back roads that, to him, were unfamiliar. When they pulled onto the highway, Jazz couldn't help turning to look off to one side. He could just barely make out the edge of the Harrison property, where Fiona Goodling's body had been found, kicking off Jazz's hunt for the Impressionist.

"Don't be surprised or overwhelmed by the city," Hughes said suddenly.

"What?"

"You were just looking a little homesick already. I'm just telling you to prepare yourself, is all. The city can be over-whelming your first time."

Homesick? Jazz snorted. "I've seen New York on TV. I

think I can handle it. It can't be worse than growing up with Billy."

"Oh?" Hughes shrugged. "It's pretty big."

"So what?"

"It can be confusing."

"Don't care. I'll be with you."

"Whole lotta people who don't look like you."

Jazz bristled. "Just because my grandmother is—" He stopped himself and started over. "I'm not like her. I'm not a racist. Dude, my girlfriend is black."

"Hey, yeah? Good for you. So's mine."

Jazz threw his hands up. "Fine. I lose. You win. Whatever."

Hughes grinned, and Jazz suddenly realized what was *really* going on. The detective was poking and prodding, looking for weaknesses. Trying to find Jazz's pressure points. And Jazz had given him one. *Cops and crooks*, Billy whispered to him, *always usin' each other's tools.*

All right, then. Lesson learned. Hughes liked to pick around in other people's heads. Well, Jazz was no slouch at that, and he'd done a decent job keeping Billy out of his head back at Wammaket. It was tough to catch Jazz with the same trick twice. He adapted easily. A sociopath's best trick— adaptation—and one that Jazz couldn't help being damn good at.

"Kid," Hughes said, his tone friendly now, "you gotta stop taking everything so seriously. Otherwise high blood pressure'll kill you before your pops ever gets a chance."

Ah, high blood pressure. What a way to go. Somehow a heart attack or a stroke sounded positively peaceful and bucolic compared to what Jazz knew Billy to be capable of. Still, Jazz didn't fear his father. Or, more accurately, he had no *personal* fear of his father. Billy was convinced that Jazz would someday take up the family business and be the serial killer that other serial killers looked up to. Jazz knew his father would never jeopardize that by harming his only son. Billy had too much of himself—his ego, his madness, his genius—invested in Jazz to risk killing him.

"My dad would never hurt me. Not physically, at least."

"So, no spankings when you were a kid?" Hughes said it with a lightness so deft and so false that even Jazz thought for a moment that it was just curious conversation. But it wasn't. This was a skilled detective, a trained interrogator, digging for information. Jazz was impressed—he was tough to fool, and Hughes had come close.

"Nope. Not once." It was harmless enough information to give to Hughes. It was also true. Billy had never laid a hand on Jazz as a child.

"So where do you think your dad is these days?"

Now Jazz shot him his best I-don't-talk-about-my-dad look. Hughes was visibly rocked by it.

"Sorry." He recovered nicely; they made 'em tough in NYC. He refocused on the road ahead. "Just making conversation."

"You make conversation like the Inquisition."

Hughes laughed. "Occupational hazard. Could be worse— I dated an ADA once and she couldn't ask what you wanted for dinner without it feeling like a cross-examination. You've got a hell of a glare, kid. But I guess that's to be expected."

Jazz shrugged and looked out the window.

"Look, I'm not pumping you for info or anything. I'm not trying to find your dad. But I'm a homicide cop. It's like if I had A-Rod's batting coach in the car; how am I *not* supposed to ask questions? And I know the fibbies have already bugged you about him. I'm just curious. Not putting together a case or anything."

Jazz blew out a sigh. "I'll tell you what I told them: He's nowhere they expect. He's not near the Nod, watching over me or Gramma. He's not in any of the places he used to prospect. He's got to go somewhere where he can become invisible. A city."

"New York?"

Jazz shrugged. "Could be. Heck, if the murders hadn't started before he broke out of jail, I'd say maybe he was even Hat-Dog."

"Nope. I can guarantee that's not the case. We have consistent DNA from multiple scenes that doesn't match Billy's. Our unsub isn't Billy Dent."

Jazz snorted. *Unsub.* It was short, he knew, for "unknown subject," the shorthand law enforcement used to describe their quarry. "You guys and your jargon. Makes you think you know something. Makes you think you can catch, define, and calculate the invisible world."

He expected it to rattle Hughes, but the cop merely drummed his fingers on the steering wheel. "I've read *The Crucible*, too, kid. This isn't a witch hunt. It's real."

On that, they both fell silent for the remainder of the drive. At the airport, Jazz watched closely as Hughes negotiated security so that he could carry his service weapon on the plane. Jazz had never flown before; he'd heard that airport security was stronger than it had once been, but if that was true, then he could only imagine that it had once been possible to carry automatic rifles openly onto planes. He lingered, watching, and made a decision.

Once his belongings were on the conveyor belt to the X-ray machine, Jazz waited until a TSA agent motioned him through the scanner. Jazz hesitated. "I'm not going through that thing," he said. "My girlfriend told me that those full-body scanners were never fully medically tested."

Clearly exasperated, the TSA agent said, "I assure you, they're totally safe."

"Right. And you're a doctor and you can guarantee me that I let that thing scan my nads and I don't end up sterile? Or having kids with six fingers someday?"

"So you're opting out?"

"Yes."

"Male opt-out!" the TSA agent called out to the universe in general.

Jazz was shunted aside to another spot. Hughes, already through security, gathered up his own stuff as well as Jazz's and waited, frowning. Jazz didn't react. He just lingered until a second TSA agent came over, this one wearing latex gloves.

"You're opting out?" the agent asked.

"Yes," Jazz said, his voice nasal and clogged. Part of it was a put-on. Part of it, though, was the little bit of shampoo he'd shot up his nose before getting into line. "Opting out."

And then he coughed—a really convincing, wet-sounding hack that made the TSA agent wince and turn away slightly.

The TSA agent talked Jazz through exactly what he was about to do and where he would be touching him. When he asked, "Do you have anything in your pockets?" Jazz said, "Just a Kleenex," and then proceeded to produce it and blow his nose noisily into it. He left it open just long enough for the TSA agent to see the disgusting yellowish shampoo goop before folding it up.

"Just, uh, hold on to that," the agent said, and proceeded to give Jazz the quickest, most perfunctory pat-down in the history of pat-downs. Jazz noted three spots on his body where he could have easily concealed some sort of contraband.

By the time he rejoined Hughes, the cop was shaking his head in amusement. "You are Homeland Security's worst nightmare," he said as they made their way to their gate.

"You could have intervened."

"Yeah, but I know you're harmless."

Jazz shrugged. "You know how you said before that you have a black girlfriend, too? That was a lie. You don't. And you never dated an ADA, either. You're just trying to keep me out of your head because you know where I come from. You know just enough to know that I'm anything *but* harmless. So you make jokes and you drop in what seems like personal stuff to keep me off guard." Jazz grinned the grin he used when he wanted to put people at ease. "You're pretty good at it. But I'm better."

Hughes gaped at him.

Jazz let the grin linger for another moment, then said, "I'm gonna hit the bathroom before we board," leaving Hughes alone with his thoughts.

Later, in the cramped space of the plane, he surprised himself by falling asleep almost immediately. He didn't even wake up when the plane took off.

He dreamed.

Touch me
   says the voice
   again
   His fingers
   Oh, the flesh
   So warm
   So smooth
   Touch me like that
   His skin on hers.
   Hers.
   He knows her flesh.
   like that
   So warm
   like that
   it's all right
   it's not all right
   it's right
   no, it's wrong

but the wrong makes it right
and the right makes it wrong
and

Jazz woke up as the plane landed and groggily grabbed his bag from the overhead. They had an hour-long layover before their next flight; Hughes tried to strike up a conversation, but Jazz withdrew. He was off-kilter, slightly airsick, and definitely dreamsick.

Who was it in his dream? What was he doing? Why did this dream keep recurring? He actually preferred the old dream, the one where he'd cut someone, maybe even killed someone. At least it was familiar. He had become accustomed to its specific nauseating qualities. The new dream kept knocking him down every time he tried to get up.

What did it mean? What was lurking back there in the cold, dark recesses of his memory? What secrets were hidden in his past? Jazz felt as though his own life was a minefield, one he'd lost the map for. One wrong step and he'd lose a foot or a leg.

Or his mind.

When Jazz awoke from the cutting dream, he felt confused. Guilty. A bit sick. When he woke from the sex dream, though, he felt a tiny bit of guilt, sure. But otherwise just… aroused. And he hated himself for it. Other guys his age could have dreams like that, sure. That was okay for them. But not for Jazz.

Because... *This is how it starts*, he thought. Dreams. Fantasies. Seems harmless at first. But then the dreams and the fantasies aren't enough. And the next thing you know, you're Jeffrey Dahmer, drilling holes in the heads of corpses in an attempt to make sex zombies, and the crazy thing isn't that you're drilling the heads to make sex zombies—the crazy thing is that doing so seems completely and utterly normal and necessary.

"You're awful quiet," Hughes said, edging back into conversation after they'd not spoken for hours. Jazz respected that the detective could recover from being busted before, but he had more important things on his mind. When he didn't respond, Hughes gave up and left him alone.

They boarded the second plane, and this time Jazz stayed awake, peering out the window, feeling the sudden lurching rush as the plane ramped up and left the ground. It made him slightly dizzy, and it felt like waking up from the dream all over again. He closed his eyes and gripped the armrests and told himself that it would be over soon.

He didn't mind the landing as much. At first, it seemed almost gentle, but then stabbing pains started in his ears from the change in air pressure and the plane touched down, the cabin roaring with the sudden speed. The violence of it was almost soothing. Distracting.

They gathered up their bags again and emerged into the terminal at JFK. As soon as they walked through security, Jazz froze, unable to believe his eyes.

"What?" Hughes asked. "What's wrong?"

Grinning, Connie said to them, "What took you guys so long?"

Part Three

5 Players, 3 Sides

CHAPTER 9

The killer sat quietly in his apartment. The walls were thin. Through them, he could hear two different television programs. One, from the sound of it, was some sort of singing competition. The other could have been a movie or a cartoon of some sort—high-pitched zinging noises that were either laser beams or the zip of something moving fast.

Children, in either case.

The killer shuddered.

On the table in front of the killer, there were four cell phones. Cheap. Disposable. The killer did not know which one would ring, so he kept them all charged. They had come to him along with several others in a box delivered from somewhere upstate, with instructions to keep them charged and turned on at all times. "Upstate," to the killer, might as well be the moon.

New York City was home.

New York City was safe.

New York City was the hunting preserve.

One of the phones rang. Third from the left. The killer let it ring two more times, then snatched it up.

"Hello?" The killer wondered, idly, which voice it would be this time.

"Eleven," came the response. The *new* voice again. It had been the new voice for a while now.

The killer did not wonder what had happened to the old voice.

"Eleven," the voice repeated calmly. "Six and five. Eleven."

The killer's eyes flicked to the part of the table beyond the phones. His lips moved silently. . . . *Eight . . . nine . . . ten . . . and . . .*

"Eleven," he said back to the phone. "Eleven." In a sudden fit of inspiration, he added, "As the crow flies."

The voice at the other end was gone already, leaving silence in the killer's ear.

The killer took the battery out of the phone. Then he put the phone on the floor and smashed it to pieces with a hammer.

"Eleven," he said again. Well. So it would be.

CHAPTER 10

Billy held a cell phone in one hand and a pair of dice in the other. He tucked the dice into his coat pocket, followed by the phone's battery.

He looked around. At three in the morning in early January, Union Square Park in lower Manhattan was no one's idea of a comfortable hangout. Still, there were a few junkies doing their nervous dance over in the shadows, waiting for the connection they prayed would come.

Billy didn't care about the junkies. He made sure he was out of the cone of light thrown by a streetlight and dropped the phone, crushing it under his foot. Stooping, he picked up the pieces and discarded them in a half-dozen different trash cans as he made his way to the NQR subway entrance.

Eleven, he thought. *Eleven as the crow flies*...

CHAPTER 11

Before returning to the Dent house the next day, Howie realized he would need armor to deal with Jazz's crazy grandmother. He had seen her slap and punch Jazz, as well as throw everything from stuffed teddy bears to skillets. She was surprisingly strong for a woman who looked to be five or six inches away from death. Maybe it was some kind of death adrenaline. Whatever the case, Howie didn't plan on letting her turn his hemophiliac body into her own personal bruise-n-contuse plaything.

Since it was January, he got away with wearing long sleeves—flannel. Nice and thick, for protection. Just in case, he strapped on some wrist guards underneath. They were supposed to be for people who typed a lot, but they had hard steel inserts and would do him well if he had to suddenly protect his face. He also wore gloves, which he promised himself he would leave on even while inside. Heavy denim jeans, of course: That stuff really felt like armor. Howie figured he could go ride out in the Crusades with his heavy-duty Levi's on. He scrounged around the house until he found his dad's old hunting cap, right down to the earflaps. *Oh, yeah.* He would look like a serious dork, but he didn't care—his skull would be protected.

"I can't believe the crap I go through for this guy...." Howie muttered to himself as he parked at the Dent house. He had spoken to Jazz's aunt Samantha briefly over the phone before coming over. She had said little about her flight or rental car drive to the Nod or anything at all, really, despite Howie's endless, helpful patter. Taciturn ran in the family. Well, except for Billy. Howie remembered hanging out at Jazz's house when they were kids. Billy never stopped talking. Howie's mom used the phrase "talk a blue streak" to mean someone who talked incessantly. Billy Dent talked streaks in all kinds of shades of blue: sky blue, navy blue, midnight blue. You name it, Billy Dent said it. The man never shut up.

Howie marched up the front steps, gave a warning knock at the front door, then let himself in with the key Jazz had given him, steeling himself for the crazy that was Gramma Dent.

Instead, he found Gramma Dent and Samantha sitting cross-legged on the parlor floor, playing "patty-cake."

"Bake me a cake as fast as you can!" Gramma chanted in time with Samantha. "Roll it! And prick it! And mark it with an *A*. And put it in the oven for me and Sammy J!"

Jazz's grandmother hooted with delight.

"Josephine," Sam explained to Howie.

"What's the *A* for, then?" he asked.

Sam shrugged. "She likes it to rhyme."

"Again!" Gramma shrieked. "Again!"

Howie ended up on the floor with them, playing a nearly endless round of patty-cake that concluded only when Gramma mumbled "Nappy time" and crawled over to the couch to conk out.

"I've never seen her like this," Howie told Samantha moments later in the kitchen, where Jazz's aunt was washing dishes. "She gets childlike sometimes, but she usually goes all temper-tantrum at some point, you know?"

"I wasn't sure what to expect," Samantha confessed. "I knew she was getting worse—I had stopped writing and calling years ago, before all of the...well, you know. But I knew...I knew that she wasn't going to be getting better as time went on, you know?"

"Was she always like this?"

Samantha shrugged. "She was always crazy. But you know...you know, the whole family was crazy, so it didn't really stand out. I mean, Billy was going around"—she shuddered—"being Billy. And back in the seventies, you could be some crazy lady spouting all of her nutty racist crap and people would just sort of nod politely and pretend they didn't hear it. She was never delusional, not like now. But crazy? Always?" Samantha smiled ruefully. "How do you think Billy ended up the way he did?"

Howie returned the smile. Samantha was in her late forties, he knew, but she looked good. Prime cougar material, really, and he had to admit he liked what he saw. His hemophilia having marked him as a freak from early days, not many girls in Lobo's Nod paid him any mind, much less were willing to get naked and sweaty with him in the way nature prescribed. But hey—maybe he'd have a shot with someone who didn't have the hang-ups and the history of those who'd known him for years.

"It's sort of a miracle that you ended up normal," Howie told her as smoothly as he could, leaning against the counter with as much savoir faire as he could muster. He figured he cut a pretty dashing figure in his jeans and heavy shirt. And gloves. And hat. Not like a page out of a catalog or anything, but it showed how he thought ahead. He was prepared. Women dug guys who were prepared.

His advance preparations were lost on Samantha, who was paying attention to the dishes.

"Normal?" Samantha's laugh was short and harsh. "Normal. Not a chance. I got the hell out of this house and this town as fast as I could, but it didn't matter. I didn't know how to be around normal people by that point. I've spent my whole life figuring it out. And once Billy got caught, suddenly it was like I had to start all over again."

Howie saw his chance; he took off his gloves and nabbed a wet, clean dish from Samantha's hands, allowing his fingers to linger on hers for a moment. It was a good, subtle move— he'd seen it in a bunch of movies.

"What the hell are you doing?" Samantha asked.

"Taking this dish."

"Why?"

He was still touching her. He realized he didn't have a towel to dry the dish with. "Um."

"Howie, you're the same age as my nephew."

"Actually, I'm six weeks older."

She shook her head. "It's not going to happen."

"You say that now."

"I do."

"We're both two lonely people," Howie said seductively, "trapped in a world created by Billy Dent."

Samantha howled with laughter. Howie figured that wasn't a good sign.

CHAPTER 12

Jazz was surprised that he absolutely hated New York City.

No, that wasn't quite accurate. Being from a small town like Lobo's Nod, it was no surprise that he hated New York. What really surprised him was *how much* he hated it. He didn't dislike New York with the simple diffidence of a small-town kid or the tragic ignorance of a yokel—he loathed it with the entirety of what he hoped was his soul.

The streets—cramped with cars and buses; with all the traffic, it took them almost two hours to get from the airport to some place called Red Hook, which looked like every bad 'hood in every action movie Jazz had ever seen.

The buildings—either run-down to the point of ruin or so overwrought that he felt like they'd been built not to serve any purpose but rather just to prove a point.

The smell—Jazz figured even New Yorkers had to hate the garbage and urine smells, but it wasn't just that. The city managed to ruin even the *good* smells; at one point, while walking from the cab to the hotel, Jazz had smelled the most delightful bread baking, but the smell vanished as quickly as it teased his nose, and no matter where he looked or how much he tried, he couldn't recapture it. He had never realized how odorless Lobo's Nod was. Other than the occasional car exhaust, the town smelled utterly neutral.

The noise—it was perpetual.

But the worst thing about the city, the thing that poleaxed him, the thing Hughes had warned him about, the thing he should have been prepared for and yet—he acknowledged—never could have been prepared for...

The people.

Look at 'em all, Jasper, Billy whispered in his head.

So...many...people.

Look at 'em. You could take one. Easy. Or more than one. As many as you want, really. There's so many, it's not like anyone would miss one. Couple thousand go missing every year in this country—man, woman, and child alike. So many. Most of 'em, no one knows. No one cares. It's like grabbin' up blades of grass in the park. One more, one less. Makes no difference.

"You all right?" Hughes asked suddenly, and Jazz whipped around like a kid caught unscrambling the adult channels.

"I'm fine," Jazz said. It came out weak and unconvincing.

"He's overwhelmed," Connie jumped in, grabbing his hand. "He'll be fine."

Connie. She'd been here before for short trips and seemed to be in love with New York already. She had managed to grab an earlier flight, a direct one, beating Hughes and him to JFK. An important lesson for Jazz: Connie wouldn't stay put just because he said so.

There's ways to change that, Jasper. Ways to make her listen. And the best part is, you know them ways already. You know them real well....

"I'm fine," Jazz said again, and tightened his grip on Connie's hand as Hughes led them into the hotel.

Movies and TV shows had prepared Jazz for two kinds of big-city hotels. There were the ostentatious, gilded palaces for the wealthy, and the rank, decrepit hovels for the itinerants and the junkies and the hookers. So he was mildly disappointed to find himself ensconced in neither—the hotel the NYPD had chosen for him was a bog-standard Holiday Inn that wouldn't have looked out of place along the highway that ran past and beyond Lobo's Nod.

"You okay?" Connie whispered as they waited for Hughes to check them in.

"Yeah."

"You've been squeezing my hand like it's putty."

"Sorry." He released her. "Trying to find amusement in our setting."

She looked around. "Yeah, doesn't feel very New York, does it?"

Maybe that was a good thing.

Hughes approached them, brandishing two keycards. He

hesitated for a moment and sized them up. "How old are you guys again?"

"Seventeen," Connie answered.

The detective clucked his tongue, then shrugged. "I only have the one room. Use protection." He handed over the cards and left them to find the room and get settled in while he attended to some other business, promising to return by lunchtime to get started on the case.

As Hughes retreated, Jazz stared slack-jawed at Connie, well and truly shocked by something not involving blood for the first time in a long time. "Can you believe that? He's just gonna let us stay in the same—"

"We're practically adults," Connie said with an air of urbane sophistication. "What did you *think* he was going to do—call our parents? It's New York. It's a whole different world." She waved her card in the air and led him off to the elevator.

The room had two beds. Jazz wasn't sure if that was a good thing or a bad thing. He had stayed in hotels only as a child, on occasional "road trips" with Billy. Billy never flew anywhere, if he could help it. *Too many security checks. Too many people checkin' your ID. Too much damn nosiness, Jasper.* So they had driven to any number of places, usually so that Billy could impart some sort of lesson to his son. Hands-on experience, Billy called it, turning Jazz into his assistant and his accomplice on more than one occasion.

Those hotels had usually been out-of-the-way rattraps, the sheets musty, the bathtubs stained even before Billy showered off the grime and the blood of his most recent prospect. This place was pleasant, if boring. There was a large framed photo of the Statue of Liberty over the bed.

"Why would you want to look at a *picture* of the Statue of Liberty when you're in New York?" Connie demanded. "You can go see the real thing."

Jazz shrugged and poked his head into the bathroom, half expecting to see his father emerging from the shower, dripping wet and grinning.

"On a scale of one to ten," Connie said, "how pissed are you at me?"

"I don't have time to be pissed at you," Jazz said, more curtly than he'd intended. "I need to help the NYPD and then get the hell out of this city."

"Settle down, big guy. You've seen a chunk of Brooklyn from the cab and a grand total of two whole blocks on your feet. Give it a chance before you hate it."

"It's not that." He pushed away her comforting hands, forcing himself to do it gently. "This place isn't good for me. It's a hunting ground. It's a...It's a prospecting gold mine."

"You're not a killer," she told him, grabbing a hand and imprisoning it with both of hers, then holding it to her chest. "Listen to me: You're not a killer. It doesn't matter what this place is."

He stared at the Statue of Liberty. Flicked his eyes to the lamp on the nightstand between the two beds. Anything to avoid looking at Connie. "Remember how I told you once that the problem with people is that when there's so many of them, they stop being special?" She nodded. "Well, take a look around and do the math."

You could slaughter a thousand of them and never be caught, Jasper, m'boy. You could do all those things I taught you. You could—

Connie dragged him into the middle of the room. "You know what? Ten out of ten Lobo's Nod boys would be splitting their pants right now at the thought of being unsupervised in a hotel room with me. That's not ego talking—I saw that on someone's Facebook page. So stop thinking about killing people and start thinking about the fact that we've got a couple of hours before Hughes comes back and you have to go to work." She arched an eyebrow for added effect.

She was trying to distract him. Trying to break the cords of his inherited fears that bound him. He loved her for it.

He pitied her for it. Those cords, he knew, could be loosened and rearranged, but they could never be severed.

"Hughes said to use protection," he said, smiling weakly. "We don't have any."

"We're not going *that* far," she said, kissing him hard and sure on the lips. "We're just gonna get real close and mess up one of the beds, is all."

He surrendered to her.

True to his word, Hughes was back in a couple of hours. By then, Jazz and Connie had remade the bed and were lounging innocently as if they'd moved not an inch since Hughes had left.

Hughes wasn't fooled; he cracked a smile as soon as he

walked in the door, then hid it behind his usual stern façade. He bore a huge flat pizza box, topped with another box, as well as a satchel slung over one shoulder. "I come bearing pizza and pictures of death," he announced.

Soon they had the files spread out over one of the beds, with the pizza and drinks on the smallish hotel table. Jazz was surprised at the dearth of files—fourteen murders should have generated a lot more paperwork.

"Most of it's scanned in," Hughes told them, and handed over an iPad. "Crime-scene photos and video, reports, evidence photos, the whole nine yards. Makes it a lot easier to see what's what, and keeps me from having to schlep a metric ton of paperwork over here."

"Why are we working here?" Jazz asked. "Why can't we just go to the"—it wouldn't be a sheriff's office, not in New York—"precinct?"

Hughes shook his head. "Trust me, you don't want to go there. It's a disaster area. The task force is spread out all over the place. It's a madhouse."

Jazz thought of the state of G. William's building when the Impressionist Task Force had moved in. Yeah, maybe it was better to work here.

"If it turns out there's something I forgot or something else you need, just let me know," Hughes said, "and I'll get it for you."

"Where do we start?" Connie asked.

Hughes raised an eyebrow. "What do you mean 'we'?"

"Oh, is this work too manly for a princess like myself?" Connie's sarcasm was damn near toxic.

"Whoa! Whoa!" Hughes held both hands up in surrender and looked over at Jazz for help. Jazz just gave him a "You're on your own, pal" smirk. "Damn, I didn't think there was a girl on this planet who could handle Billy Dent's kid, but I've been proven wrong. Look, Connie—it's Connie, right?—this has nothing to do with boys versus girls. Jasper here is technically my, well, he's here at the request of the NYPD. You're not. I can't just let you go rummaging through files."

Connie folded her arms over her chest and fixed Hughes with a glare that said she wasn't buying it. Jazz figured he'd better jump in before Hughes felt threatened enough to draw his weapon.

"Look, maybe she can't go through the files with us," Jazz said, "but there's nothing that says she can't stay in the room, right? And if she hears us talking and has ideas, it's still a free country and she can say what she wants."

He wasn't sure Hughes would go for the hair-splitting, but the detective's face split into a huge, delighted grin. "Bend that rule, Jasper!" he said. "*Bend* it!"

Connie dropped onto one of the beds, and Hughes and Jazz set up at the room's desk.

"The first thing we need to do," Jazz said, "is index all of the data. So, for example, organize everything by type of file—picture, video, whatever—and then cross-index it by victim—"

"Already done," Hughes said, producing a stapled set of papers. "There's an electronic version in the Master Index file."

"Okay, then we need to make up a chart of the victims, in the order they were discovered—"

"Victim_Timeline.xls," Hughes said, producing another printout. "E-version and dead-tree version." He grinned at Jazz. "This is the big leagues, kid. We know what we're doing."

Jazz nodded. He wasn't in Lobo's Nod anymore. "Okay, I'm going to start with the paper—those are the most recent, right?" Hughes nodded. "Good. Then that means they show him at his most organized and sophisticated. I'll start with them and work my way back."

"What about me?" Hughes asked.

"You've already seen all of this. You can help clear up any questions we have. But stick to the facts. I don't want your suppositions and guesses to pollute my thinking on this."

"Got it."

They dug into the reports and photos, as well as the pizza. Soon enough, a picture began to emerge.

The killings had begun seven months ago, long before Billy escaped from Wammaket, long before the Impressionist launched his one-man assault on Lobo's Nod. Summer in New York. From the way Hughes told it, it had been sweltering since the solstice, with off-and-on rain that crept up on you without warning.

The first two victims had both been found near a place called Connecticut Bagels, a little deli in a neighborhood called Carroll Gardens. They were found two weeks apart, and at first nothing had connected them. The first victim—a woman named Nicole DiNozzo—had been killed in the alleyway behind the deli, her throat slit with a precision Jazz couldn't help but admire. A crude hat had been carved into the flesh of DiNozzo's chest. Since all of the wounds to the body were slashing wounds, there was no way to determine any of the blade characteristics; she could have been cut with a pocketknife or a samurai sword, for all anyone knew. Bruising and general trauma indicated she'd been raped, though no fluids had been found, meaning the killer most likely used a condom.

Pretty simple. Other than the carving, it could have been any number of random rape/murders.

"But this is Carroll Gardens," Hughes told them. "If this was the nineteen-eighties and DiNozzo was mobbed up, I'd say she screwed someone over and was made an example of. Used to happen all the time back then. The Mob was big around here—Italian neighborhood. Used to find bodies in Carroll Park a few times a year. But things are different now."

"And DiNozzo's *not* mobbed up, according to your own data," Jazz said. "What about the other victims? Give me a preview. How many are white?"

"Thirteen out of fourteen," Hughes said. "We're pretty sure our unsub is white."

"Makes sense. This first murder is pretty controlled."

"Yeah. Check out the second one."

The second victim—Harold Spencer—was found dead in the same alley, at the other end. His genitals had been excised. No one had found them. Also dead of a slashing wound across the throat, this one not as precise as DiNozzo's.

"So what are the odds your crime-scene guys just missed the penis in their search?" Jazz asked.

Hughes shook his head. "Zero. Are you kidding me? Two murders in the same alley in the same number of weeks? We went over that place with a magnifying glass. If it was there, we'd have found it."

"So what happened?" Connie chimed in from the bed. "Did he—gross—take it with him?"

"Maybe," Jazz said. "Or maybe he just tossed it somewhere else."

"The FBI profile says he's terrified of his own power. Rapes the women, makes up for it by castrating the men. Punishing himself."

"No," Jazz said immediately. "Doesn't track. In that case, why take the penis with him? If he's punishing himself, he wouldn't take it. He would shun it. He's not terrified. He's proud of his male power. He revels in it. Cuts off the penises to show his dominance."

"But for the eighth victim," Hughes pointed out, "he left the penis at the scene. Cut it off and tossed it aside. Same for number eleven. Our profile—"

"No profile is perfect."

Jazz and Hughes stared at each other. Jazz could have kept it up all night, but he shrugged and flipped to a photo of the second victim. A crude dog had been carved into Spencer's shoulder.

"These guys usually get better with each murder," Jazz pointed out. "But the cut that killed the second guy is jagged, not smooth like the first one."

"We think Spencer fought back. Struggled. Made it tougher to kill him. He was older and he was a guy. The signature led us to connect the two right away," Hughes went on. "Slashing throat wounds in the same alley...Too much of a coincidence. We checked for a connection between the two vics right away, but there were none."

"Nothing?"

"Nope. Other than that they were both white. Spencer was forty, DiNozzo in her twenties. It's all on the timeline. DiNozzo was a neighborhood girl; Spencer lived in Manhattan and was in Brooklyn visiting friends. No work connections. Nothing. Complete strangers to each other."

Jazz absorbed that, and then they fell silent and went back to work. The only sounds in the room were pages being turned and the occasional slurping of soda and munching on pizza. Eventually, Connie turned on the TV, occasionally offering an opinion when she heard something interesting.

As the victim count increased, the crimes became more and more violent. Slashing wounds gave way to multiple stab wounds, choking, and—later—disembowelment. The women were raped (in some cases, it appeared, repeatedly). Astonishingly, the killer didn't always bother with a condom—postmortem examinations had recovered good semen samples from some of the victims. It was possible that the killer used a condom with some victims but not others, though there was no trace of spermicide or lubricant.

"Which means nothing," Hughes said, "because they make condoms without spermicide or lube. So that doesn't tell us anything."

"Any match to the DNA in the system?" Jazz asked. The federal government maintained a database (CODIS) of criminal DNA that state and local authorities used to match up potential suspects. Jazz knew the answer already—if there'd been a match, there would be a name for the Hat-Dog Killer—but he wanted to see how Hughes reacted.

The homicide detective shrugged. "No, but that's not our prising. This guy is careful. He's stayed out of the system."

Realistic. Not flying off the handle or getting depressed. Okay, that was good.

"Are we sure it's just 'this guy'? Two carvings, two perps?"

"No. We tossed that one around at first. Thought maybe a copycat. But the second murder had characteristics of the first that never made it into the press. And the DNA evidence doesn't bear it out."

Jazz skimmed his screen. "You don't have DNA from every crime scene." Contrary to what TV and movies made people believe—and despite Locard's Exchange Principle—not every crime scene was a vast repository of criminal DNA. Sometimes there was no way to find a DNA specimen. Or to isolate it from others. Sometimes it was just a fluke and there was nothing at all.

"That's true," Hughes admitted, "but we *do* have DNA from a bunch of them, including both Dog *and* Hat killings. All of the samples match one another, regardless of the kind of killing, regardless of the carving on the body. No tag team. No copycat. Same guy."

Jazz frowned, studying the file before him. "Well, if you

ever have a good suspect and can get a DNA sample from him, you'll have something to match it against. I see here that he didn't ejaculate in all the victims...."

"This is disgusting," Connie said, as if to herself, and turned up the volume slightly. He could almost hear her stomach lurching.

"Mm-hmm," he agreed. And it was. The photos. The reports. All of it. No doubt about it. But unlike Connie, Jazz only understood that disgust; he didn't—couldn't—feel it. Sure, a picture of a human being with its abdomen cut open and its intestines drawn out like pulled taffy was—definitively—disgusting. Grotesque. But Jazz didn't have a visceral reaction. There was nothing that made him want to stop scrutinizing the pictures. They were photos of dead people in horrific repose and that was that. End of story for Billy Dent's kid.

"There's video of the crime scenes, too," Hughes said, wiping his grease-slick hands on one of the room's towels. "Want me to load it up on the laptop?"

Cops weren't particularly bothered by crime scenes, either, Jazz reminded himself, and they weren't sociopaths. Then again, they had long careers and years of experience to inure them to the horrors of the defiled human body. Jazz had both nature and nurture.

"What are you thinking?" Connie asked. "Do you need to see the video?"

He couldn't tell her what he'd really been thinking, so he shrugged and waved one of the photos in the air. It was the tenth victim, a woman—Monica Allgood—found near a church in a neighborhood called Park Slope. She'd been raped, slashed across the throat so deeply that her head almost came off, her gut cut open, her intestines piled neatly beside her. A hat had been carved on her forehead.

"Is this when he started paralyzing them?" Jazz asked, brandishing the photo.

Hughes's jaw dropped. "What did you say?"

"I said, is this when he started paralyzing them? Or, I'm sorry, was I not supposed to figure that part out yet? Did I pass your test, Detective?"

Hughes blushed but had the grace and decency to look Jazz in the eye as he apologized. "I'm sorry. I had to be sure. I deleted the paralysis references from these copies of the reports. He actually started paralyzing with victim eight— Harry Glidden. Guy was a freakin' tax attorney, can you believe it? Most boring guy in the world, dies like that." He passed over a sheet of paper. "Here's the missing deets."

"You wanted to see if I would pick up on it. That's okay. I get it." His respect for Hughes rose a notch. He hoped the detective was returning the favor.

Connie leaned over. "Paralysis?" She stared at the crime-scene photo. "How can you tell? It's a picture. *Nothing* moves."

Hughes didn't tell Connie to back off, so Jazz let her keep looking over his shoulder. "Void pattern," he said. A void pattern was an area defined by lack of blood where blood should have spattered...meaning that something had been sitting there at the time of the bloodletting, then moved. In the crime-scene photo, there was a void pattern that outlined a pair of human legs. The victim's. "In the early crime scenes, there was blood smeared all over the place as he disemboweled them and they thrashed and kicked and fought. But at later scenes, there's a void pattern instead, indicating that they weren't moving their legs when they bled out."

"Maybe he drugged them," Connie suggested. "Or knocked them out."

"No. Toxicology shows nothing exotic in their systems. No blunt-force trauma to the head that would indicate a blow strong enough to result in unconsciousness." Aware of Hughes's eyes on him, Jazz reconsidered. "Well, no *consistent* blows to the head. Some of them were hit hard, but not all of them. So I'm saying paralysis. It's probably not hard, if you know what you're doing." He studied the new report for a moment. "'Knife wound at thoracolumbar junction... T-twelve, L-one...' Slip a knife into the spine, I guess. Right above where the belly button would be from behind." He twisted to point to the spot on his own back as best he could. "Am I right?" he asked, turning to Hughes.

"Yeah. ME says severed spinal cord at L-one/L-two," Hughes said. "Damn," he said, almost involuntarily.

"It's just a little thing," Jazz said modestly.

Little things can mean nothin' or little things can mean everythin', Dear Old Dad whispered. *And the only one who knows for sure is me. Ain't that special?*

"Yeah, but what does it mean?"

"Mean?" Jazz shrugged. "It probably means he was tired of them kicking and getting blood all over the place while he gutted them. Just making his job easier, is all."

"Just making his job easier?" Hughes blew out a long,

exasperated breath, and Jazz finally saw the annoyance and anger that had been lurking under the surface. "Just making his *job* easier? So I'm looking for a lazy serial killer? Is that it? It just doesn't make any sense. None of it makes sense."

It makes sense to us, Billy said. *And that's all that matters. Don't matter what anyone else thinks.*

"It makes perfect sense to him, though," Jazz said. "It's probably the only thing in the world that makes sense to him, actually."

"Look, I could..." Hughes hesitated, as if he knew what he was about to say could be explosive. "I could arrange for you to meet some of the victims' families. If you want to. If that would help."

Jazz stared at him far longer than people usually stare. "Why on earth would I want to meet the victims' families?"

"Sometimes it makes it more real," Hughes said.

"It's plenty real. Don't worry about that."

The two of them glared at each other until Connie cleared her throat and brought them back to the task at hand.

"Not to interrupt this macho stare-down, but I'm wondering...why hats and dogs?" Connie asked. "And why alternate?"

"He doesn't alternate," Hughes said quickly. "He did for a while, but if you look at the chart we put together, you can see—"

"He alternates until victim seven," Jazz said. "He gives her and the next victim hats, then switches back to a dog. Does the same thing later—two hats in a row before a dog."

"Why?" Connie asked.

"Don't know." Jazz leaned back against the headboard, staring up at the ceiling. *Hats are for gentlemen*, Billy said quietly. *My daddy wore a hat every day of his life.* Pictures of Jazz's grandfather floated in his mind's eye. "Hats are for gentlemen," he murmured.

"But he put hats on women, too," Hughes complained.

"Top hats," Connie specified. She had dragged a chair over and sat with them now, part of the group. "At least, that's what they look like. They're actually pretty good. I mean, when you consider they're being cut into someone's skin and all."

"Ever seen prison tats?" Hughes asked, and Jazz's memory flickered for a moment, remembering the words LOVE and FEAR tattooed across Billy's knuckles at Wammaket. "A lot of those are done with just a paper clip," Hughes went on. "Or even a staple. It's possible to get some real consistent art just with—"

"Hats are for gentlemen," Jazz said again, interrupting, "and dogs are for..."

"For bitches," Connie said with finality.

They stared at each other, then over at Hughes.

"No," the detective said, shaking his head emphatically. "He hatted women and he dogged men. It doesn't track—"

"It's not about their actual gender," Jazz protested. "It's about how he sees them. It's about his perception of them. Maybe he decides which they are before he kills them— maybe that's part of what sets him off. Or maybe he decides based on *how* they die. How they act. Like this one..." He flipped through data on the tablet. "Look—victim six. A woman. Elana Gibbs. A dog. He raped her, but the ME found less vaginal tearing and fewer bruises than the hat, Marie Leydecker, he raped three weeks later."

"So if they fight back, they're a gentleman, and if they don't they're a bitch?" Hughes said doubtfully. "You'd think that's the opposite of how it should be."

"Yeah, to *you*," Jazz said. "To you, it makes sense to go the other way—a woman who fights is a bitch. But what if after that second victim struggled, he learned he liked it? That the resistance arouses him even more? If they struggle, he has an excuse—justification in his mind, a rationale—to hurt them more, to be more violent with them. So they're giving him what he wants, which makes them gentlemen. Hats."

Connie shivered next to him. Her face had gone ashy. "I think I'm gonna go get some more ice from the machine. And maybe a Coke. You guys need anything?"

Jazz and Hughes both glanced at the six-pack of Coke Hughes had brought, half of which was still unopened. The three cans sat next to a nearly full bucket of ice.

"That's a good idea," Jazz said after a moment. "Stretch your legs, too."

After the door closed on Connie, Hughes shook his head. "Can she handle this?"

"She'll be okay." *I hope.* "What's this thing in here on the fourth murder? The bit about a flashing light?"

"Yeah, that's the only real bit of eyewitness testimony we

have. Witness saw a bright flash down on the subway tracks where we later found the body. Thought it was a train at first, but it was coming from the wrong direction."

"He took a picture...." Jazz mused.

"Yeah, that's what we think. His trophy."

"But that doesn't...that doesn't quite track."

"How do you mean?"

"I mean, he already has a trophy. The penises."

Hughes rubbed his eyes. "He doesn't always take them. Sometimes he does. Sometimes he doesn't."

"Yeah, but..." Jazz frowned. "Why *two* different trophies? It's not unheard of, but it has to mean something."

Hughes took the last piece of pizza. It was cold and stiff, like rigor mortis. "I wish I had more to tell you. But this is why I wanted you involved."

"I?"

"I. Me. We. Whatever. I was the one who lobbied to bring you in, is all."

Hughes ate the pizza, chewing with a thoughtful look on his face. "Okay, look, let's do the rundown one more time. The things we know for sure, all right?" He started ticking facts off on his fingers as he spoke, reciting from memory. "Based on the direction and angle of the slashing wounds, as well as the footprint we found at the third crime scene, he's between five-ten and six-one, probably something like a hundred ninety, two hundred pounds. He's right-handed. Most likely white. He's escalating and he's smart, so he's older—mid-thirties. Very organized, so he may be married.

Most likely in a stable relationship of some sort. His kill zone seems to be centered on the Red Hook/Carroll Gardens area, but he's killed as far away as Coney Island. His comfort zone is clearly Brooklyn, which makes him a local. That's what we know for certain."

"Wrong," Jazz said. "Those *aren't* things you know for certain. Those are things you *think* you know for certain. For all we know, those are things he wants you to think you know. Staging the scenes to maximize your confusion. Like here"—he pointed to a photo—"this scene. This murder. He dumps the guts into a KFC bucket. Why do that? Just to mess with you, I guarantee."

"Or he just likes KFC, 'cause he did the same thing with another one a little while later. Not everything can be faked," Hughes scoffed.

"Wrong," Jazz said again, insistent. "Everything and anything can be faked. Billy avoided capture for decades. Every time he killed, some cop somewhere sat down and said, 'Well, here's what we know for certain.' And every time, they were wrong, and Billy lived another day." *Livin' another day is what it's all about, Jasper, m'boy, 'cause every day we live is another chance to kill.*

Hughes slumped in his chair, defeated. "I've spent months chasing this bastard and you're telling me I'm no closer than the first day."

"No. I'm just saying you can't assume you're any closer. Once you start making assumptions, a guy like this owns you. You were right about one thing: He's highly organized.

But...he's also picked on some street people—a bunch of homeless, some prostitutes. High-risk victims, if the guy is settled and married like you think."

"A random middle-class white dude hanging out with homeless people would stick out," Hughes agreed. "But so far, we don't have any witnesses. Nothing."

"You should announce that you *do* have a witness," Jazz said. "They almost caught Billy that way once. Cops had nothing, but they leaked to the press that they had an eyewitness and they were closing in. Billy felt like he had to go in and give them some cock-and-bull story about why he was in the area and how he couldn't have been the killer."

"What happened?"

Realized it was better to run, Jasper. Billy laughed in his memory. *You remember that: Sometimes, the best thing to do is just run. Don't look back. Don't look over your shoulder—they're either there or they're not, and lookin' ain't gonna change that. Run.*

"He changed his mind. But it was close."

"I'll see what I can do about that. The fake-witness idea. We'll see." Hughes stood and stretched.

Jazz took the momentary break to change the subject. "I've gotten everything I'm going to get out of papers and screens. I need to see the crime scenes. I need to be where it happened."

Hughes nodded slowly. "Yeah. Yeah, I know. You have to understand: We have dump sites, but only some of them are also murder scenes."

Jazz understood. Most crimes had three actual "scenes"—

98

where the crime was planned, where it took place, and where it ended. Sometimes they overlapped.

"And furthermore," Hughes continued, "a lot of these crimes happened months ago. He'd sometimes go weeks between murders. He's accelerating."

"All the more reason—"

"But what I'm saying is, these dump sites were mostly public areas. After we finished up our forensics and everything, we had to turn them back over to the public, you know?"

"I get it. I still need to see them."

"No problem. I'll show you everything you need."

CHAPTER 13

His first big-city crime scene. Maybe it should have been special or memorable somehow, but it was just an alleyway. Nothing remarkable about it. Nothing to distinguish it from any alleyway in any city in any country in the world.

Except that the Hat-Dog Killer had left his first two victims here.

Crime scene meant a lot of things. Technically, it was the place where a crime was committed. But a crime scene doesn't necessarily mean the *only* place where a crime was committed. Each individual act of murder could have multiple related crimes: Where the victim was first taken. Where the victim was raped or harmed or injured. Where the victim was actually killed. And where the victim's body was left. Each one could be a separate scene. Or one scene could combine any or all of them.

Right now, the sun was going down, but the day wasn't finished blushing, and the alley was cold. Jazz tried to picture it as it had been months ago, in the hottest, dampest days of summer, with the sun gone, the moon high, and the heat rising from the streets in tortuous waves. What had drawn the killer to this alley, to this place behind—what was it called?—Connecticut Bagels? And why, a weirdly nagging part of his brain insisted on wondering, was the place called Connecticut Bagels when it was in New York?

"Two of them here," he murmured.

They say lightning never strikes twice, Billy's voice whispered. *But that ain't actually true. It can and it does; that's science. But not us. We don't. We don't drop bodies in the same place. We don't pick up prospects at the same place. That's a routine, Jasper. And routines get you killed.*

"We're not sure why," Hughes confessed. "Might have just been opportunity....It's a good dump site. No street cameras nearby."

"Subway entrance over there," Jazz said, pointing. "So he picked them up coming out of the subway, I guess? Everyone I see here, they come up the stairs with their iPods on, or the first thing they do is check their phones. They're not paying attention to anything. Easy prey."

Hughes turned and looked at the subway stairs as though seeing them for the first time. "That makes a lot of sense, but...no. That stop, this stop here, it was closed all summer long. For maintenance and upgrades. The closest working station is about, uh, eight blocks that way." He pointed west. At least, Jazz *thought* it was west. He was having trouble orienting himself—Brooklyn looked the same in every direction.

So. No watering hole for the lion in the summer, then. It had been dry. Why leave your prey here, then, in this alley?

"The alley means something to him," Jazz said, pacing its width. He stroked his fingers lightly against one concrete wall, as if he could read something written there in Braille. "There's a significance to it. Otherwise, why bring them here?"

"Like I said—it's a good dumping ground. It's—"

"He didn't just dump them here. He killed them here, too."

"What?" Hughes shook his head. "No. You have to remember the chronology. He started out dumping bodies. It's only later that he evolves to killing them and leaving them at the murder site."

"Wrong."

"Wrong? Wrong? Are you going to tell me that the sun rises in the north, too? I'm talking *facts*, Jasper. There was no evidence, no blood, no—"

"There wouldn't have been. It rained the first night, right?"

Hughes paused, then—clearly frustrated—skimmed through the iPad. "Ah, hell. Okay, yeah. I forgot that. It was months ago. First body, it rained, so no blood, but the second body—"

Jazz hushed Hughes and closed his eyes; the crime-scene photos floated before him, a garish, ghoulish panorama of phosphenes. "DiNozzo's heel. Her left heel. It was broken."

"You *remember* that? Seriously?" Almost more exasperated than impressed. Almost.

"It's visible in the third photo taken at the scene," Jazz said, and walked over to where her body had been found. There was no trace of it now, of course. She had been moved months ago. Still, he sank to one knee and put his palm where her chest would have been, as though he could somehow feel the last beats of her heart. "Right here. And her left heel was broken. But you didn't find it here. It wasn't on the invoice."

Hughes stood over Jazz with the tablet, skimming through data. "It's not that I don't trust your memory...."

"You never found the heel, and rain wouldn't wash that away. Not on a flat surface like this. Blood, sure. Not something solid. She broke it when he grabbed her somewhere else. Or when he dragged her here."

"It could have broken when he dragged her dead body," Hughes pointed out.

"No. The lividity's all wrong. If he dragged her so that her left heel broke when she was dead, there would have been evidence of blood pooling along her left side. But there wasn't. She was alive when he brought her here."

"Sonofa..." Hughes looked as though he wished he could literally kick himself. "Spencer, too, then? Was he alive?"

"I don't know. Probably." Jazz remembered something new. "The newspapers reported the first one as a dump job, didn't they?"

"Yes."

"And your crime-scene guys," he said, turning to a Dumpster at the end of the alley, "they found a spot of Spencer's blood on the Dumpster, right?"

Hughes swallowed, looked as though he wanted to say something about Jazz's memory...then consulted the iPad. "Right. Spot of blood. Probably...we *thought* it flew off the body when our guy dropped it."

"No. He saw the newspaper story. Realized what he'd done, that he'd gotten lucky and thrown you off, had you running around looking for a murder site when it was right here all along. So he kept it up. The second time, he was prepared. A drop cloth, probably. Covered the alley floor with it to make it look like a dump job. But a little spatter got away from him when he cut the throat. Hit the Dumpster."

"You're basing a hell of a lot on a spot of blood and some rain." But Hughes wasn't protesting very hard.

"This was more than just a dump site to him, Hughes. He brought them here—and here specifically—to kill them. It's holy ground to him, for some reason."

"I hear you. The only problem is, given the other dozen murders we've got...so is about half of Brooklyn."

The NYPD and the feds had been working under the assumption that Hat-Dog's earliest victims were killed at one site and dumped at another, that as he became more comfortable with his skills and his kills (and, no doubt, his selection of sites), he began to leave his victims where he'd murdered them.

Jazz's observation destroyed that pattern. It became clear as he visited the sites where the various bodies had been found that Hat-Dog's decision to leave a body in a particular place had nothing to do with his evolution as a killer. Each decision made sense only to him.

A rooftop in Brooklyn, for example, didn't seem like the

sort of place for a murder, but the medical examiner was certain that Marvin Candless had been killed up there, and Jazz tended to agree. Literally pints of blood had pooled around the body, and a void pattern that fit the body precisely—poor old Marvin had died on that rooftop, the second to die atop a building (along with an earlier victim named Jerome Herrington). Jazz noted that the ME speculated Mr. Candless had lived long enough to experience his own intestines being removed, based on the amount of blood at the scene. That was probably right.

"Why not just tie them down instead of paralyzing them?" Hughes asked, staring up at the sky. He clearly had no need or desire to look at this crime scene again, even though it had been weeks since Candless's death and anyone on the rooftop wouldn't find anything to indicate a crime had ever happened here.

"Probably more fun for him this way," Jazz said. He peered around. "Candless died when it was warmer. What have we got over there?"

"Where?" Hughes asked.

Jazz pointed to two large, squarish wooden structures, covered in plastic tarps against the winter.

"Oh. Roof gardens."

"*Roof* gardens?" It was as alien a concept to country-boy Jazz as life on a desert island.

Hughes shrugged. "City folk like green, too. Gotta get it where you can."

"Nothing here. Let's move on."

And they did. Moving on, then on, then on. Alleyways.

An open-air parking space tucked behind an old ramshackle fence that provided just enough privacy for dirty business. Some of the crime scenes, Jazz believed, were clearly thought out and picked out far in advance. Some, it seemed, were chosen on the fly, as good opportunities. Like the new alleyway he stood in.

"He took his time," Jazz muttered, remembering the file on Aimee Ventnor, the fifth victim. Aimee had been on her way home from a friend's house. A judiciously placed subway camera showed her making a bad turn coming off the R train, one that took her to a locked subway gate. The cops believed—and Jazz thought it, too—that Hat-Dog had probably "acquired" her then, watching her head down that blind passageway, knowing she would have to come back his way.

"Grabbed her right when she left view of the camera," Jazz said.

"That's what we think," Hughes agreed. "Then it's a straight shot up to the alley, if you're willing to dance around some trash cans from the bodega on the corner."

Oh, he's willing to dance, I bet! Billy crowed.

Like so many of the Hat-Dog crime scenes, this one was a public space. It had been months since Ventnor was found, so the space had long since been released back to the public. Hughes stood at the end of the alleyway to keep away any onlookers as Jazz paced and watched and thought.

"Anything?" Hughes asked eventually, joining Jazz.

"It stinks."

"It's an alleyway in Brooklyn. I'm not sure what you expected."

"No, it's just...it stinks even in the winter. He killed her in the late summer. It would have smelled even worse then, right?"

"Probably."

"Showing his contempt for her. Not leaving her in a nice place. She meant nothing to him."

"Right. He *killed* her."

"Some killers have feelings for their victims. Take care of the bodies. Close the eyes, stuff like that."

"Well, this guy cut off her eyelids, so he didn't care about *that*." Without even looking at a file, Hughes rattled off the various crimes committed in this alley by Hat-Dog. "Last victim before we started recovering semen."

"So, condom for her, but not others?"

"Maybe he thinks some are clean and some aren't? Gibbs—the next vic—was married. Maybe he figured she wouldn't have an STD?"

That made some sort of sense, but it wasn't anything Jazz could solve now. "I think I'm done here." They toured the rest of the crime scenes as the early winter night fell around them.

One of the body sites wasn't outside at all—it was inside what had been an abandoned office building, now being refurbished and converted into apartments. Hughes flashed his tin to a security guard and they trooped inside, where they found that the crime scene was now a half-painted, half-completed studio unit.

Hughes handed Jazz the iPad. "By the time we got to this one, we had the FBI involved. They did some computer hoodoo on all the photos on here. It's supposed to work like some kind of augmented-reality thing...."

Jazz fiddled with it and soon saw what Hughes meant—the camera on the back of the tablet picked up whatever he pointed it at, and showed him on its screen what that part of the studio had looked like when the police had arrived. Very cool. Jazz walked the perimeter of the apartment, unraveling the past as he went.

"Broken window." The screen showed glass on the floor, and footprints consistent with footprints found at some of the other scenes.

"Yeah. He broke the glass and came in through the window."

Jazz stared at the image from the past in front of him. Something was wrong....

Something's always wrong, Billy said. *I make sure something's wrong....*

"He didn't come in through the window. He broke it after the fact."

"But, Jasper," Hughes protested, "the glass was on the inside. That means he had to break it from the outside—"

"Right. So he opened it from in here, crawled out onto the fire escape, and broke it then."

"Why do you say that? There's not a shred of forensic evidence—"

"Ha! You know what Billy used to say about forensic evidence? Hell"—he dropped into an eerily perfect impression of his father—"forensic evidence is like snappin' together five pieces from a hundred-piece puzzle and sayin', 'That's close enough.'

"You can't trust anything you find," he went on in his own voice. "Especially the obvious stuff. Check out this picture. It shows a partial footprint *under* one of the shards of glass. If he'd broken the window and then come in, he would have either stepped on the glass or avoided it. But the only way for his footprint to be under the glass is if he was already in the room."

Hughes stared.

"Every conclusion we draw is based on something we find, Billy used to say." *If you start muckin' up what they find, then you're muckin' up their conclusions, too, Jasper. It's basic chaos theory—outcomes depend on initial conditions.*

"What do you know about chaos theory?" Jazz asked, and Hughes sighed. "Never mind. Not important."

"I actually know all about chaos theory," the detective said. "Sensitive dependence on initial conditions, right? I'm just aggravated that we missed this somehow."

"Well, I'm not sure what it means. It's just him trying to throw us off. I'm not sure it gets us any closer to him, but it shows how he thinks. A little."

Hughes made a note in a little notebook he carried in his breast pocket. "I'll get some guys to come talk to the workers tomorrow. See if anyone noticed anything when they started working. Also interview some of the building people, nose around, see if we can figure out how he *did* get in, if not through the window."

"What's next?"

Hughes checked his watch. "It's late. The only place you haven't seen yet is the one way down in Coney Island."

"Is that far?"

"Far enough. Let me get you back to the hotel. Get some rest. We'll hit the Tilt-A-Whirl tomorrow, okay?"

Jazz checked the time. "Yeah. I better call my aunt. I totally forgot to do that today."

When Hughes dropped him off at the hotel, Jazz found a quiet corner of the lobby to call home. Aunt Samantha picked up. They talked briefly about Gramma, who seemed to be doing well, having apparently forgotten that her daughter hadn't been home in decades. "We sort of picked up right where we left off," Samantha said.

"I guess that's good. And Howie's helping?"

"Um, yeah. He's...friendly."

That sounded like Howie. "Good. Look, just one more thing, Aunt Samantha. I don't think this'll be an issue, but just in case—don't talk to any reporters, okay?"

"Oh," she said, as if the idea hadn't even occurred to her. "Right. Okay. I won't." A moment passed, and then she said, "Not even the ones you're friends with?"

Friends?

Before she could answer his next question—before he even asked it—Jazz knew what was about to happen. "What friends?" He had made it an unbreakable policy not to befriend anyone in the media.

"The guy..." she said, uncertain. "The guy from the local paper. Weathers."

Of course. Doug Weathers. Jazz nearly went blind as his vision turned red. "Doug Weathers," he said. "You talked to Doug Weathers."

"He came by this afternoon. He didn't seem like the national people. Just wanted to check in, he said. He said he hadn't talked to you in a while and was wondering—oh, Jesus. Jasper, what did I do?"

You gave information to the enemy, you idiot! Jazz wanted to scream. He took a deep breath, then another. She didn't know. Aunt Samantha had been hit with the media sledge-hammer four years ago, but that had been it. She hadn't lived under the constant threat of press intrusion like Jazz had.

"What did you tell him?"

"I am so sorry," Samantha said. "God, I was an idiot, wasn't I? He seemed so nice. And I thought, I thought, well, *He's just a local paper.* And he said he knew you, that you were friends."

"He was telling half the truth. Which, to be fair, is about fifty percent more than usual. What did you tell him?"

"Nothing. Well, not nothing. But nothing important. He asked if you were around and I told him you were out of town."

"Is that it? Did you tell him where I went?"

She sighed, resigned and defeated. "I said you were in New York. But," she said hurriedly, "I didn't tell him you were there for the police."

It didn't matter. Weathers was a sleaze, a bottom-feeder, and a poor speller, but he wasn't stupid. He knew that if you added Jasper Dent and New York, you could only come up with one solution: the Hat-Dog Killer.

"Okay, thanks, Aunt Samantha," Jazz said as calmly as he could. Connie walked through the lobby just then, carrying two bottles of soda and a bag of chips. She arched an eyebrow at him as she headed to the elevator.

"I'm so sorry," Samantha said again.

"Don't worry about it. Tuck Gramma in, and I'll talk to you again tomorrow."

In the room, Connie was at the desk, a neatly ordered stack of paperwork before her. "I can't believe I came all this way to play secretary," she began, but when she saw the look on his face, her snark fell away and she went to him, wrapping him in her arms. "What happened?"

"I think it's all gonna hit the fan," he told her.

Later, they lay in bed together, curled into each other. They had snuggled in the backseat of the Jeep before and had napped together at the Hideout or—on occasion, when her parents and Whiz were away—at Connie's house. But this was—would be—their first time spending an entire night together. Jazz suddenly wished he'd thought to bring condoms.

He was also glad he hadn't. There was no way Connie would let them have sex without protection, so he was safe.

You could talk those pretty legs open if you wanted to, Billy told him, licking his chops. *She wants it so bad, she's*

*drooling for it. And you know it. You know it in your gut
and in your balls. It'll feel so good, and the best part of it is
that you'll be making her do it, making her want it. That's
the best part, Jasper. When they can't help themselves.*

"What are you thinking?" Connie asked.

"You don't want to know."

"You're thinking about the murders."

"Yeah," he lied. It was easier, the lying. It spared her so
much.

She sat up in bed. "Do you want to talk about it?"

"No. I don't want to bother you."

"It's okay. I'm here to help."

He ransacked his mind for something he could discuss. It
wasn't difficult. The case files were jam-packed with contra-
dictory and nonsensical bits of information, so he latched on
to one of them.

"It's the disemboweling," he told her.

"Because he didn't do that right away," Connie said, and
Jazz smiled in the dark, proud of her.

"Right. He didn't start disemboweling until his sixth
victim."

"So why start then? Is that what's bothering you? He
didn't start the paralysis until later, either."

"Yeah, but that's a practical thing. He doesn't feel an urge
to paralyze them—I really believe he just does it to make
things easier."

"And by 'things,' you mean gutting them."

"Yeah."

"But wouldn't paralyzing them make them not feel pain? I thought these kinds of guys got off on causing pain."

"He's paralyzing them from the waist down. Then cutting open their bellies. Trust me—they felt plenty of pain."

Connie shivered next to him. "Does this mean he's getting worse?"

"Escalation like this isn't unheard of. A lot of these guys take time to refine their fantasies. He's been thinking about all of this stuff for a long time. Maybe he thought that raping and killing and cutting off the penises would be enough. But by the time he hit number six, it wasn't doing it for him any more. He needed something else."

"So he adds in disemboweling."

"Right. But here's the thing: When he gutted number six, he was sure, confident. The cuts were precise. Almost surgical. When he killed number seven, there were hesitation cuts."

"Like he was unsure of himself. Or maybe unsure of what he was doing?"

Jazz squeezed her hand. "Right. And that's just weird. These guys usually get *better*, not worse. So why did he hesitate to gut number seven?"

Connie thought for a while. Jazz allowed himself to enjoy the quiet and the radiating warmth of her. "Maybe," she said, "something distracted or startled him. No one is consistent all the time. Not even your dad."

Variety's the spice of life, Billy admitted.

But Jazz wasn't buying it. "It's not just the gutting," he told her. "It's other things, too. Like the rapes."

Connie stiffened next to him, and Jazz cursed himself

inwardly. To him, rape was just another crime visited upon Hat-Dog's victims, but of course to Connie it would resonate more viscerally than that. "We really don't have to talk about this now," he said as gently as he knew how.

"I want to help," she told him. "Keep going."

He drew in a deep breath. "Okay. Well, rape is about power," he told her. "Power and dominance." *And fun, Billy chortled. Heaps and heaps of fun!* "But this guy doesn't seem to enjoy his power. At least, not all of the time. If you look at the medical examiner's reports, his rapes fall into two categories—some are violent and repeated while the victims are alive. Others are perimortem."

"What does that mean?"

"It means at or around the time of death."

"He's raping corpses? Jesus Christ."

"No, not corpses. Just raping them at their weakest, so he doesn't have to struggle as much. So part of the time, he's getting off on the power and the domination over them while they're still alive and fighting. The rest of the time, he waits until they're practically dead so that he can do it without any trouble. It doesn't make sense."

"The guy's crazy, Jazz. It doesn't always have to make sense."

The same thing Hughes had said earlier. And the answer was still the same: "Not to you, no. But to them—to *me*—yeah, they should always make sense."

"Are you saying your *dad* made sense to you?" she asked, horrified.

"I'm saying…"

This is a special thing, Jasper. For us and only us. Not for anyone else.

"I'm saying that I can understand it. I can live in his head. That doesn't mean I agree with it." *I don't think.*

Because a part of him couldn't stop thinking about Billy's voice. Before. Urging him to sucker Connie's legs apart and slide between them...

"I can live in his head," Jazz told her, "because that's where I grew up. With that kind of thinking. It was my normal. Like being in a cult, I guess. All the normal things, all the things that made sense to you or to Howie, were things I was taught didn't apply to me. Like...like, did your parents ever tell you stories?"

"You mean, like 'Goldilocks' or 'Sleeping Beauty'? Yeah, sure."

"Well, Billy used to tell me stories, too. Stories about his prospects. And there was even..." He drifted off, suddenly lost in his own past. The Crow King...He had forgotten all about the Crow King. How could he forget that? It had been a mainstay of his childhood, that story. That myth. He'd loved it, not for the story itself but rather for the way Billy had told it, changing his voice and his facial expression to match the different characters as he went.

"You still there? Earth to Jazz..."

"I was just remembering, is all. When I was a kid, after Mom died, Billy used to tell me this story. Like a fairy tale, or a fable. It was about a crow. The king of crows, really."

"The king of crows?"

"Yeah. It started out with the Crow King, who was surveying all he ruled..."

...and he saw it was good, Jasper. There was peace where there was supposed to be peace, and war where there was supposed to be war. Because the crow is a wise bird, the crow knows that someone's always killin' someone else somewhere. That's the way of the world. That's the natural order of things. And the Crow King was the wisest of all the wise birds, so there wasn't no way no how he was gonna dispute the natural order of things. And so the world turned and the crows ate carrion and the young squirrels still a-sleepin' in their nests and the vegetables growin' in the fields (and you need to eat your vegetables, too, Jasper, to grow up big and strong).

Now one day, into this perfection, into this natural world, there came a red robin. Red like a sunset, Jasper. A more beautiful bird you could not imagine, not with all the thinking in all the world. And the robin decided that it wanted to be like a crow. More than that, it wanted to be the Crow King.

And so the robin went off and the robin killed. It killed a great many birds. It slaughtered, bringing war where there had been peace.

And the Crow King said, "No, this is not for you. This is only for me." And he hunted down the robin, and when he found him, he held down the robin and pierced its breast with his beak and drank from it, draining it until its red feathers turned white.

And that, Jasper, was the first dove. And this is why the

dove is a bird of peace—because it knows better than to try to be otherwise.

"That's...that's a *horrible* story!" Connie said.

"That was my bedtime story," Jazz said, without inflection.

Connie wrapped her arms around him and Jazz let her and then—thankfully—he fell asleep, just like a little boy who's been read to by his father.

CHAPTER 14

Lips on his
   (oh, yes)
   shoulder and trailing a line of cool heat
   (oh)
   down farther and his fingers touch something so soft and
familiar
   (there, touch me there)
   and also somehow unknown and a groan
   his groan?
   or
   hers?
   He reaches out, back, around
   (Oh, yes)
   and opens his mouth
   and licks

He awoke to find himself pressed tightly against Connie, terrified and horrified and aroused all at once. She was awake, too, whether because of him or not he didn't know, but he kissed her and she kissed back just as urgently and fumbled with the drawstring on his pajama bottoms and reached for him there, and he would have let her, he needed to let her, but at the last minute he drew in a breath and

—like cutting—

Oh, yes, just touch—

he pulled back, pulled away, shoving Connie more violently than he'd intended.

Both dreams. Both of them at once—

He rolled out of bed, arms flailing, smacking into the nightstand, pulling the alarm clock and the phone down to the floor with him.

Both of them. Killing and sex and—

"I'm sorry," he said. "I'm sorry."

Sorry's not enough. Never enough. Never, ever...

Connie crawled over from her side of the bed to look down at him, her hair covered by the satin bonnet she wore to sleep. In the murky light that bled through the thin curtains, she was chocolate cream and he wanted to devour every last inch of her, wanted to run his tongue over her, wanted to sink his teeth into her and suck out everything of her, ingest it into him.

No. No! Stop it! That's crazy.

Take it, Jasper, Billy cooed. *Take her. She's yours. She's your prospect. This is what you've been waiting for. And best of all, Jasper? Best of all is that* she's *been waiting for it, too.*

Not true. He couldn't believe it was true.

But then there was the naked lust, the yearning in Connie's eyes, in the parting of her lips, in her pose on the bed. It was less than human, this electricity between them. It was primal, as it was meant to be, as it should be.

That's when it's best, Jasper. When they come to you. When they want it as badly as you want to give it.

"Why are you afraid?" Connie whispered, and her voice tasted like warm pie. "Why are you so afraid of me?"

"I'm not afraid of you." And he wasn't. Jazz was afraid only of himself.

"I know it isn't easy," she said. "I know it's complicated for you. But this—this thing, this moment—this is supposed to be easy. So easy."

"We can't."

"I brought condoms," she said, the words an electric prod to his heart. "I thought . . . I knew we'd be alone here."

Jazz closed his eyes. It was as though he could see the future. But not just one future. He could see so many of them. He could see himself, happy, with Connie, two normal people living normal lives, drawn closer together and connected by their shared intimacy, the way it was supposed to work, the way it was supposed to be.

But he could also see . . .

But here's the thing, Jasper, Billy's voice purred, speaking from the last time he'd spoken to his father, at Wammaket

121

State Penitentiary. *I bet you're a nice, responsible kid, 'cause I raised you that way, but are you always the one buyin' the rubbers? Hmm? Or maybe she's on that pill? 'Cause you can't always trust 'em, Jasper. You look at them rubbers real close-like, see? You watch her take that pill, Jasper. Hell* (and here Billy had roared with laughter), *how you think* you *was born?*

He could also see sex as the ignition moment, the fulcrum upon which his own career of serial murder would lever.

None of Billy's victims had been black. There had been Latinas and Asians and a great profusion of white girls, but not a single African American. Jazz thought that made Connie safe.

He'd thought that... until now.

Now he was no longer certain.

He wanted her so badly. And was that because he was a boy and she was a girl and they were in love and that's how it was supposed to work?

Or was it because the deepest part of him, the Billy part of him, champed at the bit, strained against its tether, eager and desperate for freedom, to begin what it had been born and made to do?

He squeezed his eyes shut tight, as tight as he could. As tight as the night Billy had skinned poor Rusty alive. The howl of the dog as Billy's knife did its gruesome work...

Phosphenes again behind his eyelids, this time not of the crime scenes from the pictures, but rather as he'd seen them tonight.

I did something good tonight. I helped tonight. Doesn't that mean I should be getting better, *not worse?*

Sex and killing. The two dreams, conflating. What did *that* mean?

When Jazz opened his eyes and spoke, his voice was deep, sure, emotionless.

"You should throw those condoms away," he said.

And then he crawled into the other, empty bed to sleep.

CHAPTER 15

Billy Dent roamed Brooklyn, the day having dawned clear and cold. He turned up the collar of his coat and tugged his hat down around his ears.

The cold weather made hiding even easier. Everyone all bundled up. Everyone in such a hurry to get to where they were going. No one stopping to look at anyone else. Everyone wearing gloves, how convenient. Cover up those prison tats. Cover up LOVE. Cover up FEAR.

Cover 'em up, but they're still there. Love and fear. Equal. Maybe even the same.

It wouldn't have mattered if anyone had been looking at him, anyway. Billy didn't fear the human eye. The human eye was a fickle, foolish thing. His goatee and mustache, along with a set of muttonchop sideburns trimmed and shaped just right, changed the angles and configuration of his face. Cutting down his eyebrows made his eyes more prominent. And, of course, he'd dyed his hair.

Billy chuckled to himself when he thought of the vanity of

women, and how they'd made it easier on folks like him. God bless Miss Clairol and her endless variations of hues and shades! Billy had—by mixing together a specific set of colors—managed to turn his dirty blond hair into graying brown. After thinning it out with an electric razor, he looked ten years older. The final touch was a pair of black, heavy-rimmed glasses, the kind Billy's own father had once worn. To the idiotic hipsters of Brooklyn, these glasses were "fashionable." They also distorted Billy's features in a way that pleased him and made him harder to recognize. Oh, glorious fashion!

Disguising yourself wasn't just about making yourself look different; it was about making yourself look different from what people were looking for. The cops could imagine Billy growing a beard or shaving a beard or growing out his hair or coloring his hair, but would they imagine him making himself look older?

He'd studied the FBI and police procedure most of his life. He knew how cops thought and, more important, how they thought *he* thought. They thought him a creature of immeasurable vanity, and they couldn't imagine that he would be willing to make himself look worse in order to evade recapture.

Billy was willing to do *anything* to evade recapture.

After years in prison with nothing to do but exercise, Billy was in top condition, but he dressed to hide his physique. Walked with a slump. When he was out and about, he made sure to wear a watch and checked it constantly, communicating that he was in his own world.

Plus, he had the perfect bit of camouflage: a stroller and a diaper bag.

This part of Brooklyn was called Park Slope, and Billy had noticed quickly that damn near everyone here had either a dog or a baby carriage or both. He had no interest in actually taking care of anything living, but he had a big interest in blending in, so he'd bought a used stroller at an antiques store, then wrapped up a bundle of blankets to look like a baby. Since it was winter, he could keep the top down; anyone looking through the little plastic window would see what appeared to be a well-tucked-in child, napping.

And the diaper bag actually held diapers. Under the diapers, Billy had stashed three different-sized knives, a Glock he'd bought on the street, and a length of rope.

Ambling along the streets of Brooklyn, no one gave an older dad a second look.

People. Ha.

Billy worried more about facial-recognition software than he worried about a human being recalling his face from TV. Cameras were everywhere in "free" America—at ATMs, at street intersections, at banks, behind convenience-store counters. The bastard cops and the FBI were supposed to need search warrants and court orders to look at those cameras, but Billy was no fool. He knew about the Patriot Act. And he knew something even more sinister—he knew the fear that ruled in the hearts of all prospects. The bastard cops needed a court order only when someone said no to them. And these days, all you had to do was wave a flag or say "keeping Americans safe" and anyone owning those cameras would let the cops look all they wanted. No hassle. No fuss, no muss. So Billy took no chances. He wore sunglasses and a hat whenever possible.

And he smiled.

Facial-recognition software, for some reason, had trouble distinguishing between two faces if one of them was smiling. There were even states where you couldn't smile for your driver's license photo. So, Billy smiled everywhere he went.

This was hardly a chore. Billy liked smiling. Billy was a happy guy.

In his coat pockets, he had a total of five different throwaway cell phones. One of them buzzed for his attention as he pushed his stroller past the umpteenth coffee shop on Fourth Street. This place was obsessed, Billy had noticed, with coffee shops. There were three of them on every block, not to mention the occasional Starbucks.

He paused as he groped for the proper phone. Only one person had the numbers to his various phones, and that was just for emergencies. He shouldn't be receiving phone calls—he gave them.

Finding the right phone, he flipped it open, and before he could say anything, the voice at the other end said, almost saucily, "Guess who's in town?"

And then told him.

And Billy Dent's smile grew even wider.

CHAPTER 16

The pounding at the door woke Jazz from a deep slumber that morning, gasping awake as if he'd forgotten how to breathe. Connie bolted up in the other bed, startled.

"Who—" she started.

"NYPD!" a voice barked. "Open up! Now!"

"NYPD?" Connie whispered. "What?"

Jazz shook sleep from his head and rolled to his feet. Was Hughes playing some kind of joke? Or...

Or was he being Fultoned again?

He left the chain on the door, opening it just enough to peer out. Two uniformed cops stood there, along with an older white guy in a suit and tie. The white guy pushed at the door. "Jasper Dent," he said. It wasn't a question. It was more like a command, as though he were ordering the kid at the door to be Jazz.

"Let me see some ID," Jazz said, but before the words were even out of his mouth, he was looking at the name card and badge for Detective Stephen Long.

"Homicide," Long snapped. "Brooklyn South. Open the door."

Brooklyn South. Homicide. The same division Hughes came from.

Or claimed to come from. The badge and name card looked similar to Hughes's. How hard would that be to fake? Probably easier than Jazz thought, but harder than made it worthwhile.

"What can I do for you, Detective?" Jazz asked, stalling. He could hear Connie behind him, throwing on clothes, no doubt.

"I said open the goddamn door. Do it now or we'll bust it down. Seriously."

"Do you have a warrant?"

Long blew out an annoyed breath. "Okay, we're knocking it down."

"Wait, wait." Connie had stopped moving around. Jazz unchained the door and stepped back. "Come in. What can I do for—"

"You can come with us," Long said as he and the other two cops came into the room. Long looked around, spied Connie, who was in bed, the covers pulled up to her chin. The detective raised an eyebrow. "You guys," he directed the uniforms, "check the room and the girl. Dent, put on some pants. You're coming with me."

"What's going on here?" Jazz asked.

Long looked at his watch. "You have thirty seconds to put on real clothes. Dressed or not, I'm taking you with me."

Bristling, Jazz grabbed his clothes from the previous day

and retreated to the bathroom to change. Outside, he could hear the cops going through the dresser and desk drawers. One of them must have started to go through Connie's suitcase because he heard her shout, "Hands off the panties, you perv!"

He emerged from the bathroom, dressed, to find one of the cops triumphantly brandishing the iPad and papers Hughes had brought over the day before. From the crestfallen expression on Connie's face, Jazz realized that she had hidden them in her suitcase while he'd stalled at the door.

"We're done here," Long said, and tipped an imaginary hat to Connie. "Ma'am," he fake-drawled, and grabbed Jazz by the arm and led him out the door.

Connie handled the cops dragging Jazz away with an aplomb that both surprised and impressed her. *Good for you,* she thought. *You totally didn't do the whole shrieking girlfriend thing while they hauled your boyfriend out of here. That would have been pretty low-class.*

Then again, Jazz had a history of being dragged away by the cops, and it always worked out. He had been arrested once a couple of months ago during the Impressionist case, at the same time that Howie struggled for his life after being knifed. And she had been there in the school auditorium when Deputy Erickson had pulled Jazz out of play rehearsal one afternoon, all because Jazz had done too good a job predicting the Impressionist's next victim. Both times, he had returned safe and sound.

As she did at home every morning in her own room, she switched on the TV to listen to the news and weather while she got dressed. She would have to figure out where he'd gone, of course. Even though he always came back to her, that didn't mean he didn't need help. After all, the Impressionist had managed to hold Jazz hostage in his own home, and only Connie and Howie's last minute heroics had saved him.

Or had they? Maybe Jazz could have saved himself. Put that one up there on the list of things she would never know. She sighed. *You could have chosen an easier life for yourself, Conscience Hall, than falling in love with a guy who packs the kind of baggage Jazz packs.*

Nah. She was kidding herself. It hadn't been a choice—she had fallen desperately in love with Jazz early on. Tried to hide it. From her father especially, but even from herself. In love with the son of the world's most notorious serial killer? For reals? Maybe *he's* not nuts, but *you* sure are, Connie!

The first time they kissed, though...

God, that first kiss!

Connie's driveway. Evening bleeding into an unusually cool summer night. She was sixteen at the time and he wasn't the first boy she'd kissed, but he was the first one to make her feel cold and warm all at once, the first one to make her want to dissolve into him.

He'd groaned somewhere deep in the back of his throat as they kissed, and she thought that groan was surrender.

And speaking of surrender, she thought, pawing through her suitcase for a shirt, *what the hell happened last night?* A less confident girl might have curled up in a corner with her *Cosmo* and wept and snuffled her way through some idiotic article with a title like "How to Make Him Your Boy Toy." But not Connie. She wasn't self-centered, but she also wasn't blind. She knew she had it going on and that there were basically only two good excuses for a guy not wanting to take advantage of her willingness: gay or dead.

She checked herself in the mirror. Not that it mattered. She would be bundled in a heavy coat when she went outside. And she didn't know anyone in Brooklyn, anyway.

Mirror Connie looked pretty damn good. She pouted, then puckered up and blew herself a kiss. And then felt like a stupid little girl.

Had she been unfair to Jazz the night before? Was she still being unfair to him? He'd made it pretty clear that he wasn't ready for the big step to Real Sex. What kind of girlfriend was she if she couldn't understand and respect that?

Then again...maybe *he* was the one being unfair to *her*. All kinds of people had traumas in their pasts. Not all of them were completely unable to connect with other people. And Jazz had proven many, many times in the past that he had no problem making out—they'd kissed, touched, probed, and groped each other in every way imaginable. He had drawn a line he refused to cross for no good reason and she was on the other side of that line, begging him to cross over.

Why couldn't he—

And just then, the TV, burbling in the background, said her boyfriend's name.

Connie spun around, reaching for the remote so that she could turn up the volume.

"—son of Billy Dent," a very, very blow-dried anchorman said. "Needless to say, this news comes as something of a shock to New Yorkers, prompting questions as to the possible involvement of Billy Dent in the Hat-Dog murders."

You moron. Hat-Dog's been killing since before Billy broke out of jail.

"In the meantime, police sources tell WPLX that Jasper Dent will be arriving at the Seventy-sixth Precinct in Carroll Gardens soon to discuss the case. We expect a press conference with task-force commander Captain Niles Montgomery later today to brief us. We'll have details of that press conference on our website, of course, along with a wrap-up and commentary tonight at five."

Connie turned off the TV—news anchors had a bizarre, sing-song way of talking, a constant up-and-down of weird word emphasis that nauseated her. She could only take it for roughly the length of time it took her to get dressed each morning.

So, Jazz was safe. With the NYPD. As usual, no one could be bothered to fill her in, and she figured she wouldn't hear from him until he was done. Odds were it would take him all day. What should she do in the meantime?

Come on, Connie. You're in the coolest city in the world for the day.

Just then, her cell phone burbled for her attention. It was her father.

"Hi, Daddy!" she chirped, making every effort to sound like a girl who had *not* skipped off to New York with her boyfriend and lied about it to her parents. The only problem was that Connie didn't know what that girl would sound like.

"Something you'd like to tell me?" her father asked without preamble or greeting. That was how her father operated: He always gave his kids an opportunity to come clean. Connie had never noticed a difference in the punishment, though, so she usually gambled on trying to get away with it.

"New York is *amazing*," Connie effused, trying for "breathless and overwhelmed." "Last night we went to Rockefeller Center, which is *so* much cooler than on TV—"

"I was reading the paper today, and guess what it says?"

"Well," Connie said, "I bet it doesn't say anything about the *awesome* Chinese food I had for dinner last night."

"It says that Jasper is in New York. Right now."

Ouch. Of course. That made sense. The news probably leaked from Lobo's Nod to New York, not the other way around. "Really?" She aimed for surprised, but came closer to "oh, busted." Cleared her throat for a second try. "Really? That's a weird coincidence."

"I'm sure," her father said drily. "And right now, you're where?"

"At Larissa's place."

"Let me talk to her, then."

Double ouch.

"She's in the shower."

"I can wait."

"Dad..."

"Seriously. I have all kinds of rollover minutes. I can wait."

Damn.

"Okay, Dad. I'm not with Larissa. I'm at a hotel in Brooklyn."

"With him." Her father's anger was palpable, even over the phone.

"No. I'm not with him. Honest." It wasn't a lie. Present tense was your friend when it came to lying.

"Do you really think I'm going to believe anything you tell me? This isn't like you got caught doing something and lied to avoid punishment, Conscience. This was premeditated. You set this up. You set *me* up. You planned this and then you executed your plan, a plan based on deception and dishonesty. So explain to me why I should believe anything you say. Go on. Explain."

"Because I'm telling the truth. He's not here. He's with the police."

"That's where he belongs."

Connie considered explaining that Jazz wasn't under arrest—not really—but figured she'd just let it go. "Dad, the whole reason we're here—"

"The paper says—"

"It's Doug Weathers, Dad. Jesus, you can't believe anything that guy—"

"Do *not* take the Lord's name in vain, Conscience. You're in enough trouble with me as it is already. And I don't *care* why you're there. What I care about is this: My child lied to me, deceived me, in order to run away with her boyfriend. That's what I care about. I want you home five minutes ago, do you understand?"

"I can't—I have a plane ticket. I won't be home for—"

"Give me your confirmation number. I'll call the airline and see about getting it changed."

"But, Dad—"

"What? What are you going to say? Are you going to tell me that this is unfair? That I'm inconveniencing you? That you can be trusted to handle this yourself?"

She'd been planning on saying pretty much all of that.

"Well, let me tell you something." The rage in her father's voice had grown more and more potent as he spoke, as though each word stoked a fire in his heart. "Let me tell you something: Fairness is for people who don't lie. Convenience is for people who don't lie. And trust is sure as hell for people who don't lie."

Connie dropped onto the bed Jazz had slept in. "I'm seventeen," she said quietly. "You can't control me for—"

"I can control you for five more months. And if it means protecting you from the world and that boy and yourself, I will damn sure control you right up to midnight on your birthday. Do you understand?"

She turned to her left. Cheek to Jazz's pillow. She could smell him. Not his deodorant or his shampoo—him. The pure, unadulterated scent of him.

"I love him, Daddy." The simple, unvarnished truth.

"I'm sure it doesn't surprise you to hear that I. Don't. Care."

There was nothing else she could do. Her father wouldn't be persuaded by logic and he wouldn't be persuaded by love. At least she'd tried.

Connie surrendered. She gave her father the confirmation number.

CHAPTER 17

In a depressingly short amount of time, Connie's father called back to let her know that he had managed to get her a seat on a flight out of LaGuardia late that night. It had cost him $150 more than the cost of the original ticket, a sum he made sure she understood would be deducted piecemeal from her future allowances and summer jobs until paid back.

An hour went by, and Jazz still wasn't back from the police station, though he did text to say nothing more helpful than that he thought he would be a while. Connie had hours to kill and nothing to do. She couldn't stand the idea of being cooped up in the hotel room all day by herself, with only the TV and its pathetic selection of cable channels for company. Even through the grayish window, Brooklyn looked hard and bright in the winter sunshine. Despite the bundled pedestrians, she could hardly believe it was cold out at all, so warm was the sunlight.

The police had confiscated all of the materials Detective Hughes had brought the day before, but they hadn't taken anything actually belonging to Jazz or Connie. Just stuff that had NYPD markings or logos on it.

Which meant that they'd left Connie's laptop.

The police didn't know that the previous night, Connie had taken pictures of much of the evidence and then transferred the photos to her laptop, along with notes she'd taken while listening to Jazz and Hughes. She hadn't minded pretending to play secretary as long as she got something out of it. She was pretty sure even Jazz and Hughes weren't aware of what she'd been doing. The two of them had been off in some kind of grim, downbeat type of Narnia reserved for those obsessed with crime, an alternate reality where shadows concealed murderers and the sewers clogged with unreadable clues.

She skimmed through the images and notes, then double-checked some things on the maps app on her cell phone. Sure enough, many of the crime scenes were nearby—within walking distance, even.

Connie told herself that she was just going to get out of the hotel room. Get some fresh air. Wander the streets a little and see whatever it was Brooklyn had to offer. She had been to New York before, but always with her family and always to Manhattan, never Brooklyn.

If her perambulations took her to some of the closest crime scenes, well…that was just a happy coincidence, right?

A man pushing a baby carriage nearly collided with Connie on the sidewalk, swerving at the last minute. He wore a wide smile and hilariously awful facial hair and the same heavy-framed retro-hipster glasses as half the guys she'd seen. He seemed so obliviously happy that she didn't even feel the need to shout, "Watch where you're going!" after him as he trundled down the street with the carriage. Instead, she just took a moment to look around her, taking in the city.

Connie liked the city, at least what she'd seen of it so far on her impromptu tour of old crime scenes. She had spent some time in Charlotte before her family moved to Lobo's Nod, but even a big city like Charlotte had nothing on the Big City of Big Cities: NYC. She liked seeing black faces as she strolled the streets, liked not feeling as alone as she sometimes did in Lobo's Nod, where she often felt conspicuous for more than just the infamy of her boyfriend's father. Here in New York, she was one more tile in a mosaic of black, white, yellow, brown.... It was exhilarating.

She had always imagined herself here. Here or in LA. If she was going to be an actress, it would have to be one or the other. LA was where you went for the big money and the kind of fame that required bodyguards and came with hot-and-cold-running stalkerazzi: Hollywood. The movies. Endless and eternal.

But New York was home of the stage. Broadway. Performing night after night in front of a live audience. That immediate reaction, that visceral feedback, as relentless and reliable as a tide. She'd first tasted it during a talent show in first grade and she'd hungered for it ever since. While Jazz sought refuge in hideouts and shadows, craving anonymity, Connie longed for the stage, the screen, for everyone in the world to know her face and her name.

Would that keep them together? Would it drive them apart? *"We go together 'cause opposites attract,"* the old song said, and Connie couldn't think of two people more opposite than Jazz and herself.

She paused outside a hair boutique that advertised PRODUCTS FOR AFRICAN HAIR in enormous letters in its front window. A woman in a dashiki with braids longer and more impressive than Connie's stood outside, huddled against the cold, but clearly willing to suffer it for her cigarette.

Just seeing the words *African hair* in a window made Connie feel warmer. It was the sixth or seventh such shop she'd seen along this stretch of busily trafficked road. The hair salons back in Lobo's Nod had done the best they could with her hair, but she couldn't expect much from them. She had eventually turned to her mother for braiding and general hair care, and thanks to the Internet she could have braid spray and detangler delivered, but to live in a neighborhood where dozens of shops catered to her needs? Where she could roll out of bed and walk down the street for balm or relaxer? Have her hair cut and styled by someone who looked like her, someone who knew what it was like to have this hair?

"Can I help you?" the woman asked suddenly. "I'll just be a second." She gestured with the cigarette and her expression said, *C'mon, kid—don't make me put this out even a second early.*

Connie gazed longingly into the window of the boutique.

She could probably spend hours in there, but she had a mission.

"Actually..." she said, and launched into the cover story she'd concocted for herself when prowling around the other crime scenes: She was a high school student writing a paper about the reliability of eyewitness testimony over time. "So, anyway, there was one of the Hat Dog murders over that way...." She pointed toward the alley less than a block from where they stood. "I was just wondering, Miss—"

"Just call me Rabia."

"Great. I'm Connie." They shook hands.

"Who's Puerto Rican? Mom or Dad?" That caught her off guard for a second. Back in the Nod, almost everyone assumed Connie was short for Constance. She'd never been hit with Consuela before.

"It's actually Conscience."

Rabia smiled. "Nice. Who does your hair, honey? It's not bad, but let me fix you up with some extensions and—"

"I really sort of need to work on the report...." Connie said, biting her lower lip as if she regretted having to interrupt.

"Oh, yeah, that night," Rabia said. "I remember that." She dragged on the cigarette with practiced, sensual ease. Her fingernails—visible through the ends of her fingerless gloves—had the hard yellow cast of a serious nicotine fiend. Connie could only imagine what her lungs looked like. "The cops already asked me about it." She sniffed and snorted smoke out through her nose, waiting expectantly as though for applause.

Connie widened her eyes a bit and said in the tone of a younger sister, "That's pretty cool."

Ill concealing her pleasure, Rabia shrugged. "No big deal. Look, it was months ago, okay? A lot warmer."

"Right," Connie said, egging her on. "It was warmer. So maybe you were outside later at night. On a smoke break. And…" She let it hang, let Rabia fill it in. Something she'd learned from Jazz: If you leave a sentence unfinished, people will want to finish it for you. It wasn't a hundred percent guaranteed to work, but more often than not, people would pick up the thread without even thinking about it.

Connie hoped it would work this time. She'd been to five of the crime scenes and hadn't been able to find anyone who'd been around at the time of the murders. Or at least, anyone who had been willing to admit it to a random teenager on the street. Rabia was her best shot so far.

And Rabia did not disappoint.

"And I was standing right about there," Rabia said, grabbing the thread of conversation, pointing across a middling busy street. "Over near the mailbox. It wasn't a bad night. Just having a smoke and looking at my window. Figuring out if it worked from across the way." She craned her neck to look at the window now. "Still not sure about that display. Do you think—"

"So you were across the street," Connie said quickly, before she could be dragged into a discussion about retail window displays. "And…"

"And it happened over there." She pointed again, this

time to the alleyway. From the mailbox, it would be a pretty easy sightline. Connie already knew that the victim had been left there, guts in a Kentucky Fried Chicken bucket nearby. "I told the police—I saw a guy coming out of there. Maybe six feet, maybe a little less. Wearing a hoodie. Gloves. I remember thinking it was too warm for gloves. That part I remember real well. And that was it."

"You didn't see anything else?"

"I told you."

"Or hear anything?"

"Look—"

"Maybe you saw something that you didn't really connect to it," Connie urged her. Then, yanking something from her memory: "Maybe some kind of light or something."

"No. I told the cops every—" She paused mid-drag, then lowered the cigarette without puffing. "Oh. Oh, wow. I forgot. How could I forget?"

"What didn't you tell them?"

Rabia looked ill. "Lord, how could I have forgotten? I forgot right until you just asked me. It was so crazy that night...."

"What, Rabia?" Connie's heart sped up a bit. She felt silly; did she think she would really crack the case all on her own? "What did you not tell them?"

Rabia shuddered, then shrugged, as if deciding then and there that it couldn't be important. "You said a light, right? But it was probably nothing. Right? The alley lit up. For just a second before he came running out."

Another flash. He took a picture again. Why? Is Jazz right—are these just his way of taking trophies? Or is it something else?

"That probably wasn't important, right?" Rabia gnawed at her cuticle, her cigarette dangling ash. "They couldn't have stopped him with just *that*, right?"

Connie told her probably not, then thanked Rabia and headed to the alleyway. A shiver surprised her as she entered—the body had been dumped here months ago and there wasn't so much as a scrap of crime-scene tape to mark what had happened, but she still felt as though she trod on either haunted or hallowed ground. She couldn't be sure which.

The alley looked depressingly like it had in the crime-scene photos, as though time had frozen here when winter came. The Dumpster was the same, although—as she glanced at the pictures on her phone—the bags of garbage spilling out of it were piled differently, of course. And there was no leftover snow in the picture of the original crime scene.

Connie sighed a cloud into the cold air and turned around. She wasn't Jazz. She had no idea what mattered here and what didn't. Jazz could imagine crime scenes the way they had been before the criminal left them, before he'd done whatever he could to throw off the cops. Jazz could tell when something was a clue or a coincidence, intentional or accidental. He could think like crazy people. What could Connie do?

Maybe, just maybe, I can think like Jazz.

She paced the alleyway, trying to imagine what Jazz would

do. He would mumble something about Billy. Then he might do that thing he did sometimes, where he silently mouthed what looked like both sides of a conversation. It wasn't all the time, but she noticed it because she was with him so much. She was pretty sure he didn't even realize he did it.

He wouldn't look for something small. He would look for the thing that didn't fit, no matter what size it was. Or maybe he would look for the thing that fit just a little too well. Sometimes, Jazz said, a killer tried too hard to make the scene look a certain way. In real life, things are rarely perfect, so if you see something at a crime scene that looks too good to be true, it might be.

Connie walked the length and width of the alley. She flicked through the pictures on her phone as she did so, matching up the images with the areas of the alley. It wasn't easy—without the body and the crime-scene team's equipment, the alley had a different character. She used marks and graffiti on the alley's walls to try to match things up, which is how she ended up standing exactly where the body had been propped against the wall.

This is how the killer would have seen it, she thought. *Right before he took the picture and ran off.*

That's what Jazz would say. And then he would furrow his brow and stare at the space until...

Until what? Until his brain exploded?

So the killer had stood here. Right here. A few years ago—before moving to Lobo's Nod—Connie's family had gone on a vacation to London, where they had taken a walking tour of Whitechapel, the London neighborhood haunted in the

Victorian Age by the legendary Jack the Ripper. The tour guide had enjoyed spilling the most lurid details of the crimes and had been sure to remind the tour group—repeatedly—that these parts of London had not changed much if at all since the Victorian Age.

"Jack may have lurked in this very doorway," he'd said in his heavy English accent. "Jack trod the very cobblestones under your feet right now!"

Hat-Dog lurked in this very alleyway, she thought. *Hat-Dog stood on the same dirty pavement under my feet right now.*

What had he seen? Connie flicked through until she found a picture from her current vantage point. She held the phone out in front of her. The body. Framed by a concrete-block wall festooned with an exploded rainbow of profane, silly, artistic, and just plain incomprehensible graffiti.

Look for the thing that doesn't belong.

—this very spot—

For the thing that belongs too well…

She went ahead and took her own picture, just as Hat-Dog had. The darkness of the alley flared to life for a moment and something caught her attention.

Did something else just light up? Or did I just blink at the right moment or…?

Checking her photo, she didn't notice anything at first, but then she compared it to the original crime-scene photo. There, in the morass of graffiti on the wall behind where the victim had slumped, there was something new. It wasn't in the original photo.

It's just new graffiti. That's all.

But as best she could tell, it was the *only* change. What were the odds?

She crept closer to the wall. Now that she knew what she was looking for, it was easy to find.

Connie had never tagged a wall in her life, but she knew from TV and movies that guys who tagged used spray paint. Sometimes they did funky stuff with neons, but usually it was just a can of whatever flat matte crap was on sale. She didn't feel one way or another about graffiti, but she imagined it was tough to make such stable, consistent lines with a spray. It took some skill.

The new graffito, though, was shaky. Thin. Small. And even her untrained eye could discern its major differences from the surrounding tags: This wasn't spray paint. It was some kind of plain white semi-gloss, like the stuff her dad used to paint the kitchen. It had been layered on with a brush, not sprayed on. It overlapped the original graffiti, so it had been added after the police descended on the alley.

More important, it had no style to it. Most of the other graffiti consisted of loops, whorls, arrows, and daring serifs. This was just slapped up there.

Five letters, in boring, somewhat shaky block print.

UGLY J

CHAPTER 18

And everything—predictably—went to hell for Jazz. Straight to hell, full speed.

This hadn't been the first time he'd been manhandled by the cops, but it was definitely the coldest. Hauled out of the hotel, he'd started shivering almost immediately, the cold January air nearly choking him. Long shoved him into the backseat of an unmarked car and drove them away.

Minutes later, they pulled up to a dingy brick building with an NYPD shield on the outside and a sign reading 76TH PRECINCT. Jazz wondered briefly if he was under arrest. But he hadn't been cuffed or read his rights, just pushed around.

Inside, the precinct was a madhouse, alive with chaos and noise. Uniformed cops, detectives in shirtsleeves, and a couple of men in ties who could only be—based on their stick-up-the-butt bearing—FBI agents milled about. The entrance to the precinct was clearly a sort of gathering area/lobby that had been pressed into duty as a command center; whiteboards and corkboards on wheels were parked against the walls, pinned and markered and taped with photos, names, dates. Jazz recognized it all from the information Hughes had brought him yesterday. And it was there that Jazz sat for more than an hour, waiting to be seen by...someone. The cops and agents cast cursory and disinterested looks in his direction, until at some point someone must have realized who he was. At that point, a buzz of excited conversation stirred the stale, overheated air of the precinct, making Jazz want to curl up and vanish.

He texted Connie: *I think this is gonna take a while....*

Directly across from him, unavoidably in his line of sight, was a series of plaques mounted to the wall, along with various badges and a trifolded American flag in a frame. It was a 9/11 memorial, he realized, reading the plaques. In honor of those from this precinct who'd died that day.

Jazz was too young to remember 9/11 itself, but Billy had been periodically obsessed with it. Throughout Jazz's youth, he would sometimes sit and watch video of the World Trade Center towers collapsing over and over, the explosion of glass and flame from the side of the North Tower like a gush of arterial blood. Over and over.

So efficient, Billy would mumble. *But no style. No flair.*

It was the difference between serial murder and mass murder, as far as Billy was concerned.

"All these jackasses have done," Billy told Jazz once, "is make people afraid to fly and afraid of New York. Which they already were in the first place. Takes real talent to get up close and personal and make you afraid of something brand-new."

Jazz didn't think the cops here would appreciate Billy's insights into the tragedy that had claimed their brothers. He kept his mouth shut and waited.

Eventually, a door flew open down a hallway and Hughes stormed out. At first he didn't see Jazz there, but as he got closer he spied Jazz and his expression softened for an instant.

"Sorry, kid," he said, passing by.

Jazz realized in an instant what had happened.

I wish I had more to tell you. But this is why I wanted you involved.

I?

I. Me. We. Whatever. I was the one who lobbied to bring you in, is all.

Long dragged Jazz into the office Hughes had vacated, much more harshly than was necessary for someone coming willingly. *Nothing like a little embarrassment to ramp up the aggression*, Jazz thought.

A cop sat behind a desk, his uniform festooned with more bric-a-brac than the other cops Jazz had seen. CPT. NILES MONT-GOMERY read the sign on his desk.

"Here he is, Cap," Long said, shaking Jazz a bit by his arm.

"Easy, Long. Don't take it out on the kid. Have a seat, Jasper. Long? Give us a minute."

Long left, closing the door. After a brief hesitation, Jazz decided to sit.

Sighing, the captain said, "I'm sorry to do this. You're not supposed to be here. You were never supposed to be here...."

And then it all came out, just as Jazz had imagined it:

Doug Weathers's story—headlined NYPD SEEKS TO "DENT" HAT-DOG?—had hit the Lobo's Nod newspaper's website overnight. It was a matter of a couple of hours before a New York reporter came across it and, scanning it, realized its implications. The reporter called the New York mayor's office and woke up a press person there, demanding a comment on the insertion of Billy Dent's son into the Hat Dog Killer investigation. The mayor's office, caught completely off guard and totally flabbergasted by the very idea of involving Jasper Dent, had immediately contacted Captain Montgomery, the titular head of the task force, waking him up an hour before his alarm.

"As you can imagine," Montgomery told Jazz, "I was a bit surprised to find out that a newspaper was reporting you were helping my investigation."

Jazz said nothing. He knew what would come next.

"I don't know what Detective Hughes told you, but the fact of the matter is this: He doesn't speak for this precinct, this department, or this task force. He was supposed to visit you in Lobo's Nod and show you a limited subset of our investigatory data. He certainly wasn't supposed to open his kimono. And especially not to bring you to New York."

Jazz still said nothing.

"I'm sorry that it had to come to this. This neighborhood...these *neighborhoods*, really...the ones that are at the center of this. Nice, peaceful. For the most part. Biggest crime we usually get around here is purse snatching. Now we've had seven months of bodies. Gun permit applications are up—literally—four *thousand* percent. Every couple of nights, I get to go to a different school auditorium and try to calm people down, and they just yell and scream and demand answers I can't give them. They're scared. It's my job to reassure them, and it's not very reassuring when the media starts saying that now I'm relying on the teenage son of a serial killer for help. It reeks of desperation. You understand?"

Jazz shrugged.

"This isn't about you. You didn't do anything wrong," Montgomery assured him. "But I can't have you involved in this. I'm going to send you home."

Now it was time to speak. Jazz picked his words with cautious precision and leaned forward in the most urgent yet restrained way he could. He'd perfected this pose/expression combination over years of practice. It almost always worked. "Captain? Sir?" he began. "I understand everything you've said, but can I suggest you keep me on anyway? I know you think it's crazy, but I really am good at this. You can call Sheriff Tanner back in Lobo's Nod—he'll tell you. I've already helped get one of these guys. If you let me, I can lead you places you'd never go otherwise. And no one has to know it's me. You can keep me in that little hotel where Hughes set me up. I'll never set foot in this building again. The press will never see me. And God knows I will never talk to them. Not once. Let me help. Please."

Montgomery leaned back in his chair. "Look, it's not like I'm saying we don't need help—"

"Exactly," Jazz said, pouncing. "Not that you guys aren't qualified or anything," he added hurriedly, "but when you get something like this, in a neighborhood like this, it's all hands on deck, right? So you've got your local guys and your Homicide guys and you pull in the FBI. Why not go all the way?"

The captain was on the edge, Jazz could tell; he could go either way.

"When you stand up in those schools, I bet you tell people you're doing everything possible, don't you?" Jazz said, and when Montgomery's head inclined in the slightest nod, Jazz knew he had him. One more push. "How can you go back out there and tell them that if it's not the truth? You've got one more resource sitting right in front of you. How can you not use it?"

On a good day, Jazz could talk his way into or out of just about anything. This was a good day.

But he hadn't counted on one thing.

"I can't do it," Montgomery said, with a tone of real regret. "The mayor, the commissioner, the chief of Ds...they've made it clear: They want my head or they want yours. And I've grown attached to mine."

"But—"

"Thanks, but no thanks. And please stop talking. Your freakin' Jedi mind tricks are giving me a headache. I'm going to ask you not to talk to any of the media in New York or when you get back home. Not about this case, at least. And please turn over anything Detective Hughes may have given you."

Jazz wasn't sure what to do, how to react. He'd never been shot down like this. *Bureaucracy. Who knew that bureaucracy would be my kryptonite?*

"I told you," he said, "I never talk to the press. And your

guys took everything Hughes gave me. Unless you count the pizza and pop from yesterday."

Montgomery cracked a grin at that. "No, no. You can keep the pizza and, uh, pop. I'll have someone drive you back to the hotel. But first, if you don't mind, one of the FBI agents would like to speak with you."

Moments later, Jazz found himself in a tiny office jammed with four desks. A Hispanic-looking woman in a skirt and blazer, her hair tied back in a bun, closed the door behind her and perched on the edge of a desk, crossing two shapely and distracting legs.

"I'm Special Agent Jennifer Morales," she said. "Thanks for talking to me."

"Just because I'm a hormonal teenage male doesn't mean you can use your legs to get me to talk," Jazz said, offended. "What was your next move? Taking down your hair? Is that a *special* tactic they only teach to the *special* agents?"

His sarcasm hit home—she knew as well as he did that there was actually no difference at all between an agent and a special agent. The titles were mere flukes of FBI history and meant nothing. Morales's lips pursed and she narrowed her eyes...then nodded once and slid into a chair. "Okay, good call. Sorry. No BS, then. I was one of the agents involved in hunting down your dad, back when he was going by the name Hand-in-Glove."

Hand-in-Glove had been Billy's fourth alias. He had killed mostly in the Midwest, mostly blonds, and had made a practice of swapping their undergarments, so that his fourth victim wore his first victim's bra, and so on. Jazz didn't know why he did this. Billy claimed "it was all just in good fun" when he confessed to those murders, and then he'd grinned at the prosecutor.

"You should talk to Special Agent Ray Fleischer," Jazz told her. "He's the guy who debriefed me when I was fourteen. Or maybe Special Agent Carl Banning. Or Dr. James Hefner. They're the guys who talked to me after Billy escaped. They can tell you what I told them—I don't know anything. I can't help you find him. I can't even find him myself."

Drumming her fingers on the desk, Morales said, "I don't believe you. Not entirely. I think you know things. They just may not be things you know you know."

"Well, my subconscious isn't cooperating these days."

"You could tell me about growing up with him. You could tell me how he was as a father. Something to give me insight."

Inwardly, Jazz bristled, but he didn't let Morales see it. His past was *his*. It was fractured and weird and a typhoon of emotions and fragments of memories, but it was his and his alone. No one else had the right to go trolling through it, sifting the garbage for the golden memory that could lead to Billy Dent.

"I can't help you," he told her with false contrition.

She bought the contrition. Of course she did. Women. *Even the ones wearin' badges and britches still think with their wombs.*

Shut the hell up, Dear Old Dad.

"Look," she said gently, "I think you have a lot to offer. If it was up to me, I'd have you on this task force in a heartbeat. You've heard of natural born killers, right? Well, you're a natural born profiler."

155

"There are lots of good profilers out there." Jazz wasn't sure where she was headed now.

"Not like you. They get how these guys think, sure. But you get how they *feel*. What it's like for them, what they like. Why they like it. You took one look at my legs and you knew what I was trying to do to you. And you called me on it. Most guys wouldn't have gotten it. Maybe subconsciously they'd've understood. Even the ones who understood it consciously wouldn't have said anything about it. Because they think they can master their impulses. They think, 'Yeah, she's trying to distract me with her body, but I can get past that, and if I don't say anything, I still get to check her out.' What they don't realize is—"

"—is that if you've gotten that far, you've already won," Jazz finished for her. "I know."

"See?" Her chair was on wheels and she pulled herself closer to him, squeaking just a bit. "You understand the impulses. You feel them. But you master them. You overcome them. Give me some help."

"I offered to help Captain Montgomery," Jazz said with genuine confusion. "He told me he couldn't use me. Are you going to pull rank on him? In his own precinct?"

She batted away the thought of it. "This stuff? This Hat-Dog guy? He's nothing. Compared to your dad. I mean, yeah, he's led the NYPD on a merry chase and we're still getting our bearings, but we'll catch him. And soon. They have a dozen good suspects already, and soon we'll narrow it down. He's small fry. I want the big game."

"You want Billy."

"Everyone wants Billy," she said. "But he killed three girls while I was hunting him. He knew my *name*, Jasper. Sent me text messages. 'Looking good today, Special Agent Morales.' 'I like your hair better in a ponytail.' 'I walked by you in the Seven-Eleven today. I could have touched you.'" She shivered with the memory. "I want him. You want to find him, too. Well, I can help. I have resources. Use me, Jasper. Help me find him and I'll help you once I have him."

"What do you mean? Every cop and fed in the world is looking for Billy. You think you'll make a difference?"

Morales leaned in close, so close that Jazz could taste the old coffee on her breath. "They're *looking* for him. You want to do more than find him, don't you? You want to kill him. Well," she said, smiling a mirthless smile, "I can help with that."

On his way out of the precinct, Jazz made sure to pay special attention to the whiteboards and corkboards he'd skipped on his way in. When he spotted the one he wanted, he stooped to tie his shoes, taking his time.

Gazing at the twelve photos—blown up from driver's licenses—pinned to a board under the double-underlined word SUSPECTS.

Twelve white men. Ages ranging from late twenties to early forties, from the looks of them. Jazz tried to memorize names, but the uniformed cop assigned to return him to the hotel nudged him and said, "C'mon," and he had to move.

They smuggled him out a side door. By now the New York

press had caught wind of the story and had besieged the Seven-six, so Jazz had to sneak back to the hotel. The room was empty when he got there, and a sharp panic jabbed at him. He checked the room quickly but thoroughly: A change of clothes was gone, as were her purse and cell phone. That boded well, but it was entirely possible that someone had forced her to dress and bring her things when abducting her.

When he went to call her, though, he saw a text message waiting from her—*out 4 a bit back soon*—time-stamped a few hours ago. He still wasn't used to the gadget; he hadn't even heard the text chime in all the ruckus at the precinct.

Relieved, he plopped down on what he thought of as his bed and stared up at the ceiling. Morales's offer had been tempting. But in the end, he couldn't accept. He just wasn't sure that she would be able to give him the kind of help he needed.

And besides: He didn't know if he could trust her to follow through.

The thought of being able to kill Billy, though...God! To see the end of his father, to write *finis* to the man who'd made Jazz the bundle of nerves and fear and frightening strength that he was...It could save him. It could destroy him. Billy's death could show that Jazz had a soul or prove that he had never had one.

That thought kept him up nights. Some nights because it thrilled him. Others because it terrified him.

He wondered: When next he saw his father, would he be thrilled or terrified?

CHAPTER 19

The killer sat in his easy chair, the remains of a home-cooked meal on the coffee table before him. The TV blathered the sorts of banalities his wife enjoyed—so-called reality TV, in which people competed to prove their superiority over one another. The killer tolerated the show, even pretended to enjoy it. One player and one alone captured his attention, a dental hygienist from Spokane, who spoke with a slight lisp and had hair the color of clarified butter and eyes so big and blue that he wanted to pop them out and eat them.

The killer had never eaten eyes. Or any other part of a human body. But he now desperately, desperately wanted to. The thought consumed him in a familiar, caressing way. He knew this feeling. It had been with him most of his life. He could not remember a time in his life when he could look at a woman and not want to possess her. *Possess* was an important word. It meant much. It meant to own. It meant to maintain one's calm. It meant to captivate and enter like a demon, though the killer did not believe in such bogus and repugnant claptrap.

It also meant to have intercourse with.

The killer wanted to own women. In every way. And he had, indeed, owned many. Even the ones he found possessed (that word again!) of subpar appearance he yearned to own, for to own meant to be able to destroy.

Tall, short, thin, fat, ugly, gorgeous, black, white, all shades between and beyond...He wanted them all. For his own. So that no one else could have them. His to use and to keep or discard as he saw fit.

He had spent much of his life dreaming of this. Dreaming of captive women, compelled to do as he commanded. Dreaming of them on their knees before him, subject to his whims—beaten or comforted, killed or succored, raped or loved.

The dreams could not be sated. Not by anything he watched or touched or knew. Only finding her (any "her") and owning her, making her his in every way, could satisfy his needs.

The first time he'd owned a woman, he'd thought it over at that. Thought that with the realization of his dream, he could and would now be like all the others he saw around him. He would now be what they called "normal." He discovered relaxation; he learned that with his fantasy fulfilled, he could breathe and settle and close his eyes at last.

But his calm, his repose, did not last. The fantasies returned, first as niggling daydreams, then as all-consuming compulsions, until every woman he saw on the street, on the subway, anywhere, was a target, a victim waiting to happen. And he resisted. He resisted as long as he could. As best as he could. Until...

Until...

Until he no longer had to.

Until the message and the voice...

Just then, a phone rang. The killer stiffened. It was not his cell phone or his wife's. It was something else.

"Is that yours?" his wife asked.

"Yes," he said, and swiftly went to the small, cramped bedroom, where he closed the door and dug into the bottom of his chest of drawers. Three cell phones were there. One rang again. The killer answered, trembling.

"The number is six," the voice said, and the killer felt a trill of anticipation—six!—until the voice said, "Six. Five and one."

"Six," the killer repeated. Five and one. Not three and three.

"And," the voice went on, "a little something special this time."

Shocked, the killer almost dropped the phone, but held tight and kept listening. He wrote nothing down—that would be foolish—but memorized every word.

"I understand," he said when the voice had finished, then removed the battery from the phone. On his way back to the TV, he stopped in the kitchen and tossed the phone's battery into the trash. Then he quickly snapped the cheap plastic hinge and tossed both halves of the broken phone into the garbage compactor.

"Who was that?" his wife asked.

He ignored her. She ignored him back, caught up in her show.

The killer stared at the TV. The dental hygienist from Spokane was staring back at him.

CHAPTER 20

Even though she wanted to, Connie didn't bring up what had happened between them at the hotel overnight. She said nothing about it in the car on the way to the airport, nor at the airport itself, as they went through security and then waited for their flight. The NYPD—eager to get Jazz out of its jurisdiction as quickly as possible—had made some calls and arranged for his ticket to be switched to Connie's flight, so they were in a rush from the time she returned to the hotel.

She tried to pretend that nothing had happened, that nothing had changed. She started to tell Jazz about her mini-tour of the crime scenes, but he clearly wasn't focused. He kept interrupting to bring up something about Long or Hughes or the captain guy—Montgomery—who'd kicked him out of New York, and she eventually realized that he just needed to vent. So she listened as he told her about his encounter with the NYPD. And Special Agent Morales of the FBI.

"Do you think she was serious about helping you kill your

dad?" she asked in a low voice. They were at their gate, and it was crowded. She didn't want anyone to overhear.

Jazz shrugged. He was wearing sunglasses indoors and had bought a Mets cap, which he kept pulled over his forehead. Being recognized would—in a word—suck. "I don't know."

"Would you..." She stopped herself. This was neither the time nor the place for such a discussion. The amount of hatred in her heart for Billy Dent surprised her, though. She felt an immediate and powerful kinship with Special Agent Morales, whom she'd never even met. Any woman who wanted Billy Dent dead badly enough to risk her career—for surely if Jazz reported what she'd offered to a superior, she'd be out of the FBI—was a woman Connie could learn to love. Conscience Hall was well named by her parents, but even *her* conscience had its breaking point. The man who had mauled the childhood of the boy she loved definitely occupied a spot beyond that breaking point.

So she wasn't surprised to find that she wanted Billy Dent dead. What surprised her was how happy the thought made her, how liberated it made her feel, even though she knew that Jazz killing his own father would send her boyfriend into a darker place than even *he* could imagine.

But if Jazz didn't do it...If this Special Agent Morales was the one to do it...

Well, that wouldn't be so bad, would it? The world would be rid of Billy Dent. More important, *Jazz* would be rid of him, without adding to the burden already on his too-full back.

Maybe this FBI lady is a gift from God, Connie wanted to tell Jazz.

She settled for squeezing his hand. After a moment, he squeezed back.

Jazz said nothing on the flight, staring moodily out the window instead, as though answers or resolutions had been inscribed in the billowy curves of the clouds. Connie, for her part, stared just as moodily at him, willing him to turn and look at her.

She so badly wanted to discuss what had happened the night before, in the hotel room. She still didn't know who was being more unfair to whom, but one thing was certain— she wouldn't figure it out until they actually opened their mouths and talked about it.

Had it been presumptuous to bring the condoms to New York? Probably. She could admit that. But she couldn't shake the memory of the giddy, stomach-twirling elation she'd experienced at the drugstore when she'd bought them. *They'll have condoms in New York,* she had thought. *Why buy them here, where someone you know might see you?* Then she dismissed it. She didn't *care* if someone saw. She was in love. So what if people knew she was having sex with the man she loved? Her parents were both at work, so they wouldn't see her—it would be a friend or an enemy, and it just didn't matter.

She'd bought them and packed them and thought of them

on the flight to New York. This was the right way to do it. Responsible. She and Jazz were both virgins, and they would do this the right way. The adult way.

It was time.

She knew in her head and she felt in her heart and in other, more primal, parts of her body. She was ready. When this state of readiness had been obtained, she couldn't say. But after the Impressionist nearly killed Jazz, and after Jazz finally faced the demon of his past—his father—she sensed a change in their relationship. A growth. A maturation. They were ready for the next step, and once she knew that, she was desperate for it.

Still. She hadn't planned on springing it on him the way she had. A late-night/early-morning grope-fest gone manically passionate. Blurting out that she had protection. *Wrong way to go about it*, she thought. *I should have brought it up before. Been cool about it. Like, "Hey, I think it's time. I think we're ready. How about you?" And when he said, "Yeah," then you say, "Great, we're covered; let's go."*

All of that was true, but no matter how badly she'd bungled it, his reaction—his refusal to talk, his sulking in the other bed—pained her. Intellectually, she knew that it was fear driving him, that it had nothing to do with her. But emotionally and with all the yearning in her body, she felt rejected. Harshly.

When the plane landed, she hoped that maybe they could talk while waiting for Howie to pick them up, but to her absolute mortification, her father was waiting as they passed through security.

"I just need a second—" she started.

"You had a first, a second, and a third," her father said with barely concealed rage. "No more chances. Come with me. Now."

"But, Dad—"

"No buts, Conscience."

Jazz cleared his throat, "Mr. Hall, if Connie and I could just have a minute to—"

"To what?" Dad said, rounding on Jazz, that rage now no longer concealed at all. "To do what, Jasper? Abduct her to Chicago this time?"

"I didn't abduct her," Jazz said with amazing calm. "In fact, I told her not to come at all."

"I'm sure you did," Dad said sarcastically. He loomed over Jazz like a hawk on a high branch. Connie didn't know for whom she was more afraid: Jazz or her dad. Jazz seemed harmless, although she knew he was anything but. Her dad knew it, too. Or should have.

"Dad, let's go." Connie stepped in and took her father's hand. "Let's just go."

Dad shook her off. "Listen to me, Jasper Dent. I haven't said this before, but I'm saying it now: Stay the hell away from my daughter. Or else."

"Or else what?" Jazz said with an infuriating, dead calm that belied his words. Connie knew this voice. "More history lessons about Sally Hemmings?" Almost bored. Contemptuously so. "Maybe this time a video on lynching?"

Connie pulled harder at her dad, who wouldn't budge. Jazz's calm was a gimmick, a trick. It was a Billy Dent tactic—forcing your prey to overreact by seeming completely unaffected. Jazz was trying to—

Oh, God. Jazz wanted Dad to take a swing at him. Maybe so that he could hit back and feel justified doing it. Maybe just because he was so pissed about everything that had and hadn't happened in New York that he wanted to take it out on someone, anyone, and why not the man standing between him and Connie?

"Or *else*," Dad said, in a threatening tone Connie had never heard before, "I'm going to make you wish you'd never seen her."

And Jazz stared at her father. Connie had never seen such a stare. He didn't move; his expression didn't change. It was something ethereal, something in his eyes, or in his soul. Something had shifted, and Connie suddenly realized that she'd been wrong before—her father wasn't the hawk on the high branch.

Jazz was.

"You think you're scary?" Jazz said quietly, his lips quirking in a little smile.

He said nothing else. He didn't have to. Connie's dad swallowed visibly, his Adam's apple bobbing.

"Stop it!" Connie hissed at Jazz. She knew him better than anyone else in the world—well, maybe except for Billy—but right now she didn't know *what* she was witnessing. "Cut it out. Now!"

Her father pulled his arm from her.

"You don't scare me," he told Jazz, but his voice had mellowed just a tad.

And now Jazz smiled a full smile. It terrified Connie, because to anyone not listening in, it looked as though Jazz had just heard something funny. But there was nothing funny here.

"You tell yourself that," Jazz said. "That's okay. Keep telling yourself that."

"Dad," Connie said, tugging again. "Let's go."

This time, he let her pull him away. Connie glared at Jazz over her shoulder. "Knock off the nonsense!" she stage-whispered. He sure as hell wasn't making it easier for them to be together by pulling this kind of crap. "Seriously!"

But for his part, Jazz just watched them go, still smiling.

CHAPTER 21

As soon as Connie and her dad disappeared around a bend, Jazz blew out his breath and slumped against a nearby wall. What the hell had he been thinking? Was he nuts? Goading Mr. Hall like that? This was the man who could keep him from Connie. Well, at least until Connie was eighteen.

But he had to admit that, deep down, there was a part of him that had loved the confrontation. He hadn't been able to manipulate Montgomery—the pull of his pension and his career had outweighed Jazz's "Jedi mind tricks"—but he'd come pretty close to getting Mr. Hall to take a swing at him. If Connie hadn't been there, Jazz was sure he'd have had her father roaring and punching. And then...

And then what? You beat the crap out of him? Or he beats the crap out of you? What, exactly, was your plan, you dumbass? Or is this just what you do now—you goad and manipulate people just for the hell of it.

No. Not anymore. People aren't your playthings. People are real. People matter.

Not cool to go all Billy on him, Jazz. Not cool at all.

And the way he'd treated Connie. *Double not cool.* But he hadn't known how to talk to her, how to explain his fears. How to explain the role her race played—or had played—in their relationship. They'd been together long enough now that he didn't think he loved her just because she was black. But he couldn't in good conscience deny that that had been the original attraction. Her safety, whether real or perceived, had drawn him in. He couldn't talk to her about sex without talking about his concerns, and he couldn't talk about his concerns without—

"Hey, man!" Howie said, loping to his side. "Just saw Connie and her pops. That man looked pissed with a capital *P*, and I thought to myself, *That means Jazz must be nearby.* And I was right. So, score for me. I should totally be the one the NYPD calls on for help 'cause I kick it all detective sty-lee."

"Turns out the NYPD didn't actually call for me," Jazz reminded him as they headed to Howie's car. "Why the hell couldn't you keep my aunt away from Weathers?"

"Ninja, please! It's Christmas break. I have family obligations. I couldn't watch your aunt twenty-four-seven. Not that I would mind."

Howie's salacious tone was nothing new, but it triggered a memory for Jazz, of Samantha saying that Howie was "friendly."

"What did you do while I was gone?" he asked.

"Do? Me? I didn't do anything while you were gone."

If Howie had been in an interrogation room, the cops

171

would have charged him before the first word was out of his mouth. His poker face was nonexistent. He didn't just look like he'd been caught with his hand in the cookie jar; he looked like he'd been caught sticking his whole head in there.

"Dude! You hit on my aunt!"

"That depends on how you define 'hit on.'"

"You totally hit on my aunt."

"Was that wrong? Was I not supposed to do that?"

"You should think about what you just said. Think about it, Howie."

"I'm just not seeing where I went wrong. For an older woman, she's got a nice body, and she must moisturize like a mofo because her skin is—"

"Howie. She's my *aunt*."

"You get to have a super-hottie girlfriend. Why can't I get a little action?"

"My *aunt*! What are you not getting here?"

"I'm not getting any—"

"Enough!" They were at the car by now. "Take me home so that I can try to scrub the idea of you and my aunt out of my brain."

"Man, you grew up with a guy who taught you how to carve up the human body and used to show you *Faces of Death* for a bedtime story and you think the idea of me in bed with your aunt is gross?"

Jazz slammed the door. "Yes. And doesn't that tell you something right there? Drive."

They had left New York late in the evening, so by the time Howie dropped Jazz off at home, the sun was just beginning to burnish the horizon. Jazz stood on the front porch for a moment as Howie pulled away, staring at the dawning day. A part of him wanted to throw his suitcase in Billy's old Jeep and just take off. It seemed easier, somehow. Easier than dealing with Connie's dad, figuring out how to make up for his idiocy at the airport. Easier than dealing with the weirdness that now vibrated like a plucked harp string between him and Connie. Easier than living with Gramma, for sure. And easier than finally being face-to-face with the aunt he'd never known.

The front door opened and Samantha stood there with a coffee mug, dressed in a loose shirt and yoga pants. "Are you coming in or do you like the cold?" she asked.

Jazz shrugged. "I'm coming in."

Inside, they sat at the kitchen table. The house felt small all of a sudden. It had been Jazz and Gramma for more than four years, ever since Billy went to prison. Now another presence made itself felt.

"She's asleep," Samantha said, in answer to his unasked question. "I've always been an early riser, though."

Jazz sipped from the coffee cup she'd handed him and gazed across the table at her.

"So you're my nephew," she said sheepishly, offering him a lopsided grin. "Your friend—Howie—he calls you Jazz?"

"Yeah."

"Which do you prefer? Jasper or Jazz?"

"I guess Jasper. From adults. And, uh, about Howie…"

Samantha made a sound somewhere between a chuckle and a snort. "Yeah, about Howie..."

"He's totally harmless. He's more than harmless—he's completely...I'm just sorry. I didn't know he would be a jackass around you. He doesn't mean anything by it. I mean, you should hear the stuff he says to Connie. It's just how he is. There's no filter between his mouth and his brain."

"And his hormones, from the sound of it."

"Well, yeah. I know it's weird."

Samantha nodded. "Speaking of weird...I guess *this*"— she gestured between them—"is as weird for you as it is for me, huh?"

And then they both said, in the same instant: "You look like him."

They didn't have to say who "he" was. Jazz had never thought about his resemblance to his father, and he could tell from Samantha's sudden obsession with studying her coffee mug that she hadn't thought about hers, either.

Howie was right—Samantha looked younger than her years, which surprised Jazz. He'd've figured being Billy Dent's sister would age her prematurely. But other than some gray, which she'd left uncolored to grace her Billy-colored hair, she looked ten years younger.

Of course, Billy also looked younger than forty-two. Maybe it was a Dent family trait.

Maybe we're immortals. Maybe every time Billy kills someone, he sucks up their life force. Right, Jazz. And maybe Billy really is the god he always claimed to be.

"Look, if this is none of my business," Samantha said,

"just tell me. And God knows I'm not really in any position to help, but…you're a kid. And Mom's basically an invalid. Moneywise, are you two—"

"We're all right," Jazz lied. Every month was a struggle. The house was paid for, thank God, but there were still bills—utilities, Gramma's medications, clothes, food.…There was Gramma's Social Security and some kind of "death benefit" thing from Grampa, and Billy had actually stashed away some cash that the cops never found, but each month was still like balancing a chainsaw on his forehead. While it was running.

"I never thought I'd be back here," Samantha said slowly, still staring down into her coffee. "This house. This town. Nothing's changed, has it? I mean, there's more crap in the house because she never throws anything away and there's a Walmart now and the highway's a little wider, but it's still the Nod I grew up in. And this house is still…" She looked up at the ceiling, as though something lurked there.

"Still haunted," Jazz said for her.

"Yeah."

"He's like a ghost, isn't he? Even though he's still alive?" He realized neither of them had said the name Billy yet. He wondered if she ever would.

Samantha nodded. "I hope you don't mind—I've been sleeping in your room. It used to be mine, and I just couldn't stand the thought of sleeping in *his* old room."

There were three bedrooms in the Dent house—Gramma's, Jazz's, and a spare. The spare had been Billy's, growing up.

"That's okay. I'll sleep in the spare. How long are you planning on staying?"

175

"Well, my return flight isn't for two more days. Do you mind if I stay that long? It would be a pain to change it."

"No, no, that's fine," he said with a swiftness that caught him off guard. More than the additional help with Gramma, he realized he craved the contact with Samantha. A Dent who had managed to escape the gravity of Billy and of Lobo's Nod. "Stay as long as you want."

"Those pictures on the wall in your bedroom," she said hesitantly. "His victims, right?"

"Yeah."

"I tacked up a sheet over them. Couldn't sleep otherwise."

"That's okay."

Samantha smiled a sad little smile. "I think this is where I'm supposed to get all parental on you or something. Make sure you're all right. Ask you why you have those pictures right where you sleep."

"To remind me," he told her, thinking of the words—I HUNT KILLERS—he'd had tattooed on his body. "I guess it's morbid, but..."

"Morbid?" A shrug. "Yeah, probably. But I get it. You grew up with him as your dad; I grew up with him as my brother. And with *her*, when she was just as crazy, but not as childlike. And with your grandfather."

Jazz leaned forward. "Tell me about it," he said, too intensely. He dialed it back. "I want to know."

"About growing up here?" She shuddered. "I wouldn't know where to start. And besides, you're better off not hearing that crap. Trust me on that. I spent a big chunk of my life trying to deal with it, trying to understand it. And you know what? It got me nowhere, and it made me miserable. It was only when I started putting it behind me, started purging it, that I started feeling better."

"Yeah, but you have something to purge in the first place. All I've got are fragments."

"All these FBI guys and shrinks used to come to me. All they wanted to know was 'What was it like growing up with him?'"

The same questions they asked him. The same questions—the same intrusions—he resented so much. Jazz loathed himself for putting Samantha in the exact position he hated occupying. But he couldn't help it. He had to know. It wasn't a matter of clinical or academic curiosity; it was self-preservation.

"Please," he said, and he figured she knew all of Billy's tricks, so he didn't even bother trying to manipulate her. "Please."

She slugged back her coffee and went to the counter for a refill. "Fine," she relented as she sat back down. "Fine." Checked her watch. "Mom should be asleep for a while. Fire away."

Suddenly Jazz didn't know what to ask. "Did you know?" he blurted out.

"Did I know he was killing all those people? No. I had no idea. I moved out two days after my eighteenth birthday. You don't know what it was like. Small town. Before the Internet. Very isolated. Your grandfather was a terror. Drop your fork at the dinner table and the belt would come off. Mom was always scattered. Petrified of blacks, Hispanics, Asians, you name it."

"How did you end up normal?"

"Normal? Ha. Maybe. I don't know. I don't know. I never felt like I fit into the family. And I had good friends at school, used to spend as much time as possible at their houses. And I realized early on that the way my family lived wasn't the way other families lived. And I sort of... it's like I sectioned off one part of my life from the other, put up a wall there so that I could live in both places when I needed to."

"Yeah. Me, too. Compartmentalization."

Samantha grinned. "So, you've had some therapy, huh? Good for you. Anyway, moved out at eighteen, left town, never looked back. I tried to stay in touch with Mom. Especially after Dad finally keeled over. I guess I didn't think she was dangerous. She seemed like the least crazy person in the house. Which is saying something."

"And when the killing started... you didn't know?"

She shook her head. "No. No idea. Look, I'd cut myself off, okay? I knew he was getting married. Mom sent me an invitation, but I didn't respond. I was surprised to get the invite at all. Mom really hated *your* mom."

"I know. She says that's where Billy went wrong."

"Well, I'm here to tell you it's not true. Never met your mom, but I know it's not true. The closest I came to coming back was when I heard you were born. I almost booked a ticket then. Honest."

He didn't know if he believed it, but he appreciated the sentiment.

"You have to remember," she went on, "that no one connected the killings. It wasn't a national story until he was caught. Before that, it was regional, and nothing popped in the news that would have connected for me."

"What was he like? As a kid?"

Still not using the name.

"I don't know what he was like with you," she began, moving her coffee cup in little circles. Jazz's, neglected, had gone cold. "But living with him, I could tell. Early on, I could tell there was something wrong with him. I didn't know *how* wrong, obviously, but I could tell he was...off. And for a long time, I thought there was something wrong with *me* because no one else seemed to notice. Not Mom and Dad, not that I'd expect them to. But not my friends or their parents. Not teachers. No one. They all thought he was this... this gregarious, funny kid. But I knew the truth."

"He was hiding it for them," Jazz said quietly, "but he let down his guard around you."

"I guess. I don't know why. Maybe he thought it was funny, to let one person see the truth....I don't know. He pushed things, but he never crossed a line. Not while I was around, at least. I know he killed some pets, some stray cats and dogs. But I could never prove it. And back then, you did that and people just shrugged and called you high-strung. It was different.

"From the outside, he seemed normal," she went on. "He

would tease me and bug me. I was his older sister. That's normal. He messed with my Barbie dolls...." She shivered suddenly, chilled by the memory. "I mean, I've heard...I've been told that a lot of boys do that to their sisters' dolls. But there was something.... It wasn't just cutting off their hair or drawing on them. He used to...he used to cut the, y'know, the breasts off...."

"Like he did later," Jazz whispered in awe. "As Green Jack."

Samantha shuddered. "Green Jack. Oh, God. That's what he called himself sometimes. I remember he was just a kid and there were days when he would say, 'I'm not here anymore. It's just Green Jack now.' Mom and Dad didn't notice or didn't care, but it always freaked me out. I used to think that's why he did it—just to freak me out. And when he got arrested, a part of me was like...was like, 'He did all of this just to freak me out.' Which is crazy, isn't it?"

Jazz considered himself an expert on crazy. As best he could tell, Aunt Samantha didn't come close.

"If only I'd seen a newspaper or read a website from back east, when he was calling himself Green Jack. Maybe he would have been caught earlier...." She struggled to regain her composure.

"Aunt Samantha..." he cautioned. He sensed—knew—that they were headed into dark territory, down into the memory mines, where the ore was densest and the danger greatest.

But he couldn't stop her. Not now. She went on. "One night I woke up and he was standing there, in my bedroom.

In the dark. I was fourteen, so he must have been eleven. Maybe ten. I don't remember when it was in the year. But he was just standing there. Naked. Staring at me."

"Did he—"

"No. No, he never touched me. And I was never afraid of that, if you want to know the truth. Somehow I knew I was safe. I think...I think because I was related to him, I was somehow off the list. Back then, at least. Now, who knows? Maybe he's changed."

Could he have changed? Jazz thought it possible. But change wasn't always for the better.

Just then, they heard a light thump from upstairs. Aunt Samantha jerked as though awakened gratefully from a nightmare, and the kitchen somehow became brighter than the sunlight through the window should have allowed.

"She's early," Samantha said brusquely, and rose, setting her coffee cup in the sink. "I'll help her get started. Maybe you can get breakfast going?"

"Sure. Hey, Aunt Samantha?"

She paused in the doorway. "Yeah?"

"I changed my mind. You can call me Jazz."

181

CHAPTER 22

Connie sat on her bed in a lotus position, legs folded over each other, her wrists resting lightly on her knees, eyes closed. There was a single yoga studio in Lobo's Nod, and Connie didn't like the woman who led classes there, so after three she'd bailed. Ginny Davis—poor, dead Ginny—had lent Connie a set of yoga DVDs that looked like they'd come from the ancient 1990s. Then again, yoga was an ancient practice, so maybe that was appropriate.

At any rate, she'd learned a lot from those DVDs, techniques she'd used over the past year to relax herself, especially before a performance. But right now, she was having trouble centering herself. She couldn't get those deep, cleansing yoga breaths she craved.

Images of Jazz flashed through what was supposed to be a clear and passive mind. Jazz in the hotel room. Next to her in bed. On the floor. Jazz at the airport, with her father...

It was no good. She couldn't relax. She blew out a frustrated breath and opened her eyes.

"Whiz!" she yelped. She must have been more relaxed than she'd imagined. Or at least more distracted—her younger brother had managed to sneak into her room without her hearing the door open.

"You are in *so* much trouble!" Whiz said, with something like awe in his voice. He wasn't even taking delight in his older sister's travails. He was just impressed at the sheer level of trouble, like a man reaching a mountaintop only to see a taller peak in the near distance. "I didn't think you could *get* in this much trouble!"

"I know," Connie said, pretending not to care. She couldn't keep up the pretense for long. "Uh, exactly what have you heard? What did they say while I was gone?"

Whiz scampered over to her bed and plopped down next to her. "Dad was cussing."

Ouch. Never a good sign. As if Connie needed to know, Whiz proceeded to reel off the exact words Dad had used. Connie blinked. She hadn't even known Whiz knew some of those words.

"What about Mom?"

"She cried. Not much. Just a little."

Connie deflated. Her father's anger was one thing. Bringing her mother to tears was another. She didn't know why, but those tears touched her more deeply than her father's anger ever could. In a way, she was glad her parents didn't know this. Such knowledge would make controlling her

183

almost trivially easy: *Don't do X, Y, or Z, Connie—you'll make your mother cry.*

"Was it worth it?" Whiz wanted to know. "You're gonna be grounded until, like, you're eighty years old."

"They can't ground me that long," Connie said.

"But was it worth it? You know"—and here Whiz looked around as if under surveillance and dropped his voice to a near whisper—"S-E-X?"

As much as she wanted to drop-kick Whiz into a garbage chute most days, Connie had to admit she loved the little snot monster, who was simultaneously too grown-up and too childlike. After busting out a plethora of Dad's four-letter words, he still felt the need to spell out *sex*.

"We didn't have S-E-X," she informed him. "Not that it's any of your business."

"Well, that's good. 'Cause Mom was really worried about that."

"Dad wasn't?"

"Dad was…" Whiz hesitated. "Never mind."

"Come on. Tell me."

Whiz shook his head defiantly.

"God, it's more of his black/white crap, isn't it? It's not the nineteen-sixties. It's not like when his parents were growing up or even when *he* was growing up. It's—"

"That's not it," Whiz said quietly.

"What's not it?"

"The black-and-white thing. The racial stuff."

Connie stared at her kid brother, searching his expression

for signs of one of his pranks or tricks. But he was utterly solemn, totally serious.

"What do you mean? Ever since I started dating Jazz, it's been 'white men this' and 'black women that,' and 'Sally Hemmings' and—"

Whiz shook his head. "He doesn't care. He said, 'She can date a whole platoon of white boys, just not that one.'"

Connie set her jaw. She knew what was coming next. "How do you know this?"

Whiz rolled his eyes. "Jeez, Connie. I listen to them at night through the air-conditioning vents. Don't you?"

Actually...no.

"It's the serial-killer thing."

Well, of course it was the serial-killer thing. Her father didn't trust Jazz. So typical. No matter how much Jazz had proven himself—

"And," Whiz went on, "he told Mom that the idea of you getting hurt scares him so much that he can't even talk to you about it. And all the race stuff is just the only way he can think of to keep you guys apart without thinking about you..."

Without thinking of me raped, tortured, mutilated, and murdered by my own boyfriend. Ah, crap. She couldn't find it in her heart to stay angry at her dad. Not anymore.

"Jesus, Whiz. Talking to you is better than yoga sometimes."

"Don't take—"

"—the Lord's name in vain. I know. Sorry."

"It isn't gonna happen, is it?" Whiz asked.

"What's that?"

Whiz swallowed. "Jazz isn't gonna hurt you, is he?"

Aw, man... As big of a pain in the butt as her little brother could be, she knew he loved her in that stunted way little brothers have. It killed her to see the conflicted pain in his eyes as he asked. She saw more than merely her brother's concern; she saw Dad's fear reflected there, too. All her life, her father had been so powerful, loomed so large, that she'd never been able to imagine him afraid of anything. Not even Jazz. Not even something...

"No one's gonna hurt me," she told Whiz. Seized by a rare impulse, she hugged him to her, pleasantly surprised that he didn't pull away.

She kissed him on the exact center of the top of his head and said it again, this time louder, loud enough to convince herself, too.

CHAPTER 23

For the first time in recent memory, Jazz had the run of the house. After breakfast, Gramma had fallen into one of her periodic obsessions with Grampa's grave. Sometimes she believed that he'd risen from the grave—"Like Jesus and Bugs Bunny!"—and could only be persuaded otherwise by a trip to the cemetery. Jazz hated those days; Gramma would spend hours crawling around the headstone, inspecting the dirt and individual blades of grass for some sort of perfidy. It was a lousy way to spend a day.

But Aunt Samantha cheerfully volunteered to take Gramma, meaning that Jazz was alone in the house without having to worry about his grandmother. He almost didn't know how to act. It was so quiet—true quiet, without the foreboding of a potential Gramma eruption lurking. *Maybe I should call Connie and we can fool around in my bedroom for a change.*

It was an automatic thought, and it made him pensive almost immediately. He *should* call Connie. But what could he say to her? Especially after the way he'd treated her father at the airport. Combine that with the hotel-room fiasco and he'd be surprised if she ever wanted to speak to him again.

Oh, you could make *her talk to you....*

No. Shut up, Billy. Not Connie. I don't do that to Connie.

He meandered around the house, straightening things here and there. Inspired, he started throwing away some of the old junk that his grandmother had accumulated over the years. The serial-killer pack-rat tendency ran strong in the Dent genetics, and Gramma would never tolerate Jazz throwing things away while she was around. But with her gone for the day, he could do some cleaning and she'd be none the wiser. It's not like she was lucid enough to memorize her piles of crap.

He thought about Connie as he roamed the house with a garbage bag. He'd been unfair to her, he knew, but how to fix that unfairness was beyond him. He relived the night in the hotel room, running it through his damnably perfect memory over and over. Waking from the dream. Pressed deliciously and deliriously against Connie. Her turning to him, eyes wide and full and dark. Reaching for each other. Familiar touches gone explosively unfamiliar, explosively craved.

And then...pushing her away, falling backward onto the floor, lust twisted to panic, to fear.

Yeah. How could he fix that? How could he erase in Connie's mind the memory of her boyfriend fleeing from her in terror?

He hauled the garbage outside and set it by the mailbox for pickup, then returned to the house, where he wheeled his suitcase into the spare room. He didn't blame Samantha for not wanting to sleep here. The room had lain unused for close to two decades, its surfaces gray and textured with dust. More than that, though, the room seemed to vibrate, ever so slightly out of sync with the rest of the house, the rest of the universe, really. As though something fundamental and primitive and crucial had broken here, and never been patched.

Billy's room. Billy's bed. Jazz didn't have to wonder what Billy had dreamed and fantasized, lying awake at night. He knew all too well—Billy had written his fantasies in the blood and screams of innocents from Nevada to Pennsylvania, from Texas to South Dakota. No secrets remained.

He dusted a bit, then unpacked. He needed clean clothes, so he went across the hall to his room. True to her word, Samantha had hung a sheet over the wall of Dear Old Dad's victims. Jazz found himself liking his aunt more and more. Wouldn't most people seeing them for the first time—most normal people—have taken down the pictures? Connie thought they were morbid. G. William thought they were a disturbing tie to the past. Howie thought they were a buzzkill.

Gramma thought they were Santa's elves.

He fired up his computer and checked his e-mail. Other than the usual spam and porn links from Howie (*delete, delete, delete*...), there was nothing, which meant that no one had figured out this e-mail address yet. Good.

On the desk lay two sheets of paper. Photocopies of evidence from the sheriff's office. The first one was the letter Billy had left at Melissa Hoover's house:

189

Dear Jasper,

I can't begin to tell you what a pleasure it was to see you at Wammaket. You've grown into such a strong and powerful young man. I am so proud of what you will accomplish in this life. I already know you are destined for great things. I dream of the things we'll do together. Someday.

For now, though, I have to leave you with this. Never let it be said your old man doesn't know how to repay a debt.

Love,
Dear Old Dad

PS Maybe one of these days we'll get together and talk about what you did to your mother.

The PS still stabbed at him, cored him. When Jazz had point-blank asked Billy "Did you make me kill my mother?" Billy had just laughed. Later, he had said, "You're a killer. You just ain't killed no one yet."

Which statement was true? Was it all Billy screwing with his mind?

Well, of course it was Billy screwing with his mind. That's what Billy did. Dear Old Dad had a PhD in mind screwing. The question was, was it *just* Billy screwing with his mind?

He shook his head and actually said "Stop it!" out loud to

himself in his strongest voice. What had happened? How had Janice Dent died? By Billy's hand, or by her son's?

That'll be the first thing I do. The next time I see him, the first thing I do will be to ask him that.

And the second thing?

He remembered Special Agent Morales leaning toward him. She wore no perfume. Her face was smooth and unblemished by makeup, and her grin had revealed big, strong teeth. "You want to do more than find him, don't you? You want to kill him," she'd said. "Well, I can help with that."

The second thing—he would figure that out when the time came.

The other piece of paper was the letter found on the Impressionist. It was two pages long, but the sheriff's department had reduced it to fit both pages on one sheet. Handwritten in a careful, neat, and unfamiliar hand. Most of the letter was a listing of the major characteristics of Billy Dent's first victims, with notations as to possible doppelgängers for the Impressionist to use in his harrowing of Lobo's Nod. But there was an appendix at the end, one that still mystified Jazz:

> UNDER NO CIRCUMSTANCES ARE YOU TO
> GO NEAR THE DENT BOY.
> LEAVE HIM ALONE.
> YOU ARE NOT TO ENGAGE HIM.
> JASPER DENT IS OFF-LIMITS.

He stared at the letter for a while, willing the letters to rearrange themselves into something that made more sense, then gave up, grabbed some clean clothes and the letters, and headed to his temporary quarters. He figured he'd delayed the inevitable long enough.

Sitting on the floor, his back against his father's childhood bed, Jazz called Connie.

"Hey," she said.

"Hey," he said back.

Neither of them said anything. Jazz ran through his options. Pretend nothing had happened? Apologize immediately? The nuclear option: break up. He'd written and rewritten the speech in his head a million times: *I know you love me and I love you, but I'm broken, Connie. I'm defective. I'm the toy you got for Christmas that's missing pieces, and even if it was complete, no one bought the batteries to go with it.*

"Before we talk about anything else, I need to say I'm sorry," Connie said.

"Excuse me?"

"I shouldn't have pushed you. I know you have...issues with sex. I get it. And, I mean, don't get me wrong. I totally think we're ready, but I went about it wrong. It wasn't cool. So I'm sorry."

Jazz closed his eyes and thumped the back of his head against the bed. "Con...it's not...you didn't do anything wrong. It's me. It was me. And then with your dad...I just..."

"I know. And we'll talk about that in—look, you don't have to...In New York. I just thought that with me, it might be okay. It might be safe. For you."

He sat upright. "What do you mean? What do you mean by that?"

"Well, I know that your dad never...never prospected any African Americans. Right?"

Jazz's heart thrummed. *What?*

"And I always figured that that maybe meant that I wouldn't...that I couldn't..." She blew into the phono, exasperated. "I know what you're worried about. You're worried that he somehow, like, programmed you to be a serial killer. And that there's all this crazy lurking under the surface—"

"It's not just under the surface," he said seriously.

"I know. But anyway, there's this stuff buried in you, and you're afraid it'll erupt if you have sex. Like, sex is the trigger, right? But Billy never killed any black women. It's like he just skipped over us. Almost deliberately. Like we don't exist to him. So I thought maybe that made me safe for you." She paused. "Didn't you ever think that?"

Jazz held back a laugh of commingled relief and horror. His big secret! His hidden fear! That Connie would someday find out why he'd first dated her. How long had he been terrified of telling her this, only to learn that not only did she know but she was okay with it and thought it was a good idea.

"I don't know what to say," he admitted. "I was just sitting here thinking how I needed to apologize to you—"

"For what? For freaking out?" She said it like it was no big deal.

"For that. For the way I freaked out. And now, I guess, for the way we first started dating. Which seems pretty racist, now that I think about it."

193

Connie laughed. "Jazz, if you liked—I don't know—blond girls or girls with big boobs—"

"Your boobs are pretty big."

"*Any*way. If you had a thing for one of those girls and saw her across a crowded room and went and introduced yourself, would that be a bad thing?"

"I don't know."

"Well, I do—the answer is no. So, in my case, you saw a really foxy-looking black girl across a crowded room—"

"It was the Coff-E-Shop and it was close to closing, so no one was there."

"—and you were like, 'I like black girls, so I'm going to introduce myself.' No big deal."

"Yeah, but what if the reason I like black girls is because they're, you're, safe—"

"So what? Who knows why anyone likes what they like? Guys who are obsessed with, like, redheads. Why? Because they're rare? Because they had a redheaded babysitter? Because they watched too many Emma Stone movies? Beats me. Who cares? I mean, why do I like white boys?"

"I'm the only white boy you've ever dated."

"And I'm the only black girl you've ever dated. So there."

"So, we're good?"

"We're beyond good."

"Is your dad gonna come at me with a shotgun the next time I come over?"

"Probably." She waited for a moment. "You went too far, you know. At the airport."

"I know."

"You crossed the line."

"I know."

"It's one thing to mess with a teacher's head to get out of detention or to charm that girl at the police station to get you some file you shouldn't have, but—"

"I know."

"—this is my *dad*, Jazz. He's my *father.* And you were, like, like, waving a cape in front of a bull."

"It was totally wrong."

"And you know what they do to the bulls, right? And that's how you were treating my dad."

"I'm sorry. I really am." *Nah,* Billy whispered, *you ain't sorry. You just know sayin' it gets you what you want.*

Jazz shook Billy away. He *was* sorry.

He was, like, 99 percent sure he was really sorry.

"I shouldn't have done that," he said. "I'll apologize to your dad right now."

Maybe 98 percent.

"That is *not* a good idea. He's still on fire. He's so pissed it's ridiculous. He *just now* stopped lecturing me. If you'd called five minutes ago, he would have grabbed the phone and you'd be talking to him instead."

Ouch.

"But anyway," she went on, "every couple has their thing, you know? My dad doesn't like you. And your grandmother thinks I'm the spawn of Satan. We'll deal."

"What about..." He didn't even want to bring it up, but he had to. It was in the open now. "What about sex?"

"Yes, please," Connie deadpanned.

He laughed. "Seriously. Come on."

"We'll take it slow."

"We've *been* taking it slow. Because of me. You know it's true, Con. Any other guy would have been all over you after a week. We've been together for almost a year."

"Maybe those guys would have been all over me, but they wouldn't have gotten anywhere. And you wouldn't have gotten anywhere, either. Not that soon. I wasn't ready. Not then. Now I am. Any man worth having will wait for his woman to be ready. How can I not return the favor?"

And that was when Jazz knew Connie was more and better than he deserved.

"I'll just have to get by thinking about you while I'm in the shower," she went on. "It's gotten me this far."

Jazz groaned. "You just had to put that image in my head, didn't you?"

"It's a pretty great image," she admitted. "All that lather and soapy bubbles making me slick and shiny." Her voice dropped, low and sweet.

Jazz adjusted uncomfortably. "I surrender. We need to change the subject. You're killing me."

He could almost hear Connie's delicious smile over the phone. "What are we supposed to talk about?"

"I don't know. Tell me what you were doing while I was with the cops yesterday."

"Oh, yeah. Right." She quickly filled him in on her mini-tour of some of the murder sites.

"Crime scenes," he corrected her. "It's possible they were murdered elsewhere and dumped there."

"Right, right. Anyway, there was this graffito—"

"*Graffito?*"

"It's the singular of *graffiti*."

"Now you're just messing with me."

"I swear to God. *Graffiti* is plural. It's like *data* and *datum*."

"No one says 'datum.'"

"People who speak properly do," Connie sniffed. "Anyway, someone had painted *Ugly J*."

"*Ugly J*? Why did you even notice that?"

She explained how it had stood out. "So someone went back afterward and left that tag," Jazz mused.

"Maybe the killer? They go back to the scene, right?"

"Sometimes. Not always. It's just as likely it's some smart-ass tagging crime scenes. Some kid's idea of a sick joke."

"I don't know. It wasn't stylized or artistic. Like, most taggers have a style. A little finesse. They want it to stand out, to be noticed. But this was just *there*. It was like doing your homework in Arial or Times New Roman. And before you asked: I already Googled *Ugly J*. Didn't find anything."

"It's probably some New York thing."

"I love the way you say 'New York' with such contempt," Connie said, laughing. "You were there, what, thirty-six hours? And you already hate the place."

"Can we talk about something else?"

"Sure. Let me tell you about the bath I took the other day...."

He groaned. Eventually, they hung up, and Jazz went to take the coldest shower in the history of cold showers. He tried not to think of Connie in the shower, too, but that task wasn't particularly easy to accomplish. He had a very, very vivid imagination.

Emerging dripping and freezing, he wrapped a towel around his waist and headed back to Billy's old room. His clothes were scattered on the bed, so he picked through them for an outfit, shoving aside the sheets of paper.

But he just couldn't let them go. Every time he touched those papers, it was as though they had some sort of psychic/magnetic attraction to him. He felt compelled to read them every time. This time was no different—cold and half-naked, he scanned his father's letter, then looked over the Impressionist's vile "shopping list" and its strange appendix.

And that's when he saw it. And once he saw it, he couldn't unsee it. In fact, he wondered how he could have possibly *not* seen it until now.

UNDER NO CIRCUMSTANCES ARE YOU TO
GO NEAR THE DENT BOY.
LEAVE HIM ALONE.
YOU ARE NOT TO ENGAGE HIM.
JASPER DENT IS OFF-LIMITS.

He blinked and looked again. It was so obvious:

UNDER NO CIRCUMSTANCES ARE YOU TO
GO NEAR THE DENT BOY.
LEAVE HIM ALONE.
YOU ARE NOT TO ENGAGE HIM.
JASPER DENT IS OFF-LIMITS.

In his relatively short life, Jazz had disturbed crime scenes, stolen and tampered with evidence, broken into the morgue, and illegally photocopied official police files. Now he broke most of Lobo's Nod's speed limits on his way to the sheriff's office and compounded his criminal career by breaking the state law about cell phone use while driving; he just kept getting G. William's voice mail.

"Lana?" he demanded, now having gotten through to the police dispatch line. "Lana, it's Jasper Dent. Where's G. William?"

Lana had a thing for Jazz—even seeing him handcuffed late that one night for breaking into the morgue with Howie hadn't dissuaded her. Now she was flustered, stuck halfway between trying to make small talk with him and answering his question. "Well, he's—he just stepped—are you okay, Jasper? Can *I* help you, maybe?"

"I need to see G. William. Is he coming back to the office?"

"Sure. I just saw him pull up. He's—"

"Tell him I'm on my way," Jazz said, and hung up. Soon, he pulled into the sheriff's department lot, parking Billy's old Jeep right next to G. William's cruiser. *Someone should get a picture of* that, he thought.

Inside, he blew past the reception desk, blowing off Lana, who smiled and tried to get his attention. He found G. William in his office, grinning and leaning back in his chair. The sheriff saluted Jazz with a massive mug of coffee that said SUPERCHARGED! on it.

"G. William—"

"Settle down, Jazz. You got ants in your pants again."

"Is Thurber still here? Has he been transferred yet?"

G. William slurped some coffee. "He's here. Catch your breath. Stroke at your age is a hell of a thing."

Jazz took a deep breath and compelled himself to calm down.

"You come on a social call, or is this business?" G. William asked. " 'Cause I do have some news for you. Somethin' you might find interesting."

Okay, sure. Jazz let out that deep breath and let the tension all along his spine dissipate. "Is it about the new coffee cup?" he said with forced friendliness.

"And there's the keen powers of observation that brought down the Impressionist."

"You're stoned on caffeine, aren't you?"

"I gotta admit—when there's more coffee in the cup, I tend to drink more coffee. You think this is why my leg feels all numb and tingly?"

"Could be." Without being asked or invited, Jazz slid into one of the chairs across from G. William's desk.

"In all seriousness, though," G. William said, leaning forward, "I should tell you about a couple of things been going on in town."

"Oh?"

"Yeah. We had three cars parked in no-parking zones yesterday. And Erickson pulled over the Gunnarson girl for texting while driving."

"And…?"

"Not a goddamn serial killer among 'em!" G. William guffawed, slapping a meaty palm on his desk. "Not a murder, not a maiming, not a missing person! It's almost like being the sheriff of a small town!"

Jazz allowed himself a tiny grin. "You're positively giddy."

"I think I'm entitled. Don't you?"

It was true. For a small-town sheriff to go after two serial killers in one career was unprecedented, as far as Jazz knew. A return to the petty, mundane crimes of Lobo's Nod should be celebrated, and G. William had every right to do so.

"I'm glad for you. I really am. But I need—"

"You need something so big and important that you called my cell half a dozen times and then scared the poop outta Lana and then barreled in here like you were on fire. Jazz, you're seriously gonna give yourself a stroke."

"Please listen to me," Jazz said, and then quickly explained Connie's discovery in New York, along with the acrostic he'd uncovered in the Impressionist's pocket.

G. William listened, occasionally sipping at his coffee.

"It could be the world's most incredible coincidence," he said.

"You don't believe that for a minute."

The sheriff shook his head. "I want nothing more in this world than to believe that. I want to believe that there's no connection between the guy in lockup waiting to be transported to court and the guy killing people in New York. Mostly 'cause that would probably mean there's a connection to your

201

daddy, too. So, yeah, I want to believe it's all a coincidence, but I'm not as dumb as I look, which is a hell of a good thing." He heaved himself out of his chair. "Let's go."

Jazz rose to follow him. "Don't we have to check with his lawyer first?"

"Usually, yeah. But the Impressionist has made it clear that he's always available to see you. As long as there's no cops present, you can talk to him whenever and however long you want. You just can't report it to us or tell us about it, 'cause then it'd be off-limits in court. But hell—he'll talk to *you* all day long, if you want."

"Lucky me," Jazz muttered.

G. William led him back to the holding cells, which were empty except for the one farthest from the door, in which sat Frederick Thurber, the Impressionist.

He'd been in the Lobo's Nod jail since his arrest before Halloween. Lawyers from the Nod were fighting with lawyers from just over the state line—where the Impressionist had murdered a woman named Carla O'Donnelly—over which state got to try him first. And then there was a district attorney in Oklahoma who claimed that the Impressionist had also killed someone in Enid, long before taking on his Billy Dent–inspired sobriquet and modus operandi. Fortunately, the federal government was staying out of it—for now—preferring to let the states waste their time and resources. All three jurisdictions in question had the death penalty, so Thurber was heading for Death Row one way or the other, the feds figured.

The whole thing was a snarl of legalese and lawyerly posturing, the upshot of which was that Thurber remained in Lobo's Nod until everyone could agree who would get the first pound of flesh from him.

Thurber glanced up as the door to the holding cells opened, then sat up straight when Jazz came through the door. Jazz thought maybe there was a small smile playing across his lips, but who knew what it looked like when a madman like the Impressionist smiled? Jazz kept his face impassive, his spine stiff, as he approached the Impressionist's cell. The Impressionist stood and turned to the front of the cage, staring as though the bars didn't exist and he could walk right up to Jazz if he wanted.

"Now, I can't stick around, so I'm just leavin' you with a warning," G. William said sternly. "Don't even think about hurting him."

"I won't get close enough to the bars for him to touch me," Jazz assured him.

"I wasn't talking to *him*," G. William said wearily, and left.

Alone, Jazz didn't get the chance to speak before the Impressionist said, in a voice oddly high and thin from disuse, "Jasper Dent. Princeling of Murder. Heir to the Croaking."

The *Croaking*? Was this crap for real? He'd almost forgotten how completely delusional the Impressionist was. Thurber thought that Billy Dent was a god, that Jazz was destined to the same divinity.

"Come to learn the truth?" the Impressionist asked.

"Come to accept your destiny? It's not too late. It's never too late. Jackdaw!"

The man was babbling. He was falling apart, Jazz realized. That made no sense. He should have been doing well. Serial killers tended to thrive in rigid, institutional settings. He'd read all sorts of case studies on guys like Richard Macek, who had turned into a model prisoner once incarcerated. When given limited options and no freedom, sociopaths tended to default to a sort of relaxed ennui. But the Impressionist was blowing the curve for the rest of the class. His eyes were glassy and possessed.

Well, there's an exception to every rule. And you just met him. Jazz almost felt sorry for the man, but he thought of Helen Myerson and he thought of blowing air into Ginny Davis's lungs, his hands slick with her blood. He thought of Howie, near death in an alley, slashed open by the Impressionist.

"I want to know about Ugly J," Jazz said firmly.

Sociopaths never revealed anything; they were masters at concealing their emotions or of feigning emotions to cover when they knew a lack of affect would draw attention to them. He'd expected either a calm, savvy, knowing grin or a flat, reactionless glare.

Instead, the Impressionist actually took a step back; his hands twitched as though he would bring them up to shield himself, to ward something off. If Jazz didn't know better, he would say the Impressionist was actually…afraid.

"Ugly J…" the man whispered. "No. No. Oh, no. Not Ugly J. We won't talk about *that*. You're not ready for *that*.

Even *I* know that. I defied for you. I touched when I was told not to. But not Ugly J. I won't."

Jazz stepped closer to the bars. "Talk to me. What is Ugly J? What does it mean? Or is it a person? Is it a serial killer? Is it what Billy calls himself now?"

The Impressionist shook his head, mute. Jazz came right up to the bars, aware that the Impressionist could make a lunge and grab him.

"Tell me! Tell me about Ugly J!"

"Not ugly!" the Impressionist screamed. *"Beautiful!"* Considering what the Impressionist thought to be beautiful, that could mean a lot. "Beautiful," he said again. "But the way you *die* is so ugly...! So ugly, Jasper!"

Ugly, Jasper. Ugly... "Am *I* Ugly J? Is that it? Talk to me. Tell me what you know. Who sent you that letter? Who gave you the list? You're working with whoever helped Billy escape. I know that. You know things. You know things. You know things!"

"Jasper!" G. William shouted. When had *he* come back? He cried out Jazz's name again, and Jazz realized it had been a long time—more than four years, the night G. William had arrested Billy and nearly shot Jazz—since he'd heard such panic in the big man's voice. "Get the hell away from there!"

The Impressionist and Jazz both jumped back from the cell door at the same time. So close. He'd been right on top of the Impressionist. *What could I have done to him? Reached right through the bars? What else, if G. William hadn't showed up?* The Impressionist now cowered near his bunk, shaking his head over and over like one of the deluded, driven-mad homeless people Jazz had seen in New York. *What did I do to him? It's like the idea of Ugly J flipped a switch—*

"Goddamn it, Jazz!" G. William growled as he grabbed Jazz by the elbow and jerked him farther away from the cell. "I warned you, didn't I? Didn't I tell you?"

"Look at him. Look. He's not a danger to me. He's—"

The Impressionist chose that moment to make a liar out of Jazz, bellowing with rage and flinging himself at the bars of the cell with such force that Jazz flinched at the sickening thudding sound it made. The Impressionist staggered backward, groaning, his nose spurting blood. "Corvus!" he cried. "Corvidae!"

"Jesus H. Christ," G. William swore. He hauled Jazz back into the station proper and barked into his shoulder mic for a deputy with a medical bag to the holding cells. "...and have an ambulance sent over, too, just in case. Got that?"

"Got it," Lana's voice came from the mic. "Is, um, is everyone okay?"

Snorting with disgust, G. William said, "The boy prince is just fine, Lana. Get back to work."

Moments later, they were back in the sheriff's office, Jazz leaning against the wall as G. William railed. "—told you to stay away from the cell! He's dangerous! Just because you *think* you're invincible doesn't mean you *are* invincible—"

"G. William," Jazz said calmly, "why did you come in there in the first place?"

The sheriff paused mid-rant and blinked. "What?"

"Why did you even come into the holding cells? You weren't supposed to be there."

G. William's mouth opened and closed, opened and closed, and then he gasped. "Oh, crap. I forgot! There was a call for you!" He grabbed up the receiver on his desk and punched a blinking light. "Are you still— Okay. Thanks. Sorry. We had a situation. Hang on." He held the phone out to Jazz. "For you. FBI looking for you."

"Uh-uh." A shake of the head. "I don't want to talk to them anymore. I'm tired of the feds."

"This one says she knows you. Morales?"

Jazz's curiosity got the better of him. Taking the phone, he answered, "Hello?"

"Dent? That you?" Morales's breath came fast, her words stumbling on their way out. "I need your cell number. Now. Quick. I have to send you something."

Jazz gave her the number, and a moment later his cell tickled his thigh.

"You have to see it to believe it," Morales went on. "This changes things."

He flicked on the phone and opened the text message from Morales. A photo was attached.

"...dumped last night, but as best we can tell," she went on, "she was killed *before* the media started talking about you being here in New York...."

It was a crime scene. A body. Easy enough. Young woman. Brown hair. Naked. Gutted. The usual.

Written in lipstick over the sagging, dead lumps of her breasts was:

WELCOME TO THE GAME, JASPER

Part Four

5 Players, 4 Sides

CHAPTER 24

Connie's grounding wouldn't last until she was eighty, but it would probably feel like it. She knew she'd been grounded for a good, long time, no matter what clever lies or stories she conjured for her parents. Once school started on Monday, it would be school, then home. Period. When play practice started for the spring musical, she would be allowed to attend rehearsals, but that was it.

All in all, she thought, it wasn't a bad deal. Sneak off to New York, have a lusty bout of almost-sex with your hot boyfriend, get grounded. There were worse things to get grounded for. And fortunately her parents hadn't decided to take away her phone. It rang now, TLC's "Waterfalls" blaring out too loud. Connie's mom loved that old song, sang it around the house all the time, until it was ingrained in Connie's brain. She wasn't sure if she loved the song or not, but she was obsessed with it just from hearing it all the time.

"Don't go chasing..."

She turned down the volume on her phone. It would suck

if her parents heard the ringtone and thought, *Oh, yeah, we should confiscate her phone, too.*

Caller ID said BLOCKED.

"Don't go chasing..."

Connie answered. It was Jazz.

"I'm calling from the sheriff's office," he explained when she asked why the number was blocked. "You're not going to believe what just happened."

In rushed, run-on sentences, he told her all of it: the possible connection between her Ugly J discovery and the Impressionist, then about the phone call from Morales, followed by the photo.

"...so I'm headed back to New York, and this time it's official. I'm going to help them nail the Hat-Dog Killer to the wall."

"But, Jazz..." Connie protested. "This isn't just about Hat-Dog anymore. If the Ugly J stuff is connected—"

"I know," he said. "There's a chance this all ties into the Impressionist somehow."

"More than that. It ties into the guy *behind* the Impressionist. Your dad."

Jazz went silent for a moment. "Yeah. I know."

"What if your dad *is* Hat-Dog? What if he's doing all of this to draw you out? So that he can"—*torture maim kill*—"hurt you?"

Jazz chuckled without mirth. "He can't be Hat-Dog. He was in Wammaket when those killings started. And if Billy wanted to hurt me, he wouldn't have to go through all this trouble. He could just come at me. He knows where I live."

"And he knows there are a million FBI agents watching your house on a regular basis." It wasn't a million, but Connie didn't feel like being accurate right now. Her boyfriend was talking about walking into the lion's den while wearing raw-steak underwear.

"So he's not the Hat-Dog Killer. But maybe they know each other. Or knew each other."

"What, did they meet at a serial killer convention or something?" Connie stretched out on her bed, staring at the ceiling.

"No, Miss Sarcasm. But Billy traveled a lot. And I've been thinking—it wouldn't be *too* much of a coincidence if he'd met someone like him along the way. And sometimes serial killers take on partners or allies. It doesn't happen a lot and it doesn't last for long, but what if Hat-Dog is someone out there who owes Billy a favor? Or who just thinks it's funny to do stuff for Billy? Hat-Dog could be the one who sent the Impressionist to Lobo's Nod. The one who arranged Billy's escape from Wammaket." Jazz's words came faster and faster. "This could be the linchpin to everything Billy's been up to, to everything he's planning as he goes forward. I *have* to go to New York, Con. I have to find this guy and make him talk. He could be the only way I have to get to Billy."

"And what will you do then?" she asked quietly. "What do you do when you finally see him face-to-face, on the outside? With no prison guards?"

"I'll figure that out when the time comes," he said, and she wished he'd said it with some kind of passion or heat. Some rage or violence in his voice. Those were all things she could deal with, things she could say something about.

But Jazz's voice in that moment had gone cold and dead. She hated when he did that. Hated when he reached for the knob in his soul that read COMPASSION and dialed it all the way down to zero. She could handle anger. Soullessness? That was beyond her comprehension.

She rolled over and flipped open her laptop, which lay on her bedside table. The desktop image was of her and Jazz in one of their rare scenes together in last year's production of *The Crucible*. Reverend Hale takes Tituba's hands and implores her to give up the names of the devil's children in Salem. Powerful scene—man of God begs slave woman to do evil in the name of good. She hated it, all of a sudden.

"If you kill him, he wins."

"No, Connie. If I kill him, he's dead."

"Don't go chasing…"

She closed her eyes. "Just promise me you'll be careful in New York, okay?"

"Please stick to the rivers…"

"When am I ever not careful?" he teased, suddenly a Real Boy again.

"You mean other than letting an NYPD detective lie you into going to New York? And other than letting a serial killer into your house? Do you need more examples?"

He laughed. "I guess not. Don't worry, Con. It's all good. I'm going to be surrounded by FBI agents and cops. I'll be the safest guy in New York."

"If anything happens to you, I'll kick your ass so hard you'll poop from the front," she threatened.

"That sounds like something Howie would say."

"I think he did once."

"Okay. I have to go pack. I love you."

"I love you, too."

No sooner had she put the phone down than a mocking chortle assailed her. Twisting around, she saw that Whiz had quietly opened her door at some point and was now laughing at her. "I love *you*," he mimicked, and made smooching noises.

"Stop spying on me, Wisdom!" she shouted, and threw a pillow at him.

He ducked. "I'm gonna tell Mom and Dad that you're talking to your *boyfriend*." He drew out the word *boyfriend* into something almost salacious. Connie couldn't believe how her brother could—in the same day, in a matter of hours—go from sweet and concerned to mega-brat. Had *she* been such a shapeshifting creep at his age?

"And *I'm* gonna tell them that you're spying on me in my underwear," she said.

"You're not in your underwear," Whiz countered.

"I will be in *my* version of the story," Connie said, utterly convincingly. Whiz blanched and ducked out of the room, closing the door behind him as he went.

Connie sighed. Great. Jazz was off fighting the good fight and she was trapped here in the Nod, engaged in a battle of wits with her witless younger brother. Life wasn't fair.

She spent some time online, poking around again for information about Ugly J, but still found nothing helpful. Then she started looking into the Impressionist's history. Since his capture and the revelation of his true identity, there had been a small avalanche of historical information revealed about the Impressionist—where he'd grown up, how his parents had died (in a word: gruesomely), and more. Connie figured that maybe there would be a clue either to Ugly J or to how the Impressionist had hooked up with Billy Dent. But she could find nothing. Cross-referencing Billy's "career path" as a serial killer to the Impressionist's travels netted exactly zilch.

Her parents would probably freak if they walked in on her doing this. *This is exactly what we're trying to protect you from!* they would protest. *You shouldn't even be* thinking *about these things!*

Whatever. There was death and horror in the world. Her parents could try all they wanted to shield her from it, but Connie knew it was there. She wasn't going to close her eyes and wish it away. Especially not when she happened to be in a position—maybe—to shed a little light on that darkness.

After hours staring at the screen, Connie finally took a break, stretching and rubbing her eyes. Was she chasing waterfalls? Or did Billy Dent and the Impressionist count as the rivers and the lakes she was used to?

Speaking of her phone...she had silenced the ringer a little while back so that it wouldn't go off if Jazz called or texted late at night. But maybe she'd missed something. She checked the phone for messages. There was a single text that had come in.

BLOCKED.

Connie swiped at it to read it, then realized: Jazz couldn't text her from the sheriff's department's landline.

Then who—?

It said: *r u game?*

CHAPTER 25

One of his remaining disposable cell phones rang, and the killer answered.

"Eleven," said the voice. "Eleven. Six and five." There was a lilt to it, a joy, a buoyancy that was lost on the killer, who could not sense such things. The sounds and the nuances of human beings meant as much as did color to the blind.

The killer repeated "eleven" in his mind, fixing it there, and stared at the laptop screen before him. Eleven. Eleven meant...

The killer gaped and gawped and stared for moments protracted and elongated by the shock of unknowability.

"I," he said, "don't understand."

"Well, I'll tell you what," said the voice. "I'll tell you what. We're gonna have some fun, okay?"

The killer didn't quite understand "fun," but he said nothing and simply listened.

"Saw on the news today," the voice went on, "that the bastard cops say they have an eyewitness. Just came forward, they said. They tried to sound real convincing, and I bet they think they were, but they're not. They're bluffing. That's okay, though. That's okay."

And then the voice began to explain things. To describe things. And the killer did not understand, but the killer did not need to understand.

The killer needed only to obey.

To accede.

To win.

To *ascend*.

CHAPTER 26

"Dude!" Howie exclaimed, throwing his absurdly huge hands into the air. "I can't believe you're doing this to me again!"

"I have to go to New York." Jazz threw clothes into his borrowed suitcase. He'd barely had time to unpack. "I need you to help watch Gramma. I'll let you tattoo my freakin' *ass*, okay?"

"I am totally sleeping with your aunt. I don't care what you say. I know she doesn't seem interested right now, but trust me: She will succumb to my wit and charm, and I will know her. In the biblical sense."

"Right."

"You *do* realize that means I'm going to bone her. In the biblical sense."

"I'm aware."

Howie noticed the shadow of a grin on Jazz's face and crossed his arms across his chest in defiance. "I'm totally serious here! Not only will I sleep with her, but I will knock her up, too. I'm gonna be the daddy to your cousins. So there."

"Sounds great, Uncle Howie." Jazz went to clap Howie on the shoulder, thought of the bruise it would cause, and settled for a handshake.

"Your cousins will be tall and handsome and have bigger dicks than you do," Howie said very solemnly.

"I'm sure. Thanks, man."

"Have you forgotten that school starts again on Monday?"

"With any luck, I'll just miss a day or two. I'll help them narrow the profile, look over the new crime scene for stuff they might have missed...get them pointed in the right direction. Boom. Done. Home."

"And I'm still gonna tattoo your ass!" Howie shouted after him as he left.

On the plane, Jazz didn't even have time to enjoy or dread his flight. He was busy pondering the message left for him at the latest crime scene. Morales had e-mailed him all of the preliminary information, including crime-scene photos.

"We're bringing you in," Morales had told him on the phone. "I don't care if I have to go over Montgomery's head to the governor. This guy has called you out. So you're in."

Less than a half hour later, it was official, and Jazz was on his way back to the airport after a call to Connie to let her know what was going on. Aunt Samantha was good to watch

Gramma for a little while. Jazz truly regretted leaving her so soon. He felt like they had much more to talk about.

When he'd told Aunt Samantha that he had to go back to New York, he'd only had time for a quick talk. The topic had been Howie. "I'm sorry to leave you with him. I know how he is, but he's actually a good guy—"

"You act like I've never been around a horny boy in my life," she'd said. "I think I can handle him. I would actually find it sort of flattering if I didn't know for sure that he does this to *every*one."

"Not everyone. Just, like, ninety percent. Maybe ninety-five."

"I'll humor him. It's no big deal. Go do what you have to do."

During the flight, he flicked through the screen of his phone, looking at the crime-scene photos Morales had sent. This one was different. For one thing, the body wasn't even in Brooklyn. It had been found on subway tracks in Manhattan, on something that at first he'd read as *the Sline*—which sounded strange even for New York—but then realized was actually *the S line*. Jazz didn't know what that was and he didn't particularly care, but Morales had helpfully annotated one of the photos: *S line: shuttle between Grand Central and Times Square along 42nd St.* Jazz had no idea how far apart Grand Central and Times Square were, so that told him nothing. Still, it was nice to see that Morales was thinking of him and his general ignorance of all things Big Apple.

One thing he did know, even with his limited experience with New York geography: This part of New York—this part of *Manhattan*—was even farther from Hat-Dog's jeopardy surface than Coney Island had been.

The ME's preliminary examination of the body at the scene indicated that the murder had taken place several hours earlier, elsewhere. The victim's intestines had been removed and were not with the body. Paralyzed, as usual. Eyelids cut off, like the others. White female, between twenty-five and thirty. Five-four. Maybe one hundred twenty pounds (when all those innards had been in their proper places).

And because it wouldn't be the Hat-Dog Killer without some kind of escalation: The eyes were missing. Jazz sighed. He knew from Billy's stories over the years what was involved in that. Eyes were actually pretty easy to scoop out, assuming you had your victim conveniently unconscious or dead. Just some tendons and nerves holding the eyes in; nothing you couldn't cut easily with whatever was lying around the house. He wondered if they'd been removed pre- or postmortem? He supposed the autopsy would tell them.

So, he killed her and gutted her and de-...eyed her somewhere else. De-eyed? Un-eyed. Anyway. Then hauled her to the S line and dumped her.

A hat was carved into her sternum, between her breasts. Above was written the message to Jazz.

WELCOME TO THE GAME, JASPER.

Game.

It's not a game, you sick lunatic.

The best estimates as to the death were that the victim had died in the early morning hours. So that meant she'd

223

been killed before the New York press had glommed on to Jazz's presence in the city and (unofficial) involvement in the Hat-Dog case.

"So there's no way to know," Morales had told him, "if this guy left the message for you before the press reported you were in town or after. If before, then that means he saw the story Weathers did on the Lobo's Nod website. If after, then he's still calling you out. Either way, he's obsessed with you."

WELCOME TO THE GAME, JASPER.

It almost—almost—sounded like something Billy would say. If not for that word—*game*. Billy never thought of what he did as a game. It was fun, yes, but the sort of fun to be taken deadly serious. There was a reason he referred to it as "prospecting." The prospectors of olden times had been involved in life-or-death stakes for the most part, and when they succeeded, they celebrated.

Jazz could remember Billy returning from prospecting trips, flush with excitement and success. He would dump out of his suitcase a mélange of clothes, trophies, newspaper clippings of his exploits, and the occasional body part, then collapse in the big easy chair in the living room to obsessively watch TV coverage of his "adventures" while eating take-out Chinese food and drinking bottle after bottle of cream soda (one of Billy's other obsessions).

Jazz would innocently play with the contents of Dear Old Dad's suitcase, then arrange the trophies carefully in the rumpus room.

When the plane landed, Jazz was surprised to find Hughes standing there at the gate, waiting for him.

"Didn't bring the girlfriend this time?" the detective asked.

"Thought for sure you'd be on suspension after the reaming out your captain gave you."

"I'm too valuable," Hughes joked. "But, yeah, sorry about that," he went on as they walked to his car, which was parked obnoxiously in a no-parking zone, watched over by a TSA agent. "I didn't mean to lie to you. But I'd been banging my head against this case for months and getting nowhere and I wanted to bring you, but Montgomery—"

"I get it," Jazz said, climbing in. "It's not like I've never broken the rules before."

Hughes nodded and gunned the engine. "So, I understand you've met our FBI liaison?"

Jazz wondered briefly if he should mention Morales's offer to help kill Billy. But no. Hughes might be maverick-y, but he didn't think the detective would countenance outright murder. "Yeah. She tried some mind-screwing on me, but changed her tune pretty quick."

"She likes doing that. Messing with guys. She's a dyke, you know."

Jazz squirmed at the word. "Didn't know that," he said casually, wondering how Hughes would feel if he went all Gramma and dropped the N-bomb.

"It's statistically proven that of all the law enforcement agencies in the country, the FBI has the largest percentage of lesbians. Isn't that interesting?"

That actually *was* interesting. "Really?"

Hughes guffawed. "No. I made that up. But it sounds like it could be true, doesn't it?"

Dyke. Invented FBI stats. Hughes had his psychological guard up again. Jazz didn't blame him.

"You're a true wit. Anything new happen while I was in the air?"

"Nope. Still waiting on toxicology, autopsy, all that stuff. Still going over the scene."

"What's the plan?" It was getting dark outside, but Jazz didn't want to let the fall of night slow him down. He was buzzing to get out on the street.

"Well, first I'm going to get you to the crime scene. The S doesn't even run some weekends, and this is one of them. So we're taking our time with crime-scene analysis. Body was still on-site, last I checked. I asked them to hold her there as long as they could, so you could see."

"Good. Then what?"

"Then back to the precinct. Montgomery and Morales want to bring you up to speed on everything. Officially."

Jazz nodded, staring at the photo on his phone. "This guy. Whoever he is..."

"He's getting cocky," Hughes said. "Which means he'll slip up."

"Maybe. I hope so. Sometimes they get cocky because they deserve to be."

CHAPTER 27

By now, she knew, Jazz had made it to New York. Connie tried to focus on getting through her punishment and thinking good thoughts in the general direction of Brooklyn, but no matter what she did, she kept coming back to that message. She stared at her phone.

r u game?

WELCOME TO THE GAME, JASPER.

What in the *hell* was going on here?

r u game?

It could mean a couple of things. *Game* was something you hunted in order to eat it. So, hell, no, she wasn't that kind of game.

But it could also mean "Are you up for something?" "Are you ready?"

To which Connie could say only, "Hells, yes."

She was sick of being told to sit on the sidelines, play the good girlfriend, "stand by your man." Sick of watching the crazy stuff from the outside. She had sneaked off to New

York to help and that had worked out pretty well, right? Her exploration had discovered...something. And now it appeared that someone knew what she'd found. How?

I could have been followed in Brooklyn. Someone could have been watching. She shivered at the idea that she might have been under observation the whole time. Who could it have been? The Hat-Dog Killer himself? Billy Dent? Someone named Ugly J?

Her first instinct was to call Jazz and tell him about the text, but she knew exactly what he would say. Jazz would assume he had all the answers because Jazz *always* assumed he had all the answers. One day shortly after their encounter with the Impressionist, he had sat down with her and very seriously explained to her how to survive a serial killer.

"First thing is," he told her, "run. Just get the hell away. Even if he's small or seems weak or crippled somehow. It's all an act. These guys don't come after you unless they're sure they can take you, so run. Bundy used to wear his arm in a sling. Fooled people. Made him seem helpless and harmless."

"I know to run away," she'd said, more than a little bit exasperated.

"If you can't run, if he's already got you," Jazz pressed on, ignoring her, "then your next line of defense is verbal. Be firm. Tell him to leave you alone. Don't try to hit him or attack him. Not yet. He's probably stronger than you and hitting him will just flip his switch. But there's a chance he might not be used to a woman being firm with him."

"Or maybe tough chicks make his little pee-pee hard," Connie said.

"I'm trying to help you," Jazz said, and then proceeded to describe the escalation of her options: from moderate physical force if possible to verbally puncturing the fantasy ("Nah, why rape me? Let's go get a drink instead") to absolute fight-for-your-life, scratch-his-eyes-out panic.

"It's all going to depend on the situation," he'd admitted at last. "Some guys will get turned on by you fighting back. Some will be scared by it."

"So, basically, be careful and don't do anything stupid," she'd said, and he had agreed.

Be careful. Don't do anything stupid. Exactly what Jazz would say right now. Along with: *Show it to G. William.*

Well, she *would* show it G. William. Eventually.

But right now...there wasn't really anything to show, was there? Just a random text. It could be anything. It might even have been a mistake, something not meant for her, something not even remotely related to what was happening in New York. That had happened to her before, people accidentally texting the wrong number.

You're making excuses, Connie. Excuses to keep this to yourself.

Yeah. Yeah, she was. Because...because...

Because I'm sick and tired of being treated like I'm a doll made out of cheap plastic, like I could break at any moment. By Jazz, always trying to protect me. By my dad, who doesn't even trust me to pick a boyfriend. Even by Howie.

And Howie's the most breakable person I know! Jazz and Howie go off and break the rules whenever they want. But I'm supposed to be the rule follower. The good girl. Since when did I become the freakin' mom? Just once I want—

Her phone vibrated in her hand.

i kno something abt ur boyfriend

Chills radiated up Connie's arms, and the fine, light hairs there stood on their ends. She shivered involuntarily.

"Don't go chasing..."

Another vibration. Another message.

no police no parents

She figured that went without saying. And for now she was fine with it. She would call G. William when she knew more, she decided.

Another vibration.

Whoever was at the other end was just going to keep sending her messages, apparently. She could play or not, but she would be given the pieces to put on the board either way.

let's play came next, followed by more.

CHAPTER 28

Hughes drove carefully but quickly, wending their way through what he called Queens, then to Brooklyn, then to a bridge that seemed vaguely familiar to Jazz. He was sure he'd seen it in movies.

"This is the East River we're driving over," Hughes lectured, "and yeah, this is the world-famous Brooklyn Bridge."

"I'm not here for a geography lesson," Jazz said.

"Just thought I'd give you the tourist package as long as you're in town."

"Whatever."

In silence, they headed to the most recent crime scene, in Midtown Manhattan, far out of Hat-Dog's comfort zone. This is where they'd found the woman in the picture Morales had sent to Jazz. They were loading the body into a body bag as they arrived. "She was ready to be moved a while ago. I can stop them, though. Do you need to see her?" Hughes asked.

"Sure. Why not?" Even though it was January, it was still

hot and humid in the subway. Jazz stripped off his heavy coat and handed it to a nearby cop, then went to duck under the crime-scene tape. The area was cordoned off and crawling with crime-scene techs. Jazz idly checked his cell phone and saw that he had no signal. Connie had been right about that.

"Whoa!" Hughes stopped him. "Can't have you stomping around in there."

Jazz grinned. "I'll be a ghost. Believe me, I know how to walk around crime scenes. I've been doing it since I was a kid."

At a flash of Hughes's badge, the techs allowed Jazz to crouch down next to the body bag. It wasn't zipped up yet, so he could see the victim. He flashed back to a few months ago, when he and Howie had broken into the Lobo's Nod morgue to see the body of Fiona Goodling, the Impressionist's first victim in Jazz's hometown. Back then—it seemed so long ago already!—Jazz had refused to see her as a person, preferring to imagine her as a thing. Now, though, he knew better.

I'm not going to rest, he thought, gazing at where her eyes should have been, staring into the black pits. *I'm going to get him. Because that's the only thing in this world I'm any good at, I think.*

The medical examiner, noticing where Jazz was staring, cleared her throat. "As you can see, she's been enucleated."

That was a new word to Jazz.

"Try it in Spanish," Hughes said. "I'm more fluent in that."

"Sorry," the ME said, "it's just that you don't get to use that word a lot. Means her eyes were taken out."

"Are they still here?" Jazz asked, glancing around as though he might see them lying on the ground.

"I just said—"

"You said that they were taken out. This guy cuts off penises, too, but he doesn't always take them with him."

The ME, clearly miffed at being upbraided by a kid, went stiff and formal. "Immediate area canvass found no eyeballs with the body or in the immediate vicinity. But that doesn't mean one of the unis won't stumble across them somewhere. There's also a chance we'll find them during the autopsy. I had a case once where some toes were missing and we found them in the victim's throat. They were stuffed down there postmortem."

If the ME was expecting a reaction, Jazz disappointed her, merely nodding at the thought of severed toes jammed down a dead man's throat.

"Did a decent job removing the eyeballs..." Hughes commented. "I mean, the eye sockets and the skin around the sockets don't even look disturbed."

"Yeah," Jazz agreed with a shrug, "but it's not that difficult, really. Billy used to do it with one of those grapefruit spoons. You know, the kind that are serrated?" He mimed dishing out a spoonful of grapefruit and was rewarded with—for the first time—a nauseated look from the Homicide cop. "All that's back there are a couple of muscles and a big optic nerve. Piece of cake. Your eyes aren't really all that secure in the first place."

"It's true," the medical examiner agreed grimly, as though personally offended by the fragility of the human body. "You just cut the lateral tendon—same thing as in a lateral canthotomy—and you can pop—"

"Enough!" Hughes said, pressing his thumb and forefinger lightly against his eyelids, as if assuring himself that his eyes weren't about to spontaneously pop out. "I get it. I get it. We done here?" he said to Jazz.

"Give me a few minutes." He prowled the crime scene, playing a borrowed flashlight over the walls and ceiling, along dripping pipes. He even hopped down from the platform, avoiding touching the rails because he didn't know which one was the electrified one, and walked a hundred feet or so in either direction. Other than smashed-up plastic bottles and discarded chip bags, he didn't find anything.

Well, he did see the single largest rat he'd ever seen in his life. It glared at him with defiant, completely unscared eyes before scampering off into a crevice somewhere.

"Find anything?" Hughes asked, giving him a hand back onto the platform.

"Just the biggest rat in God's creation." Jazz measured off the rat's length with his hands.

Hughes chuckled and said, "That's not big, Jasper. That's average."

"I was looking for..." Should he tell Hughes about Ugly J? Yeah, he decided. It might not turn out to be connected—there was still a chance that Ugly J had multiple meanings, after all—but it wouldn't hurt. He filled in Hughes about

Connie's discovery and the acrostic on the Impressionist's letter. "I guess it could be a coincidence. It might just be an Impressionist thing and also be some kind of New York thing and they might have nothing to do with each other. But maybe there's a connection."

"Between Hat-Dog and the Impressionist?" Jazz gave Hughes a moment to catch up; the detective did not disappoint. "Oh, Lord. Then there would be a connection to your dad, wouldn't there?"

"Maybe. It all depends what Ugly J means. If it's some random urban legend or something, it could just be something Hat-Dog and the Impressionist both happened upon. Billy might not be involved at all. Does it mean anything to you?"

Hughes pondered. "No. How about you guys?" he asked the uniforms. They walked beats—they would know.

Fancy-ass detectives with their shiny gold shields and their shiny suit pants from sittin' on those fancy asses all day long, Billy said, *ain't the real problem. The real problem's the bastard cop in the bag, the guy on the street who notices your car don't belong on that block. The guy who realizes you drove past the same building twice and slowed down both times. He's your real enemy.*

The uniforms gathered around. Head shakes from everyone. "Nah. Nothing. Maybe check with IU?"

"What's IU?" Jazz asked.

"Intelligence Unit. They handle gang stuff," one of the uniforms answered. "But it doesn't look like a gang tag to me."

"Like you're an expert," Hughes said. "Can't hurt to check."

"What's the deal here?" the second cop asked. "There's graffiti all over this city, a lot of it the same."

Jazz told them what Connie had seen.

"Jesus," the first cop said, "now the *girlfriend* is a profiler, too? Maybe we should just turn this over to the kids at P.S. One-thirty-eight."

"Settle down," Hughes told him. To Jazz, he said, "E-mail Connie's photo to me and I'll have IU look at it."

"I didn't see Ugly J anywhere, but that doesn't mean anything. It seems like he comes back and adds it later."

"We'll get a hidden camera set up in here. Keep some undercovers circulating after we leave. Maybe we'll get lucky. I'll also have some unis recheck a bunch of the crime scenes. Just in case."

Jazz looked up and down the track. "Tell me about this again? This S line? Does the *S* stand for something?"

"Short," one of the cops joked feebly.

"It's just a letter," Hughes said. "I guess it might stand for *shuttle*. This is a short shuttle line from Grand Central to Times Square. Just a couple of blocks."

"Anything unique about it?"

"Depends on your definition of unique. It's unique in that it isn't unique, really." Before Jazz could even splutter, "Huh?" Hughes continued: "Unlike the other trains, there are actually *three* S lines. This is just one of them. There's another S shuttle in Queens that goes out to Rockaway Park, and a third one in Brooklyn, runs...where does the Brooklyn S run?" he called over his shoulder.

Three cops started to answer. One spoke loudest: "Starts on Franklin, runs through Park Place to Prospect Park."

Prospect Park, Billy said. *Sounds like my kinda place. Heh.*

But Jazz actually couldn't believe the other name mentioned, and laughed out loud despite himself and despite Billy's intrusion. "*Park Place?* There's actually a Park Place? Is it near Boardwalk?"

"Ha, ha. You're a riot, kid. No, Park Place is where we found victim number...seven."

Number seven. Marie Leydecker. White female, twenty-seven years old. Raped. Strangled. Gutted. It was almost like checking things off on a list. Jazz remembered now. Remembered walking the crime scene. Hat-Dog had waited more than two weeks after killing Leydecker before moving on to Harry Glidden, the poor, boring tax man, white male, thirty-one. Throat slit. Etc. Same tune, different key. Except for the paralysis, which began with Glidden. Had Leydecker done something to make Hat-Dog think he should start paralyzing victims?

Hughes hustled him out of the subway so that the crime-scene guys could work undisturbed. Back in the car, Jazz settled into the seat and watched Manhattan drift by him. Even late at night, the city's streets were clogged and choked. In the distance, he saw what he now knew to be the Brooklyn Bridge and experienced a strange feeling of homecoming. His hotel room and bed waited on the other side of that bridge, and he was bone-tired.

"We have too much information," he said. "It's like this guy has decided to drown us in evidence and theories and ideas. So much crap that we can't figure out what's really important."

"That's why I wanted you on board," Hughes told him. "To cut through the nonsense."

"You guys have already done a great job," Jazz said, and meant it. Sure, he'd found some things and noticed some details that they hadn't, but in general the NYPD and the FBI had done an incredible job. They'd gathered not just a mountain, but a mountain *range* of evidence, collated it, narrowed down a possible suspect pool of millions to a mere dozen....He was blown away by them. Raised to fear and respect law enforcement, yet hold it in contempt, Jazz had never thought he could be impressed by cops. Billy had told too many stories of hoodwinking them. Yet Billy had never ventured to New York. How would Green Jack and Hand-in-Glove and the Artist have fared against the NYPD?

Ugly J. The Impressionist. Hat-Dog.

Jazz wondered: If there was a link, then maybe—just *maybe*—they were finding out right now how Billy would do against the NYPD.

Even this late at night, the 76th Precinct was surrounded by press. Hughes, having planned ahead, arranged to sneak Jazz in through a back door.

Montgomery and Morales pulled him into a conference

room littered with papers, cardboard file boxes, and dead laptops. It smelled of printer toner, stale coffee, and body odor. He got a crash course on the Hat-Dog Task Force and how it worked.

Montgomery was in charge. No question about that. When it came down to "Do we do X or do we do Y?" he was the man with the authority. It was his jurisdiction and his original case, his Homicide detectives putting in double overtime. The FBI had come in on request—Montgomery and Morales knew each other from a previous case.

"We divvied up the job, basically," Montgomery explained. "My guys know the neighborhood, so they're handling interviews, canvassing, stuff like that. We're sharing evidence collection, depending on how spread thin we are at any point in time."

"There are four agents assigned to the task force on a more or less permanent basis," Morales said, "including me. I can pull in others as needed. We help out with evidence collection when we have to. And since the Bureau has better analysis resources and computer resources, we're in charge of collating and analyzing the data the NYPD brings in."

"And profiling," Jazz added.

"Yeah. We have a BAU guy who's seen everything. You saw the profile report, I assume?"

Jazz had, indeed, read the profile from the FBI's Behavioral Analysis Unit. Parts of it he agreed with. Parts of it he didn't. They would get to that shortly, he figured.

They took him out to the main lobby of the precinct, where there were more bodies in motion. There was a large whiteboard against one wall, divided into a grid. It was nearly identical to the document Hughes had shown Jazz at the hotel, but with one difference—pictures. Down the leftmost column, there were fourteen crime scene photos, shot to show the entire body of the victim. Each body had a row of information associated with it:

#	VICTIM INFO	NAME	TAG	DATE	Δ	LOCATION	NOTES	DNA
1	C/F/24	Nicole DiNozzo	Hat	6/11	–	Behind Connecticut Bagels	First victim	
2	C/M/40	Harold Spencer	Dog	6/25	14	Behind Connecticut Bagels	First penectomy	
3	C/F/15	Lucy Donato	Hat	7/16	21	Parking space on Clinton	Hat on left hip	
4	C/M/52	Brian Florio	Dog	8/2	17	Liberty Ave. subway stop @ Pennsylvania Ave.	Penectomy	skin/blood
5	C/F/14	Aimee Ventnor	Hat	8/21	19	Alleyway 4th Ave		
6	C/F/33	Elana Gibbs	Dog	9/7	17	Alleyway off Flatbush	First disembowelment. Guts in KFC bucket near body.	semen
7	C/F/27	Marie Leydecker	Hat	9/29	22	Park Place & Classon		hair
8	C/M/31	Harry Glidden	Hat	10/19	20	@ victim's tax prep office	First paralysis/discarded penis	

#	VICTIM INFO	NAME	TAG	DATE	Δ	LOCATION	NOTES	DNA
9	C/M/40	Jerome Herrington	Dog	11/6	18	Rooftop North of Carolina	Penis taken	hair
10	C/F/25	Monica Allgood	Hat	11/20	14	Abandoned bldg. across from St. James Church		
11	C/M/20	Chad Jordan	Hat	12/2	12	See vic #6	Penis discarded @ scene. Guts in KFC bucket.	hair
12	C/M/51	Charles Bollanger	Dog	12/12	10	Boardwalk @ Coney Island	Penis taken	semen
13	C/M/19	Marvin Candless	Hat	12/22	10	Rooftop near Luquer St.	Penis discarded @ scene	
14	A/M/37	Gordon Cho	Dog	12/29	7	Carroll Park	only non-white victim	
15	C/F/28	Sheila Riggs	Hat	1/3	5	S line	Eyes missing	pending

"The delta is—"

"How long between killings," Jazz said, standing before the whiteboard, staring. "In days. The deltas are generally shrinking, so he's getting more and more comfortable. Getting better at what he's doing." *Preparation is everything, Jasper,* Billy had said so many times. *Spend a month gettin' ready for what'll only take ten minutes. Or an hour. Measure twice, cut once, I always say. Unless you want to cut a whole bunch, in which case, sweet God, there's so many places to cut!* Pity swelled inside him. When hunting a serial killer, you looked for patterns. Elements that connected under the surface, sometimes, but they were there anyway. You looked for a killer who killed due to certain triggers. There were guys who murdered when their wives had their periods. Guys who killed when they got their paychecks. Guys who killed like clockwork every three weeks, or when the moon was full or whatever. Even if the timing wasn't regular, there were patterns in the victims, in the signature, in *something.*

But there was no pattern Jazz could find. The poor cops and feds had spent months with this data, poring over it, massaging it, running it through computers and databases. And all they had to show for it was a dead body on the— what was it called?—the S line.

"You can see," Montgomery said, "that we have matching DNA from a variety of both Hat and Dog killings. Still waiting to see if we get anything tonight. All of the hairs indicate Caucasian male, brown hair. No dyes. Nothing to really hang our hats on there."

"We're going to modify the chart tomorrow morning," Hughes said. "While we were on our way back from the city, unis were checking the other crime scenes for that Ugly J tag."

"Oh? And?"

"Found evidence of it at some of them. Not all. And get this—only at sites identified as Dog killings."

"I'm still not convinced this ties in," Morales said.

"It's something," Hughes argued. "It's finally something

that distinguishes Hats and Dogs. There have been no Ugly J tags at any Hat sites."

"Or you just missed them," Morales countered. "Or they were painted over. And they weren't at *all* of the Dog sites."

"Or we just missed them," Hughes mimicked pointedly. "Or they were painted over."

Jazz groaned. One more mystery piece in a puzzle growing more and more bizarre. It sparked nothing for him, to his frustration.

The victims ranged in age from fourteen to fifty-two. In some cases, the body had been found at the murder site. In others, it had been moved. There were days between some murders, weeks between others. Penis cut off and taken; penis cut off and left at the scene. Guts removed and left piled on the rooftop. Guts removed and gone, gone, gone. Guts removed and left at the scene twice in—believe it or not—those KFC buckets.

"Guy must *love* KFC," someone deadpanned. "There's a better fried chicken joint just three blocks over. He had to go all the way to Fort Greene to get an actual—"

"Shut up," Montgomery advised.

Jazz appreciated the silence. Guts. And eyelids. And penises.

And now, the eyes missing.

"He's escalating," Jazz said, and then felt idiotic for saying it out loud. *Obviously* he was escalating. That's what serial killers did—they started slow and small, then expanded their domain as their confidence increased. And, more important, as living out their original fantasy proved not to quell whatever raged and rioted within them, they added new elements, like an addict who needed more and more drugs to get the same old high.

"Penis, guts, eyes. What connects them?"

"The FBI profile says—" Montgomery began.

"Yeah, I read the profile." It was a good profile, as profiles went. The killer was considered mixed organized, based on his moving of the bodies and ability to evade capture for so long, but also his propensity to leave messy crime scenes. Jazz differed there. He thought the killer was actually highly organized. The messy crime scenes weren't showing a lack of control—they were the ultimate expression of Hat-Dog's control. He could make a crime scene look any way he wanted, as organized or as disorganized as he wanted, when he wanted.

WELCOME TO THE GAME, JASPER.

He's playing.

Definitely male, as semen had been found in some of the raped women. No semen in the male victims, so no male rape, so...

"He's expressing male power," Jazz murmured.

"Yeah, we think that's why he cuts off the penises," Morales said. "As a way of defining himself as the alpha male."

"But then why take some and leave others?"

"He takes them when they're dogs, leaves them when they're hats. But we're not sure what that might mean."

Jazz furrowed his brow and stared at the whiteboard until

his eyes lost focus and all the gridded boxes blended on top of one another. *Is this what it's like inside his head? Is it all mixed up and mashed up? Chaotic? Is that why it makes no sense?*

No. That's what he wants me to think. Even if he's not consciously aware of it. He wants me to think none of this makes sense because if it doesn't make sense, then I stop trying to figure it out. And then he gets to keep on doing what he wants.

"He's the alpha male," Jazz murmured. "Top dog. Top dog? Top hat?"

"Yeah, someone mentioned that a while back," Montgomery said. "Anyone remember who?" he called out to the precinct in general.

"Doesn't matter," Jazz said. "I'm just thinking out loud. Somehow, it makes sense to him. It's the most obvious thing in the world to him." He stared at the whiteboard a little while longer, then rubbed his eyes. "Tell me what you have planned for your next step."

"We've got a dozen possibles," Hughes said. "Guys who fit the profile—"

"More or less," Morales inserted.

"Agent Morales thinks we're being a little too liberal in our interpretation of the profile," Montgomery explained. "We prefer to think of it as casting our net a little wider. Just to be sure."

"Anyway," Hughes went on, "there's a dozen guys. We're bringing them in one by one, starting tomorrow. Setting it up so that they'll never see one another. Each guy will think he's our only suspect."

Jazz nodded. Good.

"We notified them tonight that we'd like to speak with them first thing tomorrow."

"Then you'll stick 'em in a room and watch 'em for an hour or so, right?" Jazz speculated. "The guilty guy won't be able to sleep tonight, so there's a chance he'll nod off while waiting for you."

"That's the theory."

"It might work." Jazz shrugged. "But Hat-Dog is cold-blooded. There's every chance he got your call and rolled over and slept like a drunk baby."

"We're just using everything in our arsenal."

"Who's conducting the actual interrogations?" Jazz asked.

Without a moment's hesitation, Morales spoke up. "I am. Along with a male NYPD detective. This guy has issues with both sexes. We're going to play off of that."

"I want to be in the room, too."

"Not a chance in hell," Montgomery pronounced, in a tone that said he was used to having even jaded New Yorkers obey him. "Not risking it, for one thing. For another thing, you're like a celebrity. These guys see you, recognize you, who knows what it's gonna do to the interrogation?" Before Jazz could protest, he held up a hand. "You watch with the rest of us through the glass. If you have a problem with it, don't even bother leaving the hotel tomorrow. That's it."

Jazz appealed to Morales, hoping for an override, but the

special agent shook her head. "It's the right call, Jasper. You know it."

"Fine. Give me whatever you have on these suspects. I'll look at it all tonight. For now, I need some sleep." He hadn't even realized how tired he was until the words were out of his mouth. But something like fifteen hours ago, he'd been sitting on the floor of his father's old room in the Nod, talking to Connie on the phone. He'd done so much since then that he couldn't sort through it yet.

"Yeah, sure. Let me take you to the hotel," Hughes offered.

Hughes ended up staying with Jazz at the hotel. Hat-Dog knew that Jazz was involved in the investigation, after all, and the last thing the task force needed was for Billy Dent's kid to be killed while assisting on the case. The detective sacked out on a rollaway cot while Jazz slipped into the bathroom for some privacy while calling Connie.

But Connie didn't answer. Jazz wondered if maybe her dad had confiscated her phone again. He left her a quick voice mail, ending with, "Miss you. I love you." As he hung up, he wondered about that. When had it become so easy to say "I love you"? At first, he had stuttered and struggled to say it in person. Now he could toss it out to voice mail. Was that a good thing or a bad thing? It could go either way, he realized. It could be that the words passed so effortlessly through his lips because he meant them deeply and truly.

Or it could be that he didn't mean them at all. And that— like all the lies we tell ourselves—it was easy to repeat.

He crawled into bed. It was better this way, he knew, the two of them separated. With Connie back in the Nod, it was safe for Jazz to lust after her, to yearn for her, to be weak for her. No one could be hurt if they were apart. And that was good.

Hughes's snores already filled the room. Even though it was still relatively early and he was slightly horny from the mere thought of Connie, Jazz drifted right off to sleep.

CHAPTER 29

Connie stared at her cell phone. A message. From Jazz. She couldn't believe she had just let her boyfriend go to voice mail as she watched.

But she knew what would have happened if she'd answered. He would have known something was up, the way he *always* knew something was up. That bizarre, slightly creepy sixth sense he had. He could read your mind by reading between the lines. And she would have told him about the texts and then he would have warned her off—*It's too dangerous, Con! Call G. William!*—and Connie wasn't about to be waved off. Not this time.

I can do this. I can help. I saved Jazz from the Impressionist. I found the Ugly J clue in Brooklyn. I. Can. Do. This.

She would be careful. She would be *more* than careful; she would be super-careful. And she would let Howie in on it, so that someone knew what was going on, where she was headed.... That was the responsible way to handle it. Almost eighteen, almost a legal adult. Who could tell her *not* to handle this?

i kno something abt ur boyfriend

Simple as that. That made it Connie's business to find out. *And maybe...*

The little voice tickled at the back of her brain, right on the edge of her thoughts. She chased it away, but she knew what it wanted to say.

And maybe you get on TV doing this. It's like a reality show, but better because it really is real. And maybe...

Stop it.

And maybe that's how you get noticed and get famous.

The voice, having had its say, went silent, and Connie pretended she'd never heard it in the first place.

Convincing her parents to let her out of the house would be nearly impossible, Connie knew. But the mystery texter had given her her first instruction—*go 2 where it all began*—and Connie was damn sure that whatever "it" was, it hadn't begun in her bedroom, where absolutely nothing remotely interesting or important had ever happened.

It was getting late, but Howie would most likely still be awake, so she called him. He answered on the fourth ring, just as she had resigned herself to being sent to voice mail.

"Sorta busy here, Connie," he said brusquely.

She glanced at her clock. It was almost eleven at night. "Doing what? Masturbating?"

"Jeez!" he exploded. "No! Gross! I don't do that. I'm saving myself for that special someone, and that special someone is not me."

"Howie, you'd jerk it if you saw your mom's bra in the dryer."

"I would not. I so totally would not. My mom's bras are like, like *grandmother* bras, okay? Strictly utilitarian. Functional. Not like that sexy lacy number you wore last week when we all went to Grasser's for burgers."

Connie felt herself blush. "Howie! You peeked!"

"If you wear a white shirt with a red bra underneath, you're just asking for it. I'm sorry, but in this isolated instance, you really, really can't blame me."

Connie made a mental note to watch what she wore around Howie. She liked being sexy and looking good, but she didn't want one of her best friends thinking about her bras. *Ew.*

"In any event," Howie went on, "I'm busy, doing the exact opposite of playing with myself, for your information."

"What's the opposite of that?"

"Trying to get Jazz's aunt into bed," Howie said with a matter-of-factness that was both hilarious and horrifying.

"You're doing *what*?"

"She's hot," Howie said. "Older-lady hot, you know? Cougar-y? MILF-y? Plus, Jazz doesn't want this to happen, so she's got that whole 'forbidden fruit' thing going for her, too. I just can't resist that. I'm, like, a slave to my passions and stuff."

Connie's head spun. Howie...and Jazz's *aunt*? Billy Dent's *sister*? "How the hell did this happen?"

"Well, nothing has happened yet. But I'm over here helping her get the crazy racist lady to sleep and I'm using all my

251

best moves. Trust me, this is happening. The ladies always eventually succumb to Howie Gersten."

"When has anyone *ever* succumbed to you?"

"The succumbing part is strictly theoretical at this point," he admitted. "But I have high hopes."

"If you can stop thinking with the contents of your jock strap for a second, I need your help."

"Yes," Howie said solemnly, "I can teach you how to be more 'street.'"

"For God's sake..."

"Or is it 'urban'? I can't remember. Anyway, I can teach you, grasshopper. Or hip-hopper."

"Be serious for just a minute. I need help in your area of expertise." Before Howie could say "pleasing women of all ages," she pressed on. "I need to sneak out of my house."

"How do you get to the ripe old age of seventeen without knowing how to get out of the house?" Howie demanded. "Hell, your bedroom is on the first floor! You don't even have to climb down a trellis or sneak down squeaky stairs."

"But once I'm out, I'm screwed—I don't have a car."

"Ah." Howie chuckled. "You've come to the right place, ma'am."

An hour later, Connie slipped silently out her window into a frigid January midnight. She willed her teeth to stop chattering. At Howie's suggestion, she'd lubed the tracks of the window with some hand lotion (good stuff, too—fifteen bucks a bottle) so that it would open and close quickly and quietly as she came and went. Howie was a goofball of the first order, but a lifetime of parental fascism had inculcated in him some truly spectacular sneaking skills.

She darted to the cover of a cluster of firs at the end of the driveway and waited. Soon Howie's old car drifted into view, its headlights and engine both off. Connie wasn't sure how necessary this next part was, but Howie insisted.

As the car passed, coasting down the hill, Connie emerged from cover and then, jogging alongside, wrenched open the passenger-side door and threw herself in.

"Close the door!" Howie said. "Close it!"

Connie managed to slam the door. "This is ridiculous," she panted, catching her breath. "You just wanted to be able to say you pulled this off."

"You want your parents to see or hear a car driving by this time of night?"

"My parents are asleep."

"People wake up."

Once they were out of sight of Connie's house, Howie gunned the engine and flicked on the headlights. "Where to, Miss Daisy?"

"I think you have a couple of things reversed," she told him drily. "And I'm not sure where we're headed yet."

In short, clipped sentences, she told him about the Ugly J discovery at the dump site, as well as the note in the Impressionist's pocket, followed by the mystery texts. In the dim light of Lobo's Nod's ill-spaced lampposts, Howie's face became more and more pale as she went on.

"Are you nuts?" he asked. "Is Jazz's kind of crazy an STD

or something? This isn't something for you to mess with. It's for the cops. This is G. William territory."

According to Jazz, Howie always balked at first but invariably caved in the end. She hoped she could be as persuasive as Jazz.

"I'm just going to do some preliminary investigating." She liked the way that sounded. Very official. Very safe. "Then I can point G. William in the right direction."

"Some crazy person—probably a serial killer—is texting you and you want to get the cops *started*? Not sane, Connie. Not sane at all. This is Jazz-level idiocy."

"You broke into a morgue with him. I'm not asking you to do anything illegal."

"Jazz is my bro."

"I respect that. But maybe a little of his bro-hood rubbed off on me." She regretted it as soon as she said it. Howie's eyes widened and he started to speak, but she said, "Can we just stipulate that you made a killer double entendre with 'rubbed off' and then move on?"

"I guess." Howie's shoulders slumped in disappointment and Connie almost felt sorry for him. Howie lived for innuendoes. He signaled and took a right turn out of Connie's neighborhood, onto the main road that cut directly through the center of the Nod.

"This is for Jazz," she reminded him. "It's about him, at least."

" 'I know something about your boyfriend,' " Howie quoted. "That could be anything. That could be someone who knows where he buys his underwear. Or it could be that jackhole

Weathers trying to lure you into an interview. Cell number was blocked, so it could be coming from somewhere around here for all we know. Probably is."

Connie hadn't considered that. Doug Weathers was just the sort of devious, bottom-feeding scumsucker who would plant a string of clues to pique her curiosity and try to trap her into some kind of compromising position that he could splash across a newspaper: BILLY DENT'S SON'S GIRLFRIEND IN CONTROVERSY! Or maybe just lure her into an interview. "If that's what it is," she said with measured cool, "then all he's gonna get is a pissed-off sister all up in his grill."

"I love when you go all hard-ass." Howie shot her a pleased smile.

She returned it. "So does that mean you'll stick around and see this through?"

"Well...I mean, if you're gonna do something stupid, I guess I should stick around. That seems to be my function. And besides, Sam went to bed already."

"Sam? Is that what she goes by?"

"It's what I call her. If you give a girl a nickname, it's endearing and forges a bond between the two of you." He glanced over at her. "I read that on the Internet."

Connie melted. Howie was so desperately pathetic in so many ways that she could never stay angry or disgusted for long. She reached out to pat his shoulder, but he flinched and said, "Whoa! Careful."

"I'm going to be gentle," she assured him, and then stroked his shoulder so lightly that even his hemophiliac blood vessels didn't rupture. "You're a good guy, Howie."

"Will you tell Sam that? I also read that women trust other women more than men."

She sighed. "Help me out tonight and, yeah, I'll put in a good word for you." Not that it would help. She couldn't imagine a woman Samantha's age hooking up with Howie. Although stranger things had certainly happened in the world.

"Score!" Howie fist-pumped. "What did the text say again?"

"It said 'go 2 where it all began.' "

Howie frowned. "Where is *that*? Where *what* began?"

"That's what I've been wondering. But it first said that this was about Jazz. So I've been thinking about Jazz's past. Where it all began for *him*."

"Hospital where he was born?" Howie asked.

"Too literal. I think it's his house."

"I just came from—ah. Oh, right." Howie nodded grimly. "Got it."

He flipped a uey and gunned the engine.

According to the dashboard clock in Howie's car, it was three in the afternoon. Connie mentally subtracted the fourteen-plus hours by which the clock was always wrong (thirteen-plus during the summer) and decided that it was twenty of one in the morning when they pulled up to what had once been the Dent house. Not the house where Jazz lived now, the house Billy had grown up in—that was Jazz's grandmother's. The short gravel drive Howie's wheels now crunched led to the house owned by Billy Dent himself.

"Don't go chasing..."

Billy Dent, Connie mentally substituted. The rhythm still worked. *Don't go chasing Billy Dent. Please stick to the normal and the sane that you're used to....*

Denuded tree branches seemed to clutch at the car as they drove along, almost as though the spirit of William Cornelius Dent possessed them.

Stop thinking like that, Connie.

"How long do we have?" she asked Howie. Anything to break the silence.

Howie shrugged. "My parents think I'm spending the night at Jazz's grandmother's house."

"*Your* parents? Your overprotective parents?"

"They know Jazz is out of town. They figure it's safe."

"Yeah, but... with his aunt?" Connie was shocked. Howie's parents, letting their son (try to) shack up with an older woman?

"Oh, that. They think she's an ugly old crone." He shrugged. "This might be because I told them she was an ugly old crone. I'm not entirely sure. Man, it's been a while since I've been here...."

The spot where Jazz's childhood home used to be was marked out by a series of stakes with caution tape strung between them. A sign read NO TRESPASSING! Another read PRIVATE PROPERTY.

Finally, one read: THIS PROPERTY IS CONDEMNED.

Condemned. Yeah, in so many ways, really...

Where the house had once stood there was now a blank, a blighted sore on the face of the earth. A wealthy father of one of Billy Dent's victims had bought the house at auction after Billy went to prison. Then, to great fanfare and with the press in attendance, he'd had the house bulldozed and the wreckage burned to ash in a controlled fire. Connie hadn't lived in Lobo's Nod at the time, but Jazz had told her about it. He'd watched his home go up in smoke on the evening news.

"It was like a party," Howie said, his voice a mixture of memory and rage as he gazed through the windshield. "Watched it on TV with Jazz. People treated it like a Memorial Day barbecue. Brought hot dogs and marshmallows and roasted them over the flames. *Kegs*. It was nuts. Like burning the guy's house brought any of them back."

Connie reached for Howie again. This time he didn't flinch and she briefly massaged the back of his neck, wary of his fragility. "You're a good friend," she said.

Howie snorted. "I know. Why do people keep telling me that?"

To that, she had nothing to say.

Howie parked with the headlights glaring at the bare, burned earth and the hole that had once been Jazz's basement.

"What do you expect to find here?"

"I don't know." She got out of the car. In every direction, there were trees and hedges. To the east and west, she could just barely make out houses. Billy Dent's neighbors.

They planted all that stuff to block off that lot after he went to jail, Connie remembered Jazz saying. *Like they could erase what he'd done if they didn't have to look at where he'd lived.*

Howie joined her by the foundation of the house. A few broken, burned cinder blocks littered the hole. In the glow of the headlights, they could see empty beer and soda bottles, as well as snack chip bags and what looked like used condoms.

"People come out here for privacy, I guess," Howie said. "Figure no one else would, right?" He inhaled deeply. "Still smells kinda burny. Even three years later."

Connie squatted down near the edge. Howie suddenly grabbed at her, but she brushed him away. "I'm okay. I'm not gonna fall."

"I'm more worried about the ground giving way."

"It's pretty frozen." Her breath painted the air misty white. "Don't worry."

"Yeah, right." Howie shivered and hugged himself. "Picked the wrong place to say *that.* I don't believe in ghosts or demons, but if they existed anywhere, it would be here."

Connie grinned. "I'll protect you, big guy."

"Much appreciated. What'd the next text say?"

"Next text and *last* text." She showed it to Howie.

cherry. sunrise. jasper. down

CHAPTER 30

"What the hell does *that* mean?" Howie's earlier fear had been replaced with exasperation. He bit down on his lower lip—lightly—but even so, Connie saw a bruise begin there. He turned in circles, taking in the surroundings. "It was crazy to come here without telling anyone. I hate puzzles. And codes. And mysteries. And riddles. And—"

"It's not tough," Connie told him. She scanned her surroundings as best she could in the dark, with only the headlights to pierce the night. "I bet there's a cherry tree around here. We go to it."

"And then wait until sunrise? No way. I gotta get *some* beauty sleep."

Ignoring Howie, Connie peered through the middle-of-the-night murk of the Dent property, searching out a cherry tree. With her luck, she realized, there would be more than one.

Wait a sec, she thought. *Wait. What—*

"What does a cherry tree even *look* like?" Howie whined, voicing her inner thought.

A look of sheepish guilt/stupidity passed between them and then they both went for their cell phones.

Connie's Google-fu was better and faster than Howie's. "Here," she said, holding up a photo on her phone. "A cherry tree." She scowled, "But it talks about the leaves and…" She gestured around the winter landscape, the frost-rimed ground, the trees with their naked branches.

"No worries," Howie said, grinning. "I remember. Over there." He pointed to a large, many-limbed tree not far from the hole in the ground that had once been the Dent house. "That's it. Right there. I remember what it looked like back then. It used to be in the backyard. Y'know, when there was a house here to be in back of."

Together they made their way to the cherry tree. Howie stared up into its branches, lost in thought and memory. "We wanted to build a fort up there," he said, his voice quiet, as though he were murmuring in church. "We were like eleven, I guess. Right up there." He pointed with a shaky hand. "And I remember his dad was all for it. He said…" Howie suddenly turned away, savagely. "Damn! I can't believe…I can't believe I was such—"

"Howie." She put her hands on his shoulders, a bit firmly, trusting the padding in his winter coat to keep him from bruising. "Howie, it's okay. You were just a kid. You couldn't have known."

"That bastard." Howie bit through the word like bitter

citrus peel. Connie had never heard him so distraught. "You know what he said? He gave that big crap-eating grin of his and he said, 'Ain't a bad idea, Jasper. A boy should have a private place all his own. Just him and his secrets.'"

Connie thought she could feel the memory, reliving it through the shudder of Howie's shoulders.

"I thought that sounded so cool," Howie said. "God-damn...I thought Billy was the coolest dad in the world. What was *wrong* with me? Everything normal and good in Jazz's life, Billy made it evil and disgusting." He shook off her hands, spinning around, looking not at Connie but up into the tree instead. "We lost interest because, hell, we were eleven. But I bet Billy was picturing Jazz dragging cats and stray dogs up there and cutting them open." He snorted. "Maybe even me. Figured I'd go missing one day and no one would know what happened, but Billy would know. That was Billy's dream, right? His fantasy? For Jazz to turn into him?"

"Still is," Connie said quietly.

Howie nodded once, firmly. "You know what, Connie?"

"What, Howie?"

"We can't stop Billy Dent. Not the two of us."

"Yeah. I know."

"But we can ruin him. We can piss him off and take away the thing he wants more than anything in the world. Can't we? Can't we do that?"

Connie thought of kissing Jazz. Of her hands on him, of his on her. Of their hesitant first kiss and of the passionate ones that followed.

"Yeah. We can take away his dream, Howie. We can keep Jazz from becoming Billy." Mostly, she knew, because Jazz would do the heavy lifting. He would have to—the danger signs and the tools were all locked up in his head, and no one else had the key.

"We can make it easier for him," Howie said. "That's what we do, right? We make it easier for Jazz to be normal."

"Yop."

She took his hand in her own. It was almost comical, the two of them wearing gloves so heavy that their fingers couldn't entwine. But that was okay. It wasn't about the contact. It was about the solidarity.

"So that's the cherry tree," she said after a while.

"Sure is. Sunrise."

"I think that means we face east."

Howie nodded and released her hand after a brief squeeze. At the cherry tree, they used the compasses on their phones to find east. "Now what?" Howie asked. "The next clue is 'Jasper.'"

"I think we're supposed to walk. And the last clue is 'down,' so we're supposed to dig."

"Sure, that makes sense. But walk how far? His age? Seventeen steps?" Without waiting for an answer, Howie immediately loped off to the east, counting out until he hit seventeen.

Shaking her head, Connie caught up to him as he looked around. "The ground doesn't look disturbed at all."

"Whatever was buried was buried a long time ago, I bet."

"Why do you say that?"

Connie wasn't sure why she said that—it just made sense.

It was the kind of thing Jazz would say with complete confidence, and when someone questioned him, he would rattle off an explanation that was *duh*-worthy.

Channeling her inner Jazz with all her might, she said, "Well..." and then it hit her.

"Look," she said, speaking rapidly, before the idea could flit out of her mind as quickly as it had flown in, like a bug sucked into and out of an open car window. "We don't know for sure who's leading us on this wild-goose chase, but odds are it's Billy or someone connected to Billy, right? So the first thing that happened after Billy broke out of prison was the FBI and the cops landed on Lobo's Nod like it was D-day. They covered this place for weeks. So no one would be able to get here, of all places, to bury something. Which means that whatever we're looking for here was buried at least before Billy went to jail."

Howie nodded. "Yeah. All right, that tracks." He stomped the ground with his huge foot. "And, yeah, if anything's buried here, it had to be long enough ago that all the ground settled."

Glancing back at the cherry tree—seventeen Howie-steps to the west—Connie shook her head. "It's not right here. It can't be."

"Jazz is seventeen," Howie protested. "I took seventeen steps—"

"Right. But first of all, we're assuming seventeen is the right number. Think about it—if whatever it was was buried a long time ago, there's no way the burier could know when we would come looking for it. Unless whoever it is specifically planned on doing something when Jazz was seventeen. But that's ridiculous because—"

"—because what if something made it so that this 'game' had to be triggered earlier?" Howie finished. "I get it. So maybe it's Jazz's age when the thing was buried?" Howie groaned. "How are we supposed to know *that*?" He turned away from her, morose.

"Come on, Howie. Don't punk out on me. Whoever's doing this *wants* us to play the game. We *can* figure this out." She hoped. What if this wasn't a game, but a joke? What if this was a setup, designed to get Jazz's girlfriend and best friend out here where something could—

"The cherry tree..." Howie spun around. "We were eleven!"

Before Connie could stop him, he counted back toward the cherry tree, taking six steps. He jumped up and down at the new spot, excited.

"This is it! Eleven steps away from the tree! This is the spot!" He stomped hard, then winced. "Oh, man, that's gonna bruise!"

He was so happy that it broke Connie's heart to tell him he was wrong. "This isn't the spot," she said, walking over to him.

"But we were eleven when we wanted to build the tree house. That's why Billy or whoever chose the cherry tree as the starting—"

"Yeah, and I believe that you're right that eleven is the answer to the 'Jasper' clue. But eleven *what*?"

"Eleven *steps*," Howie said, frustrated. "It's always 'take three paces this way and ten paces that way.' Jesus, Connie, haven't you *ever* seen a pirate movie?"

"But *whose* steps, Howie? Billy's? Jazz's? Yours? Look at your NBA-length legs, man." Howie looked down. "When I walk next to you, I have to take, like, a step and a half for every step *you* take."

Howie blew out an annoyed breath, clouding the air for a moment. "Jeez. You're kidding me. So, what? We have to figure out Billy Dent's *shoe size*? Is that what's next?"

"I bet he'd choose something simple to remember. I bet it's just feet. Not, like, *his* feet. Real feet. Twelve inches."

"Then we're in luck," Howie said, and rushed back to the tree. By the time Connie got there, catching up to his long strides, he had already lined up his back at the tree and started walking east, carefully placing one foot directly in front of the other like a tightrope walker. "My feet are size fourteen, which is pretty much exactly twelve inches."

"And you know this because...?"

"Because you know what they say about guys with big feet." He waggled his eyebrows. "Anyway, this should get us close, right?"

"Yeah."

Howie counted eleven. "Okay. Then this should do it. Bring me that stick."

Casting about in the dark, Connie caught sight of the stick he was referring to, a large branch that had fallen off a tree, perhaps even the cherry tree itself. She walked it over to him and watched as he fruitlessly and with much comical grunting tried to spear it into the frozen ground.

"This—uh—marks the spot—uh—or at least within a few inches—uh—so we can come back with a shovel—uh—damn it!" He wiped cold sweat from his forehead.

Connie sighed theatrically and took the branch from him, then crouched down, gripping the end of the branch near the ground. Twisting and pushing at the same time, she was able to drive it a few inches into the ground, though it winded her.

"I was about to try that," Howie explained.

"Right."

"You grabbed it from me before I could."

"Right."

"You'll never know!" he called after her, following her back to the car now. "I was *just about* to try that!"

"Sure." But she wasn't paying attention anymore. She was thinking of coming back with a shovel, when it was light out. When the ground would be a little warmer and less solid in the light of the sun. Thinking of digging.

Wondering what she might find.

Howie pulled a reversal of his clandestine extraction, drifting headlightless and engineless down the gentle slope toward her house.

"You'll call me tomorrow, right?" he asked, and yawned.

"I'm about to jump out of a moving car and you're yawning."

"We're going, like, a mile an hour." He checked the speedometer, squinting. "Maybe a mile and a half."

"I'll call," she said, and hopped out, jogging alongside the car until she had the door closed.

She felt very conspicuous, standing literally in the middle of the street. Howie had dropped her off ("inserted," he insisted on saying, demanding they use spy lingo) three houses up from her own, just in case someone was awake and looking out the window in the Hall home. She moved to the side of the road and approached her house carefully. With the exception of the light near the front door, it was dark. And quiet.

She had a feeling, again, that someone was watching her. Not her dad or her mom. Not even Whiz. No, she had a sudden, foolish feeling that *Billy* was out there. Which was ridiculous, because the odds seemed to be that Billy was in New York. And even if he wasn't, he wasn't stupid enough to hang around Lobo's Nod, the one place on the planet where almost every person would recognize him on sight.

But maybe he has magical powers and he can be in two places at once or can see across vast distances....

She shook herself and came just short of slapping her own cheek. She was exhausted. Thinking stupid things. Childish things.

As Howie had promised, her lubricated window opened easily and silently. With a small, nearly inaudible "Oof," she hauled herself over the sill and into the quiet familiarity of her own bedroom. With the window closed, the room went warm and still. She enjoyed it for a moment.

If this had been a horror movie, she knew, there would be something here. Like, a clue. A note from the person who'd texted her, maybe.

Or a severed head. Or maybe a finger from the Impressionist. Or maybe...

She was suddenly completely convinced that her family was dead.

Isn't that what would happen? she thought. *Lure me out of the house and then—*

She didn't let herself think further. Paranoia pumped through her like blood and she struggled against it, stripping off her clothes and slipping into boy shorts and a T-shirt for bed.

No one is dead. No one is dead. Stuff like that only happens in movies and in books.

And in real life.

Even as she told herself that she wouldn't do it, she sneaked out of her room. *Just going to the bathroom, is all. That's all. And the bathroom is next to Whiz's room....*

She put an ear to Whiz's door. Heard nothing.

Cranked the door open a bit, wincing at the slight creak. Why was the creak absent during the day, present only when she needed to be absolutely quiet?

In the glow of a street lamp coming through the window, she saw a lump under the covers.

Doesn't mean anything. Could still be dead. Might not even be him.

Stop it, Connie. Stop being so ridiculous.

It's not ridiculous. Billy Dent has done worse, hasn't he?

She didn't want to, but she suddenly remembered something Billy had done as Satan's Eye. Jazz wouldn't talk about the things Billy had done—not to her, at least—but she'd done some research. She couldn't help it. And she remembered how in one night, Billy had kidnapped two women, murdered them, and then put them into each other's beds, where they were discovered the next day by a husband and a boyfriend.

I'm doing this.

She crept into Whiz's room. The form in bed seemed not to move, but as she came closer, she was relieved to find that it was, in fact, moving—the rhythmic, soft up and down of sleep-breathing.

The street lamp picked out her younger brother's face, so much less obnoxious and peaceful in repose. Connie sighed.

Whiz's eyes snapped open so suddenly that Connie almost screamed. She gasped and took a step back in shock.

"What are you doing?" he whispered accusingly, as if he'd caught her emptying his piggy bank.

"I...thought I heard something."

"You're a freak," Whiz shot back, then rolled over to face away from her. "Get out of here."

I love my brother, and I'm glad he's not dead, Connie told herself as she went back to her room. *I love my brother, and I'm glad he's not dead.*

She intended to repeat it over and over in her head until she believed it, but she fell asleep first.

CHAPTER 31

Lips on his
   (oh, yes)
   down farther
   Touch me
   says the voice
   again
   His fingers
   Oh
   so warm
   Oh

Jazz woke early. Not because he wanted to and not because he felt compelled to, but rather because Hughes shook him roughly by the shoulder and said, "Wake up," in a commanding voice devoid of sympathy. The detective was already dressed.

Tangled in the sheets, clutching a pillow, Jazz blearily looked around the room. "What time is it?"

"Five of seven. First suspect is scheduled for interrogation at eight. And you still have his file to look at."

Groaning, Jazz rolled over and pulled a pillow over his head. Hughes snatched away the pillow and tossed it over his shoulder.

Fifteen minutes later, Jazz was on his way to the precinct, flipping through the files on the dozen men suspected of being Hat-Dog. They all lived in Brooklyn, well within a specific computer-plotted jeopardy surface that contained most of the crime scenes thus far. The two extreme outliers were Coney Island and the S line in Midtown. "Why Coney Island?" Jazz asked. "Why Midtown? Why go outside his comfort zone?"

"Midtown, we're thinking it's a crime of opportunity. The girl lived nearby. We think maybe he works in Midtown, stays late at the office or something, sees the girl..."

"Hmm." Jazz didn't like that theory. Hat-Dog had been at this too long to go off half-cocked like that. He was too organized, too mature. But sometimes the impulses could scream and hoot and holler like monkeys in a cage, and the only way to shut them up...

I had to go and get me one, said Dear Old Dad.

That's what Billy had said the night he'd returned from killing Cara Swinton. He had drummed into Jazz from an early age that "we don't crap where we eat," meaning "no prospecting in Lobo's Nod." And then one night, soon after Jazz's thirteenth birthday, Billy went out and did exactly that, crapping right there where he ate, killing poor Cara.

The only explanation he ever offered: "I had to go and get me one."

The compulsion. The urge. The need.

"...Coney Island," Hughes was saying. "We're thinking he might have been on vacation...."

"Any of these guys married?" Jazz asked, refocusing on the present and the suspects. "Kids?"

"Six married. Four divorced. Couple girlfriends. That's the profile, right? Highly organized, probably married or in a relationship. Four of 'em have kids."

"Start with those guys."

"We plan to."

"Do these guys know they're suspects?"

"Nah. We've talked to all of them informally. They all had quote-unquote legitimate reasons for being around one or more of the crime scenes, so we're pretending we just want to clear some things up. And then we get them nice and relaxed," Hughes said grimly, "and we pounce."

The precinct had transformed when they arrived. No longer chaotic, it now looked like something out of a movie or a TV show—two giant HDTVs showed crime-scene evidence in a sort of animated PowerPoint presentation. The men had shaved; the women had done their hair. Jazz felt the undercurrent of tension and chaos, but it was well-suppressed. The precinct had the air of a crisp, flawless operation. Evidence

boxes were neatly stacked, and the whiteboard with the vic-
timology chart had been redone to look so professional that
it almost seemed to be selling something.

"This is good," Jazz said. "Show the evidence against
them. Are your people instructed how to act when the suspects come in?"

"They'll get real quiet and murmur among themselves,"
Montgomery said, walking over to him. "We know what
we're doing. A show of overwhelming evidence and force.
Make these guys feel like we know everything, even the
things we don't know."

"Billy would laugh at it."

"Not every serial killer is your dad." The captain put a
hand on Jazz's shoulder. "Let me show you our fine accom-
modations."

He guided Jazz to a small observation room. Through a
one-way mirror, Jazz could see into the interrogation room,
a dingy, dull-walled box with a table and three chairs. There
were more boxes stacked around here. For all Jazz knew,
they were packed with old take-out menus and blank copier
paper. But what mattered was that they were all labeled HAT-
DOG. If Hat-Dog came into this room, especially after being
walked through the "command center," he would be overwhelmed by the mountains of evidence accumulated against
him, possibly so shaken that he would confess. Or at the very
least, drop some sort of clue.

That was the theory. Jazz wondered if it would actually
work. Billy had once been interrogated by the police, in
association with a Green Jack murder. *They thought they*

had me fooled, he said, *but all they did was show me how desperate they were.*

Jazz realized his upper lip was damp. He wiped at the sweat. Montgomery was right—not every serial killer was Billy. Billy was the exception, not the rule.

Just as he settled into a chair for a day of watching interrogations, Morales came in. She was wearing a severe black pantsuit with a white blouse buttoned almost to the throat. Her hair was tied back in a bun.

"Any last-minute advice?" she asked Jazz. He was both flattered and relieved that a seasoned FBI agent was looking to him for help.

He gave her a quick up-and-down appraisal. The nearly sexless look was the right approach. Hat-Dog had serious sexual issues. Gender hang-ups. His rapes of women varied from violent and desperate to perfunctory and almost gentle. The penectomies of his male victims indicated either a fear or an exaltation of male sexual power and prowess. He was a messed-up dude, as Howie would say.

So going with a sexually neutral image to start was best for Morales. If she felt like the interview was headed in a certain direction where her feminine charms could be of assistance, it would be easy to remove the jacket, let down the hair, unbutton an extra button or two. Far more difficult to go from sexy to dowdy; that genie never goes back into the bottle quietly or easily.

"You know what you're doing," Jazz told her. "Is Hughes going in with you?"

"Yeah. He's gonna be bad cop."

"Good luck."

Jazz settled back with Montgomery and a couple of other observers, including a civilian psychiatrist who was consulting on the case. "I would love to interview you sometime," he whispered, slipping Jazz a business card. Jazz just sighed and put the card in his pocket, making a mental note to throw it away later.

The first suspect was a man named Duncan Hershey. He wore dirty jeans and a surprisingly clean black T-shirt. His winter coat was hung on a peg on the back of the door, well out of his reach. Hershey's hair was long, unkempt in the manner of a man unfamiliar with long hair. He had been forgoing haircuts for a while. "Lost his job last summer," Montgomery said, bringing everyone in the room up to speed. "About two weeks before the first murder. Could have been the inciting incident."

Jazz had the particulars committed to memory already. Hershey was white, thirty-five years old. Married for six years with two children, a four-year-old and a six-year-old. Had been a construction foreman until last summer. Now he picked up piecemeal freelance work and handyman jobs.

He had especially been flagged by the NYPD because he worked in the building where Monica Allgood had been found, the building where the glass had been deliberately broken from the outside to screw up the cops.

Duncan didn't look particularly tired as Morales and Hughes came into the room. The old cop trick of getting a guilty suspect to fall asleep in the interrogation room clearly hadn't worked on this guy. Which could mean something or nothing, really.

He was hunched over a paper cup of water, which he'd drained almost immediately. If Hershey turned out to be the Hat-Dog Killer, he'd just made a rookie mistake. Never drink something the cops ask you to drink. For one thing, they can withhold bathroom privileges to stress you. For another —

"You done with that?" Morales asked, indicating the cup.

"Oh, yeah." Hershey's voice was higher than Jazz had expected.

"Need a refill?" she asked, sounding for all the world like a waitress. Hughes had said absolutely nothing since walking in, pausing to flip through a folder and sigh theatrically.

"Nah, I'm done," Hershey said, glancing at Hughes.

"Let's just get this out of the way, then...." Morales deftly guided the paper cup away from Hershey, pushing it down the table with the tip of a pen. It looked utterly natural, but Jazz knew she was avoiding touching it.

"He's not the guy," Jazz announced. "He just voluntarily gave you guys his fingerprints and his DNA on that cup. It's not him."

"People screw up," Montgomery reminded him. "Don't be so quick."

"Not him," Jazz said, and folded his arms over his chest. "He's smarter than that."

They watched the interrogation in all its mind-numbing details. Hershey had alibis for some of the murders, no alibis for others. His memory was neither particularly good nor particularly bad, which is to say he seemed like anyone else pulled into a police station and suddenly asked to account for their lives over the past several months. If the police had hauled Jazz into an interrogation room and said to him, "On Monday September second, where were you at or about ten PM?" Jazz was pretty sure he wouldn't know, either.

Guilty people knew. They always knew. They lived in fear that they would be forced to account for their whereabouts during their crime, so they crafted their lies with great care and loving attention to detail.

"Ever been to Coney Island?" Hughes asked more gruffly than the question demanded. "Down the boardwalk?"

Hershey wasn't intimidated. "What, are you kidding me? Who *hasn't* been to Coney Island?"

"You go this past November, maybe?" Hughes leaned across the table as though he would beat the answer out of Hershey, who pulled back a bit in his chair.

"Settle down," Morales said, putting a calming hand on her partner's shoulder. "Can you just think back, Mr. Hershey, and tell us if you remember going to Coney Island? I kind of like it there in the off-season. Not as many tourists. I went myself in October. Can you remember?"

Hershey shrugged. "Hell if I can remember exactly. Probably, though. Usually get down that way a couple, three times a month, you know? My wife's mom lives in Bay Ridge."

"Of course," said Morales, smiling.

After about an hour of back-and-forth softball and hard-ball with Morales and Hughes, Hershey seemed annoyed and frustrated. Which is exactly how Jazz expected an inno-cent man to act.

"It could be a con job," Montgomery reminded him. "These guys are good at wearing masks."

Yeah, Jazz knew that. He was pretty good at wearing masks himself, and he prided himself on being able to see through them.

Then again, there was Jeff Fulton/Frederick Thurber/the Impressionist. That had been a mask made out of lead. Not even Jazz's X-ray vision had been able to see through it.

Just then, Hughes made a show of standing up and stretch-ing, as though trying to work out a kink in his neck. That was the sign that they were done with this guy.

"Not the guy," someone in the observation room said. One of the FBI guys.

Told you, Jazz didn't say.

He didn't need to. Montgomery looked over at him and lifted an eyebrow that seemed to say, *Well, yeah, okay.*

"What were the odds it would be the first one?" Mont-gomery said.

What are the odds it'll be any of them? Jazz wondered. *How many people live in Brooklyn? In the whole of New York City?* The profile was good; the task force had done a tremendous job. But they were still looking for a chameleon in heavy weeds.

"Next victim," someone deadpanned.

"Anyone need coffee?"

Jazz sighed.

⁘

The sun shone brightly overhead when Connie started digging in what had once been the backyard of Billy Dent's house. She quickly became overheated and should have taken a break, but instead she just peeled off layers and kept digging, sweat streaming down her face even though it was freezing outside.

A persistent beeping noise began, repeating over and over—three quick beeps, followed by a pause, then three again. She ignored it and kept digging.

CHAKK

Her shovel hit something, and as she peered down into the hole she'd dug, she was horrified to see a flap of hair and flesh pared away from gleaming white bone by the tooth of her shovel.

Beep-beep-beep.

"Don't go chasing..."

Someone was buried here. She had found a body.

Don't.

Go.

Cha-

-sing...

Swallowing, she kept digging, trying not to strike the body again. The police would want it intact, wouldn't they?

Beep-beep-beep.

She cleared more dirt away from the head and bit back a scream of absolute terror.

Beep-beep-beep.

It was Jazz.

She'd found Jazz buried in his own backyard. She would know that face anywhere. Recognize that nose, those lips…

But how? How could Jazz be buried here? And oh, God, if he was down here, then who—*what?*—had she been dating and kissing and almost sleeping with all these months?

Connie took a step back, dropping the shovel, and a hand came around her from behind and she tried to scream and then she opened her eyes and almost without thinking reached out to slap her alarm clock, silencing it halfway through a sequence of *Beep-beep-beep.*

Oh, God, she thought, and touched her chest, feeling her heart race exactly as it had just now in the dream. *Oh, thank God.*

"Look who's joining us for breakfast on a Saturday," Mom said, pleased, when Connie appeared in the kitchen. The rest of the family was already there at the table, Dad wearing a tie, which meant he had to go into the office even though it was a weekend. Ugh. The only work Connie ever wanted to do on a weekend was a Sunday matinee performance on Broadway.

"You're quiet this morning," said Dad as she poured milk over her cereal.

"She's tired from sneaking around the house all night," Whiz said helpfully. Connie shot him a dirty look.

"What's this?" Dad asked, clearing his throat and suddenly taking tremendous interest in his daughter. "Sneaking?"

"Something woke me up," she lied. "I thought I heard something, so I went to check on Whiz." She glared at him. "I should have let the boogeyman take him."

"I'll show you boogies!" Whiz cried, and went for his nose with one finger.

"Wisdom!" Mom said sharply. "If you stick that finger in your nose, you will *lose* it, do you hear me?"

Whiz shrugged and dove back into his scrambled eggs. He insisted on eating them topped with a nauseating concoction of ketchup, mustard, and soy sauce.

"What did you think you heard?" Dad wouldn't let it go.

Connie made a show of being exasperated, even though the direction of the conversation petrified her. Did Dad know she'd sneaked out the previous night? "I don't know. Something. It was probably a dream. Or the house settling. Or the wind."

Dad hmphed and checked his watch. That would be one parent out of the way. Mom worked at the Tynan Ridge branch of the state university, and they never called her in on weekends. Connie had to get her and Whiz out of the house so that she could escape. Howie had tormented her earlier this morning with a text that said *Ready?*, accompanied by a picture of himself standing in overalls, propping up a long-handled shovel like the farmer in Grant Wood's *American Gothic*.

After Dad was gone, Connie slipped into Whiz's bedroom, where he busily slaughtered something vaguely dragonish on his Xbox.

"I need a favor," she said.

Whiz ignored her. He was good at that when he wanted to be.

She tried again. "I need your help. I need you to get Mom to take you to the mall." The nearest mall was a half-hour drive away. Connie would prefer that Mom be gone all day, giving her a chance to get out, dig, and come back before being missed. But if Mom just dropped Whiz off and came home, it would still give her plenty of time to get out of the house, cover her tracks, and contemplate the punishment her father would eventually visit upon her.

"I don't want to go to the mall," Whiz said, aiming and swiping his on-screen sword with scary precision. Connie idly wondered if Billy Dent had ever owned an Xbox.

"Sure you do. There's that new movie—"

"Already saw it."

"And you want to see it again."

Whiz hit Pause and assessed his sister craftily. "What do you want?"

"I just told you—I want you and Mom out of the house."

"So that Jazz can come over and you guys can do the nasty?"

Jeez, even my kid brother thinks we're ready, Jazz! "No. Jazz isn't even in town. I just need to do some stuff. And I can't have you guys around."

"What's in it for me?" Whiz said, his tone clearly

conveying that he knew she had nothing to offer him for such a favor.

Connie drew in a deep breath and played her best card.

"I'll show you the code to unlock the parental controls on the satellite box," she said.

Whiz's eyes grew wide with something akin to worship.

CHAPTER 32

There were two interrogation rooms, one on either side of the observation room. While one suspect was being questioned, the next one would wait in the other room. The observers could look in on either one, and as the day crawled along, Jazz started to feel dizzy as he rotated between the two.

As the morning dragged into a cigarette-stale afternoon, Hughes and Morales ran their good cop/bad cop on four more suspects, all of whom fit the profile in various ways. It was a parade of white guys in their mid-thirties, all of them leading lives of depressingly similar dissatisfaction, all of them as empty as overpumped wells.

It took its toll on the people in the observation room, who'd begun the day with verve and excitement and a sense that New York's months-long nightmare was one confession away from ending. But as the day wore on, observers drifted out, replaced by others who watched for a little while, then left again as it became obvious to everyone that the guy in the box wasn't The Guy. Only Jazz and Montgomery stayed the whole time, the captain settling into a chair next to Jazz and leaning forward, elbows on knees, looking for all the world like a baseball manager trying to wish his team into the playoffs.

Jazz's phone rang in the middle of one interrogation, earning him a nasty glare from just about everyone in the room. He could have sworn he heard one of the loaner FBI agents mutter, "What makes *him* so special?" to another agent. The caller ID showed Connie's face, but Jazz fumbled to turn off the ringer, failing miserably. Finally, after what seemed like *hours* of that damn phone ringing, a cop grabbed it from him, pressed a few times, and shoved it back in his hands, silent and dark.

"Next up," Montgomery announced, reading off a sheet of paper like it was a scorecard, "is Mikel Angelico. That's M-I-K-E-L for those of you playing at home. White male—"

"Go figure," a cop said, to general laughter.

"—twenty-eight years old. Currently unemployed—"

"Say it ain't so, Cap'n!" someone called out.

Montgomery sighed like a father with newborn triplets who all needed fresh diapers at the same time. "No one's making you stand here, Wizniewski. There's boxes of documents need stacking over in the copy room."

"Sciatica, Cap," Wizniewski said.

"Christ," Montgomery muttered. Jazz had just opened his mouth to shoot down Wizniewski—he was tired, the cop was an ass, why not?—when the door to the observation room burst open and a youngish uniformed cop said, "Captain! Captain! You're not gonna believe this!"

What they wouldn't believe was Oliver Belsamo.

"And he just walked into the precinct?" Montgomery clarified.

The cop who had burst in—Amelio, his nameplate read—nodded. "Yessir. Walked in, ignored all the stuff out there, sat on the bench. He was waiting for a while. Noticed him right away, but he didn't say anything, just sat there, kinda twitchy, so I kept an eye on him and then—just now—he finally came right up to the front desk and said, 'I saw that story in the paper. I need to talk to someone about all the dead people.'"

Montgomery raised an eyebrow as he glanced at Jazz.

"You ran the fake-witness sting, didn't you?" Jazz asked. The expression on Montgomery's face was enough of an answer. "Awesome. And now this guy is coming in—"

"Doesn't mean he did it," the captain cautioned, trying to calm not just Jazz but also the half-dozen cops, FBI agents, and shrinks in the room with them. "Could just be a nutbar. Could be looking for publicity."

"What should I do with him?" Amelio asked.

Montgomery shared another look with Jazz. Jazz tried to dial down his excitement but was afraid it came through anyway, his best efforts to the contrary. Yeah, it was true that this "Belsamo" guy probably had nothing to do with the murders. Probably thought he saw something or was just looking for attention. Happened all the time. *And thank God for it,* Billy crowed. *More chaff in the radar! More fog in the air!*

"I say we at least talk to him," Jazz said, fully aware that at least half the room didn't care what he thought.

Montgomery nodded as though that had only confirmed his own feelings. "Set him up in room two, and get Hughes and Morales over there."

Hughes and Morales soldiered on. Jazz was impressed with their stamina. Hughes had been playing the pissed-off, barely-in-control black guy all day long, but still managed to drop in a joke or two between suspects. Morales had had to pretend to keep her partner in check and had taken her hair down and put it back up so many times that she didn't even glance over in the mirror now as she once again bunned up in preparation for the next suspect.

"Here's what Amelio got on intake," Montgomery said, and read off a blurt of stats on the walk-in: Belsamo, Oliver M. Thirty-two. White. Divorced. No kids. Currently unemployed.

They all clustered at the appropriate window for their first look at Belsamo, who was unshaven and dressed in a ratty old denim jacket. His fingernails were dirty; his eyes shifted around the room. The guy looked homeless.

He looks too crazy to be Hat-Dog. Hat-Dog would pass for normal. This guy can't.

Then again...then again, maybe he knows that's what we think, and he's playing us....

Being in a serial killer's mind was like navigating a maze made out of mirrors.

Hughes and Morales strode into the interrogation room as though they'd just come from an hour's beauty sleep. Hughes did his growly thing. Morales did her "Can I get you some water?" thing. Belsamo declined. They settled in.

"What can we do for you today, Mr. Belsamo?" Morales asked politely. Going with the good cop first.

He shrugged.

"We can't really help with shrugs," she said, putting some joviality into it.

"Saw the paper. Said there was a witness."

"That's right," Morales said, as Hughes did his best seething-with-rage act. "Someone saw the man who killed Lucy Donato. Do you know something about that?"

Belsamo shrugged again. Morales pressed some more, gently, not about Donato specifically. Harmless questions. He answered in mumbles and whispers. He kept looking around the room, startled, as though ghosts tapped his shoulders.

"You really think this guy could have planned and executed those murders?" Jazz asked. He regretted saying it as soon as the words were out of his mouth. Masks.

"I don't know," Montgomery admitted. "Could be playing us."

"Think he's on something?"

"Maybe."

"...Elana Gibbs," Morales said gently, bringing the subject back to the murders. "Did you know her?"

Belsamo said nothing.

Didn't even shrug this time.

"Hey!" Hughes shouted suddenly. "Hey, you need to talk to us, you understand?" It was a flat-out lie. Belsamo wasn't under arrest. And even if he had been, he could have pled the Fifth and clammed up.

"I don't want to," Belsamo mumbled. "I don't want to talk about that girl."

An electric spark ricocheted around Jazz's heart. *Holy...*

"Why not?" Morales asked pleasantly. "She was a pretty girl." She slid a photo of Gibbs across the table, taken from some online dating site. "We can talk about her. It's okay."

Belsamo's eyes flicked at the picture, then flicked away.

"Holy crap," breathed Montgomery, now leaning forward so much that he was almost a street urchin at a bakery window.

Despite himself, Jazz leaned forward, too. Belsamo didn't seem the type, but still...he'd reacted—a small reaction, true, but a reaction nonetheless—to the picture. Now Hughes should—

"How about *this* picture?" Hughes asked belligerently, sliding another photo over. "You prefer this one?"

It was a crime-scene photo. Elana Gibbs lay in repose, slit from pubis to breast, her abdomen an open, empty wound.

Belsamo reacted. He swallowed and shook his head, looking away. "Don't show me that. I didn't want that."

Didn't want that? "That's a confession!" Jazz whispered excitedly. "Right?"

"No," said Montgomery. "He could always claim he just meant he didn't want to see the picture. But it means we're on the right path."

"Why didn't you want it?" Morales asked calmly. "You mean you didn't want to hurt her?"

"Or maybe she's just an it to you," Hughes snarled. "Maybe you mean you got tired of it, so you threw it away like trash. Is that it?"

Belsamo shook his head violently. "Stop it. Stop talking to me."

"We're just talking," Morales soothed. "It's just talk."

"If you talk to me, I have to talk to you, and I don't want to talk to you!" Belsamo yelled. For an instant, Jazz thought the man would snap, would make a move. But he calmed as quickly as he'd flared, slumping in his seat again. He started picking at the dirt under his fingernails.

A glance between Hughes and Morales. Morales nodded a minute nod. She took over.

"Why don't you want to talk to us, Oliver?" She slid her chair a little closer, her voice pitched low and comforting. She did everything but take his hand in hers. "Are you afraid of what you might tell us?"

Belsamo shrugged.

"I've heard a lot of things, Oliver." Using his first name. Familiar. Comforting. "I've heard a lot. I can handle it. You can tell me whatever you want. This is a safe space. I know you have something to tell me. This is the place. This is the time."

"Please stop asking," Belsamo whispered. Montgomery turned up the volume on the speaker from the interrogation room.

"Why? Because you'll tell me?"

Another shrug.

"You'll tell me, won't you, Oliver? You'll tell me, and you'll tell me the truth, right? Because you wouldn't lie to me."

"I don't lie," Belsamo said, with something like pride.

"That's good. Because you know what'll happen if you lie to us, don't you? If you tell us something that's not true?"

Belsamo contemplated this for a moment, still picking at his fingernails. "I know what will happen," he said in a low, barely audible voice. "I'll go to jail." Then, more strongly: "I'll go directly to jail."

"Well, maybe not directly. It might take a little while. But, yeah, you'll go to jail if you don't tell the truth."

"It's time to open up," Hughes said in a kind tone, sensing the moment. He pushed the two pictures a little closer. "It's time to tell us."

Belsamo sighed, his entire body crumpling and deflating like yesterday's balloon. "Yeah. I know." He cleared his throat and pointed to the pictures. "I did it. I killed her."

Jazz's heart pounded. Montgomery swore softly under his breath.

"You killed her," Morales said, her voice controlled and soft. "Just her?"

For a moment, it seemed as though Belsamo did not understand the question. Struggle writhed his features, twisted his lips, and crunched his eyebrows together. But finally he shook his head.

"How many?" Hughes asked. Flat. No expression on his face. No judgment. No excitement. *How many?*

"A bunch of them," Belsamo went on. Pause. Then, as if helpless to stop himself, gathering steam: "I killed them all."

CHAPTER 33

The precinct dropped its pretense of studied, methodical calm and fell right into chaos. As Jazz emerged from the observation room, he felt as though he'd stepped into an evacuation drill. People ran in every direction. Phones blared.

Hughes slid out of the interrogation room, his eyes shining and bright and alive. "Did you hear that? Were you in there? Did you hear that?"

"Yeah." Jazz accepted a sudden and unexpected bear hug from the detective, who trembled with what Jazz could only assume was joy. Or maybe a massive overload of adrenaline.

"I mean, it's not definite," Hughes went on. "He sort of clammed up right away, like he realized what he'd said. And people confess to crap they didn't do all the time, especially in this city, where the crazy quotient is ridiculous, but—"

"Hughes—"

"—I just have a feeling, you know? He just feels right for it."

"Hughes, he doesn't fit the profile."

Hughes released Jazz and stepped back. "Yeah," he said, looking for all the world like a toddler whose birthday party has just ended. "I know. I know that. But—"

"I'm just saying. Not married. No kids. No serious relationship at all. A loner. And look at him. Did you really look at him? The hair? The dirty nails? He's not organized enough to take a shower or wash his hair—how do you expect him to be organized enough to pull off the Hat-Dog murders?"

Hughes frowned. "He confessed. You weren't in the room. You didn't see the way he reacted when we showed him the crime-scene photo."

"I saw. I was watching."

A head shake. "No, man. It was different, in the room. Ask Morales."

As if summoned by her name spoken aloud, the FBI agent emerged from the interrogation room, grabbing another FBI guy to say, "I want an NCIC check on this guy ASAP. Get a medic down here right now. I'm getting a court order for his blood, and as soon as it gets here, I want that blood out of him and in a lab."

"Is he under arrest?" Jazz said, and then felt stupid for asking.

But Morales shook her head. "No. Once he's in custody, I have to read him his rights. If he babbles something else in the meantime, I want it to count. Once the court order for his blood gets here, we'll make it official and take him into custody, Mirandize him, all that." She shouted at the other agent, who apparently wasn't moving quickly enough for her. "Get on the damn phone and get that medic! I want a

DNA match to the blood and semen samples *yesterday*, got it?"

"How long until we know?" Jazz asked her.

Morales clucked her tongue. "It'll take maybe an hour to get the court order, depending on how quickly we can find a judge on a Saturday. Shouldn't be that tough, though. I'm going to put the highest possible priority on this."

"And then..."

She cocked her head at him. "And then once I have the court order, we officially arrest him. *Then* we take our DNA samples. We match them to the samples we already have and when they match, we have our guy."

"How long will that take? Matching the DNA?"

Hughes and Morales shared a look. "Depends if we go with the city or the federal labs..." Hughes said.

"We can get a special courier to get the samples to Quantico within hours," Morales said. "I bet our lab is less backlogged than yours."

"I'll get someone to check," said Hughes. "Either way, it's gonna take a couple of days to get results back," he told Jazz. "It's not like on TV, where it takes a couple of hours."

"How long can you hold him? Can you hold him until the results come back?"

"Probably. It's a weekend. Once we officially charge him, we can keep him for twenty-four hours before we take him to a judge. By then, it's Sunday, so we get a break. Monday, we take him to the judge. If the results are back by then—"

"*If*," Hughes stressed.

"*If*," Morales agreed, "then we're golden. If not, we show

the confession and hope the judge holds him without bail pending the DNA results."

"In the meantime, we have an hour before you're actually arresting him, right?"

"Yeah."

"Then I need to talk to him," Jazz said. "You have to let me in."

"No. No way," Morales said. Hughes nodded in agreement.

"He called me out, you guys! If it's him, *he* left that message for me. You have to let me talk to him."

"No way. Sorry, but I'm not risking having a confession thrown out because of something you did or said. I want him in jail for life. Or maybe even a needle in his arm, if we play our cards right." Morales seemed to relish the idea, and her mien completely convinced Jazz that she would gleefully help him kill Billy.

"Look, once you get the DNA results back, his confession won't even matter," Jazz said. "The whole reason you brought me out here was because you think I have some kind of rapport with guys like this, right? He wants to see me. He wants to talk to me. Let's give him what he wants and see what happens."

Montgomery had joined the group while Jazz was talking. "Has anyone Mirandized this bedbug yet?"

"He's not under arrest, Captain," Hughes said. "He came in voluntarily—"

"We need to step very carefully here. I don't want him to lawyer up yet, but I don't want to step in a pile of crap that the DA's gonna have to scrape off my shoe, either."

297

"I'm sort of a legend to these guys," Jazz said, adding a dollop of embarrassment to his voice. "If this guy's a serial killer, then he called me out. He knows who I am. Just my presence alone might jostle something loose from him. I can be very careful with what I say and do, Captain Montgomery. I won't violate his rights in any way. But if we can pull some more information out of him..."

Montgomery looked over at Morales. "Well?"

"Not a chance in hell."

Jazz threw his hands up in the air. "Look, he *confessed*. Right now, he's in there realizing he made a mistake. There's a good chance that he'll recant. Hell, once you Mirandize him, you'll probably never hear his voice again, and there's still plenty to learn from him. If seeing me can make him talk some more, isn't that a good thing? Trust me, Captain Montgomery"—and he gave the captain his most potent look of trustworthiness—"I know where the land mines are. I know what areas to avoid to make sure your case is still solid."

Montgomery wiped both hands down his face. It was a gesture of surrender Jazz had seen time and time again on teachers, principals, and G. William. "Okay," the captain said, nodding. "It may seem crazy, but so is this guy. As long as someone's in there with you. For protection."

"I'm totally against this, Captain," said Morales.

"It's not your call to make," said Montgomery, and Jazz fought off the grin that wanted to blow up on his face. *Gotcha*, he thought. *Finally gotcha, Montgomery.*

"Fine. Hughes, you're on this, then."

"Let's do it."

Moments later, Jazz and Hughes went into the interrogation room. Jazz felt a moment's frisson of panic/delight. He was in control here.

Saints and sinners, all the same, Billy said. *That hard-on cops get from beatin' down a suspect is the same hard-on ol' Dahmer got drillin' holes in boys' heads.*

Shut up, Billy, Jazz thought. Couldn't he enjoy something—couldn't he feel something, *anything*—without Dear Old Dad chiming in from the past?

Belsamo sat at one end of the table, staring down at his fingernails, now picked nearly clean. He had piled a small, disgusting mound of dirt on the table in front of him. Jazz took a seat about halfway down the table, perpendicular to Belsamo. Close enough to converse pleasantly, far enough away to demonstrate the figurative distance between them.

"Oliver," said Hughes, sitting at the farthest point of the table from Belsamo, "this young man is not affiliated with the NYPD. He'd like to talk to you. Is that okay? You're not surrendering any of your rights in speaking to him, and you can stop at any time. Do you understand?"

Belsamo looked up for the first time, opening his mouth to speak. He caught a glimpse of Jazz first, and his mouth stayed open, gaping, silent.

Jazz had expected a reaction to his presence. His encounter with the Impressionist educated him as to his position in serial-killer mythology. He was the sole scion of the world's greatest living serial murderer—that position in history's most demented hierarchy meant something to a certain class of sociopath. For the Impressionist, it was worship. For Belsamo...

"You're here," the man finally said, gasping it as though he'd inhaled tear gas. "You're him."

Jazz kept his expression carefully neutral. *You show any weakness to a serial killer,* he'd once told Connie, *and they live inside you after that.* He had managed to survive interviews with his father and the Impressionist and come away essentially intact. He wouldn't let Hat-Dog break that streak.

"Of course I'm here," he said calmly. "You called to me. You sent me a message. So I came."

Belsamo's awed manner cracked, becoming confusion. If it was false, then it was a truly magnificent performance. Jazz almost stood and applauded.

"You sent me a message," he said again, still calm. "So I came. What did you want to tell me?"

Belsamo tilted his head, an archaeologist finding the wrong fossils.

"Was it about the men?" Jazz whispered, leaning in. "Did you want to tell me why you kept some of their penises, but not others?"

Still nothing.

Desperate, Jazz knew he had two powerful cards to play, his aces in the hole. His trumps. He could mention Billy. Or he could mention the thing that had made the Impressionist fling himself face-first into his cell door....

"Is this all about Ugly J?" Jazz asked. "Do you have a message"—for? to? from?—"about Ugly J?"

Belsamo blinked, then opened his mouth....

And a sound came out.

It wasn't a word. It was just a noise, loud and sharp and short. Then Belsamo grinned and made the noise again.

"*Caaaawwww!*" he cried.

Stunned, Jazz sat back in his chair. He thought he had been prepared for anything Belsamo might say. What the hell?

Belsamo jumped up, twirling drunkenly as he warbled to the ceiling. Hughes was up instantly, moving faster than Jazz thought possible, interposing himself between Belsamo and Jazz.

"I think we're done here," Hughes muttered.

"Yeah, I think so." They watched Belsamo for another moment as the man wheeled and spun and tumbled into a corner of the interrogation room, giggling to himself as he hit the wall.

Hughes held the door open, and just as Jazz went to walk through, Belsamo cried out, "Behold my power!"

Jazz turned, hearing Hughes swear vigorously at the sight of Belsamo, his pants and underpants dropped to his ankles, his turgid junk gripped in one hand and waving proudly. "Behold!" Belsamo shouted again, and cawed.

Hughes pushed Jazz through the door and slammed it shut behind them. "Great. Now someone's gonna have to clean up in there when he's done choking his chicken."

"Hughes, that guy...is it just me, or was he totally clueless when I mentioned the message he sent to me?"

Hughes grimaced. "I don't think I like where this is headed."

"It's just that... if he doesn't know about the message, he couldn't have—"

"Look, let's just wait and see what the DNA says. No point burning brain cells over it until then."

"But—"

The detective shushed him. "We have some time. Ever seen the Statue of Liberty, Jasper?"

CHAPTER 34

That afternoon was cold but sunny in Lobo's Nod, even on the cursed ground that had once belonged to Billy Dent. Connie had tried calling Jazz—this was big stuff now, she'd decided, and that dream of him buried had rattled her—but the call had gone to voice mail. Just as well, maybe. He was doing something important and most likely dangerous in New York. He didn't need a distraction.

The branch was still where she'd jammed it the night before when Connie and Howie arrived once again at the site of the former Dent house. Howie peered around in the bright of day. By daylight, the place was less foreboding. It was also less concealed, despite the trees and hedges. Anyone driving by would see them.

"You think someone's gonna see us?" Howie asked. "Chase us off?"

Connie shrugged and dropped the tools on the ground. She looked around the perimeter of the former Dent property, at the trees and shrubs. "I don't think so. But let 'em try. Hopefully we don't need long."

They started with a pickax, taking turns breaking through the hard crust of the earth. Howie had swiped the shovel from his own garage, but realized on his way to get Connie that at this time of year, they'd need to break up the frozen topsoil first. So he'd stopped off at a hardware store. ("You owe me twenty bucks, by the way," he told Connie.)

Within the first five minutes, Howie was exhausted. Connie stripped off her heavy coat and kept swinging the pickax. She tried not to imagine what she would do if it turned out this was a setup or a hoax. She would be getting in a hell of a lot of trouble with her parents for nothing.

"You're doing great," Howie cheered from the sidelines. "Look at you go!"

Resisting the urge to bury the pickax in Howie's head instead of in the ground, Connie flailed away until she'd broken up a patch roughly a foot and a half in every direction. The soil beneath was warmer and looser. She reached for the shovel. Howie helpfully handed it to her.

She dug out a foot or so down before favoring Howie with a deathly glare that got him off his butt and over to the hole. He dug for a while, maintaining a steady patter of complaints, until his phone chirped for his attention.

"It's Sam," he said, looking at it. "She needs me." His voice almost vibrated with pleasure.

"Gramma probably needs her adult diaper changed," Connie told him.

"But my fingers may gently brush against Sam's as we change the diaper together," Howie pointed out.

"Fine. Go. Just remember to come back for me."

Once Howie left, Connie allowed herself a five-minute break before taking up the shovel and attacking the ground again. She was determined to dig until she found *something*. A gopher hole. A rabbit warren. A treasure chest full of Spanish doubloons. A pocket of oil that would make her richer than Midas and solve the energy crisis. *Something.* Even if it took all day and all night.

But it didn't take that long. It took only another ten minutes.

Bodies, Connie knew, were buried six feet deep, for reasons she couldn't recall. Something superstitious and ancient and partly forgotten, like so many modern rituals. Something about being certain that the dead person couldn't get out of the grave...

She didn't have to dig six feet, thank God, only three.

Only? Ha! Her arms and shoulders ached as her shovel hit something with a *CHANNNNG* sound. She thought— briefly—of her dream, of finding Jazz buried here, then plunged ahead, spooning out loose dirt and digging around the edges of the thing to find its dimensions. With a few more minutes' hard digging, she'd managed to clear away its top.

It was a lockbox of some sort, measuring maybe twelve inches by five inches. Connie pried around the edges of it, then lay flat on her belly to reach down and pull it up. It was only a couple of inches deep, and lighter than it appeared; she had no problem hauling it out.

Once it was on the ground next to her, she stared at it for long moments. Gray and dull, with a hinged top and a stout combination lock hanging from a steel loop. She picked it up and tilted it gently from one side to the other. Something inside shifted. Something light, but relatively solid. It didn't feel fragile. She put the box back down on the ground and stared at it.

Jazz had told her once how to foil a combination lock. She didn't remember all of the details—something about sensitive fingertips and listening to the tumblers—so she just raised the pickax with the last of her strength, aimed carefully at the lock, and brought it crashing down.

And missed, gouging another new trough into what was left of Billy Dent's backyard.

Oops. Crunching up the ground with a pickax was one thing, but hitting the small target of a lock was another altogether. Especially since she couldn't afford to hit the box itself—she didn't want to damage whatever was inside it.

She took a few deep breaths, yoga breaths, clearing her mind. Then, hearkening back to her acting training to center and relax herself, she swung again with the pickax and thought, *Hey, wait, what if Billy left something* explosive *in that box?* But it was too late—she couldn't halt the momentum of her swing and the sharp, hard blade of the pickax smashed into the combination lock.

Which didn't break.

Oh, come on! Her shoulders and arms felt like slabs of meat ready for the grill. The lock was dented and twisted, but a few tugs told her that it wasn't going anywhere.

Could be something explosive in there. Could be anthrax. If Billy Dent left this, it could be just about anything. You should go get Sheriff Tanner and have him tackle this.

Made sense.

But, she countered her own internal logic, *if you get the cops, then they'll be all like, "Why didn't you call us as soon as you got that first text message?" And you'll have to put up with all that nonsense. And you might never get to see what's inside.*

Curiosity fueled her muscles as she swung the pickax again, trying not to imagine a choking cloud of something noxious and lethal erupting from the open box.

This time, the lock broke.

Connie opened the box, thoughts of explosives and gases and anthrax already fled from her mind. She needed to know what was inside. Some part of her thought that Howie would be disappointed not to have been here for the opening, but she was beyond caring now, driven. She had to know. She had to see it.

The box did not contain anthrax or a bomb or anything else exotic. A few inches shallow, it contained exactly three things: two clear plastic bags with envelopes zipped into them, and...

A toy.

She plucked it from the box gingerly, as if it were dangerous. But it was just a small plastic bird. Black. A raven, or maybe a crow. Something like that. Weren't they part of the same family? Or genus? Connie couldn't remember—her bio class interested her about as much as Whiz's video games.

A crow ... the Crow King ...

This was a cheap plastic bird, the kind of thing you bought at a gift shop somewhere. It was hollow—when squeezed, it made a halfhearted wheezing sound. Connie shrugged and put it on the ground next to the box.

She unzipped one of the plastic bags and withdrew a manila envelope that measured something like six inches by five inches. Even as she did it, she thought, *Maybe I should actually measure it and take notes for the cops*, before realizing that she had already touched and moved the evidence. Oh, well. So much for preserving the crime scene.

What crime? So far, all you've found is some junk buried in the backyard.

The envelope was only partly full, still crisp and nearly flat, fastened with a metal clasp, then sealed. She opened it as gingerly as she could, thinking of old cop shows where "the guys in the lab" managed to pull DNA samples from envelope flaps and identify the killer that way. Her hands shook.

What are you doing, Connie? Call the cops! Call them now!

But she was powerless to stop herself as she peeled back the flap, then shook the contents out into her hand.

Anthrax! screamed some primitive part of her, but all that fell into her palm was a set of photographs.

There were half a dozen of them, all of them with three people. The man Connie recognized immediately—it was Billy Dent. He was younger, but there was no mistaking that infamous grin, those piercing eyes.

The woman, she knew, was Jazz's mother. It was a shock

seeing her—Connie had seen only the one photo of her, the picture Jazz kept in his wallet and now had scanned into his phone. The only picture that had survived Billy's purge of all things "Mom" from the Dent house nine years ago. But here were more pictures of her.

Holding a baby, in the top picture.

Connie didn't need to flip the photo over, didn't need to read JASPER, 7 MONTHS to know that she was seeing something Jazz had never seen—his own mother holding him as a baby. Jazz had one fat little baby fist jammed in his own mouth, and from his free hand dangled the very same crow toy Connie had just examined. *Baby's first toy...*

The other pictures progressed from Jazz at seven months to fifteen months. Connie couldn't tell if these were special occasions or what. Each photo was roughly the same—Jazz's parents and baby Jazz in some combination. In one photo, Jazz was standing, arms akimbo in that drunken baby waddle toddlers use, as his parents crouched near him, ready to catch him if he fell. It looked so normal that Connie realized in a flash how Billy had managed to go without being identified as a sociopath for so many years. *He really did seem normal. He just seemed completely normal.*

Jazz's mom looked...unhappy. In most of the pictures, she seemed off-kilter, as if dissatisfied or distracted. Connie wondered if she was on drugs—some kind of prescription or maybe something you didn't pick up at the pharmacy along with tampons and Halloween candy. Or maybe she just knew what her husband was, what he did, and she couldn't hide that knowledge.

How many had Billy killed at this point? Did she think it would get better, that he would stop? Was she in denial?

And who, she wondered suddenly, took these pictures?

Probably Gramma. Who else would it be?

She scrutinized the pictures for long minutes, looking for some clue, some detail that would illuminate her current quest. Or maybe something that would mean something to Jazz when he saw these photos. But there was nothing. The clothing and the decor—the photos having been taken, no doubt, in the house that once stood mere yards from her—were typical of the late nineties. Nothing special.

At least Jazz would now have more pictures of his mother. That was something, right?

She tucked the photos back into the envelope, then rezipped it into the bag and set it next to the crow.

The envelope in the second plastic bag was so thin that she thought it must be empty, but when she opened it, she saw a single sheet of paper within. With the tips of her fingernails, she pulled it out.

For a moment, she didn't know what she was looking at. But then she realized: It was a birth certificate. More important, it was *Jazz's* birth certificate: DENT, JASPER FRANCIS was typed in the appropriate space, along with Jazz's birth date, time of birth, length, and weight.... It was signed by a Dr. Ian O'Donnelly at Lobo's Nod General Hospital.

Connie stared at it, and then she saw what she should have seen right away, and all her breath left her lungs and the world swam black and red.

CHAPTER 35

Morales had retreated to an empty office to harangue federal and local courthouses to find a judge who could sign the court order that even now one of Montgomery's cops was filling out on the computer. The faster that order was signed, the quicker they could get Belsamo's DNA and get that process started. Jazz needed a break, so he and Hughes sneaked out to the car and drove back to the place called Red Hook. Hughes parked in a grocery store parking lot and pointed through the windshield.

"See? The Statue of Liberty. Told you."

Sure enough, Jazz could see the statue off in the distance. Big deal. He'd seen it on TV and in movies.

"You really think Belsamo's the guy?" he asked. "Even after that little display?"

Hughes shrugged. "Could be. Some guy just wandering into the precinct like that? It's possible. Some of these guys— a lot of these guys—they want to get caught."

Most of these guys, they want to get caught, Dear Old Dad had said so many times that Jazz had lost count. *You understand what I'm saying? I'm saying most of the time, they get caught 'cause they want it, not 'cause anyone figures 'em out, not 'cause anyone outthinks 'em.*

"Yeah. Some of them."

Almost without realizing it, he rubbed briefly at his collarbone, where the reversed I HUNT KILLERS tattoo emblazoned his flesh.

Yeah, I hunt killers. Right. Seems more like they hunt me lately. Between the Impressionist literally knocking on my front door and Hat-Dog calling me out, I'm not doing much actual hunting.

"He just doesn't seem right for this," Jazz said, switching the topic to a more comfortable area. "Hat-Dog is highly organized. Belsamo...isn't."

"We don't know that," Hughes argued. "We don't know how much of what we saw in there was an act."

"Really? Pulling your pud in a police station is a far way to go for an act."

"You're the one who's always saying that the stuff we think is crazy makes perfect sense to these guys. Maybe he's spent the past year wanting nothing more than a chance to show his junk to Billy Dent's kid."

For some reason, this made Jazz think of a world in which the solution to serial murder was for him to see the exposed genitals of serial killers, leading to a brief mental image of a traditional cop lineup, sociopaths all in a row, pants on the floor, and Jazz walking down the line like the Pope blessing worshippers.

"That's insane."

"Exactly."

"Insanity alone can't account for everything. For someone as organized as Hat-Dog, there's an underlying sense to it."

"What about this Ugly J thing? You think that's some connection between your dad and this guy and that Impressionist guy?"

Jazz shrugged. "Billy was in jail when Hat-Dog started up. But he was in jail when the Impressionist was prospecting, too. Someone kick-started the Impressionist. Maybe Hat-Dog. Or maybe the other way around."

"Prospecting. You said that before. Is that...is that what he called it? Prospecting?"

And now Jazz felt like *he* was the one who'd exposed himself in public. He wanted to curl up in a corner of the car and melt away. He'd forgotten that not everyone had memorized every detail of Billy's career. Was the word *prospecting* even something in the public record? He didn't know.

"Never mind," he said.

Hughes said nothing, and they sat in silence, gazing out at the Statue of Liberty until Hughes's cell chirped for attention.

"It's Morales."

"Too soon for the court order," Jazz said. "Even for the feds."

"Text just says 'bad news.'" He started the car. "Let's find out what."

313

Jazz and Hughes arrived at the precinct just in time to watch them let Belsamo go. He shuffled out the door reluctantly, like a vagrant turned away from a shelter.

"What the hell?" Hughes demanded. "He confessed! You can't have even taken his DNA yet, and the bastard said he killed—"

"That's enough!" Montgomery barked, and dragged them into his office. "Settle down, Louis. You can't go off like that out there, whipping everyone into a frenzy."

"What happened?" Hughes asked, and Jazz answered almost by reflex, realizing in a flash of insight what must have happened.

"They found a new body," he said. "Didn't they?"

Hughes gaped at him and before Montgomery could respond, Morales breezed into the office.

"New body," she said tightly. "Three damn *blocks* from here. The bastard is laughing at us. Corner of Henry and Baltic. Right outside P.S. Twenty-nine. Assistant principal leaving school found the body fifteen minutes ago."

"But Belsamo could have—"

"Let me guess," Jazz said, interrupting Hughes. "The body wasn't there this morning."

Morales nodded emphatically. "The body *had* to have been dumped during the day. In broad daylight. The timing doesn't work—Belsamo was here most of the morning, waiting to be interrogated, seen by a million cops and feds."

"The whole damn task force is his alibi," Montgomery said bitterly.

"Just another nutjob." Hughes sounded defeated.

"Unis and evidence collection are on the scene. Want to check it out?" Morales asked.

"Let's go," Jazz said.

Morales drove Jazz to the crime scene; Hughes stayed behind to coordinate the task force gathering the day's alibis from their potential suspects.

"We also ran his name as a matter of course," Morales said, still speaking of Belsamo, clearly pissed off. "He was questioned the night of the S-line murder in connection with a drunk-and-disorderly. Unis confirm he was with them for an hour in Boerum Hill. No way he had time to schlep out to Midtown, find our girl, do his thing, and then leave her on the S."

"So . . . it's definitely not him."

Morales nodded a tight little nod. "Never even got anyone in there to take a blood sample. All happened too fast. Damn!" She slammed a palm against the steering wheel. "Thought we had this one." She grabbed her phone and stabbed out a number as they paused at a light, then barked at whoever answered to cancel the court order. "No point wrecking a judge's weekend for nothing. We might need a happy one later on."

Jazz could feel the smoldering anger boiling off her like steam. She probably thought it made her tough, but it actually made her vulnerable. Angry people weren't thinking straight. It would be easy to—

Stop doing that!

Never killed a cop before. Not even a lady cop, Billy mused. *And this one's real special, ain't she? Tried to catch ol' Hand-in-Glove, didn't she? Would be great to get to know her from the inside out, get my drift?*

Go to hell, Billy.

Hell's all around, Jasper m'boy?

As Morales had said, the crime scene was mere blocks from the precinct. A crowd had gathered, along with the usual media vultures. Morales handed Jazz a pair of sunglasses and an FBI baseball cap. Crude disguise, but maybe it would work.

NYPD uniforms had set up a perimeter around the scene and now did their level best to keep gawkers and press from getting too close. Jazz looked around quickly as he stepped out of the car. This was brazen, leaving the body here. P.S. 29 was on the corner of Baltic and Henry. Not a busy intersection, from what Jazz could tell, but even a lightly traveled New York intersection got more traffic than the busiest in Lobo's Nod. Right across the street was a Chinese restaurant— two guys in food-spattered aprons stood in the doorway, gaping at the craziness across the street.

The rest of the buildings within sight looked residential. Smallish, squat apartment buildings and some town houses.

"He's definitely getting cocky," Jazz murmured to Morales

as they ducked under the crime-scene tape. "Dumping right out in the open like this?"

"Yeah." Morales had taken in the surroundings, too. "Safe bet—well, safe-*ish*—that no one's lingering around a school on the weekend, but even so, he had to figure *someone* would pop up unexpected."

"Where's the witness?"

Morales pointed. An NYPD uniform stood near the front door to the school, holding out a cup of what could have been coffee or water or even whiskey to a woman in a winter coat who seemed to be on the verge of hyperventilating. "Dr. Meredith Sinclair. Assistant principal at P.S. Twenty-nine. She's not going to be any use to us for a few minutes. Let the unis calm her down and then we'll take a run at her."

Jazz liked the way she said "we."

The body lay almost like a snow angel just within a fence that separated the school grounds from the sidewalk along Baltic. Nothing new. Jazz went into instant assessment mode.

Caucasian female, age twenty-five to thirty. Blond. Naked. Slit open from breastbone to waist, the gaping wound of her gut revealing the shiny-slick loops of intestines. Eyelids gone. Eyes missing.

"Left the guts *in* this time," Morales mumbled, crouching down for a better look, blocking a crime-scene tech. Annoyed, the tech moved a bit and took another photo of the body. Another cop shot video.

"No," Jazz said. "Put them *back*."

Morales arched an eyebrow and summoned one of the medical examiner's men, who probed at the corpse and

317

confirmed that, yes, the intestines were no longer attached to the body. They'd been removed, then stuffed back inside.

"Evolution of his signature?" Morales wondered aloud.

"Or maybe just expedient," Jazz said. "Maybe he wanted to leave a clean murder site and he didn't have anywhere else to put her guts when he moved her."

"She was left here sometime between ten, ten-fifteen, which is when Dr. Sinclair got here to do some work before the winter break ended, and three, which is when she came out the front door. Nice little five-hour window." Morales tsked. "Anything else, Boy Wonder? You're the one who found all the stuff we missed at the other scenes."

Jazz shook his head. "There's nothing else to see here. This is just the dump site. Every clue available to you is in or on the body." He turned a tight circle, scanning the surroundings. "I don't see any security cameras pointed this way. You won't see him there. But maybe canvass the surrounding blocks, see if someone saw something as he headed this way. He wouldn't have been walking, not with a load like that. You're looking for a car that stopped at this intersection, a guy who got out...."

"Then why check around the other blocks?"

"Because he had to come from *some*where. If you can get an ID on the kind of car, maybe you can figure out which direction he came from. Maybe another camera out there somewhere on his route caught a picture of him or his license plate or something."

Morales kicked at the ground. "Yeah. Okay." He could tell by her tone of voice that she thought it was useless. And she was probably right. But they had to try something. Anything, at this point.

"He's showing his contempt for us," Jazz told her. "He knows the investigation is headquartered right down the road. He might have even known we were interviewing suspects."

Morales clucked her tongue. "How would he know that? You think he's a cop?"

She asked it so matter-of-factly that it stunned Jazz. No attempt to conceal her thoughts, no attempt to lower her voice. The New York cops within earshot all went stony-faced, offended, angered. If she noticed, Morales didn't show it.

"Nah," Jazz said lightly. It was possible, of course. But this seemed like such a risky move.... Would a cop—even a crazy cop—take such a chance? "I think he's FBI."

Morales blew out a puff of laughter. "Okay, yeah, right." She took the woman's wrist in her hand, almost as though checking for a pulse. "Her extremities are in rigor. Rest of the body's getting there."

"Given the cold temperatures, figure she's been dead six, seven hours?" One of the medical techs looked at Jazz with impressed surprise and nodded, confirming the estimate.

"So he kills her early this morning and dumps her here right away," Morales said. She moved, carefully, in order to get a better angle on the body. "Raped?"

"Won't know until we get her on the slab," the tech said, "but I'm guessing yes, based on some bruising on her inner thighs. Could have just been from rough consensual intercourse at some point in the last twelve to sixteen hours, but given the circumstances..."

"Let me know what you get," she told the tech. To Jazz, she said, "Do you need to see anything else?"

Jazz glanced over at the assistant principal again. She was gulping whatever was in the cup, and the cop with her looked bored.

"Are we sure she didn't see anything when she got here?"

"She says—"

"Witnesses are wrong. Eyewitness testimony is pretty unreliable."

"I know that."

"I'm just thinking...if I were a serial killer and I wanted to throw the cops off, I might drop a body so that it's found when I'm talking to them. Make them think I'm just some kind of crackpot."

Morales shook her head. "I would buy that if *we* came to *him*. But he approached us. We didn't suspect him to begin with. Why would anyone—even a lunatic—try to throw off suspicion by *raising* suspicion?"

To that, Jazz had no answer.

CHAPTER 36

Connie didn't even realize that she was still staring at the birth certificate until a voice suddenly shouted and shocked her back to reality.

"Hey! Hey, what are you doing?"

She looked up and around. Realized that the voice came from through the hedge to the east. A man stood there with a baseball bat.

"That's private property!" he shouted.

Connie froze. Who the hell was this guy to try to run her off? It wasn't *his* property. She opened her mouth to say "Buzz off!" but before she could, he said, "I'm calling nine-one-one!" and held up a cell phone as if he needed to prove it.

Oh...crap.

Trespassing. Disturbing evidence. Damaging private property... And those were just the crimes Connie could imagine herself. The justice system probably had plenty of other blanks to fill in.

She stooped down and gathered up the box and its contents,

then took off in the opposite direction, leaving the shovel and pickax behind. *I owe Howie more than twenty bucks now*, some crazy part of her realized.

"Hey!" the guy shouted. "Hey! Stay right there! I'm calling the cops! I'm serious!"

I know you're serious, dumbass, Connie thought as she ran like hell for the cover of the woods. *Why do you think I'm running?*

She didn't know the woods and back byways of Lobo's Nod the way Jazz and Howie did, but Connie *did* have excellent coverage on her phone. Its GPS got her through the woods and into another housing development, where she paused to catch her breath and text Howie while hidden behind someone's shed. Howie, fortunately, was done at Jazz's and easily able to pick her up, though he did complain—of course—about the lost shovel and pickax.

He stopped complaining when Connie showed him the lockbox and its contents.

And the birth certificate.

"This is the big one," she said. "This changes things."

"Why? So, it's Jazz's birth certificate. Now we know he wasn't born in Kenya. Big deal."

She pointed to a specific portion of the birth certificate. Howie's eyes widened immediately and his chest hitched as though he'd been shoved.

322

"Oh my God." He stared incredulously where she pointed. "Is this for real?"

"Yeah."

The birth certificate was completely normal and unassuming. Except for one thing.

The spot for FATHER.

It was blank.

"It shows his mom's name," Howie breathed, "but there's nothing for his dad...."

"Which means," Connie said, speaking the words out loud for the first time, "that Jazz might not be Billy's son."

Howie drove Connie home, still processing what she'd told him. "Looks like you lucked out," he told her as they pulled up. There were no cars in her driveway.

"God, it feels like I've been gone for days," she said. "But it's just been a couple of hours."

"Maybe your moms decided to stick around the mall. Run errands or something while your brother's at the movies."

"Maybe. I'm not gonna question some good luck." She got out of the car. "You're good to take it from here?"

"I'm not a complete screwup," Howie said, offended. "I can handle my part. Just make sure you send it."

She waggled her phone. "Already e-mailed. Let me know what happens. And hey—be careful."

Howie backed out and headed back to the Dent house,

doing his best to pay attention to the road, even though all he could *really* focus on was a notion that he'd never imagined possible: What if Jazz *wasn't* Billy Dent's son? What would that mean for his best friend? It seemed impossible, but that blank on the birth certificate...Why leave it blank if you knew who the father was? Had Jazz's mom had an affair? Or maybe a one-night stand with a man she didn't even know?

Another thought occurred to Howie, one that tightened his gut so much that he had to pull over for a moment until the tautness in his belly subsided: What if Billy Dent had... well, what if he had forced one of his male victims to rape his own wife? What if that's how Jazz had been conceived?

Connie had wanted to call Jazz right away. To give what might be the best news of Jazz's life. And Howie could understand that. Nothing would please him more than to say to Jazz, *Hey, buddy, you know how you're worried that being Billy's kid means you're, like, genetically predisposed to go psycho? Well, guess what? I have good news!*

But he'd stopped Connie because... *was* it good news? No matter who the sperm donor was, Jazz had still been raised by William Cornelius Dent, which was bad no matter what. And would it really be any better to know that Billy wasn't your dad... but that he'd been there for the conception, gun in hand? Howie shivered at the thought and nearly threw up on the steering wheel.

After settling his stomach and his nerves, he drove back to the Dent house. Gramma was running around in her underwear as Samantha chased her with a housedress, begging her to put some clothes on. Howie averted his eyes. Not out of propriety but just to avoid wrinkled old-person flesh. Guh-ross.

Upstairs, he used Jazz's computer to check his e-mail. As promised, Connie had sent over a picture of the birth certificate. Howie printed it, folded it, and tucked it in his pocket, then went downstairs to help Sam wrangle Jazz's grandmother.

Something in Sam's presence brought out the child in Gramma, which made her a little easier than usual to handle, though Howie still found it beyond perturbing to see a septuagenarian running around the house, giggling, her hair tied up in pigtails, occasionally trying to pinch him. (His arms bore welts and bruises from where she'd managed to succeed.)

"Can I show you something?" he asked Sam, who was in the process of getting Gramma settled onto the sofa with what looked like a big photo album.

"Jazz warned me about you, Howie. Told me how to handle you. I'm *not* falling for that old trick," Sam said. "I don't want to hear your zipper if I say yes."

"That's a little obvious for me," Howie sniffed. "I love you for your mind, anyway."

Sam was partly bent over Gramma as she paged through the album, her rear sticking out in a very fetching way. She fixed Howie with an eyebrow-raised glance over her shoulder and straightened up, annoyed. "Really? Stop staring at my mind, then, kid."

"Right." He produced the birth certificate and flapped it in the air. "But I really do have something to show you."

"Can you be a good girl and look at pictures for a little while?" Sam asked her mother, who gasped and pointed at a picture.

"Handsome man!" she crooned. "Handsome daddy!"

It was a picture of Billy's father.

"Right. Handsome daddy." A shudder seemed to run through Sam at the photo of her own father. "You see if you can find all the pictures of Daddy."

"You're my favorite sister," Gramma said, and hugged Sam with a strength possessed only by the crazy.

"And you're mine." Sam disengaged herself and joined Howie in the kitchen, positioning herself, he noticed, so that she could keep an eye on Gramma through the doorway. "What have you got?"

Howie handed over the birth certificate. He explained how and where Connie had found it.

Sam scanned it quickly. "You think it's Billy leading her around?" Her voice dipped when she spoke the name, and her eyes flicked to her mother. "Why would he want her to find this?"

"I don't know. But did you notice the space for father is blank?"

"Yeah. Probably an oversight."

"An oversight?" Howie struggled to keep his voice down. Gramma was peacefully paging through the album. No point getting her riled. "The guy who got away with killing over a hundred people didn't make an oversight. There's a reason it's blank."

"There could be a million reasons, not just one. Maybe at

326

one point Billy might not have thought Jazz was his. He was pretty pissed when Janice got pregnant initially. I remember Mom telling me that. But he got over it. But I'm sure they had *some* reason."

"Like what?"

Sam shrugged. "I don't know. Because my brother was completely insane?"

"Was?"

"Is. You know what I mean." She crossed her arms over her chest, the birth certificate dangling from her fingers like something dead or dying. "Howie, you have to promise me that you and Connie aren't going to go poking around into this anymore. Let the cops handle it."

"We're trying to help Jazz. If it turns out he's not Billy's kid—"

"Then what? He's going to suddenly be all better? His childhood will magically disappear in a puff of smoke? Please. There's a better chance of you actually getting to first base with me."

"I already got to first base with you."

Sam tilted her head to one side. *Excuse me?* the motion said.

"I touched your butt the other day. When you were washing dishes."

"You bumped me with your hip. It doesn't count, and besides, that's not first base, anyway."

Howie sighed. "Felt like heaven."

Sam groaned and massaged her temples with her thumbs. "Look, this birth certificate doesn't mean anything at all. For all you know, it's not even legit. It could be something that Billy dummied up to mess with Jazz. Or Connie. Or you. Or just something he did to amuse himself. He's crazy, Howie. His motivations don't—"

"Sammy J!" Gramma shouted suddenly. "Sammy J!" She scampered into the kitchen, flush with excitement, the photo album huge and flapping like a giant bird in her withered hands. "Look! Look!"

Sam took the photo album from her breathless mother, who jabbed a finger at a photo. "I found a picture of *you*, Sammy! See? See?"

"Very good!" Sam said, her voice proud. "Good job!" To Howie, she said, "It actually *is* me. I'm sort of surprised."

Howie bent to look at the picture. It was a young girl— maybe four or five years old—in a dress and what looked like dirty sneakers. She was very plain—no indication at all in this picture that she would grow up to be the sexy thang Howie so lusted after. "God bless puberty, huh?" he said.

"Oh, you sweet talker," Sam drawled with sarcasm. "How *do* you keep the ladies from throwing their naked bodies at you?"

"Usually I just keeping talking," Howie admitted.

"Anyway, yeah, I was a late bloomer," Sam said, turning another page. More middling photos of an awkward prepubescent Sam. "Didn't really get much better until high school. Buh—" She caught herself. "You-know-who was the good-looking one. From day one, pretty much."

As if she'd conjured it, the next page had a photo of a

younger Gramma, tired but smiling, holding a baby. Howie knew without asking or being told who that baby was.

For what was probably the first time in his life, Howie did not say what immediately came to his mind. Which was: *Dude. The Antichrist as a baby...*

CHAPTER 37

Morales drove Jazz back to the hotel. The next set of suspects would be coming in soon enough, and things were now doubly crazy due to the new body. A long night stretched ahead of all of them, so Morales was going to sneak a quick nap in the precinct break room. Jazz just wanted some peace and quiet so that he could think.

If he hadn't known better, he would swear that someone was trying to keep him from thinking. Someone was trying to prevent him from putting together the pieces.

Pieces. Literally, of course. There were body parts in great profusion, some of them taken, some of them not. But if Hat-Dog was a puzzle to be put together, he seemed to use pieces from different boxes, as though he'd opened a bunch of jigsaws and then taken whatever pieces he wanted from them whether they matched or not. It was so chaotic that it almost seemed like it had to be deliberate.

Then again...why couldn't that be possible?

He wrote *UGLY J* on a sheet of paper and circled it, then

circled it again. Ugly J was at the center of it all. It sounded like a serial killer's moniker, but no one had heard of such a person. Could this be Billy's new identity? The Impressionist had said that Ugly J was beautiful, which jibed—the Impressionist worshipped Billy, after all, and would see a free, murdering Billy Dent as something beautiful to behold.

But if Billy *was* Ugly J—which made the most sense—then what was his connection to Hat-Dog? Jazz could believe his father had planned far enough in advance to set up the Impressionist before going to jail, but to do so twice? To set up a second serial killer, this one in the biggest, most complicated city in the country? Somewhere Billy had—so far as Jazz knew—never visited even once?

No. That didn't track.

So that meant that either Billy hadn't set up Hat-Dog...

Or that Billy wasn't Ugly J.

Neither possibility made much sense. Neither possibility was any more or less comforting than the other.

Jazz reached for one of the photos. It was a close-up of one of the carvings, a hat knifed into a woman's shoulder. He had his theory about the hats and dogs—*bitches and gentlemen*, he remembered saying—and maybe that was so, but...

He was alternating for a while there. And then...

Jazz consulted the list of victims. Yes. As he remembered: two hats in a row. And then, later, two more hats in a row. No one knew why. The cops had had a theory at one point that had to do with the weather, but it wasn't a terribly good one, and ultimately it didn't pan out.

This is the key, Jazz thought. *This is where the pattern breaks down. Those are crucial. That's where we'll find this guy. What happened there? Why two hats in a row?*

And what about Belsamo? He didn't fit the profile. Other than his age and race, he was a complete mismatch. And yet he had coincidentally showed up to confess right when Hat-Dog decided to dump his latest victim four blocks away?

Right. Jazz could almost hear Howie's voice: *That's a coincidence the same way I'm the starting forward for the Pistons.*

Two of them, Jazz realized. Two of them working together. That's what it was.

But the cops already eliminated that idea. Every scrap of DNA they found—Hat or Dog—matches. It's one guy.

He thought of how Belsamo had refused the water. How he had not touched anything in the interrogation room.

Maybe the profile was wrong. Maybe Belsamo was as good an actor as Jazz, as good an actor as Billy. All of that cawing and cackling...a ruse, to make them think he couldn't possibly be the killer. Coming in voluntarily to distract the cops while someone else dumped a body in their backyard...

He called Hughes. "Hey, what happened to Belsamo?"

"Your little buddy?" Hughes started laughing. "Guy who liked to wave his dingus around?"

"Yeah, him."

"Man," Hughes said, gasping for breath, "as long as I live, I will never, ever forget the look on your face when he whipped that little Johnson of his out and—"

"I didn't know they made them that small," Jazz deadpanned.

332

Hughes exploded into deeper laughter, and it took a minute or two for both of them to settle down.

"So what happened to him?" Jazz asked.

"What do you mean? We cut him loose. You saw."

"Yeah, but did you ever get that DNA sample from him?"

"No. Of course not. You were there; we were still waiting for the court order. Even the feds can't make a court order appear in the time it took for that body to show up at Baltic and Henry. Well," he considered, "maybe for a Homeland Security thing they could. But a run-of-the-mill homegrown serial killer? Nah."

Jazz thought. "What about the interrogation room? Did he leave DNA anywhere?"

"Jasper..."

"He was masturbating. Remember? Did he finish?"

Hughes made a gagging sound. "I am grateful to report: no. No one had to clean up his grungy spooge. I guess once *you* left the room, he couldn't keep it up anymore, kid."

"Ho, ho, ho. How about hairs?"

A sustained, groaning sigh from the other end of the line. "Do you have any idea how many people were in and out of that room all day? I'm sure there are plenty of hairs in there. Which ones belong to your boyfriend, though, I can't say."

"So we have nothing?"

"We *need* nothing. He's not the guy."

They hung up, and Jazz stared at the wall until his eyes lost focus. Hughes could be sure. Jazz wasn't.

What we need, Jazz decided, *is a DNA sample from that guy.*

Connie paced the length and breadth of her bedroom, thinking. Juggling, more like. She had so many things up in the air right now, so many balls to track....And some of them, she was afraid, would turn out to be grenades.

She had worried—briefly—that Whiz might rat her out to her parents, but figured she could rely on Mutually Assured Destruction on that front. If Whiz ratted her out, she could tell her parents to change the parental lock on the satellite box, and Whiz knew it. Done and done.

If only all of her dilemmas had such simple, hands-off resolutions.

Just call him. Just call Jazz....

No. She couldn't do that. This wasn't the sort of news you delivered over the phone: *Your father might not be your father after all....*Uh-uh. She had to do it in person. Look him in the eye. Hold his hands. Show him the birth certificate and be there for him....

Checking the Internet, she assumed he was busy with Hat-Dog in New York, even though there was no mention of him on any of the websites. The task force was definitely keeping his involvement a secret. And the local Lobo's Nod news had nothing, of course. Not even a mention of Hat-Dog at all. This, she realized, was how guys like Billy got away with it. Most serial killers were local. They only made national news when they did something stupid, like forsaking their "jeopardy surfaces" for new territory. In Billy's case, he just kept changing methods and signatures as he changed geographic areas. No one was watching the news in—for example—Tennessee *and* in Utah, so no one made the connections. Until it was too late.

Hat-Dog was killing people in New York. No one in Lobo's Nod cared. Why should they?

They would care if they knew there was a connection to Billy. But there's no hard proof of that yet.

Yet being the operative word.

Connie knew that Billy was involved somehow. The *Ugly J* graffito and acrostic on the Impressionist's letter just couldn't be a coincidence. She refused to believe that. That meant there was a connection—however tenuous—between Billy and the Hat-Dog killer. Connie was even willing to bet that it was Billy who had—somehow—invited Jazz to "the game," whatever that meant. And she was sure he was the one who'd guided her to the old Dent house and its strange buried treasure. Who else could have done that? Who else *would* have done that? Who else would even know there was something there in the first place?

Her cell rang and she grabbed it. Howie was supposed to call her if he learned anything new from Sam, but when she answered, she realized immediately that it wasn't Howie.

"You broke the rules, Connie," said a voice she didn't recognize, and not because it wasn't familiar to her. She didn't recognize it because it had been filtered and Auto-Tuned to the point that it sounded both musical and robotic at the same time.

"Who is this?" she asked, not expecting an answer, and not surprised when she didn't get one.

"You broke the rules," the voice said again, sounding vaguely disappointed in its flat way. "And the rules weren't complicated. I said no police. You called the police. So simple. I thought you were smarter than that."

Connie's mind raced. She *hadn't* called the police. But someone else *had*. The guy with the baseball bat. But how on earth could her caller know that? It had just happened, like, an hour ago. Maybe ninety minutes. How...

"I didn't call the police," she said. "It wasn't me. It was a neighbor. It was—"

"Do you really expect me to believe you?" the voice asked. "Do you expect me to *trust* you? You would say anything, wouldn't you?"

If the voice knew about the police...that meant the person had to be local, right? Someone who would be aware of happenings in Lobo's Nod.

Or just someone who has a line to the Lobo's Nod police band. Or...

She flipped up the lid of her laptop and searched *BILLY DENT PROPERTY* and the day's date. Sure enough, a squib popped up on the Lobo's Nod Web version of the police blotter that the cops had been called to Billy Dent's old haunt. Attributed to Doug Weathers, of course. That weasel probably lived with a police scanner glued to one ear, just on the off chance Billy Dent's old address popped up on a broadcast.

And now it was online. Anyone in the world could know.

She expected her caller ID to say UNKNOWN NUMBER, but it didn't. She quickly jotted the number down on a piece of paper, as though it might vanish from her phone. "I'm sorry, Mr. Dent," she said. "But it really wasn't me. I can't help it that your old neighbor got agitated when he saw me and called nine-one-one."

The voice laughed. The sound was metallic and headache-inducing with all the audio processing. "You think I'm Billy Dent? Now, why would you think that?"

"Who else could you be?" She felt dizzy and sat down on her bed. Jazz's warning about letting a man like Billy into her head spun over and over in her mind. She had to be careful. Billy held all the cards, including his own identity. He could get her confused very easily. She took a stab in the dark: "Or maybe you're Ugly J."

Another laugh, this one longer and more sustained. "I like you, Connie," the voice said. "I've liked you since the first time I saw you. A few months ago. In *The Crucible*."

Connie shivered and goose bumps broke out along her arms and neck. Oh, God. In *The Crucible*. Weeks after Billy had broken out of Wammaket...In the audience? In the friggin' *audience* and no one noticed?

"I thought you were wonderful as Tituba, Connie. I stood in the back and watched you. And Jasper. Watched both of you. Fine actors. I think you may have a career in show business ahead of you, Connie. Assuming you live, of course."

"Threaten me all you like—"

"Don't show me a bravery you don't really feel, Connie," the voice warned. "It doesn't impress me. I appreciate honesty more than bravado. And I'm not threatening you. I haven't threatened you so far, have I?"

Connie waited and then realized the question wasn't rhetorical—the voice was waiting for an answer.

"No. You haven't."

"Exactly. And I'm still not threatening you. Let me tell you who I *am* threatening, though."

At that instant, Connie's phone trilled with its text message alert. She automatically pulled the phone away from her ear, just in time to catch an incoming picture.

It was Jazz.

In New York.

She knew it was New York because he was wearing that Mets cap he'd bought at the airport as a partial disguise, and because she recognized the edge of Hughes's sleeve at one side of the photo. It had been taken in New York. Recently.

Close enough to take that picture. Her throat stopped working. *Close enough for that picture means close enough... oh, God. If he can get that close without being noticed or seen...*

She put the phone back to her ear, tried to speak. Nothing came out.

"Your boyfriend will suffer for your insolence and your lying, if I so choose."

"No," Connie tried to say. A rasp. She tried again. "No. He's not even here. He's not even involved. It's not fair to—"

"I think I've been very fair with you," the voice went on. "Sent you clues to that which you seek. Complimented your acting—and I was being sincere, by the way."

Had she been wrong? Was this *not* Billy Dent after all? Would Billy threaten Jazz like that? And if he did, just to frighten her...He would never actually carry through on such a threat....

Would he?

She didn't think so.

But then again...maybe it wasn't Billy Dent.

The cadence of the voice...the vocabulary...things that Auto-Tune couldn't hide. She'd seen Jazz's Billy impression. She'd heard Howie recount the man's monologues. She'd even seen the few rare TV clips of him speaking. And this didn't...

Oh, God.

"Did it bother you, playing a slave, Connie? Did it stir something inside? Resentment? Anger? Racial memories you'd thought long buried?"

The voice, processed into neutrality, didn't sound sly or conniving, but the words did the trick. Connie struggled against it. She would not let herself be dragged into a psychological quicksand pit by a psychopath. She would do this on her terms.

"It was just a role," she said carefully. "That's all."

"But surely a part of you wondered if you only got the role because you were the only black female actor at the school. Didn't you wonder that? What if you'd not been interested? What would that pretty little drama teacher have done?"

At the mention of Ms. Davis, Connie's breath caught and her heart leapt forward a beat. Tears sprang to her eyes and she rubbed them away furiously. *No. I'm not going to be manipulated.*

"I wouldn't know," she replied, keeping her voice steady.

"I would tell you to ask Ms. Davis, but she's slightly dead." Her gut clenched as she said it; it was like pissing on Ginny's grave. But this game was too serious not to use all of her available ammunition.

The voice chuckled—it sounded like a rubber ball bouncing in a giant tin can. "Trying to keep up with me, Connie? Trying to keep me out of your head?"

"Just being proactive."

"Ever think maybe that's what I wanted in the first place?"

Great. Now Connie didn't know *what* to do.

"People are dying, Connie, and they will continue to die, while you try to play games with me. While you try to keep me out of your head, a place I've already been to. Trust me— you have no secrets from me."

I don't believe you. I can't. "Oh?"

"People keep dying and all you care about is yourself. Oh, you claim you care about your boyfriend, but really you just worry about him because he's *yours*. No other reason. You're selfish, Connie. You're an actress, after all, and they are a vain, self-centered lot.

"Let me ask you this, though, while I have you on the phone: Do you ever wonder why they always focus on the pretty *white* girls, Connie? The ones that go missing, I mean. The ones who get killed or maimed or raped or—on a good day—all three. When *black* girls go missing no one seems to care, do they? If I made you disappear—and I'm not saying I would, though I could—no one would notice."

"People would notice," Connie said through gritted teeth, and then slapped her forehead. Damn it! She was doing *exactly* what he wanted her to do! She was buying into the argument. Accepting the premise. Joining the debate.

"You'd like to think so, I'm sure. Oh, your parents and friends would notice, but no one else. It wouldn't be a national story. It would make the news in your little town, but even then they would give up reporting on it after a couple of days. They'd devote ten or fifteen seconds to it on the local news the day your raped and mutilated body was found in a shallow grave near the intersection of Grove Street and Route Twenty-seven. You know the spot, Connie?"

She didn't answer. Didn't need to.

"Ten or fifteen seconds. A picture of you from the yearbook. A cutaway to your mother weeping hysterically, and all the white folks watching shrug and wait for weather and sports. But when a white girl goes missing...oh, then they go nuts, Connie. They update you every chance they get. The cable channels get involved and it goes national. People talk about the poor pretty girl who's gone missing. They gather at work and at school and they post blogs and they go on message boards. They name *laws* after them. They give you AMBER Alerts in their honor. And when those poor lily-white girls show up dead, they spend more than ten or fifteen seconds on them. They show you the home videos. They show the parents. The friends. They take you right to the memorial service. Why is that, do you think?"

"Because this is a racist society that devalues black lives," Connie said with heat, then immediately bit her lower lip. Damn it! How many times had Jazz told her that you never let a psycho into your head? You never expose a weakness or an irritation or a rage. They live in your heads forever after that.

341

"Racism!" the voice chortled in triumph. "Racism! Of course! That must be it! Why, that's the only possible explanation! But, Connie...what if it isn't racism? What if it's just true that your life is genuinely worth less than a white girl's? What would you say to that?"

In a tone of frosty neutrality, she responded, "I would say that you definitely have the most up-to-date version of the White Supremacist Jackass app on your phone. Good for you."

A long, sustained burst of tinny, artificial laughter. "I like you so much, Connie. I really do. You give me hope for the future."

"Glad to help. Now why don't you tell me exactly where you are and who you are?"

"Heh. That wouldn't be any fun. We're playing a game, Connie. You agreed to the rules."

"I don't even know what the rules are."

"Well...basically, the rules to *this* game are whatever I decide they are. This isn't like the game being played in Brooklyn. This is *our* game, Connie. A game for you and me. Something special, just for us."

"I'm touched and honored," Connie said sardonically. "When do I get to make my next move?"

"Oh, soon. Very soon. But it'll be a little tougher on you, Connie, because you broke the rules."

"I told you, I didn't call the—"

"There must be a *penalty* for people who cheat," the voice went on, "for people who don't abide by the rules, wouldn't you agree?"

The droning, toneless roboticism of the voice was beginning to grate, sawing through her brain and generating a massive headache in its wake. "Stop playing around and tell me who you are," she said. "As if I didn't already know." A bluff. Maybe it would...

"Oh, I'll tell you. In my own way. In my own time. The first clue is in that lockbox." The voice paused for a moment. "I'm going to give you five minutes, Connie. Five minutes to find the clue and then I'll call you back. If you don't have the clue, you'll never hear from me again.

"Well...until the night I come for you, that is."

"Wait!" Connie shouted. "Wait! Five minutes? That's not fair. I can't—"

"Not *fair*?" The voice's aggravation and anger broke through the Auto-Tuning. "Fair? You broke the rules, Conscience Hall! And now you suffer the consequences! Five minutes, beginning...now."

Click.

Oh. Crap.

Connie rooted through the box. Baby pictures of Jazz with his parents...the birth certificate...was that the clue? That it was Billy? Or maybe the clue was that little crow toy...which could still be Billy, really. She shivered, remembering the creepy Crow King fairy tale.

Or maybe it was something else. Something related. What was the word *crow* in Latin? In Spanish? In French? She had taken classes in all three languages and struggled to remember, then thought, *What if it's not a crow? What if it's a raven? And what if the clue is in Russian or German? What if the damn toy isn't the clue in the first place?*

Her clock had advanced a minute. *You're kidding me.* Her heart thudded so hard in her chest that she would not have been surprised if she could have seen it throbbing through her shirt.

Less than four minutes left. The desire to speed through the contents of the box was great, but she forced herself to scrutinize each item. Same three people in each photo:

Jazz. *No. Not him. Duh.*

Mom. *Dead. Not her. Double-duh.*

Billy. *Obvious choice.* Too obvious, in fact, now that she thought about it. Billy's escape from Wammaket had been planned and coordinated and abetted by someone on the outside. So her mystery Auto-Tuned voice would be someone helping Billy. Someone on his side of the game board. Hat-Dog?

Now who's cheating, jerk wad?

Staring at the photos... Maybe someone was in a background....

Or maybe it's the person who took *the pictures....*

That was most likely Jazz's grandmother. Even though the racial nonsense her caller had spewed would have been right at home in Gramma Dent's mouth, Connie couldn't imagine her having the sense or stability to make that call.

So what was the clue? None of the photos were illuminating. She switched over to the toy. Just a chunk of plastic.

It's hollow.

Is there something inside it?

Can I get it open?

Need a knife.

Kitchen.

Time?

*Damn it. Who knows what this lunatic is going to do in...
ugh...two minutes if you don't have the special clue?*

Or was the clue the crow itself? Raven. Whichever. Maybe
that's all she had to do when the phone rang, was say,
"Crow!"

Too easy. She couldn't believe it was that easy. Or maybe
the voice just *wanted* her to think it was too easy....

Once you let them into your head...

"Don't go chasing..."

Nothing else left. Nothing except the envelopes. She
wasted a futile thirty seconds peering into them, looking for
something stuck or written there.

Was the *arrangement* of the items in the lockbox important? No, that was crazy—the contents would have moved
when it was unearthed. You couldn't rely on any particular
order once it was buried.

Less than a minute to go.

She stared at the lockbox, now not even seeing it, not even
looking for anything because it was pointless, the seconds
counting down, and she would never get it and just as her
phone rang, she saw it.

She *saw* it.

Oh, thank God. Thank God she left the lid open.

Another ring. She took in a deep breath, steadied herself
so that she would sound calm, then hit Answer.

"Bell," she said before the voice could speak.

An infinity of silence passed, and Connie was certain that

she'd screwed up, that the small image of a bell she'd spotted carved into the inner lid of the lockbox was really nothing more than a trick of the light, a shadow cast by the latch or...

"Very good, Connie," the voice said. She thought she detected some surprise through the Auto-Tuning, but couldn't be sure.

"Time for you to return to New York," it went on. "You'll want to fly into JFK if you can. The second clue to my identity is there, at terminal four, Arrivals, on the first floor. Bring cash."

"What do you—" But the voice was gone, the line as dead as Billy Dent's victims.

Time for you to return to New York...

A quick Internet check found a single seat on a flight bound for JFK the next afternoon. A center seat, of course, right smack in the middle of the plane to guarantee the worst possible experience. And booking at the last minute like this would suction the last of her babysitting and summer job money right out of her bank account, but what choice did she have?

None. This was for Jazz.

Besides, paying for the ticket would be the easy part. Connie stared at the closed door to her bedroom, imagining her parents beyond it. Oh, yeah, this was gonna be pleasant....

CHAPTER 38

According to the police file—a copy of which Jazz had of course been given (being an official task-force member was a nice change of pace)—Belsamo lived in a place called Fort Greene. On the cell phone map, it seemed close enough to Carroll Gardens. Clueless as to the subway, Jazz decided to walk it and ended up hopelessly turned around and lost on the stupid Brooklyn streets. His cell phone's maps only loaded sporadically and he couldn't get any sort of bearing. Most people were bundled against the cold and rushing along and he couldn't bring himself to stop one of them for directions. Doing so would probably involve tackling, given how they moved.

He finally managed to get to Fort Greene. The neighborhood itself seemed nice enough, but Belsamo's building was tucked deep into the darkest end of an alley strewn with trash and debris. Jazz idly checked the walls for the Ugly J graffito, but didn't see it.

The wind picked up. The sun was going down. Jazz turned

up the collar on his coat, tugged his cap down around the tops of his ears, and slipped on thin but warm leather gloves.

There was a surprisingly strong lock on the door to Belsamo's building. Ten buzzers lined up in two ranks of five. Belsamo was apartment 4A. When Jazz buzzed, nothing happened.

Good. He's not in.

The next part—getting into the building—would be easy. Billy had done it dozens of times.

Y'see, most people are lazy. And stupid. Best of all, they like t'think they're all good people, nice and helpful people.

Jazz started pressing buttons. On the third buzz, someone responded.

"UPS," Jazz said, making himself sound both bored and annoyed at the same time. "Got somethin' for Three-C, but no one—"

He didn't even get to finish the spiel; whoever lived in apartment 2B hit a button and the front door buzzed and unlocked. Jazz slipped into the vestibule.

The entryway was cramped and gray. A sickly yellow bulb gave off enough light for him to see down a short hallway to two doors, as well as up to a landing. Jazz smelled fried onions, strong and persistent.

He made his way up the stairs, moving quickly, but not *too* quickly. If someone saw him, he didn't want to appear to be in a guilty hurry.

The door to 4A was disappointingly plain. Jazz wasn't so naive as to hope for a sign reading SERIAL KILLER WITHIN! or

WELCOME TO THE GAME, JASPER! but he'd thought maybe there would be *some* indication....

It was locked. Not a problem. Billy had been teaching Jazz how to force locks, jimmy doors, and shim with credit cards since he could walk. A New York City apartment building didn't phase Jazz in the slightest. Even if Belsamo had a chain, there were ways around that. A deadbolt or a police bar would be a real challenge, though....

Despite the jog up four flights of stairs and the illegality of what he was in the process of doing, Jazz found his breath coming easily, his heart thudding along with reliable, dull predictability. With his stiff, laminated high school ID, he managed to trip the lock on the third try, not even needing to resort to the collection of hairpins and wires he'd brought with him.

He took a deep breath and stepped into Belsamo's apartment, closing the door quietly behind him.

As soon as he entered, he knew.

He *knew*.

He couldn't explain it. If called to testify in court (and he was miserably certain that would happen), he would be able to say nothing beyond, "I just knew. I felt it in my bones." Comically and pathetically psychic.

Belsamo was Hat-Dog, though. Jazz knew that now. He felt the same undercurrent of *wrong* he'd felt toward the end of his father's days of freedom. Old memories assaulted him—the teeth in Billy's nightstand drawer; the knife in the sink; Rusty's last, dying whimpers as Billy skinned him alive.

Jazz put out a hand and braced himself against a wall for a moment. He didn't believe in ghosts or demons or other supernatural, superstitious nonsense. Billy had been a hard-headed rationalist, a man who believed only in what he could see and touch and hurt. But in that moment, Jazz wondered if everything he believed and everything he disbelieved should perhaps be reversed. Maybe evil *wasn't* a chemical trigger in the brain and a jacked-up childhood. Maybe evil was, after all, something vaporous and mystical that could move from place to place on its own....

Stop being an idiot. Stop it. This is just a reaction to figuring it out. To knowing the truth.

Jazz suddenly wished Connie were there with him. Or Howie. He just didn't want to be alone in this place.

It was the neatness, he decided. For one thing, it lay in stark contrast to the filthy, unkempt near-beggar he'd seen at the precinct. "Slob Oliver" was a put-on, a sham, designed to distract the cops. This apartment...this was the real Oliver Belsamo: The to-a-pin precise placement of everything. The way a decorative mirror on the wall hung perfectly perpendicular to the floor, as if regularly straightened with a level. Such neatness had been Billy's mania, too, and even though Belsamo's tiny studio was a fraction the size of the house Jazz had grown up in, the place vibrated and shimmered with the same crazy energy, as if possessed by the spirit of the departed Dent house.

But it went beyond the neatness. The place was neat, yes, but also cramped. Too organized. Preternaturally organized, almost. Piles of magazines, their spines exactingly lined up with one another, set so that the colors of the spines ran from darkest to lightest. Books placed in precise order of height and thickness, a staircase of pages. Every bit of wall space was claimed with either shelves or piles of reading material or that freakishly perfect mirror, which Jazz avoided gazing into, lest something be in there. Something like horror in his eyes. Or his own monstrous reaction to Belsamo's lair.

Oliver Belsamo had clearly kept every scrap of paper and every piece of reading material he'd ever owned. And had it organized according to some system that had welled up from deep within.

That makes him a hoarder, not a serial killer.

Jazz had bought a small, cheap flashlight at a convenience store near his hotel, and now he played its beam around the apartment. The apartment was a studio; the only door led to a tiny bathroom that Jazz couldn't believe was actually usable. In order to get to the toilet, he had to squeeze through a gap of mere inches between the sink and the shower. It was impossible to turn around at the sink at all.

Still wearing his leather gloves, he opened the medicine cabinet and pawed around with impunity. Nothing. Belsamo used Crest toothpaste. *As far as I know*, Howie would have joked, *that's not one of the diagnostic criteria of sociopathy.*

He abandoned the bathroom. There was a tiny stove with a half-height fridge in a little nook that could not be called a kitchen by any reasonable standard. Jazz realized Belsamo must have to wash his dishes in the bathroom sink.

He opened the fridge, half expecting to see a collection of penises and intestines, and perhaps an eyeball or two. But no. Just a container of yogurt, some celery, and a pack of energy drinks.

One step up from hobo at the precinct, but in real life... other than the energy drinks, he seemed to eat healthily.

He keeps everything. But what about the trophies? Where does this packrat keep his favorite cheese? Where are they?

Jazz examined the neatly made bed. Nothing out of order. The bookcases were crammed with mostly nonfiction—true crime. That didn't necessarily mean anything. Lots of people read true crime. He skimmed the collection anyway. No books about Billy. That did seem a bit odd. Wouldn't a *real* true-crime aficionado have at least one book about the twenty-first century's greatest living boogeyman?

Maybe. Maybe not.

An end table had a neat stack of mail on it. Bills. Jazz glanced through them. One wasn't for Belsamo. The address was right, but the name was different. What kind of man didn't throw away missent mail like that?

Jazz was beginning to regret coming here. He figured he should just go back into the bathroom and see if he could find a hair to bring back for the cops to compare to the DNA found at the various Hat-Dog scenes. Maybe he'd been wrong about Belsamo. Maybe his logic was wrong. His intuition was wrong. And that magical, superstitious buzz he'd felt on entering the apartment—maybe that was wrong, too.

But he decided to check one last place, dropping to his belly to skim the flashlight's beam under the bed. He didn't know what he expected to find, but it wasn't what was there: a laptop. Old and boxy.

He hauled it out from under the bed and opened it. There was only one folder on the desktop.

It was named *Game.*

Jazz swallowed hard. He tried to open the folder, but it asked for a password and he had no idea whatsoever.

WELCOME TO THE GAME, JASPER.

The laptop wasn't connected to the Internet, but Jazz looked at the browser history anyway. He found a bunch of links to what appeared to be S&M porn sites, but without an Internet connection, he couldn't check to be sure. He was sort of glad for that.

S&M porn wasn't Jazz's particular kink, but it didn't necessarily mean anything. Plenty of people were into that sort of thing, and the overwhelming majority of them didn't rape, kill, and gut innocent victims.

There was nothing else of interest on the laptop.

Game.

Not *Games.* You might expect someone to have a folder on their computer labeled *Games.* Solitaire and video poker and Angry Birds and that stupid minesweeper game Howie loved to play.

But "Game"? Singular?

Game *doesn't just mean something you play,* Jazz realized. Game *also means something you* hunt.

Was he looking at a folder containing information on the Hat-Dog victims? Profiles, dossiers, lists...clippings from websites about the murders? Cyber-trophies for an Internet-age madman?

But where does he keep the real *trophies? The body parts he took? Where does he keep his killing gear? Weapons? Rope? Tape? Knives?*

Suddenly, Jazz focused beyond the secure folder, noticing for the first time Belsamo's desktop pattern.

It was a crystal-clear photo of a black bird. Some sort of crow or raven.

He remembered the noise Belsamo had made in the interrogation room. Some sort of cawing sound. Just like a crow...

What is going on *here?* A chill ran up both of Jazz's arms and rippled across his shoulders for a split second. He imagined his Yosemite Sam tat shivering. A crow. The Crow King...the story...oh—

The ring of a phone made Jazz jump. Had he not silenced his phone before sneaking in here? What an idiotic—

No. The sound was coming from a corner of the bookcase. Jazz scrambled over and noticed three identical cell phones there. One of them was ringing, and Jazz snatched it up and opened it before thinking it through.

Before he could say anything, a voice said, "Nine. Five and four. Nine." A chuckle. "Looks like you'll be staying close to home again, eh?"

Jazz couldn't swallow. Couldn't breathe. He knew the voice.

It was his father.

CHAPTER 39

Jazz struggled for words—for *thoughts*—unable to filter either. He had suspected, on some level, that Billy was involved with Hat-Dog, but now to have confirmation...

"Did you hear me?" Billy said, voice now stern and icy. "I said nine. If I don't hear a response, you're going to help me redefine misery."

A response. What kind of response could Billy possibly want? Every second—every millisecond—that Jazz hesitated, his father was gathering information, processing it. Jazz had to act. Quickly.

"I understand," he said. There had to be more. "Nine is confirmed," he went on, fighting to disguise his voice. He was pretty good at this—he had a decent range of voices to fall back on, none of them related to any specific person, but all of them different from his own. Right now, he was going for as close to Belsamo as he had in his repertoire, a sort of grim yet uncertain bass. He usually used it on the assistant principal at school when he needed to get out of a class.

And now…what? Hang up? Jazz waited, just in case his father had something else to say.

Dead air for a moment. And then just a heartbeat too long. Jazz realized he should have hung up.

Belsamo would have known exactly what to say. And how to say it. Just my luck he leaves his phones home when Billy decides to call. What are the odds?

The same odds, he figured, as any other mistake a serial killer would make.

"Nine is confirmed?" Billy asked in slightly perturbed amusement. " 'Nine is confirmed,' eh?"

If he hung up now, Billy would know something was wrong, would know that it wasn't Belsamo who'd answered. Jazz had no choice—he had to try to keep Billy on the line, keep him talking. Learn whatever he could.

"Nine," Jazz repeated. *What would Billy want*—"Thank you," he said.

"Well, now," Billy said, "that's mighty kind of you to say! You're quite welcome." A beat. "Jasper."

Busted.

"I was wonderin' when I'd be hearing from you, son! Are you enjoying New York? It's a hell of a town, isn't it? I should have come here years ago."

So much for disguising his voice. Jazz shot a panicked glance at the door. Belsamo could come back at any moment. Stay here and gab with Billy? Or run?

While he tried to decide, he said, "New York's not bad. So, I know why *I* came. What brings you to the Big Apple? Just playing some kind of game with the Hat-Dog Killer?"

Billy laughed. "Oh, hell, Jasper. You like firing off words at me, thinkin' one of 'em'll get some kinda reaction, don't you? Anyhow—I didn't come to New York for Hat-Dog. I came to New York for...well, I came here looking for someone special." Now Billy sounded almost wistful. "And fortunately, I found what I was lookin' for."

Someone special. Who was Billy's latest prospect?

"But speakin' of someone special," Billy went on, "I been meaning to talk to you about your little lady friend."

"I don't know what you're talking about."

"Oh, sure you do! You think the Impressionist was runnin' around Lobo's Nod all that time, spying on you, without stuff getting back to me? You got jungle fever, Jasper! You got yourself some dark meat!" He sounded highly amused. Almost giddy.

Jazz gritted his teeth. Billy knew. About Connie. The thought terrified him more than anything else had in his life. It frightened him more than the power he knew he possessed. "I don't know what you're talking about," he lied, amazed that he could keep a tremble out of his voice.

"Oh, yes, you do. Oh, yes, you surely do, young man!" Billy sounded like a parody of a lecturing schoolmarm for a moment. "You know precisely what I'm talking about. That girlfriend of yours."

Jazz glanced around wildly, as though Billy were spying on him right now. He had to leave. Now. He made for the door and slipped out into the hallway. "What do you mean? What girlfriend?"

Now Billy's voice turned stern. "Don't go lying to me, boy.

You ain't so big and so old that I can't whup you with my belt like my old man done to me. Or maybe I'll just cut off one of your girlfriend's fingers for you. Sort of like old times, you know?"

"Stop it." He was outside by now, back in the alley. Belsamo was nowhere to be found.

"I gotta admit, after the last time I saw you, I was curious about your love life, son. The way you went to all that trouble to misdirect me and mislead me when I asked about your—whatchacallem?—romantic prospects...I never thought you'd be with a colored girl."

"No call for that kind of language," Jazz said, his jaw tightening. He spun around suddenly. He was back on the main street now—What was it called? Where was the sign?—and darkness had fallen. The sidewalk was thick with pedestrians. Baby carriages. Dogs on leashes. Jazz couldn't help thinking that Billy was watching him. But there were a dozen buildings within visual range. All those rooftops...more than a hundred windows...

"I don't mean nothin' by it, Jasper. You know that. I'm just from a, you know, a different generation. I was raised by a woman who didn't have no appreciation for, well, for *diversity*, let's say."

"I know. I'm the one who's been taking care of her since you got yourself locked up."

"And I surely appreciate it. Just like I appreciate the, well, the poetic justice of you dating a black girl. Given that I never killed no black girls. Is it okay to say 'black girl,' Jasper? Or does that offend your sensibilities? Is it 'African

American girl' instead? 'Girlfriend of color'? So many things to keep track of, and I'm such a busy guy to begin with. Things slip through the cracks."

"Say what you need to say."

"I just think it's pretty damn ticklish. I don't suppose… Oh, Jasper," he gasped, as though something had just now occurred to him, "you didn't go and put love in that poor girl's heart just 'cause I ain't never killed no one looked like her, did you?" When Jazz said nothing, Billy roared with laughter. Jazz could picture his father's head thrown back as he howled. "Did you think that magical black skin, that kinky hair, those big brown eyes were gonna save your soul? Did you think somehow being with her would stop you from turnin' into me?"

"Don't be ridiculous." Jazz used his very best annoyed voice.

"You did!" Billy wasn't buying it. Of course not. "You *thought* that. Oh, Jasper. Oh, my boy, my son. Thought I raised you smarter than that. Thought a lot of things, I guess. So tell me, Jasper—what's it like, being with a black girl? She go all ghetto in bed with you? What's it like down there? Never had the pleasure myself, you know."

"Don't have anything to compare it to," Jazz told him as officiously as possible. Trying to put Billy off balance. Shake him.

Impossible. Billy just laughed again, was all. "That what you think? You go on thinking that. Go on livin' in denial."

"I got your message," Jazz said. " 'Welcome to the game.' What was that about?"

359

"Don't recall sending you a message," Billy said, and as he did so, it finally occurred to Jazz that he should be contacting Hughes. He fumbled his own cell phone out of his pocket.

"You sent that message, didn't you? The one welcoming me. You used the Hat-Dog Killer to get in touch with me. How long have you been in New York?" Stabbing in the dark, blind, but not deaf.

Something was wrong with his cell. It wasn't working.

"Long enough, son. Long enough." Wistful. A man on a diet, watching the pile of fries delivered to the next table over.

"And you're controlling Belsamo, is that it?"

"Is that his name?" Billy asked. "I suppose you've already got him all trussed up for the bastard cops."

"No. He wasn't home." *Oh, damn! Why did I tell him that?*

He expected one of Billy's low, gruesome chuckles, but instead there was nothing. And then: "I see." Icy.

Jazz pondered that even as he realized why the phone wasn't working—that cop had turned it off during the interrogations and Jazz had forgotten to turn it back on. While he waited for it to boot up, he said, "You were expecting him—" And then stopped. The cell phones. Disposables. Of course Billy hadn't known *Jazz* would answer; he'd expected *Belsamo* to answer....

He spun around and ran back to Belsamo's building. A man was leaving just as he arrived, and Jazz slipped in past him and charged up the stairs.

"You're breathin' all heavy," Billy said. "Forget something back in that apartment you illegally entered? Been there. I empathize."

Jazz hadn't locked the door when he left Belsamo's, so he had no problem getting back in. He made a beeline for the end table, the one with the mail on it. He hoped what he was looking for would be there. ‚ ‚ ‚

It was.

He couldn't believe it. It *was*.

"Kinda quiet there, Jasper," Billy needled. "You findin' what you need there?"

Jazz stared at the envelope in his hands. The one with the wrong name. "C. D. Williams." A mash-up and switcharound of Billy's own name, William Cornelius Dent. It wasn't a misdirected piece of mail or something for a previous resident. It was an alias.

The return address said it was from something called U-STORE-IT-ALL.

I was wondering where his trophies were. Not enough room here. And we might come here. So he stored them somewhere else. That's where he is now.

"He's not here," Jazz said. "We spooked him today. At the precinct. So he went to visit his trophies, didn't he? It calms him, I bet. Always worked for you."

"We? You still thinkin' you're on *their* side, Jasper? Not enough to catch that poor jackass thought he was me? Now you gotta come here and catch this other guy?"

"That's the game, isn't it?" He caught Belsamo's laptop

out of the corner of his eye, still open on the floor. He closed it with his foot and nudged it back under the bed. He contemplated tucking the envelope into his pocket, but realized someone as OCD as Belsamo would notice it missing. He snapped a quick picture of it with his phone, which had booted up by now.

Then, just out of curiosity, he squeezed the envelope, just enough to get the plastic window to lift away from the contents so that he could get a peek inside. All he saw was another line of text: *Re: Unit 83F.*

Good to know.

"That's the game," he said again to his father. "You put another serial killer in play and goad me into catching him. You must have been pissed when the cops jumped the gun and brought me onto the court before you were ready. Were you really running all of this from prison? You never answered any of your so-called fan mail, so how did you do it?"

Billy chuckled. "You know what I love most about you, boy?" he asked as Jazz once again left Belsamo's apartment. Jazz started a text to Hughes: *I have billy on phone!!!!!* and included the names of the street signs he finally spied across the way. "I'll tell you. It's this: You're so goddamned smart, but even so, you're only about half as smart as you think you are."

"So educate me." He watched the blue meter on the screen fill—slowly—as his text crawled through the ether to Hughes. He realized now that Belsamo would probably notice the missing disposable phone, but he wasn't about to surrender this line of communication with Billy.

"It's a game, but not the kind you think. There's no court. And it's not about you. Not at all."

"Sure it is. I know all about Hat-Dog now." Time for another knife lunge in the dark, bluffing: "I know about Ugly J."

At that, Billy burst into raucous laughter. It wasn't Billy's usual laughter, the fake crap he used to catch people off guard. No, Jazz detected genuine amusement. Billy was laughing involuntarily because he thought something was truly funny.

"Glad to amuse you," Jazz told him. His phone buzzed in his hand. From Hughes: *WTF??? On my way.*

"Oh, Jasper. You have no idea. About Ugly J. But I'm impressed you got far enough that you know the name."

"I know more than the name," Jazz lied. Fast. Smooth. Sure. Best lie he'd ever told. Hell, *he* believed it.

"You don't. Because if you knew anything about Ugly J, trust me—you wouldn't be on this call with me. You'd be curled up in a corner somewhere. Or you'd be sitting in a dark room with a knife and some pretty little girlie's toes piled up next to you while she begged you not to cut anything else off."

"You talk big, Billy, but I'm still working with the cops."

"Not for long. You'll come around. You'll see how the crow flies."

Just then, a bright light exploded around Jazz; his heart

flopped madly in his chest, a strangling fish desperate for water. Billy had found him.

No. Not Billy. Headlights. Hughes, behind the wheel of an unmarked car. Jazz gestured frantically at him.

"What about crows?" Jazz asked. "Why is Belsamo obsessed with them?"

"He's not," Billy said, sounding hurt for the first time. "Don't you remember the story I used to tell you? About the Crow King?"

The Crow King...the dove...

"Of course. *That's* what this is all about?" Maybe Dear Old Dad was crazier than Jazz had imagined. "You've got this guy all twisted up over that old fairy tale?"

"Not a fairy tale," Billy said angrily. Lecturing. "And not a fable. Those are magical BS. I told you folklore, Jasper. I told you *myth*."

"And this myth is supposed to mean what, exactly?"

"If you ain't figured that out yet, well...well, then maybe my parenting was a little subpar. I'll take that. But maybe, just maybe, Jasper, you're out of your depth here. Ever consider that? Think maybe you're in over your head?"

Hughes had gotten out of the car and was rushing toward Jazz. Jazz froze, his attention split between Hughes and his father's voice. He needed to keep Billy talking until...until... he wasn't sure. Somehow he had imagined Hughes would know what to do when he got here.

"Into the car!" Hughes stage-whispered, gesticulating with wild, overblown motions. Playing the biggest, worst game of charades ever.

"I think we're done for now," Billy said.

"No!" Jazz said, headed for the car. Right. Get in the car. Get to the cops. Maybe they could trace—

"We're done," Billy said. "But keep this phone, Jasper. We'll talk again. Soon."

"Billy!" Jazz shouted even as Hughes flung open the passenger door.

But it was too late. His father was gone.

CHAPTER 40

For some period of time Jazz couldn't determine, the two of them sat in the car as it idled along the sidewalk. Jazz had gone numb, and he didn't know why.

Ever consider that? Think maybe you're in over your head?

You're the one in over your head, Dear Old Dad. You're the one I'm closing in on.

But he knew it wasn't true. Not even remotely. He hadn't *really* been close to catching Billy just now. The disposable cell phone he'd swiped from Belsamo's was disposable for a reason: so that it could be tossed and never traced. Billy would have one just like it, and the instant he hung up on Jazz, he'd probably tossed it into the...the...

"What's the name of that river again?" he asked Hughes, his voice somewhat subdued.

"Which river?" Hughes asked.

"The one we drove over. To get to Manhattan."

"The East River."

Jazz nodded. He could easily imagine Billy's disposable cell phone sinking into the East River, bound for the Atlantic Ocean and its endless anonymity.

"You kept him on the phone as long as you could," Hughes said, soothing, proving that if the cop thing didn't pan out, he could always fall back on being a phony psychic. "We probably couldn't have traced the call. Maybe gotten a ping off a cell tower, but Billy's smart—he would have been long gone by the time we—"

"He said for me to hold on to this phone," Jazz said. "Said we'd talk again."

Hughes pursed his lips and nodded. "Okay, then. We'll take it to the TARU kids. They can clone it so that the next time he calls, you can talk to him and they can be tracking him at the same time. We'll get him, Jasper. He's playing with the big boys now. The NYPD doesn't mess around."

Jazz snorted laughter, then stopped himself immediately. He didn't mean to sound disrespectful, but this was *Billy* they were talking about. Billy didn't mess around, either. Billy had gotten the local and state police forces of sixteen separate states, to say nothing of the FBI itself, all tangled up in knots. A career that spanned more than two decades. The NYPD could not "mess around" all it wanted.

This was *Billy Dent.*

The snort hadn't gone unnoticed.

"We have every terrorist in the world gunning for this city ever since Nine-Eleven," Hughes said coldly. "You want to know how many of them have succeeded? I'll give you a hint: It starts with Z and ends with a fucking zero, that's how many. Your dad is just another terrorist with a string of hits behind him and an NYPD badge ready to take him out in front of him. Bank on it, Jasper. Bank on it."

For a moment, Jazz believed him. It was quite possibly the best moment of his life.

And then reality set in.

Billy was reality and reality was Billy, the two intertwined into an interlocked set of chains that wrapped around Jazz and sent out steely tendrils to anyone and anything close to him.

"So how'd he get the phone to you?" Hughes asked. "And what are you doing over here all by yourself? Lucky no one recognized you."

Jazz gulped. He had no choice—he had to tell Hughes the truth.

As he told Hughes everything—*everything*—the detective's eyes grew wider, his expression more and more incredulous. Every time Jazz thought he'd told Hughes the worst possible thing about the evening, he would get to the next part of the story—*So then I went through his mail, oh, and here's a photo of the envelope*—and the cop's face would assume an even more tortured aspect.

"Oh, sweet Christ," Hughes said, visibly ill. "I can't even tell you how many laws you broke."

"I think nine," Jazz said helpfully, hoping to get Hughes to crack a grin.

No such luck. "More like a dozen. To start. What *possessed* you to— No, no, never mind. Don't tell me. Don't tell me...."

"Now we have an alias for him. C. D. Williams. We have confirmation that he's tied to Billy."

"We have jack. You broke—"

"I'm not a cop," Jazz pointed out. "You can use everything I found in there. There's no prosecutorial conflict. No violation of his Fourth Amendment rights. Go ahead and arrest me for breaking and entering and whatever else I did when I went in there. I poked at his mail and took a burner phone. Probably not even fifty bucks' worth. I'll plead guilty. It's my first offense—I bet I walk or get probation. In the meantime, you can use the evidence against Belsamo."

"Are you some kind of special idiot they grow down South?" Hughes erupted. "Do they fry you up with grits and whatever the hell else they deep-fry down there? No judge worth his robe is gonna let Billy Dent's kid walk on a first offense, no matter *what* that offense is. No prosecutor who likes his job—and believe me, Jasper, they *love* their jobs— would let you plead out to anything but the top count on the indictment. You *will* go to jail. That's a guarantee."

Jazz began to protest, but Hughes cut him off with a threatening gesture. "Beyond that," the detective went on, "is the fact that you've been working with the NYPD and the task force in an official capacity. Approved by Montgomery and everything. Any defense attorney in the world, even the most overworked public defender in the friggin' *Bronx*, could convince the deafest, dumbest judge in the city that you needed a search warrant to go into that apartment. None of this evidence is admissible. It's useless. It's worse than useless because it's also going to get you arrested and thrown in jail, where you won't be able to help us nail this guy and where you'll get raped and shived to death five minutes after you hit gen-pop."

"They wouldn't put me in with the general population," Jazz said with some confidence.

Hughes glared at him wearily. "Then you get stuck in solitary like your old man. That sound good to you?"

Jazz forced a grin. "Well, *he* broke out...."

Hughes slammed the steering wheel with his fist. "Don't joke about that! People *died* when your dad got out!"

"I know that!" Jazz screamed back at him, and even though he had sworn to himself that he would never break in front of anyone, that he would never show weakness, he couldn't help himself. It was as though he'd been lugging a net full of boulders for weeks in stoic silence and could bear it—and them—no longer. "You think I don't know that? You think I don't know everything that weighs on my conscience? Those guards are dead because of me! And Helen Myerson and Ginny Davis and Irene Heller are dead because I didn't figure out who the Impressionist was quickly enough. And all the people Billy killed from the time I was around ten— when I could have reported him or killed him myself—those forty-seven people are dead because of me. And Melissa Hoover," he remembered. "You can add her to my tally, too, Hughes! And let's put my mom on the list, too, because I should have been able to save her. So you add that up. Go ahead. It's more than fifty people on my list. I'm like Speck and Bundy and Dahmer combined. I'm one of the greatest murderers in U.S. history!" He kicked at the dashboard in frustration, in rage, leaving a broad scuff.

You're a killer. You just ain't killed no one yet.

Billy was right. He was right all along. Billy was always right.

I am Ugly J.

"You gonna cry now?" Hughes asked, somewhat softly

Was Hughes poking at him again? Trying to prod a reaction out of him? Or was he actually concerned?

Didn't matter. Jazz struggled to regain control of his emotions, grappling with them like a greased wrestler until he'd subdued them. Like always.

"That wasn't for show," he said evenly, "but I could. Do you want me to?"

Hughes sighed and stared out through the windshield. "No. I guess not." He started the engine. "Damn it, Jasper. Look at this spot you've put me in."

"You risked things to bring me here. This is—"

"This is different." Hughes pulled away from the curb and they headed north. "That was a calculated risk on my part. Low risk, high reward. No laws broken. And it was *my* decision. You understand that, Jasper? It was *my* decision. I made it. You forced this one on me."

"I'm sorry." It was an automatic reaction. Programmed. When people were upset with you, you apologized. It usually worked.

"I know you are." Hughes shrugged. "I *guess* you are. In any event, this is between us for now. You don't tell your girlfriend or your grandmother, even. You sure as hell don't tell anyone on the task force. Got it?"

"Got it."

"I'll take you to the hotel. You're not coming in tomorrow. I'll sling a line of bull at Montgomery and Morales. In the meantime, I'll figure out a way to get some unis to sit on Belsamo without raising suspicions."

"So you believe me?"

"What choice do I have? Unfortunately, now I have to do this the hard way. E-mail that picture to me. Now. I'll see what I can find out about the storage place."

Jazz remained silent as Hughes turned east and then south, piloting them back to the hotel. "Thanks," he said when the detective pulled up to the hotel.

"Don't thank me for this," Hughes said, and drove away.

CHAPTER 41

Early the next morning, Connie packed a duffel bag and went to her parents; she didn't even give them time to speak before saying, "This is how it's going to be...." She had spent the night trying to think of ways to trick or cajole them into letting her return to New York, but in the end decided that a blitz attack was best, so she just walked into the family room and announced that she was headed back to New York.

"Oh?" Her father's voice and expression both teetered on a precipice between amusement and anger. "You're going to tell *us* how it's going to be?" He sat back in his chair and folded his arms across his chest. If he could have snorted a burst of fire, he would have. "This should be interesting."

"It's not really interesting at all," she said. "It just *is*. I'm seventeen—"

"You live under my roof," Dad interrupted. "And you—"

"Let her finish," Mom said quietly.

"Are you on her side?" Dad turned to Mom. "What's going on here?"

"There's no 'her side' here, honey. We're a family. There's one side—our side—and we share it."

"I'm seventeen," Connie pressed, "and in a few months, I'll be an adult. Like, officially. But I've always been responsible. I've always been good. My grades have always been excellent, and I've never been in trouble."

"Until—"

"Until recently, I know," Connie said, jumping in before her dad could go off on a rant. "And that should tell you something. If I went all this time without doing something wrong, doesn't it tell you that I must have had a good reason?"

"You're our child, Conscience." He was mellower than she'd expected. Maybe he thought she could be reasoned out of this, rather than bludgeoned with parental wrath. Under normal circumstances, he might have been right. But Connie was convinced that this was a matter of life or death, if not for Jazz, then certainly for more innocents in New York. "Until you're eighteen, it's our job to take care of you. And we take that pretty seriously. When it comes to this boy"— she hated how he avoided saying Jazz's name—"you don't always think clearly."

Mom picked at the edge of her sleeve. "Honey, this isn't about whether or not you get to spend time with your boyfriend—"

"I know."

"—it's about the fact there are dangerous people—"

"There is a *serial killer* loose in New York," her father interrupted. "And your boyfriend is directly tied into, caught up in it all. How on *earth* can you think of getting yourself wrapped up in that? And what in the world makes you think we would be okay with you doing that?"

"There was a serial killer right here in the Nod," Connie said quietly. "Jazz was involved in that, too. And it worked out fine."

"Connie!" Mom exploded, her veneer of reserve finally breaking down. "Just because you survived this once doesn't mean you should go *looking* for trouble! That's like drinking and driving over and over just because you didn't kill yourself the first time!"

"People are dying," her dad added. "More than a dozen of them. You want to stand in the middle of that? Really?"

She thought of the lockbox. She thought of those quiet, tense moments when she and Howie had sneaked through the Dent house, looking for Jazz. A dead cop in a cruiser out in the driveway. Howie cradling the useless shotgun, as if it could help. Silent for the first time since she'd met him. Both of them knowing that it was entirely possible Jazz was already dead at the hands of the Impressionist.

And then, kicking down the bedroom door...Her boyfriend, bloodied but alive...The rush of her own blood and adrenaline as they got the drop on the man who'd killed Ginny Davis...

"I hear you, Daddy. I get it. But you can't look after me forever. In a few months, I'll be eighteen. What's going to change in those few months? I'm already the person I'll be at eighteen. The calendar just hasn't caught up yet." She took a deep breath. "I need to go back to New York. I need to do it now," she said in a rush, before her parents could interrupt. But she needn't have worried. They said nothing. Her mother stared down at her hands, and her father simply shook his head worriedly.

"And I'm going to go," Connie went on. "I'm going to go. The only way you can stop me is physically. That's just a fact. And I know you won't lay a hand on me, Daddy." Her father said nothing; his face remained impassive, but his eyes told the tale—he could not bring himself to harm his child, even if he thought it would save her. "So the only way you can stop me is if you call the police and have them stop me at the airport or on my way. And you can do that. I know you can. But you have to understand something: If you do, then I'll know that you love me and want to protect me, but that you don't trust me. And if you don't trust me now, if you don't trust me after seventeen years of being a good daughter, then that means that you've never really trusted me." She took a deep breath. "And *that* means you never will."

"Connie..." Mom wrung her hands.

"Let me finish, Mom. If you won't ever trust me, then that means I'm done. You can have the cops drag me back from the airport and you can keep me locked up in the house, but once I graduate, I'll move out and you won't see me anymore. Not because I don't love you—I do—but because I can't be around people who don't trust me. I'll put myself through college. Somehow. Or maybe move to New York or LA and try to get into acting. I don't know. But I won't be here and I won't come back." She hefted her bag. "It's your decision."

Her father stood, and Connie was once again reminded just how massive a man he was—solid and tall and broad through the chest and shoulders. He looked like a construction worker, not a lawyer, thanks to a strict exercise regimen he'd followed since his years playing football in college. "You're not leaving," he said.

"I am. This isn't a bluff, Daddy."

"I'm sure it isn't. I'm sure you believe it right now, as you're saying it, but you'll never go through with it. If you walk through that door, my first call is to the police. And you can threaten all you want, but we both know that you'll eventually realize I'm right."

"I love you both," Connie said, and a tear surprised her. "Tell Whiz I love him, too." She knew that if she sought out her brother in his room, she would break down completely, and she couldn't afford to do that. It might be the last time she would see him, but she couldn't put herself through that, couldn't let what might be his last memory of her be one of weeping and sorrow.

She turned and walked to the front door.

"Do *not* walk through that door, Conscience!"

Connie thought she heard her mother say, "Let her go, Jerry," but she couldn't be sure. She closed the door behind her. Howie waited in the driveway, the engine of his car idling.

"Let's do this," she said to him as she climbed in.

"We gonna be dodging Johnny Law? Gonna have five-oh on our asses?"

"Just drive."

CHAPTER 42

And
  of course
  a shoulder and trailing a line of
  (yes)
  cool heat
  (yes)
  a groan
  whose?
  He opens his mouth
  (yes, like that)
  and licks
And

Jazz woke the next morning, his mind muzzy, his emotions hacked and split into pieces. Groggy, he peered blearily at the clock on the bedside table. According to it, he actually had slept for hours. But with the dream arousing and terrifying him in alternating, equal measure, he felt as though he hadn't slept at all. He must have dreamed that he'd lain awake all night, searching for wisdom and insight in the blank white hotel ceiling.

Despite mentioning TARU, Hughes had—perhaps intentionally, perhaps not—neglected to take the disposable cell phone, so Jazz had put it on the bedside table, just in case Billy decided to call back. The phone's caller ID listed a phone number, but when Jazz called it, he only got an anonymous, robotic outgoing voice mail message. Billy had probably already tossed that phone and moved on to another one.

He thought of calling Connie. But his dream still pounded at the doors of his conscious mind, only slightly unreal in these moments of waking.

He felt poisonous.

Slick and grimy with some contagion.

To speak to Connie now would be to pollute her with the thoughts spinning in his head. Would be to lie to her and not tell her about Belsamo and what he'd done. He couldn't abide the thought of lying to Connie. Not to her.

He could have called Aunt Samantha or Howie, but he didn't want to speak to anyone. Not now. All of his focus, all of his attention, was now devoted to recalling the conversation he'd had with Billy.

Jazz's memory was good. Not eidetic like Billy's, but better than most people's. And recalling the things Billy said was sort of a specialty of his. Dear Old Dad had trained his son to lean extra-heavy on the fatherly wisdom he imparted.

Fine. You designed me to be your tape recorder. I'll use that against you, you bastard.

The problem wasn't remembering every line in the twisted play of Butcher Billy's life. The difficulty lay in figuring out which words mattered and which ones were just verbal chaff, noisemakers designed to distract attention and lead Jazz into the corners of Billy's maze where the walls closed in.

The crows... There's something there. Something real. Belsamo was into crows. Billy mentioned them. And, yeah, I remember that old story he told me. I just recited it to Connie the other day.

Billy had been adamant that the story of the Crow King wasn't a fairy tale. He'd called it folklore. Myth. The differences were crucial. Billy sounded like an inbred redneck, but his IQ was in the stratosphere and he wielded words as precisely as he wielded knives and cleavers and hammers.

Fairy tales and fables were stories for children. They involved magic. They weren't real.

Myths and folklore, though... they weren't precisely real, but they were designed to explain something that *was* real. They represented something about the real world. The origin of something.

The Crow King... what did the Crow King represent?

And then Jazz sat up straight in bed. Another chunk of knowledge had just dropped into his brain. More accurately, it had bobbed to the surface of the ocean of his memories, like a body that has broken free of its concrete shoes.

The Impressionist. In his cell in Lobo's Nod. He'd said something to Jazz....

Jasper Dent. Princeling of Murder. Heir to the Croaking.

Not "the Croaking." *Damn it, Jazz! Did you really think he was that crazy? What's wrong with you? You missed the connection right there!*

The Impressionist had been talking about the Crow King. Heir to the Crow King.

So... Billy was the Crow King, then. The one who bled the robins until they were dove-white. What the hell was *that* supposed to mean?

More important... how far back did this craziness stretch? How long had Billy been putting things in motion? The Impressionist knew about the significance of crows. So did Belsamo. Which meant that the lunacy went back at least to before Billy's arrest and imprisonment. All those years Billy traveled for murder... was he also evangelizing his particular brand of lunacy? If so, how many protégés did he have out there? How many madmen had he programmed to follow in his footsteps?

And if he was able to program them as adults, what chance does his son have?

Jazz had been aware for years now that people existed out there in what he thought of as the "real world" (the world *not* of Lobo's Nod or of his grandmother's house and deepening senility) who admired Billy, who thought he was a patsy for someone else's murders, who believed he'd been framed. And people who saw in him a strength they lacked and didn't care that that strength had been turned toward murder.

But he'd never imagined that any of these sad, damaged people would turn out to be killers themselves. Since when do groupies become rock stars? Maybe they end up as roadies, sure. Maybe even an opening act or a one-hit wonder.

But for a groupie to become the main attraction...?

It chilled Jazz.

He thought—fantasized, perhaps—that he had plumbed the depths of Dear Old Dad's sociopathy by dint of growing up in Billy Dent's house. Now he had to face the frightening possibility that the Dent insanity bored a deeper hole in the core of one's psyche than he'd ever imagined.

Where does it end? he wondered. Every pit, no matter how deep, had a bottom.

Where was the bottom to Billy's madness?

Jazz had to know.

How many of them are out there? The Impressionist and Hat-Dog...that's two. Is Ugly J a third? How many did he train? How much time did he have?

The story of the Crow King went all the way back to Jazz's childhood. Had this all started then? Was it somehow connected to his recurring nightmares—the death, the sex? Or was the story of the Crow King just something that Billy had made up back then on a whim and was now exploiting for his own amusement?

But then something occurred to Jazz. A nugget of information nudged from the rough walls of his memory:

No one held my hand and taught me how to play.

Billy had said that. When Jazz visited him at Wammaket a few months ago. Jazz had been trying to manipulate Billy and had asked...had asked for help with something relating to the Impressionist. Billy had scoffed.

Dear Old Dad wasn't interested in teaching. So then what *was* he doing with Hat-Dog?

Jazz rolled over in bed in frustration. He needed to *talk* about this. It was no good to ricochet ideas in the spaces of his mind—he needed feedback. The task force was forbidden to him now, through his own actions. So he did the only thing that made sense.

"Lobo's Nod Sheriff's Department," Lana said a moment later. "How may I direct your call?"

"Sheriff Tanner, please," Jazz said.

"Just a...Jasper? Is that you?"

Jazz groaned inwardly. Leave it to Lana to recognize his voice. Her ability to obsess over a man, combined with her inability to weed out the bad boys, would probably get her killed someday.

"Yeah, it's me. Can I talk to G. William?"

"Sure. So, how's it going in New York?" she asked, almost giddy.

"It's great, Lana," Jazz said enthusiastically. "I've seen the Statue of Liberty, and I'm also tracking a guy who takes people's eyes, cuts off their dicks, and—on two occasions—leaves their guts in a KFC bucket. It's awesome."

A normal person would have quickly transferred the call. "Oh. Okay. Um, when do you come back to the Nod? Kinda quiet around here without you."

"Lana. G. William. Please?"

The line went silent for a moment and then G. William's booming drawl: "Haven't even had my coffee yet. It's damn indecent to call a man before his coffee."

Jazz checked the bedside clock again. "I knew I could count on you to be in this early."

"Old habits. NYPD got you out of bed this early, too?"

Jazz bit his lip. He couldn't go into his extra-legal activities with G. William. "Well, I'm working hard, that's for sure," he said amiably. "But I wanted to run something by you."

"Shoot."

"It's about the Impressionist."

"Speaking of whom...he's back to being mute. And all patched up after you last saw him."

"How nice for him. Remember when we were trying to find him and we were talking about him?"

"Which time?"

"Most of them. I've been going over it in my head and I keep thinking how we talked a lot about him playing us."

"He wasn't playing *us*. He was playing *at* being Billy."

Jazz grunted. True. "But I keep thinking now...it's almost like it was a sort of game to him, wasn't it?" He was falling from a window, grabbing for ledges as they zipped by, trying for some connection between the Impressionist and Hat-Dog.

"You're not making any sense, Jazz. What game? He wasn't really cluing us in like some of these guys do. Yeah, he guided us to some of the bodies and he taunted you, but the only rules he followed were the ones your dad laid down years ago. And Billy himself pointed out to you how the guy didn't even follow *them* very well. Hell, if he was playing a game, it was...like solitaire, I guess. He was playing a game he could only play by himself."

Jazz shot out of bed. "That's it!" he shouted, loud enough

that someone on the other side of the wall pounded on it for quiet.

"What's it?"

"Oh, man, I gotta go, G. William. And thanks," he said hurriedly, and hung up before the sheriff could say anything more.

He flung himself to the room's desk, where his copies of the Hat-Dog files lay scattered. He pawed through them, organizing them, riffling through the papers to confirm the details he needed.

It all came together. It was beginning to make an insidious sense.

Just as he'd been saying all along, it made perfect sense to a crazy person. And now Jazz believed he'd found a way to make it make sense to someone rational.

He glanced at the clock again. He'd been working for three hours without even realizing it. He needed one more thing to confirm his suspicions, then probably another couple of hours of work before he could tie it up nice and neat and take it to the task force.

A toy store. That's what he needed—a toy store. There had to be one nearby. After all, a random walk on the street revealed legions of baby carriages everywhere he went.

He picked up his phone to call 411 for the nearest toy store and stared at its screen for a moment, cogs and gears clicking in his imagination. It was a smartphone, right? Its various icons shined up at him. He'd used maybe two of them since getting the phone.

Howie. He would call Howie.

CHAPTER 43

With a half hour still to go to the airport, Howie finally stopped checking the rearview mirror for the flashing lights and sirens of Lobo's Nod's finest.

"I think they believed me," Connie said quietly.

"Would you really cut them off if they narced on you?"

"I don't know."

She had been quiet the whole way, arms folded over her chest, staring moodily out the window. He was trying to think of something very stupid and very funny to say—his usual tactic—when his phone buzzed in his pocket. Since his mom worried about her baby boy talking on the phone while driving, she'd installed a really kick-ass hands-free system in his car roughly ten seconds after he'd bought it, so at the same moment, a pleasant and very sexy robotic voice said, "Phone call. Jazz Matazz." Howie had put Jazz into his contacts list that way because he liked the way the speakerphone said "Jazzmatazz."

Connie perked up in the passenger seat for the first time

since they'd left her house. "Whatever you do—" she started, but Howie had already hit Answer.

"Jazz Matazz!" he cried out.

"Does that dumb thing still call me that?"

"Of course not. I was just funning with you."

"What are you up to?"

Next to him, Connie shook her head wildly and cut her hands back and forth in the universal "No!" gesture.

"I'm driving Connie to the airport."

"What?"

"Jesus, Howie!" Connie exploded.

"Connie," Jazz said from the speakerphone, "where are you headed? Back here?"

"Yeah," she said, glaring at Howie.

"Don't."

"Well, I need to—"

When Jazz spoke again, it was in a voice so cold and so commanding that for a moment Howie thought maybe Billy Dent had grabbed the phone at the other end. "Do *not* come to New York. This isn't something we're talking about. Just turn around and go home. Howie, I need your help with something."

Howie risked a look over at Connie, whose eyes had grown wide with fury, her lips pressed together as if to keep from breathing out flames.

"Um...sure, man, but you should know—"

"I don't know how to download apps on my phone," Jazz said with peculiar urgency.

Howie laughed nervously. "Is that really an issue right now?"

"I need a specific one. I'm pretty sure it exists. Can you walk me through it?"

"Jazz, this is kinda—" To his right, Connie was now back in arms-over-chest mode, glaring through the window.

"Please!" from the speaker.

"Fine, fine. What do you need?"

He told him. Completely confused, Howie nonetheless explained how to locate and download the app in question.

"Thanks," Jazz said. "You're gonna turn around and go home now, right? I'm counting on you. And Connie? Con?"

Howie studied her grim posture. "Now's not a real good time, buddy. From the looks of things, you won't be getting laid for a long, long time."

"Con, I know you can hear me. I get that you're pissed. But I'm in the middle of some crazy stuff here, and at least knowing that you're safe keeps me going. All right? I love you."

There was silence on the line as he waited for her to say it back. When she said nothing, the line went dead.

"You could have talked to him," Howie said after a few minutes.

"Did you hear that voice he used with me?" she asked. "He went all Billy on me. I won't tolerate that."

Howie signaled and shifted lanes.

"What are you doing?" Connie demanded. "Are you getting off the highway?"

"Well...yeah. You heard him. I'm gonna turn around and—"

"You're doing no such thing."

"But—"

"A butt is something I'm gonna kick if you keep this up," Connie said. "He doesn't know what's going on here. I'm going to track down this mystery person and help him whether he wants it or not."

Howie watched an exit ramp go by. He could always turn at the next one....

Oh, who was he kidding?

"At least call him. Tell him what's going on."

"When he's like this? When he's all crazy like this? No way." She jabbed a finger at him and he flinched even though she didn't actually touch him. "And *you* don't call him, either. Once I'm on that plane, he can't stop me. No one can. And if he knows I'm on it, he'll freak out and get all distracted, and with everything that's going on, being distracted could get him killed."

"Fine. Fine." The next exit, it turned out, was for the airport. Howie guided the car down the ramp. "But are you sure about this? It could be dangerous." Even as he said it, Howie felt idiotic. A mysterious voice was seducing Connie into traveling to New York. Manipulating her. Of *course* it was dangerous. Either Billy Dent or someone like him was at the other end of that phone call. "Maybe you should just let the cops handle this."

"What, the NYPD? They have their hands full already with the Hat-Dog Killer. This is personal. I'll go to New York. Find this clue at JFK, then get to Jazz. Show him what we've got, what we know. In the meantime, just to be safe and cover all the bases..." She twisted around in the car seat and retrieved the lockbox from the backseat. "I want you to wait until my flight is off the ground and then take this to the sheriff."

"Got it. Will do. Sammy J and I will hold down the fort here in the Nod," Howie promised.

Out of the corner of his eye, he caught Connie turning to stare at him. "What?" he asked defensively. He knew that look—it was Connie's Guilt Glare, usually employed when he said or did something stupid or offensive or both. "What did I do?"

"What did you just say?" she asked, her tone insistent, with an undercurrent of panic.

"I said I'll hold down the fort with Sam. We be keepin' it one hundred, dawg. We'll keep Gramma cool; we'll check in with G. William to see if the cops learn anything else from that lockbox; we'll—"

"No. Exactly. What did you say *exactly*?" Before he could recall his exact words, she filled him in: "You said 'Sammy J and I.' Sammy J."

"Right. It's just a nickname." Howie signaled and pulled off the highway onto the access road that led to the airport. "It's what they called her when she was a kid."

"And doesn't Sammy J sound like someone else we know?"

Traffic was light, so Howie risked taking his eyes off the road. Connie strained against her shoulder belt, leaning toward him intensely, staring as if she could burn the answer into him with her eyes. "What are you talking about?" he asked. "Why are you all freaked out all of a sudden? It's just a nickname."

"Sammy J. *J*," she said, emphasizing the last letter.

The connection clicked. "Jesus, Connie. You think Sammy J is Ugly J? Just because they share an initial? That's crazy."

"I'll tell you what's crazy: Auto-Tuning your voice if there's no reason to. Billy wouldn't do it because I already know who he is. The only reason for someone else to disguise it—"

"Is if you know the voice already," Howie interrupted. "But you've never met Sam "

"Or to disguise your gender," Connie told him. "And yeah, I've never met her, but I *might*. As long as she's in town, staying at Jazz's, the odds are I *would* meet her. And hear her voice."

"That's nuts," Howie said in a tone that wasn't convincing even to him.

"Who's new to town who I haven't met yet, but probably will at some point? Who's the only person in this whole mess who would have a reason to disguise her voice from me?"

"You're assuming a lot. I mean, Mr. Auto-Tune—"

"Or Ms. Auto-Tune."

"—could be anyone. I mean, maybe he—or she," he amended quickly, "is just worried that you're recording your conversations. Or just doesn't want you to be able to identify him or her by voice someday. Or..."

"You can keep throwing 'or' out there as much as you want, but face it—the most likely scenario is that it's someone known to me. Or to us. Maybe that's not one hundred percent guaranteed, but come on, Howie."

Howie hated to admit it, but she had a point. And all he could think of, suddenly, was the photo album Gramma had showed him. The pictures of Sam as a little girl. *I was a late bloomer....*

"We know Billy had a confederate out there," Connie went on. "Someone who coordinated his escape from Wammaket. Someone who was in contact with the Impressionist. What if it was his sister?"

Howie shook his head. "No. I don't buy it."

"Because you want to sleep with her."

"That's beside the point. I don't buy it because Sam *hates* Billy. You should see her when he comes up. She despises that guy. Jesus, she said in public that she would pull the lever if they executed him."

"Yeah, and I just told my parents that I would never speak to them again if they called the cops on me. I sounded serious enough that they didn't."

Howie said nothing as he guided the car into the drop-off lane and stopped. "God," he said at last. "Have I been macking on a serial killer's right-hand man? Woman? Are there even... is there even such a thing?"

"I think so. Jazz mentioned one once. Some woman in England, I think. Sam could be a serial killer."

"Watch it. That's the mother of my illegitimate children you're talking about."

"Howie."

"But really—what are the odds of a brother and sister serial-killing tag team?"

"Same parents. Same genetics. Same environment. I don't know the odds, but it's not impossible."

"How do we find out? Do we just ask her?"

"Not a chance. There's got to be some way to find out without confronting her directly."

"I'll ask Gramma," Howie joked.

"Hell, what if she's involved? I was thinking that before—what if she's been faking all this Alzheimer's crap, hiding in plain sight?"

"No way, Connie. Uh-uh. You haven't been around her as much as I have. Trust me—the woman's nuts. And not in the way *you* mean. Not in like an evil mastermind–slash–Hannibal Lecter kind of way. She's completely off her rocker. Sometimes Jazz has to change her adult diaper, for God's sake. You think she's gonna go through that just to keep up a cover story?"

They sat in silent thought in the car, staring at each other until a horn honking from behind them brought them out of their reverie.

"Maybe I *should* stay here...." Connie said hesitantly, almost unwillingly.

"No. Go to New York. Figure out this bell thing. Get the other clue. This stuff is all connected. What's happening in New York is connected to what's happening here. You work the New York angle with Jazz and I'll figure out what's going on here."

"Are you sure?" She was worried, that much was obvious. Howie didn't blame her; he was worried, too. He sort of liked being alive. He also thought Sam was hot and it would really suck if she turned out to be crazy like her brother.

"Sure? No. But go." He popped her lock and the horn from behind blared again. "You better get going. And for God's sake, be careful! There's crazy-bad juju going down."

"Howie..."

"I'm serious, for once. Now go. It'll be all right. I'm not as fragile as I look."

"I know. That's the problem—you're *more* fragile."

"This is true." He leaned over impulsively and kissed her cheek. "Get out of here. You have a flight to catch."

Once she was through security, Connie had to run for her plane, boarding right before the door closed. She apologized to her row mates and slid into her middle seat.

Was she doing the right thing? She had left Howie—Howie!—completely unprotected, with Gramma, who was crazy enough for any three people, and Samantha, who quite possibly could be crazy, too. Even though he'd encouraged her to go, was it the right thing to do?

She dug into her purse. Howie was right. Time to set aside pride (no matter how righteous) and anger (ditto) and call Jazz. See what he thought. Didn't it make more sense for *him* to go to JFK, after all? Sure, it would be a distraction from the Hat-Dog Killer, but Howie was right—these cases were interconnected. It was *all* interconnected, as cables stretched from the past to the present, from Lobo's Nod to New York, entangling and binding all of them: Jazz, Billy, Sam, Howie, the Hat-Dog Killer, the Impressionist, Connie herself, the victims....She couldn't untangle the knots just yet and see where they'd come from, but she knew they were all connected.

"Miss, no electronic devices," a flight attendant said just as Connie hit the Call button under Jazz's name.

"But—"

"Off, please. Now." Said with a grim little smile that seemed to broadcast *Try me, sister.*

Connie ended the call before the first ring, then made a show of shutting down her phone. Now she had the entire flight to think about how she might have sent Howie to his death.

And how she might be voluntarily winging her way to her own.

By five that evening, Jazz's hotel room looked like an evidence locker had exploded inside a math classroom.

But he had the answer. It all worked out.

He stared at the new app on his phone, then shifted over to the sheet of paper covered with his most recent scribbles. Yeah. Yeah, it all made sense.

Crazy sense. But sense nonetheless. Somehow, it was fitting that Billy and G. William had said the things that made it all click for him.

Hughes had warned him away from the precinct, but this was too big.

He gathered up a few critical pieces of paper, double-checked his phone, then grabbed Belsamo's disposable cell before heading out the door.

CHAPTER 44

The 76th Precinct was still mobbed by press. Jazz gnawed on his bottom lip, watching from half a block away. He had no choice but to plunge right in.

For a disguise, he turned up the collar of his coat and pulled his hat down low over his forehead, then slipped on his cheap sunglasses. He pushed into the throng, eyes down, jostling reporters out of the way. Two NYPD uniforms stood at the front door, keeping it clear for civilians, and they ushered him into the precinct without realizing who he was.

Morales stood just inside the front door, leaning against the wall as she swapped a high-heeled shoe for a sturdier sneaker. She recognized Jazz as he whipped off the hat and glasses. "Feeling better?" she asked, only slightly surprised to see him.

"What? Oh, yeah. Much better." He scanned the entryway. "Got a minute?"

"Headed out," she said, putting on the other sneaker and

dropping her heels into a bag. "Field office wants a report in person, and you don't keep the field office waiting. First rule of the FBI."

"But—"

"First rule," she said again, and breezed out the door.

Jazz ground his teeth together. Should he follow her? She was the one he should convince now, because there was no way Hughes would listen—

"Dent!"

Speaking of Hughes...

Jazz grinned apologetically in Hughes's direction as the detective bulled through the lobby toward him. "Sorry! I was just leaving." Yeah, he'd go after Morales and—

"You're not going anywhere." To prove it, Hughes clamped a powerful grip on Jazz's wrist. Jazz tamped down his first reaction, to break the grip in the most painful way possible. Crippling an NYPD detective wouldn't solve this case any sooner.

"I can go," Jazz whispered. "Let me—"

"I *told* you to stay away from here." Hughes dragged Jazz unwillingly into a smallish office. "Everyone thinks you have food poisoning. And I still haven't figured out what to do about you after last night."

Jazz calculated the odds of being able to persuade Hughes that he'd figured out the Hat-Dog Killer before the pissed-off cop tossed him out of the precinct. *Hit him with something he won't expect.*

"Belsamo's on Atlantic," Jazz said, and Hughes released him

immediately. He was in control right now, whether Hughes liked it or not. "There's an Atlantic Avenue around here, right?"

If Hughes's reaction weren't so predictable, it would have been fascinating to watch as he visibly deflated, his face realigning from righteous anger to incredulous shock. "How do you *do* that?" It was as close to a whine as Jazz could imagine coming from the detective. "He's been walking up and down Atlantic Avenue all day. Not doing anything illegal. Just walking from the river to over by Flatbush, over and over. Like he's casing the whole avenue."

"Not the whole avenue," Jazz said. "He's looking for his next dump site."

It was raw, bloody meat to a starving wolf, and Hughes could do nothing but bite into it. "So it's him? He's definitely the Hat-Dog Killer?"

Jazz considered taking mercy on Hughes and just spilling it all at once. But . . . nah. Where was the fun in that?

"He's not the Hat-Dog Killer," Jazz said with authority, and watched the shock return to Hughes's face, along with a soul-crushing distress.

Jazz gave it a couple of seconds to sink in, then said, "He's the *Dog* Killer."

"There *can't* be two of them," Hughes said. "We've been through this already. We considered that months ago and had to discard it. We've got DNA from various scenes and it's all a match. It's one guy."

"You found that DNA because they *wanted* you to find it," Jazz explained. "They planted it. To make it look like one guy was doing this. This is a game and there are two players: Hat and Dog. You have Dog's DNA. So even if you catch him, Hat is still free and clear."

Jazz could imagine it perfectly, as though he'd been eaves-dropping on the phone call. It must have been a panicked call, from Dog to Billy, the games master.

"There's a problem." Dog would have done his best to cover his worry with calm and reserve. Because that was how Billy would have taught him to act.

"I don't like problems." Jazz imagined Billy saying it jovially, with a slight lilt to his voice. A dad ruffling his kid's hair after a tough Little League at bat. "Why don't you fill me in and we'll see what we can do."

"I didn't realize. Until I came home. But . . . he scratched me."

"What?"

"I have a scratch. On my hand."

"Didn't you wear gloves?"

"Yes. The scratch is high up on the hand. Over the wrist. He must have clawed down the glove. I didn't expect it. He fought like a bitch, not a man. I didn't realize until just now. . . ."

And Billy would sigh, resigned to working with amateurs. "Okay. Okay, let me think. Let me think."

"They have my DNA now."

"I know. That's not actually a problem. Evidence is only good when you have something to compare it to."

"So we make sure they never have anything to compare it to?"

And Jazz could hear the familiar chuckle emanating deep within Billy's chest, low and rumbly. "No. Are you kidding me? That's what they expect. No. We want to make sure they have something to compare it to...."

"It's a game," Jazz told Hughes. "And Billy's playing, but he's not on any one side or another. There are three players, but only two sides, you see? But there's a game on top of the game—Hat and Dog are playing each other with Billy watching them, but at the same time, Billy's playing with us. Four players. Three sides."

Hughes wiped down his face with both hands. "Jasper, our forensic people are really good. Every criminal makes a mistake, and when they do, we find them."

"Exactly! Don't you get it? That's what Billy was *counting* on. Look." He held up a sheet of paper on which he'd plotted the evidence found at the various crime scenes. "You had no DNA evidence at all until the fourth victim, the guy found at the subway station on, what was it, Pennsylvania and Liberty Avenues, right? That's when you found some blood and skin cells under the victim's fingernails."

"Right. And then we found semen at the sixth crime scene—"

"But not the fifth! That was a Hat crime. The sixth victim was Dog's first woman. Raped because he had to make it look like one guy, not two. Hat rapes and Dog doesn't, but for you guys not to catch on, they occasionally had to mimic each other. Dog raped the sixth victim and was so disgusted with himself that he had to reduce her to something less than human—that's why he disemboweled her. Then Hat had to keep it up. Every time one of them added something to the signature, the other one had to pick it up and run with it."

"That's crazy. He deliberately left evidence—"

"It's so crazy that it worked. Dog was giving DNA to Hat—hairs, semen samples—and letting him plant them so that you guys would think there was one guy, the Hat-Dog Killer, not two, Hat and Dog."

"If they're playing a game, what kind of game is it? And why would Belsamo voluntarily walk into—" He broke off at the enormity of Jazz's grin. Jazz silently lifted his cell phone and held it up to Hughes. A bright Monopoly board filled the screen.

"Jasper, no!" Hughes groaned. "Park Place...that's just a name. It's not—"

"I've got it on my phone. I bet Belsamo has it on his laptop, in the folder titled *Game*. They're playing Monopoly," Jazz insisted, now shoving another paper at Hughes. "Hat and Dog. Two of the player pieces in the game. They carve their symbol into the victims to prove they did it. First two victims, remember? Found behind some place called Connecticut Bagel. Well, both killers started at Go and rolled nines. Bang. Connecticut Avenue. Third victim, in an empty parking space. Free Parking. That's a Hat. They take turns. Fourth victim, first DNA: a rail stop on Pennsylvania Avenue. That's the Pennsylvania Railroad, man."

Hughes scanned the paper, but Jazz could tell he was

being humored, not believed. "They don't always alternate. There are two hats in a row."

"Right. He rolled doubles, so he got to go again."

Hughes uttered a single syllable of laughter, without mirth or joy. "So let me get this straight: You think your dad has got these guys playing a game of murder Monopoly, killing people or dumping them based on where they land on the Monopoly board?"

"Follow them. Each murder matches a spot on the board in some way. I did the math—every murder is reachable by a roll of the dice from the one before it... *if* you assume there's two players. Look—Park Place," Jazz said, jabbing a finger at the paper. "A murder at the Coney Island *boardwalk*."

"I told you—those are just coincidences. Do you know what apophenia is?" Hughes asked, somewhat paternally.

"Yes." Apophenia was a form of insanity that made people see patterns where there were none, or imbue meaningless patterns with great import. Like crazy conspiracy theorists. "I know what it is. But this isn't—"

"Finding these ridiculous patterns... stretching this to fit a *board game*, of all things... I'm worried about you. Maybe we pushed you too—"

"It's not apophenia if the pattern's real," Jazz protested. "Look, it's not important that it's Monopoly. It could have been anything. All that matters is that they have some kind of structure. It could have been checkers or chess, but Billy would find that too simple. Cliché. Everyone does chess, he would say." Hughes shivered, and Jazz realized that—without intending to—he had once again done his dead-on Billy impression. "This is more like...like *reverse* apophenia."

"Oh, really?" Hughes folded his arms over his chest.

"Yeah. It's not seeing a pattern where there is none—it's *hiding* a pattern where there doesn't have to be one. These guys don't need a Monopoly board to kill people. They would do it anyway. He's just making them dance."

In the face of Hughes's obvious skepticism, Jazz pressed on. "Two murders with the guts left in KFC buckets? Kentucky Avenue. Dog did one, rolling a six to get there. Later, Hat rolled a five and landed on the same spot. One of the other cops even mentioned it. You were there: The nearest KFC was a mile away. Why bring the bucket and do it twice? Hell of a lot easier than transporting the body all the way to the nearest KFC, right? They only move bodies when they have to, in order to comply with the rules of the game." Hughes said nothing, so Jazz kept going. "He left that body on the S line in Manhattan because—"

"—it's the shortest line," Hughes mumbled. "Short Line Railroad." The detective's finger skipped down the page. "Saint James...the church. Right..."

"And look at where Belsamo landed right before coming into the precinct."

Hughes skimmed the list and looked up, puzzled. "Community Chest?"

"He drew the Get out of Jail Free card." Jazz grinned triumphantly.

"But he wasn't in—"

"Right. So Billy had to *send* him in. He had to put him right in the precinct. Remember what he told you guys in the interrogation room? That if he lied he knew he would go *directly* to jail? It's right out of the game, a direct quote. Billy sent him in so that he could play the Get out of Jail Free card and keep playing the game."

Hughes took a step back, exhaling a long, shuddery breath. "Jasper, this is...this is nuts. You know that, right?" He favored Jazz with a look Jazz had by now gotten used to, a look that said, *I knew this kid would snap someday.*

"Hat left the body on the Short Line, on the S," Jazz said. "Then Dog got the Get Out of Jail Free card and came in to confess. Billy probably promised him it wouldn't last. If he'd gotten—I don't know—the beauty pageant card, he would have killed a model. But he didn't. So it was a calculated gamble on Billy's part: Belsamo could have botched his whole confession act. Or maybe you guys could have really cracked him and led us to Hat. Hell, Hat could have even been caught dumping the body at Baltic." Hughes said nothing, so Jazz kept talking. "But Billy himself was never at risk, so it was a gamble worth taking. *Especially* since it meant he got to mess with your heads. He knew we already had Dog's DNA, so if he was going to sacrifice either of his players, it would be Dog anyway. Plus, he knew Belsamo was either so unhinged or so good at playing unhinged—I don't know which yet—that he would give us nothing worthwhile. Plus, he had a secret weapon: Hat. We didn't know there were two killers. And then the dice helped Billy tremen-

404

dously. Hat rolled an eight and ended up on Baltic. So close, it was perfect."

"So he left a body at the corner of Henry and Baltic, four blocks from the precinct, to alibi Dog." Hughes thumped the wall with the flat of his palm. "Really? All of these coincidences just pile up into a plan? You want me to believe that Billy Dent, the most meticulous lunatic in history, lets a roll of the dice determine what happens next?"

"Of course he does!" Jazz exploded. "He doesn't care about these guys! It's a *game*, and they're just pieces on the board. This amuses him. He saw a way to march Belsamo right in here under our noses and then right back out again, so he took it. If Hat hadn't rolled an eight, Billy would have come up with something else. You cannot *imagine...*" He took a deep breath and started again. "You can't *begin* to imagine the contempt he holds for you guys. He respects you as a group, as a collective with resources that can stop him, but individually? You're all pathetic, stupid fumblers, groping in the dark for clues."

Hughes raised an eyebrow. "That your daddy talking or you?"

"I'm trying to help you!" Jazz couldn't believe this. He couldn't believe Hughes wasn't with him. "I've got it all worked out, right down to the next dump site! When Billy called me, he said the number nine, then five and four. So he's rolling for these guys. He rolled a five and four, which adds up to nine." He held up the cell phone Monopoly app again. "Nine spaces from Community Chest is Atlantic

Avenue, Hughes. That's where Belsamo—Dog—will leave his next victim."

"But you *talked* to him!" Hughes said. "He knows you know the number nine is next, so why wouldn't he just change it?"

"Look," Jazz said patiently, "the fact that Belsamo is casing dump sites on Atlantic Avenue tells you that he's still on the board and planning on moving to the same spot. He still rolled a nine. So, what? Billy called him back on a different phone and gave him the number."

"That doesn't make any sense. Why not change it up? To mess with us?"

"Because Billy knows I know the number nine, but he doesn't know that I know what it *means*. And he doesn't think I'll figure it out. As far as he knows, I still think Hat and Dog are the same guy. Besides, I'm getting the feeling... the way he risked sending Belsamo in here, I'm getting the feeling that Billy's getting tired of the game. He's ready for it to end, and maybe Belsamo's the loser."

"Isn't that a *good* thing?" Hughes asked. "Ending the game, I mean? When the game ends, the killing stops."

Jazz shook his head. "This is Billy. I think once the game ends, that's when the *real* trouble begins."

CHAPTER 45

Howie waited until the airline website on his smartphone told him that Connie's flight was in the air before making a beeline for the Lobo's Nod Sheriff's Office. He spent most of the drive trying not to think about two things: the implications of the blank FATHER field on Jazz's birth certificate, and whether or not Sam was just as nutso as her brother.

Man, if that's the case, then I'm totally swearing off hitting on my friends' relatives.

He pondered this at a stoplight for a moment.

Well, unless they're smoking hot.

The sheriff's office was quiet, and only one car lingered in the parking lot. Tiny town like the Nod, you didn't expect a lot of action on a weekend night, as long as guys like the Impressionist were locked up. The only reason the place was open at all was because it also served as the basic nerve center for the entire county's police force. Otherwise, it would be shut down like the rest of the Nod.

Howie sucked in a deep breath. He really hated the idea of

saundering into the office with a lockbox of evidence that had been obtained under less than entirely legal circumstances. Then again, the last time he'd been here, it had been to break and enter with Jazz. Followed by stealing and duplicating a medical examiner's report, then opening a murder victim's body bag. Was he really going to get into any more trouble for this?

"I'm totally tattooing 'I Heart Howie' on Jazz for all this nonsense," he said aloud, then got out of the car before he could change his mind.

Inside, he found only his least-favorite member of the Lobo's Nod sheriff's department, Deputy Erickson, lingering at what was usually Lana's desk, idly clicking away at the computer. Jazz had forgiven Erickson for all of the stuff that went down during the Impressionist hunt last year, but Howie still couldn't get over the way Erickson had slapped cuffs on him, leaving bruises he'd had to cover for a week.

Now the deputy looked up as Howie approached. "Hey, Howie. What can I do for you?"

"Your friendly veneer doesn't fool me." Howie made a show of sniffing the air. "Is that bacon I smell? Or maybe scrapple?"

"Right, right, I'm a pig. You're hilarious. Do you actually need to be served and protected or is this purely an antisocial call?"

Howie filed away the idea of an "antisocial call." He liked it. "I need to see G. William," he said as officiously as possible. "I have a matter for his eyes only."

Erickson gestured to the empty office. "The boss is probably already fast asleep. What, you think he lives here? Even he gets a night off every now and then."

Howie frowned at the way the universe constantly foiled his plans.

"Look, Howie, whatever it is, I'm sure I can—"

"Nope."

"Honest to God, all of that stuff from October is water under the bridge. Jasper and I—"

"Nope."

Lana's chair creaked as Erickson leaned farther back than it was accustomed to. "You're not going anywhere, are you?"

Howie chose to punctuate his point by planting his butt on the very same bench where he and Jazz had once been cuffed.

"When the big man locks you up for annoying the police, don't come crying to me," Erickson said, reaching for the phone.

"That's not a real crime," Howie said confidently.

Oh, crap. What if it is?

"Hey, G-Dub!" Howie called cheerfully a little while later. "What's the happy-hap?"

G. William, it turns out, was not already asleep when Erickson called.

"I've got the last ten episodes of Letterman on my DVR," he grumbled on his way into the office. He glared at Howie. "It took me a week to figure out how to record and play back on that stupid thing. This better be good."

"It is," Howie promised, raising the lockbox.

G. William nodded as if he'd been expecting this. "Would this have anything to do with the nine-one-one call that came in about the old Dent property?"

Howie managed to communicate volumes of distrust and distaste with a single glance in Erickson's direction.

"Oh, for Christ's sake!" Erickson complained.

"My office," G. William relented. "Double-time it, Howie. I love me some top-ten lists."

Settled into G. William's office, Howie clutched the lockbox to his chest.

"You have to give it to me at some point, Howie," said the sheriff.

"First, I want immunity." That's what they always said on TV.

"Immunity from what?"

That was a good question. "Well, the death penalty, for starters."

G. William actually thumped his forehead against his desk. "Howie, unless you've got a dirty bomb in that box, I doubt there's anything in there that would lead to you getting the death penalty."

"I'm just being careful."

"Give me the damn box."

Howie reluctantly handed it over. "I'm pretty sure you're violating my civil rights."

"You're not under arrest. You came in here voluntarily." G. William popped the lid. "If anything, *you're* violating *my* rights to a peaceful evening at—" He broke off. "Ah, hell. Goddamn it all."

As G. William methodically removed each item from the lockbox with a pair of tweezers and held it up to the light, Howie recounted how he and Connie had expertly and with much savoir faire followed the trail of mystery texts that led them to Billy Dent's backyard

"That place is a real eyesore now, by the way," he added. "The town should do something about—"

"Howie!" Tanner yelled. "Stop bitching about the appearance of the crime scene!"

Howie jerked at the bellow. "Sheesh, G. William. It's just a hole in the ground. It's not really a crime scene."

Tanner jabbed one thick, threatening finger in the air between them. "You disturbed evidence. That's a crime, Howie. Then there's trespassing—the guy who owns this land didn't give you permission to go diggin' it up."

Oh. Right. That was all true. How inconvenient. Howie's mom had never found out about his brief arrest at Erickson's hands, but he was pretty sure if G. William cuffed him now, there'd be no way to avoid telling his parents.

"Sorry 'bout that, Sheriff. We were just—"

"And this." Tanner lifted the birth certificate with the tweezers. "This could be explosive for Jazz, you know?"

"Do you think..." Howie started, then stopped.

Tanner shrugged as though he'd said what was on his mind, anyway. "I don't know what to think," he said. "But we're gonna look into all of it." He started talking as if Howie

411

wasn't even in the room. "Go to the phone company and try to trace the texts from there... Probably go back to a burner... Maybe track where it was bought... Might give us a lead." He clucked his tongue. "Damn, boy. Wish you kids'd come to me right from the get-go."

Howie suddenly felt very small and very young. G. William's calm, measured disappointment somehow stung worse than his outbursts. "Yeah, I know. But it was for Jazz, you know?"

"Just... just get Connie in here right away so that we can get elimination prints from her. We'll need them from you, too."

"I didn't touch anything," Howie said. "Well, just the box, but I was wearing gloves. I've seen *CSI*. Plus, it's cold out and my hands get all scratchy."

"Fine." G. William picked up the phone on his desk. "You call Connie, and I'm gonna call—"

"That might be tough. She's out of touch right now."

G. William paused with the receiver halfway to his ear. "What's that supposed to mean?"

Howie suddenly realized that it would be bad if he told Tanner where Connie was headed, but he didn't have a lie prepared. Not for the first time in his life, he wished he had Jazz's think-on-his-feet-edness.

"Um..."

"What are you not telling me, Howie?" Tanner asked, his voice quiet and serious. "Now's the time. Remember: I can always decide to file charges later. Evidence tampering. Maybe obstruction. You're a minor and it's your first offense, but trust me when I say this: Going into the system is no fun."

412

Well, hell, there's something else Jazz and I would have in common—juvenile records.

"There's nothing else, sir. I swear it." His voice didn't sound convincing even to himself. "Oh, wait! I almost forgot. There's a chance Jazz's aunt is also totally a psychopathic serial killer, too. I sort of have my fingers crossed against that one, though."

"Stop trying to distract me with nonsense!" G. William thundered. "Tell me where Connie…Oh, Lord. She's gone to New York, hasn't she?" G. William's eyes widened with horror. "Jesus God, Howie! How could you let her do that? How could her *parents*—"

"She didn't really give them much of a choice."

"Erickson!" G. William bellowed with all his considerable lungpower. The deputy appeared almost immediately in the doorway—Howie figured he'd been loitering nearby, listening in.

"Yeah, boss?"

"Get the state lab on the phone and tell 'em I've got evidence I need fingerprinted and run through the state database and IAFIS ASAP. Plus, sweep this thing"—he gestured to the lockbox—"for any possible DNA." As Erickson moved to scoop up the lockbox, Tanner said, "But before you do that, call the Halls and tell them that we're getting their little girl back safe and sound."

"Yessir." Erickson vanished as quickly as he had appeared.

"Which airport is she landing at?" Tanner asked Howie. Howie realized that he didn't know, and also that he would never be able to convince Tanner of this. But before he

413

could say anything, the sheriff waved him off. "Just get out of here, Howie. I don't have time to deal with you now. I'll track her through her credit card." He started jabbing buttons on the phone.

As Howie made for the door, Tanner said, "And don't leave town!" Howie nodded meekly, biting back the urge to say, "Did you really just *say* that?"

He slipped out of the sheriff's office into the night. He stared up at the sky, the same sky being navigated by Connie's plane on its way to New York.

Fumbling his smartphone from his pocket, he quickly tapped out a text to Connie:

go ghosty, girlfriend. 5-0 headed your way

CHAPTER 46

"If this is all true," Hughes told Jazz, "and I'm not saying it is...then who ran things before Billy escaped?"

"I don't know. Maybe the Impressionist. I haven't figured that connection yet. But Billy was able to communicate from prison, somehow. So maybe he's been running this all along."

"Then who's Hat?" Hughes still sounded skeptical, but at least he was asking the right questions.

"I don't know. He could be anyone. The FBI profile might match him or it might not. You guys were profiling two killers at once without realizing it. One of them the woman-hating rapist with supreme organizational skills. That's Hat. Then there's Dog, Belsamo—women might as well not exist for him. He's obsessed with men and their power, his own power and the power of other men. No wonder there were so many apparent contradictions—you were looking at a portrait painted simultaneously by two different artists.

"Belsamo's the one who helped me figure it out," Jazz went on. "It wasn't just the game aspect—at first I thought he was playing a game *with* Billy, not being played with *by* Billy. But then I thought about him waving his dick at me in the interrogation room. Talking about his power."

"And?"

"And I thought about how Hat-Dog performed penectomies, but only Dog ever *took* the penises with him. As trophies. Hat just tossed them aside. Chop and toss. He didn't care. He was just doing it because Dog did it and it had to look like the same guy. He probably didn't even know Dog was keeping the penises. Hat has contempt for maleness. Dog exults in it. He sees power in maleness and he takes it with him."

"But they both raped women—"

"Sort of. The ME reports show differences between the two. More bruising with Hat's female victims. I think he actually raped them. As an aspect of control. He wants to possess them, and raping them is a way of establishing ownership. He enjoys it. Dog's victims weren't bruised. I don't think rape excites him. I don't think women excite him. I bet he used a sex toy to rape them, probably perimortem."

"What about the paralysis?"

"A Hat innovation. He hates touching men. He didn't want to kill men at all—he had to, in order to keep up the pretense of the game, that there was just one killer. In his own mind, he probably thinks of himself as the only man who matters, the only one who deserves to dominate women. Also, he was used to dealing with girls and women; it was probably easier for him to deal with men if they were incapacitated."

Someone in a shirt and loosened tie—probably an FBI

agent—opened the door and peered inside. "Oh. Didn't know someone was—"

"Give us a minute," Hughes said wearily.

The fed glanced at Jazz appraisingly and backed out, closing the door.

"This is all interesting—"

"Because it's true. Look, there was only one non white victim, right? One Asian. Gordon Cho, victim fourteen, killed by Dog right before you came to get me in the Nod. And what space did Dog land on, if you do the math?"

"Very interesting—"

"He landed on *Oriental Avenue*, Hughes." Jazz shook the paper at him.

"—but it's just that," Hughes said. "Interesting. It's not evidence. It's not proof." Hughes made a show of folding the paper in half and then in half again as he spoke. "Like my old man used to say: I ain't sayin' it is and I ain't sayin' it ain't. I'm going to look into this. But I have to do it on my own and I have to be careful how I do it. You better actually hope you're wrong about this, kid."

"What? Why?"

Hughes stood and walked to the door. "Because," he said, turning to Jazz, "if you're right, we only know it because you broke the law to gather evidence while an official representative of the task force. Which means that piecing this all together in a legal way that will stand up in court *and* put Dog behind bars *and* lead us to Hat before he gets his next die roll..." He shook his head. "It's all going to be ten times tougher than it would have been if you'd done this the right way. That's why. Good enough answer for you?"

He didn't wait for Jazz to respond, leaving Jazz alone in the office.

Jazz kept the office to himself for a few minutes after Hughes left, pondering. On one level, Hughes was right, of course. Jazz had "gone off the reservation," as the cops put it. He'd gone rogue. Endangered the prosecution's ability to put Belsamo and the still-anonymous Hat behind bars.

And yet...he knew he was right. He had taken the quickest, most direct route to Dog. Billy had rolled a nine for Dog, meaning that he would commit a crime that had something to do with Atlantic Avenue. Worst-case scenario, the cops knew where to wait for Dog when the time came to dump his body. One more victim would be his last.

No. No, that's not cool. That's Billy thinking. "One more victim" is one more too many. People are real. People matter.

Yes, Jazz had obtained evidence illegally, but that wouldn't matter if they caught Dog in the act and snatched him up. All Hughes had to do was sit on Dog. Eventually, he would lead them to his next victim and the cops could swoop in and grab him. Make him tell them who and where Hat was. Maybe even...

Maybe even lead us to Dear Old Dad.

And Jazz wondered: Had that been his motive all along? Deep down, had he decided to forsake justice for Hat-Dog's victims in order to hack out the quickest, most direct route to Billy? He could claim he'd simply been so excited at the thought of catching Dog that he'd ignored the law, but maybe there was a part of him that no longer cared about Hat's and Dog's victims, a part that wanted only one thing....

That final confrontation with Billy.

I don't know.

He slipped out of the office. It was getting late, but the precinct still buzzed and bustled. Jazz suspected it was like this 24/7, with fresh agents and cops spelling each other at regular intervals. He knew that task forces worked around the clock, generating tens of thousands of pages of documents and evidence. It was a logistical nightmare, fueled by adrenaline, caffeine, and what G. William called "pure cussedness," that human condition which makes it impossible to quit even when the odds are long and the hours longer.

Jazz wondered: If he stood on a table and shouted out Dog's name and address, how many of these fine, upstanding officers of the law would be tempted to go put a bullet in the guy's head? How many of them would actually go and do it?

Ain't all that much difference between them and us, Billy used to say. *'Cept we're more honest about what it is we do. We admit it drives us, turns us on. They pretend they do it for the good of "the people," whatever that means, but they really do it 'cause they like it. They like the authority. The power. The guns. Just like we do, Jasper.*

Outside, the press had settled into a sort of languor. With no news and none forthcoming until Montgomery's usual 9:30 press briefing (timed to let the local ten o'clock news run with it), they had nothing to do, but couldn't just leave the scene of the biggest story in NYC.

I've got a scoop for you guys. The name and location of one half of the killing duo that has paralyzed Brooklyn.

Could he do that? Could he use the press to his advantage? Jazz had already pushed through them to the street but now paused and looked back. It could be done. There were ways to manipulate the media to the advantage of the good guys. Whoever Hat was, he would obsessively watch the news, read the papers, scan the websites for mention of the Hat-Dog Killer. Billy had done the same, at one point amassing a set of four huge scrapbooks filled with tales of his exploits. He'd burned them late one night when his inborn paranoia finally conquered his all-consuming pride.

The press was a powerful tool, but a dangerous one, too, as apt to blow up in your face as function properly. Jazz had been taught a healthy respect for the cops—along with hatred of them, of course—but he'd been raised to fear and shun the media. He had learned many things at the feet of William Cornelius Dent, and most of them fell into the category of "Bad Things," but avoiding the media was something Jazz was pretty sure made sense.

It was too risky. Using the media to find Hat would be like playing with nitroglycerine.

On his way back to the hotel, he bought a slice of pizza from a shabby, run-down shack of a restaurant, certain that it would have roaches embedded alongside the mushrooms he'd requested. Instead, it was the best pizza he'd ever had in his life. *Okay, New York,* he thought. *I'll give you this one. I'll never be able to eat that delivery stuff again.*

Howie would have loved the pizza, he knew, wiping his

greasy hands on his jeans as he entered his hotel room. Connie, too. Thinking of them made him suddenly, surprisingly homesick. He'd been too busy and too distracted to miss Lobo's Nod or his best friend and girlfriend, but now a slice of pizza brought it all home to him. New York wasn't the place for him. He needed the wide-open skies and narrow boulevards of his hometown. He could be anonymous in New York, he realized, unknown and unsuspected. Ever since Billy's arrest, that's what he'd fantasized—being somewhere (being some*one*) that no one knew or recognized. New York should have been his Shangri-la.

But now he realized that being anonymous was the worst possible future for him. Dog's anonymity had allowed him to kill with impunity for months. That little studio apartment reeked of insanity, but how many people had ever set foot within?

Jazz needed to be surrounded by people. Yes. And they needed to be people who knew him, people who could see the signs. People who could tell if—when?—he was tipping into Billy territory.

Connie. Howie. G. William. Maybe even Aunt Samantha, if she could be persuaded to stay in the Nod.

Could this be his family? His support system? Jazz had always thought that his past was his own burden to bear, but could it be possible that he was meant to have people around him? Was *this* the true meaning of "People are real. People matter"? Not that they mattered in order to be safe *from* him... but to be safe *for* him?

The phone rang, so sudden and shrill into his thoughts

that he jerked like a marionette, fumbling for his cell. He swiped at the screen, but nothing happened.

Another ring.

Oh. Not *his* phone.

The Billy phone.

"Hello?"

"Jasper!" Billy cried, sounding like a man who's not seen his child in years. "M'boy! How *are* you? Still doin' well, I hope? Not too disappointed that the bastard cops aren't givin' you much help, I hope?"

"I don't know what you're talking about."

"Of *course* you do. You were right in ol' Doggy's doghouse. Saw it all up close. Nosed around his food dish. Saw his *chain*, Jasper, m'boy. I know you—thinkin' you're some kinda... some kinda *white knight*, ridin' to the rescue. White knight, Jasper. And then the cops do nothing. How do I know that? Well, I guess 'cause I just spoke to Doggy and he's still breathing that sweet, cold, free air." Here Billy inhaled deeply—a pot smoker's hearty toke, a gourmet drinking in the contents of a roiling, aromatic kettle. "Ah! Yeah, he's still out there. He's *prospecting*, Jasper, and ain't no one trying to stop him. Unless you have designs on that for yourself. Is that it? You thinkin' you can take down ol' Dog all on your own?"

"The police know all about him," Jazz said with conviction. It wasn't even really a lie—Hughes knew everything Jazz knew at this point. By now, the detective may have come clean to Montgomery. By now, the police could... "They're probably loading up SWAT and ready to roll on him any minute now."

422

Billy blubbered laughter. "I would like to see that! I truly, truly would. You know, I would like to be there when they knock down his door with their battering ram—"

"I'd like you to be there, too," Jazz said savagely.

"Ha! Good one! Nice! But if I could be a blowfly and buzz around, I would get a hell of a chuckle, Jasper. You've been there. Tell me—what evidence are those good ol' boys gonna find in his place?"

Nothing, Jazz knew, and didn't say.

"And girls," Billy amended. "Good ol' boys and girls. They got lady cops and they got that cutie FBI agent, Morales, don't they? It's a hell of a diverse task force, ain't it? Got Morales and they got that big ol' *Negro* Hughes, don't they? Is it okay to say 'Negro,' Jasper? I'm wonderin', 'cause it sounds a lot like that *other* word that people get so het up about. I gotta ask you, you bein' my expert on such things on account of sticking it to that pretty little kinky-haired girl."

"You bastard," Jazz seethed. "You just keep talking and talking and talking, don't you? Talking in circles and spirals and trying to keep everyone on their toes, babbling nonsense to cover up the fact that you've killed and tortured so many. People *died* when you escaped. You made me complicit in that. People died."

"Were they important?" Billy asked blandly. The voice of a man asking for vanilla ice cream.

"They mattered!"

"Why? Because they were alive? Because they were people? Is that all it takes? If everyone's special, ain't no one special, Jasper."

Jazz realized he'd dropped to his knees at some point during the call, the weight of Billy's voice, the sheer mass of his psychic venom dragging Jazz down, down, down. He had trouble breathing. Billy's voice was relentless, eternal, and it brought back every half memory and barely recalled figment from his childhood. Jazz was a boy again, not a man. He was a toddler, waddling around the house, following a mother who would soon be gone, reaching chubby arms out to a father glowing with the satisfaction of having slaughtered— at that point—dozens.

"You still with me, Jasper?" Billy said, not pausing, not giving him a chance to recover. "Hate to think I could be talkin' to a dead line, you know? Hate to think of this fatherly advice bein' wasted."

"We're tracking this call," Jazz said, hoarse. A pathetic lie, obviously told. Jazz didn't expect his father to buy it, and sure enough, Billy didn't even acknowledge it, just kept on talking:

"I still have so much to teach you. There are days when I sit here, when I sit here and I think, *There's so much I still haven't taught him. So much I need to give him.* We lost time, Jasper. Lost four good years, four important years. And that's on me. That's *my* fault, y'hear me? I take that blame and I carry it on my shoulders every day and it makes me stooped and weak, to think that I let my needs and my urges come between us. I'd'a been able to control myself better, those two sunny, silly bitches'd still be alive and I'd be home and we'd be doing just fine, learning together."

Jazz fumbled with his cell, flicking to where the pictures

424

were stored, tapping and swiping until he found the one he was looking for: a scan of the picture of his mother. The only thing left of her.

And what about Mom? Jazz wanted to ask. *Would we be one big happy family?* But there was no point. Billy had killed Mom—had *erased* her—years before he killed in Lobo's Nod, years before he'd been captured by G. William.

"You don't have anything to teach me," Jazz managed. "You taught me enough."

"It's never enough. When you have your own kids, you'll understand. You'll be fifty, and you'll still be my boy, Jasper, and I'll still wish I could take you and put my arm around you and teach you what you need to know in this ugly, evil world."

Jazz swiped his mother's picture aside. A new photo: him with Connie and Howie, all grinning for the camera. The shot was bittersweet—he enjoyed seeing the honest smile on his own face, the camaraderie with his closest friends, but the picture had been snapped by Ginny Davis one day after school. Poor, dead Ginny, her death caused by the Impressionist—and, therefore, by *Billy*—and not prevented by Jazz himself.

"You think you can come after me, don't you?" Billy asked. "That's why no one's tracing this call. That's why you're not screaming your head off for help. Because you want me all to yourself. Just like a crow."

A crow…Jazz slid his phone away and used his free hand to steady himself on the floor. The fog in his brain began to clear, just a little, and through the parting clouds he saw a black bird, its wings wide and all-encompassing. "A crow," he said. "Crows. Belsamo—Dog—had a crow on his laptop. He made noises like a crow. And the Impressionist said something about—"

"You been thinkin' about that story, Jasper?"

"The one you told me. About the Crow King. I looked it up once. Tried to find it in a book or on the Web. But it doesn't exist. No one knows it."

"Yeah. That's the one. That was your favorite when you were a kid."

"No."

"Well, seemed to *me* like you liked it! Always got a chuckle out of it. Anyway, like I said before—it's not just a story. It ain't just somethin' made up. It's got some *real* in it, you see?"

"No. I don't get it."

"You will." Billy chuckled. "Or you won't! Hey, who knows, right? Crazy ol' world we live in. Anything's possible, I guess. But my money's on you, Jasper. Always has been. I raised you right, boy. Raised you strong and proud and tough. Last four years or so been hard on you, I know. Been hard without your Dear Old Dad around."

"I've been fine." He forced himself up to a crouch, looking around the room for a weapon. Anything that could cause pain. He would march out of this room and keep Billy talking for *days*, if that's what it took, but he would follow his father's trail of crazy right to his hideaway and then he would do what he should have done years ago.

"You've been foundering," Billy said confidently. "You

keep goin' back and forth: 'Am I fit for other people?' 'Am I a monster?' 'Can I touch this pretty little colored girl?' Sorry— *African American* girl? Or...woman? Does she make you call her a woman, not a girl?"

Jazz decided on the chair. It was heavy and sturdy. He tilted it so that the back of it rested on the floor, then kicked at one of the legs, which splintered and cracked into a good length of wood, hefty and solid with a wickedly jagged point.

"What's that I hear in the background?" Billy asked. "Almost sounded like snapping an arm, but I know that ain't it. You tearing up the furniture? You ready to hunt *vampires*, boy?"

Somehow, the solidity of a weapon in his hand cut through the morass of confusion, a blazing trail of bloodlust leading to sparkling clarity. "You get off on this crap, don't you?" Jazz asked, the question as obvious as its answer, but his voice no longer weak. "Not just trying to mess with my head. Not just killing people. But the rest of it, too: puppetmastering these guys. You love telling them who to kill as much as you love killing yourself."

"Not really," Billy mused. "Ain't true. Not at all. And you got it wrong—I don't dictate to them. I just watch the clock and keep the rules. They decide how to play the game."

"But you started it. You inspired it."

"I did?" Billy sounded genuinely surprised at the notion. "You really think that? See, like I said before, I still got a lot to teach you. Like this: Wasn't *my* idea to set these boys playin' against each other. I just stepped in to help adjudicate."

"Yeah?" Jazz recovered his cell phone and dropped it in

his pocket, still clutching the stake he'd made. He paced the hotel room like that, powerful and impotent all at once, a wolf on a leash. "How's it work? How do you pick the winner? Or do you just play until someone gets caught?"

"We play until they can't play anymore," Billy said.

"Oh? What does the winner get? Bragging rights? A signed Billy Dent trading card?"

"Oh, no, Jasper. Better than that. *Much* better, I promise. Why, you may even get it yourself one day."

"I don't want anything you have to offer," Jazz snarled. "I won't be one of your puppets. One of your pawns. I won't be a party to any more dying."

"You're gonna be the death of that FBI agent, Jasper. I promise you that. You'll watch her die."

"Bull. I'm not killing anyone." *Except you.*

"It's all in your hands, m'boy. She can die pretty or she can die ugly. Now, if it was me, I'd start with those lips, so full and...*generous*, I guess, is the word I'm looking for. I would start with them. And I sure am curious to see those goodies she hides under those FBI blazers. Those shapeless blazers they wear. Not shapeless enough for her, eh? Bet you wonder, too, don'tcha?"

Ugh. The worst part, of course, was that Jazz *did* wonder about Morales's breasts and he *had* noticed the plush, inviting softness of her lips. Any straight man, he told himself, would have. But most straight men weren't lethal.

"Want to get your hands up under there, don't you, Jasper? Want to find the things she hides from the world, the things she won't share. Bring 'em out into the light."

Jazz shook his head with a violence that was nearly chiropractic. "Shut up, Billy." He made his voice as stern as possible, deleting the quaver that wanted to creep in, the combined weakness and strength he felt at the mere thought of peeling Special Agent Morales's clothes and armor and dignity at once. "You can't do this to me anymore. I'm my own person. My own man."

"Why, of course you are! Never said anything to the contrary!"

"Where are you?" Jazz screamed into the phone, his whole body leaning, *straining*, into the effort, as though his soul could be vomited out and up through the words, as though he could scream himself into the phone and out the other end, wherever Billy was. "Where are you? Tell me! Tell me, goddamn it! Tell me so I can kill you!"

The only response: a roar of laughter, so familiar, so damning.

"Jasper, if you really wanted me dead, you'd'a killed me when you visited me at Wammaket a couple, three months back. Coulda leaned right over the table and throttled me with your bare hands. Bet them COs woulda been real slow responding to that. Swim through molasses to rescue me, they would. Race like turtles. Lightbulb overhead—you could have gotten to that and broken it and slashed open my carotid before they took you down. Try as I might, I can't picture a jury in the world—much less the county—that would have convicted you. Poor ol' Jasper goes and offs his evil sumbitch daddy....That Sheriff Tanner, he'd've given you a medal.

429

"No, Jasper." Billy sighed, a professor who's given the same lecture for too many years. "If I'm alive right now, it's for one reason and one reason only: 'cause you let me live that day."

The worst part wasn't that it was true: The worst part was that Jazz had already known it. A part of him could excuse away the earlier deaths—the ones Billy had committed early on, some of the ones the Impressionist had committed in Lobo's Nod—but he couldn't excuse away the later ones.

All on his head. All of it.

"There is blood on my head!" Reverend Hale screamed in *The Crucible.* Jazz had screamed it, too, and in the end, it didn't matter—John Proctor still went to the gallows.

All of Jazz's strength and rage flooded out of him, sucked out by Billy's cold, twisted rationality. By Billy's truth.

"If you still got that anger in you, though," Billy continued, "I'll tell you what: Next time you see me, you go right ahead and kill me. Don't dillydally around. Don't dicker. This is serious business here, son. This is *Crow* business."

"Why are you here?" Jazz could only find a whisper in his throat. "Who did you come to New York to find?"

Billy said nothing for a moment, and Jazz wondered if his father had hung up. "That's not for you to know. Not yet. Tell you what—I'm gonna tell ol' Doggy. I'm gonna let him in on the secret. And then you can ask him. Doggy needs a bone. But first, Doggy needs to play with his toys.

"Oh, and by the by...thanks so much for movin' that birdbath. Bet it made my momma real happy."

Click.

430

Jazz dropped the makeshift stake. This particular vampire would need more than a stake through the heart, he knew. He stared at the mute cell phone in his hand, then scooped up his own cell and fumbled for a number.

"Where are you?" he asked when the line opened. "I need to see you."

"At my hotel,"

"I'm on my way."

CHAPTER 47

Connie spent the flight forgiving Jazz. Was he being an over-protective jerk? Sure. But she had to admit that if ever there was a time to be an overprotective jerk, this was it.

There's no need to distract him right now. I'll just go find...whatever it is Mr. Auto-Tune left for me. How dangerous could that be? It's in an airport, which has got to be, like, the safest place in the world these days. And then I'll bring it to Jazz. And we'll figure it out from there. Easy.

When they landed, she turned on her phone. It chirped at her immediately and a text message time-stamped from a couple of hours ago popped up:

go ghosty, girlfriend. 5-0 headed your way

Howie. She would have known even without his name on it.

WTF, Howie? What are you—

5-0. The police. Her parents must have called her bluff. There would be cops waiting for her as soon as she got off the plane. She gnawed her lower lip. What could she do?

The annoyed woman stuck between her and the window asked her rather impolitely to move. Connie automatically tucked her legs up and let the woman through.

Think, Connie. You're not an action hero. You can't escape them. So you have to trick them instead. You're an actress, right? You need to act.

And she remembered something Jazz had said once, during one of his periodic "lessons" on avoiding sudden death at the hands of people like himself: *Don't get distracted by details.* She remembered Ted Bundy and his arm-in-a-fake-cast routine. Women had seen that cast and been suckered to their own deaths.

People like details, Jazz had told her. *They notice them. They fixate on them. And they let them consume them, to the detriment of the bigger picture.*

Connie's plan formed in seconds. Too little time for her to think it all the way through, but fortunately also too little time for her to doubt it. *Worst-case scenario: I get caught. Best-case scenario if I do* nothing: *I get caught.*

The woman who had pushed past her was now struggling with the overhead bin for her suitcase, her large purse resting on the empty aisle seat, unwatched. Connie quickly and efficiently rummaged through the bag. Reading glasses. Okay, cool. Then she silently thanked God that the woman was white as she found exactly what she'd hoped to find—a makeup compact. She palmed it.

As the plane slowly emptied (and her former row mate disappeared down the aisle), Connie ducked low behind the seat and whipped out the compact, with its powdery "neutral"

433

makeup disk. Years of theater experience had taught her how to make makeup seem natural, but now she wanted anything but. It took a little doing, but within a few minutes she had managed to create a blobbish patch of beige skin that started above one eyebrow and leaked down her face, nicked the top of her nose, and came to an uneven end along the ridge of her cheekbone. It looked like a birthmark gone awry and it was pretty hideous, she thought.

Details.

She bound up her long, carefully braided hair and wrapped it in her satin sleeping bonnet. She slipped on the reading glasses and checked herself quickly in the compact's mirror. It was good, but not good enough.

Hair and makeup, done. Time to raise the curtain and start the show.

The plane had almost entirely emptied out. Connie finally rose from her seat and maneuvered out of her aisle with great difficulty, avoiding coming down on her left foot. Bracing herself on the seatbacks, she managed to shuffle up to the front of the plane, where she made sure to make eye contact with one of the flight attendants who had *not* told her to turn off her phone at takeoff.

"Are you all right?" the attendant asked, telling Connie instantly that her posture and her faked expression of pain were both working.

"I feel like an idiot," she started, "but I twisted my ankle running for the plane before. I didn't think it was that bad, but after sitting all this time..."

"Oh, God, it's probably even worse after the change in cabin pressure!"

The "let them finish your sentence" trick rides again.

"Yeah, is there any way..."

"I'll get a wheelchair for you."

Connie allowed herself to slump against one of the seats a little. "Thank you so much. I'm sorry to be such a pain."

"Not at all. Just sit in that seat there and I'll have someone get your bags."

Soon, the attendant helped her out of her seat and off the plane. There in the jetway, a man waited with a wheelchair. Connie sank into it and thanked the attendant again as she piled Connie's duffel onto a little rack on the back of the chair.

"Take good care of her," the attendant told Wheelchair Man.

"No prob."

On their way up the jetway, Connie unfolded the cheap little airplane blanket she'd grabbed from a nearby seat and wrapped it around herself like a shawl. She figured by this point she probably looked like a cancer patient. She tucked her arms together to make herself as small as possible.

Moments later, he rolled her out into the terminal. Connie immediately noticed two uniformed cops standing with a TSA agent off to one side. They were looking for a black teenage girl with beaded cornrows. Not some woman with a facial mark and glasses, wrapped up and wearing a bonnet that probably covered a bald head, as best they could tell.

Still, she held her breath as Wheelchair Man rolled her past them.

"Where to?" he asked her.

Connie finally allowed herself a grin.

"Terminal four," she said. "Arrivals."

CHAPTER 48

Morales was staying in a hotel three subway stops away from Jazz's, but he hadn't figured out the subway system yet and now was no time to try. So he had hailed a cab and—like in the movies—told the guy to floor it. The cabbie glanced over his shoulder at Jazz with an expression of mingled amusement and annoyance and proceeded to lope along at the speed limit. Jazz sighed heavily and resigned himself to the trip, watching Brooklyn bleed past him.

He should have gone to Morales in the first place, he realized. Should have texted her and not Hughes when he'd had Billy on the phone outside Belsamo's apartment. She was the one he needed. Hughes had—after much thought and stress—broken NYPD regulations to bring Jazz to New York in the hope of catching a killer.

But the very first time he'd met her, Morales had offered to break the law for him. *With* him.

She answered the door in a hotel bathrobe, her hair spilling down, un-bunned, messy, disheveled. God, she was sexy. He felt his groin lurch at the sight of her. He wanted her. Not the same way he wanted Connie. Or maybe it *was* the same way. Maybe he was kidding himself. For all his talk of loving Connie, maybe it was just some animal reaction.

She can die pretty or she can die ugly.

"I was about to get some sleep for once," Morales said, cocking a hip. "What's so important you had to race over here?"

Her lips...

Now, if it was me, I'd start with those lips, so full and... generous.

Jazz shivered.

"Is it cold in the hall?" Morales stepped aside. "Come in. I can make some, well, coffee, I guess. Do you drink coffee?"

"Yeah..." Jazz hesitated, then entered the room.

You're gonna be the death of that FBI agent, Jasper. I promise you that. You'll watch her die.

No. He would not kill her. Billy was just trying to psych him out. That's what Billy did—he planted seeds of doubt, of crazy, of dismay. And even if they didn't bloom, he still got to paw through the loam of your psyche.

As if the sound and finality of the door closing suddenly made her aware of who she was with and what she was wearing, Morales pulled the front of the robe closer together with one hand and ran the other through her untamed hair.

I sure am curious to see those goodies she hides under

those FBI blazers. . . . Want to get your hands up under there, don't you, Jasper?

Of course I do.

Want to find the things she hides from the world, the things she won't share. Bring 'em out into the light.

So what? So does every other guy with testosterone and a working penis.

And that made him think of Dog and Hat and the missing penises and he finally shook off Billy's voice and listened to himself confess multiple felonies and misdemeanors to a special agent of the FBI.

To her credit, Morales didn't interrupt Jazz as he related to her the path that had taken him physically into Dog's apartment and mentally into Dog and Hat's brutal game of "murder Monopoly," as Hughes called it. Her eyes, so dark brown they were almost black, widened and narrowed at certain points, and she pursed those plush lips that Billy wanted to "begin" with, but she said not a word until he wound and wended his story to the point at which he'd hopped in a cab to visit her in her hotel room.

"And Hughes knows all of this?" was the first thing she said, confirming.

"Except for the last phone call. Well, and that I came to you."

Morales clucked her tongue. "I have to think for a second.

And I have to go get dressed because I can't believe I'm sitting around talking about this in a bathrobe."

She grabbed some clothes from a suitcase, then disappeared into the bathroom. Jazz took advantage of the few moments he had to take a quick inventory of the room.

Standard hotel room. Nothing special. The Bureau clearly wasn't about to rent out a suite for one of its special agents. The room had the feel—no surprise—of someone who used it only to sleep and for the occasional shower. Morales had two double beds, her suitcase open on one of them. He glanced into it—dirty laundry, from the looks of it, probably ready to be sent out. Would it be terribly stereotypical—as a guy and as a potential future serial killer—to steal a pair of used panties? His amusement at the thought surprised him. Maybe if he could mock his own proclivities, he would end up all right. Billy Dent didn't seem to truck in irony, after all.

Her service revolver—a standard-issue Glock 22—hung in a shoulder holster over the desk chair. Jazz stared at it. He'd figured her for the Glock 23 instead. It was basically the same weapon with the same load—a .40-caliber—but it was about an inch shorter. Easier for women and smaller men to handle. Made more sense for her to carry one of those, and not this friggin' hand cannon in a shoulder rig that would ruin the line of those blazers Billy had taken note of. She was either exceptionally confident or exceptionally proficient. Or both.

She left that gun here with you. She deserves *what comes next, Jasper.*

Stop it.

Take that gun and hold it on her when she comes out of the bathroom. And then—I promise you—the fun starts.

Jazz turned away from the gun, away from the suitcase with its pervert bait. On the nightstand, he noticed a small frame with a black-and-white photo. Male. Caucasian. Maybe mid-thirties, lazy grin.

"My ex-husband," Morales said from behind him. Jazz turned. She was in her FBI armor now—slacks, formless shirt. Hair tied back.

"I'm sorry," Jazz said, mainly because it seemed to be the thing real people said when death and divorce were brought up. *Ex-husband. So much for Hughes's lesbian crap. Can't believe I fell for that.*

Morales shrugged.

"Most people don't keep a picture of their—"

"I still love him," she said. "He couldn't deal with..."

"With you being a fed?"

"No. It was your dad. I became obsessed. Charlie couldn't live with...he didn't—"

"You don't need to—"

"He shouldn't have had to have dealt with it. With my obsession with catching the Hand-in-Glove Killer. But he tried to deal with it and then he couldn't and then we got divorced. Okay?"

Jazz felt soiled somehow, but he merely nodded.

"So what are you thinking?" she asked. "Why didn't you go back to Hughes with the new phone call?"

"Because he's pissed enough at me."

"Like I'm not totaling up all the state laws you've broken

441

in my head? Hell, I bet Belsamo could even file a civil suit against you. He'd probably win, too."

"You said you would help me kill Billy," Jazz told her, forcing her to shift uncomfortably, like a recalcitrant toddler needing to use the bathroom.

"Killing Billy and catching Dog are two different things."

"No. They're the same. The path to Billy leads through Dog. He said he came to New York looking for someone. Said he would tell Dog who. We catch Dog—*without* NYPD, *without* the task force—and we can force him to tell us who Billy came to find. And then we get that person and we're one step closer to Billy."

"Force him, huh? You gonna go all Cheney on him?"

"I don't know what you mean by that. But I think I can be persuasive. In the first place, these freakshows are all giant Billy Dent geeks. The last one I caught thinks I'm some kind of demigod." He left out the part about the Impressionist ramming his head into the bars of his cell.

"What if Dog doesn't want to talk? Or what if he's just too crazy to tell us anything worthwhile?"

"I think his whole cawing, look-at-my-dick act in the interrogation room was just that—an act. He wouldn't be together enough to keep from being caught this long, otherwise. But you just have to trust me, Morales. We nail him down and I can make him talk. One way or the other."

Morales rubbed her temples. "You're talking about torture. You're talking about kidnapping a United States citizen—"

"A criminal."

"A United States citizen—"

"A serial killer."

"—and depriving him of his rights, his due process. Then torturing him into giving up information not related to the crimes he's accused of—"

"The crimes he *committed*."

"—and using that information to assassinate another U.S. citizen."

"You're the one who offered to kill Billy!" Jazz threw his hands into the air. What the hell? He thought she was a hard-case. All of a sudden, she was a big ol' wuss.

"Why come to me? Why not Hughes? Why not let him do his thing?"

"Like I said: Hughes said he was going to look into it, but he has to play by the rules."

She snorted. "I'm an FBI agent. I have rules, too, you know."

"Yeah, but you don't care about them," Jazz told her. "Not if they stand between you and Billy." He purposefully and significantly glanced at the photo of her ex-husband, making sure she couldn't miss it. "This is your chance to do what you've dreamed of for almost a decade. To bring down Hand-in-Glove. Permanently. To redeem all those dead girls. To redeem what you lost."

Unfair, really. Completely unfair. Using her own grief and her own compulsions against her like that. But Jazz decided in that moment that he didn't care if it was fair or unfair.

Morales had become a tool, a widget he would use in order to get what he needed—Billy.

She actually licked her lips. That was when he knew he had her.

Sexy as she was, though, he had no interest in her body. Not now. Right now, all he needed was her authority, her badge, her gun.

She flipped open her cell and made a call. A moment later, she said, "Hughes. It's Morales. You have men on this Belsamo character, right?"

Jazz nearly squealed in glee.

"No, I'm not with Dent," she said impatiently, rolling her eyes as if it added to the illusion. "I've been looking at the workup on him and going over the interrogation transcript and there's something that bothers me. And something must bother you, too, or you wouldn't have uniforms on him, right?" She paused, and Jazz could imagine Hughes twitching, trying to think of a good reason to be following Belsamo, one that didn't involve multiple crimes against the suspect.

"You're kidding," Morales said. "Okay, okay. I get it. Fine. Yeah, I'll see you in the morning. They lost him in the subway," she said to Jazz after she closed her phone.

"They *what*? Have these guys ever tailed someone before?"

"You know how tough it is to follow someone through the subway around here? You need more than a couple of uniforms, and that's all Hughes could spare without going into detail about why he wanted to tail Belsamo. So what now, boy genius?"

Jazz fumed. He didn't know what next.

"We could sit on his apartment," she said, "but he might kill someone in the meantime and then we've just been sitting on our thumbs while—"

"Doggy needs a bone!" Jazz snapped his fingers, lurching toward her excitedly.

"What?" She took a step back, as if Jazz had threatened her.

"I can't believe I totally forgot this in all the craziness. But that's what Billy said to me. One of the *last* things he said: 'Doggy needs a bone. But first, Doggy needs to play with his toys.' The storage unit!"

"You think he's gone there?"

Jazz nodded. "He needs a bone. I bet that means he's picked out his victim. He needs his murder kit. But I checked his apartment thoroughly. There was no murder kit and nowhere to hide one. So I bet he's got his tools at his storage unit." Another thought occurred to him. "I bet that's where he keeps his trophies, too."

Morales held out her hand. "You have the envelope, right? Or at least the address."

Jazz grinned. "Of course I do."

Morales fist-pumped. "Yes! Let's get going. I have a car downstairs." She grabbed her shoulder holster from the chair and wriggled into it, her shapeless shirt becoming suddenly quite shapely in a way Jazz neither could nor wanted to ignore. As she turned to pluck a blazer from the desk, Jazz noticed a second, smaller gun tucked into the small of her back. A Glock 26 from the looks of it—nine-millimeter rounds.

But she hadn't done anything since coming out of the bathroom, which meant that...

"Did you think I would leave you—or *anyone*—out here with my gun without knowing I had a backup in the john?" she asked, flashing him a knowing smile that reminded him of Connie in all the right ways. "Let's go."

CHAPTER 49

Billy Dent was not alone. He had company in his small room. He looked over and thought about discussing what was on his mind. . . .

But no. There was no point.

Oh, Jasper. Poor Jasper. Seeing only a part of the game. Didn't he know that there were many different kinds of games, games for all kinds of players?

Sure, there was the game Hat and Dog played. A game with specific rules and a very special prize. But then there was the game *above* that game. The game Billy played. The game with rules he himself had written. The best part of that game was that none of the pieces knew they were a part of it. It was a game with many sides, but only one player: William Cornelius Dent.

This is the way it was meant to be, of course. In a world filled with so many pieces of plastic, so many things—human beings, they called themselves in a great, self-perpetuating delusion—that thought they mattered, that thought they *thought*, there could be no more appropriate game than what amounted to solitaire. Billy Dent, playing alone.

Billy used one of his burner phones. When the ringing stopped, he said, "Hey there. Havin' a good evening? It's about to get better."

He didn't wait for a response, just continued on: "How'd you like to win this whole thing once and for all? Tonight?"

And, yeah, *that* got a response.

CHAPTER 50

After leaving the lockbox with G. William and making his oh-so-stealthy getaway from the sheriff's office, Howie drove the Nod aimlessly. His parents had expected him home hours ago, but he had texted to say that he was helping out with Jazz's grandmother again. In reality, he was just wasting gas money and contributing to global warming as he tried to think of a path around it all, a way through the thickets that did not involve confronting Sam.

The idea that Sam was Ugly J... the idea that she was just as crazy as Billy...

It can't be. For one thing, she really seems to hate the guy. For another thing, I think she's hot. And if I think she's hot and it turns out she's a psychopath, then what does that say about me? I'm totally not ready for that kind of therapy.

It's not that he was in *love* with Jazz's aunt. Puh-lease. Howie Gersten was horny and desperate and more than slightly clueless, but he wasn't *stupid.* He had the hots for her and he figured that the fact that she knew this and hadn't called him gross or a perv meant that maybe something could happen. Which would be great for Howie because he was a total virgin and sick of it to the tune of jerking off so much that he was worried he was going to cause some kind of penile trauma. Hemophilia extended to his entire body, after all—he'd bruised Li'l Howie plenty of times, which sucked. If sex was gonna hurt, he'd rather have someone else causing the pain.

What were the odds that Sam was involved in Billy's craziness? That she was Ugly J? Most serial killers were men. So many that it was just the first natural assumption to make in any serial killer case. So, yeah, it just made sense to assume that Ugly J was a guy.

But what if Ugly J wasn't necessarily a serial killer? What if Ugly J was just, like, an apprentice? An assistant? Howie didn't think there was a career path planned out for sociopaths like Billy Dent, but Jazz's dad had broken a lot of the typical "rules" for serial killers. Maybe it wasn't all that crazy to think that he'd turned his sister into his helper.

Maybe he had even . . .

Ugh. Gross. Don't think that, Howie.

Too late.

Great, now every time you want to fantasize about Sam, you're gonna think about Billy Dent doing his own sister. Jeez.

Incest is best, put your sister to the test. . . . Some old bit of middle school vulgarity, hopping and skipping back from his memory. *Double gross.*

He pulled over to the side of the road and killed the engine. Craned his neck to look up at the stars. But the stars weren't there. The night sky was almost perfectly smooth with clouds, the stars and the moon hidden as though they could not bear to see what came next. Howie couldn't bear it, either.

It wasn't that he was a coward. He didn't like to *think* of himself as a coward, at least. But a lifetime of overprotective parents who had every reason to be overprotective... well, that had a way of worming into a guy's consciousness. Most teenagers, Howie knew, thought they were indestructible. Howie desperately and devoutly wished he could believe that, but every damn time he woke up with a new bruise on his arm from rolling over in his sleep and bumping the night-stand... every time he went to the doctor for his latest des-mopressin shot...

Every time he relived the night the Impressionist had nearly killed him with a swipe of a knife, a swipe that any-one else could have shaken off...

Every time he thought of these things, he reminded him-self: *It's not cowardice, Howie. It's just common sense.*

But those words had started ringing hollow a long time ago. His best friend was in the biggest, scariest city in the country, hunting a lunatic with more than a dozen murders to his name. And maybe, just maybe, his own father. And Connie? She was on a plane—or maybe she'd landed by now—to that same place, determined to do whatever she could to help.

How can I do any less? How can I not handle this one

damn thing? Just figure out if Sam is a bad guy or not. That's all. Do it, you coward. Do it, you stupid, joking, horny, useless bleeder.

He stared at his cell phone for what felt like an eternity, flicking to Jazz's number over and over. He desperately wanted to call his best friend, to get his advice on this. But Connie was right—Jazz was in deep enough already. The last thing he needed was Howie calling for advice on how to deal with Sam.

And besides...shouldn't Howie be able to figure this out for himself? Being a hemophiliac didn't mean his *brain* stopped working. Just his clotting factor.

When Howie had been younger and his parents had first explained his disease to him, they had done that typical thing all parents do: They'd tried to put the best possible face on it. "Abraham Lincoln was a hemophiliac," they'd explained to him, "and look at what *he* accomplished. And Mother Teresa. And Richard Burton, the actor."

Years later, when he was old enough and curious enough, Howie had investigated these claims. Turns out the actor dude was the only one confirmed to have hemophilia. Mother Teresa was just a rumor, and an unlikely one—women carried the gene for hemophilia, but rarely had the disease. And Lincoln? No one could prove it one way or the other.

Like with Genghis Khan, another historical figure rumored to be in the Howie Hemo Club. Whenever people tried to find a connection to historical figures, funny how they always managed to skip over guys like Genghis Khan.

During this same bout of research, Howie had discovered

one other fact about his particular disease: Hemophiliacs tended to die young.

Which meant, maybe, that he should accomplish as much as possible while he still counted among the breathing.

Just cut the Gordian knot, Howie thought. It was one of his favorite bits of ancient history: Alexander the Great comes across this gigantic, complicated knot of rope and is told that whoever can untie it will rule the world. But no one has ever even come close because the knot is so friggin' big and complex.

So Alexander just pulls out his sword and cuts the knot in half. Ta-da. No more knot.

Yeah, that works, he thought, and cranked the engine.

CHAPTER 51

It started raining as soon as they headed to the car.

It was a simple matter to find directions to U-STORE-IT-ALL online. They weren't terribly far, but Morales refused to speed because if they were stopped, she would have to show her ID and then there would be a record of the two of them out to commit some sort of late-night skulduggery. Jazz champed at the bit in the passenger seat, strumming his fingers against the window.

"Calm down," she told him. "At this time of night, the traffic's on our side. GPS says we have clear roads all the way there. *He's* got to take the subway and wait for a transfer. Plus, in this weather, I guarantee he'll take a bus instead of walking from the subway, so he'll have to wait for that, too."

"We don't know *when* he gave the cops the slip. He could be there already."

"Being pissy with me won't change that."

"We need to stop off at a hardware store for a sec."

"I thought you were in a hurry."

"Just a little contingency planning."

She pulled over for him to run into the first such store they saw and then they were back on the road right away. Soon Jazz saw a flickering sign for U-STORE-IT-ALL in the distance. He leaned forward as though he could add to the car's momentum.

"I can't flash my badge to get us in," Morales told him. "You know that, right?"

"Yeah." Again, there could be no record of what they did here tonight. "Let me get us in."

She arched an eyebrow. "You gonna break in?" The word *again* was unnecessary and unsaid.

"Not if I can help it. I'm going to try something else. Cut the lights and park on the street so that the guy in the booth can't see you."

The "guy" he referred to was a rent-a-cop sitting in a dimly lit booth framed out in what had to be bulletproof glass. Morales dutifully killed her lights and glided the car to a stop along the curb of the road. Ahead, a short driveway ran perpendicular to the street into a smallish parking lot jammed with rental vans, shielding them from the view of the booth. Beyond lay a chain-link fence ten feet tall with a sliding gate and a keypad. But Jazz only had eyes for the booth and the rent-a-cop.

Never break and enter when you can just plain ol' enter, Jasper, Billy had said once.

"Do you have some paper? Anything will do."

"Glove compartment."

Jazz found a little notebook in there. He tore out a sheet of paper, wrote on it, then folded it and put it in his pocket.

"I think you scare the hell out of me," Morales said. He shrugged and she called out "Good luck" as he slipped out of the car.

Jazz hmphed. Luck. Who needed it?

It was still raining, though it had tapered off a bit as he approached the gate and stood there, hesitant, for just a beat too long, just long enough to appear awkward, confused, out of place. Without checking, he knew that the security guard had noticed him. Peering from the gate to the keypad, he feigned exasperation with little bits of body language—a shrug, a tossed-out hand.

Then he turned as though to go... and pretended to catch sight of the guard for the first time. Even though he was sure the guard couldn't see the finer details of his expression from this far away, he went ahead and widened his eyes, anyway.

Always keep the performance honest, even when no one's watching, Billy used to say.

Jazz headed to the guard. By now he could see the man leaning forward already, in anticipation. *Good.* That movement told him something in advance.

The bulletproof shell in which the guard lived had a speaker grille set into it, as well as a small slot through which one could probably slip keys or a receipt or a credit card, but angled such that a gun would fire its payload down into the desk. Jazz stood as though he thought he had to speak directly into the grille.

"Hello? Sir? I need—"

"I can't let you in unless you have a passcode or an account number," the guard said gruffly.

Interrupting. Good. The man's posture was vaguely aggressive. He was fat and resented getting up from his chair to speak. He wanted Jazz gone, and quickly.

People like that were actually easier to manipulate. They were focused on the end result of the conversation, not on the conversation itself. This guy was already imagining himself settled back in his chair, watching what appeared to be a reality-TV show in which scantily clad women lay out next to a pool for some reason.

He was also probably already anticipating Jazz's next statement, figuring on something like "But please!" or "I lost my passcode" and readying his rote "I can't let you in."

So Jazz did the one thing the guard would not have prepared himself for:

Nothing.

He simply stood there, still and quiet, staring straight ahead at the grille that shielded his face from the guard. The guard began to back away from the glass, then realized that Jazz wasn't going anywhere. He paused midway to his chair. The TV chattered. Someone said, "I was like, she is, like, so bitchy and, like, without *any* reason, you know?"

From behind the grille, the guard said, "I said I can't help you."

Jazz still didn't move.

The guard inched back toward the chair, then stopped again. "Hey. Kid. I *said*—"

Not yet.

"—that I can't help you. Scram."

Jazz waited.

The guard finally came back to the glass. He couldn't see Jazz, though, because the grille was blocking his face, so he craned his neck to peer around the grille, finally meeting Jazz's gaze with eyes sunken into the dough of his face.

"Kid! Seriously. Move it or I'll call the cops."

Jazz noted that the end of the man's tie had, due to his positioning, flopped into the slot in the glass. Easiest thing in the world to reach out, grab that end of the tie, and pull. Strangle the guy into unconsciousness, then scale the fence. Billy roared at him to do it from the depths of his subconscious.

No. That's the backup plan. I don't want to hurt him if I don't have to.

But Jazz *did* want to hurt him, if he was being honest with himself. The man was rude. Dismissive. Fat, lazy, and disinterested. Being strangled on the job by his own tie would probably be the best thing to ever happen to him.

"It's my uncle," Jazz said in a hoarse whisper, and then leaned his forehead against the glass, as if he needed the support.

Uncle. Not mother or father or brother or sister. Immediate family was expected. Con men knew that people had an emotional response to immediate family, so they cornerstoned their lies on the nuclear family. A good security guard would be wary of such a ploy. Jazz didn't know if this guard was any good—he suspected not—but as Billy said, *Assume every damn cop in the world is Sherlock Holmes and you'll never do anything stupid.*

"Look, I know you can't help me," Jazz said with quiet fierceness. "I know that. But will you at least listen to me? And then maybe you can tell me what to do next?" Now making his voice tremulous, bordering on querulous.

"I can't do anything for you," the guard said. "You need a passcode or a receipt to get in." But his voice had changed, just slightly. There was the smallest bit of curiosity in it now. A tiny rip in the fabric.

"My uncle," Jazz said. "Look, he's dead, which doesn't matter because he was sort of a jerk, okay?" Another switch-up. The guard was expecting a sob story. *Oh, my beloved uncle is dead and he always wanted me to have his collection of rare Portuguese pencil erasers! Please, sir, let me in!* "No one liked him. He was a tool. But the problem is that he had this rare comic book collection, see? And my mom is on her way here right now to get it." Now he'd brought the mom in—the guard would be tracking back to caution, so Jazz had to move quickly, establish the lie, the narrative.

"She's a drunk," Jazz said. He was thinking "junkie" originally, but for some reason drunk seemed to work better. It was less dramatic and so more believable. "And if she gets here and gets those comics, she's just gonna sell 'em for a bunch of money and buy more booze."

"So I let you in and you're gonna save your mother from herself, is that it?" Sarcastic. Incredulous.

"I just want to change the lock," Jazz said. He held up a key and a small padlock, bought not long ago at the hardware store. "There's like two thousand comic books in there.

There's no way I could haul them out. And hell, the rain would ruin 'em. I just want to change the lock so that she can't get in. And then maybe my sister and I can get her back to the treatment place next week and we can deal with all of this later. I'm just trying to buy some time, you know?"

The guard snorted. "And maybe cherry-pick the most valuable comics while you're in there?"

"I wouldn't know which ones to take," Jazz said, with complete earnestness. "You can come with me if you want. Come watch. I'm just gonna swap one lock"—he held up the key—"for another." He held up the padlock. "It'll take five minutes."

The guard hesitated. "I can't leave my desk." Relief. He doesn't have to make a personal choice—he can just fall back on the rules.

They follow their rules. They worship their rules, Billy said. *And that's their downfall, Jasper. Because we don't give two tugs of a dead dog's tail about the rules.*

"Then screw you!" Jazz yelled, suddenly boiling over with anger and exasperation. He leaned down to let the guard see his face for the first time, a face screwed up with pain and rage, a few hot tears wicking from the corners of his eyes. "Screw you like everyone else!"

Set them up. Let them think they know the rules of the conversation. They're in power. You're the supplicant. Let them think all they have to do is brush you off.

Then change it up. Suddenly. Starkly. Get them off their asses and out of their comfort zones.

He thumped the heel of his palm against the glass and

then spun away from the booth, stalking off, then whirling around to scream, "It's on you! When she's passed out in some alley in Brighton Beach, it's all *your* fault!" before walking farther into the darkness. Jazz didn't know where or what Brighton Beach was, but he'd heard someone on the task force mention it.

"Hey! Kid!" the guard shouted, his voice different now. Bewildered. Maybe a bit hurt. No one likes to be yelled at. Especially by someone who mere moments ago had been so pliable and pitiable.

Jazz spun around again and shot the double-bird at the guard. It was a calculated risk. But usually someone who's trying to con you won't flip you off. Not on a conscious level, but somewhere beneath that, the guard would now actually be a little more inclined to believe Jazz.

"Kid!" the guard shouted again, now just a tiny bit desperate. Jazz took two more steps into the darkness, then stopped. He waited a moment, then turned around, assessing the distance to the guard as though it were laced with acid pits and vipers.

"What?" he shouted back, aggressive. Accusatory.

Even from here, he could detect the slump of the guard's shoulders, the sense of defeat.

"Don't steal anything!"

And the gate rumbled as it slid open.

Jazz resisted the urge to fist-pump, and instead acted like a kid who'd just been given a way to help his drunk mom. He tossed a "thank you!" over his shoulder as he ran through the widening gap in the fence.

A moment later, the gate clanked and cranked shut behind him. Jazz stood for a moment, catching his breath. He was aware of a box to his left and a camera up high watching the gate, and him. A map of the facility was mounted on a nearby wall, and he pretended to study it, as though unsure of where to go next. As long as the guard could watch him on the camera, he couldn't do anything too overt, but while arguing with the guard, Jazz had surreptitiously examined the monitor setup. As best he could tell, there were four screens available at any one moment in time, cycling through a variety of cameras. As long as he was careful to keep out of the camera's range as much as possible, he should be okay.

He stepped under the camera and quickly called Morales, telling her what to do. A few moments later, she pulled up to the gate, her engine loud, distracting the guard, who would be watching as she stretched through her window for the keypad. Couldn't make it. She'd pulled in too far away.

With exaggerated exasperation, she climbed out of the car and walked to the keypad. She had already removed her jacket and guns. Her shirt—now wet—clung to her, all but guaranteeing that the guard would watch her, not his monitors.

Jazz darted into the camera's view for a moment, triggering the motion sensor that opened the gate from this side. As the gate cranked open, he kept running, into the shadows where he couldn't be seen.

Morales pulled in and the gate closed behind her.

They were in.

CHAPTER 52

Wheelchair Man was a young guy, maybe a couple of years out of high school, who couldn't keep from referring to "a fine sister such as yourself" repeatedly as he wheeled her more slowly than was necessary to terminal four. Connie did her best to ignore him as he kept up a steady stream of increasingly flirtatious patter, but finally couldn't take it anymore. By now she was in another building entirely, the TSA and the cops far behind her. She hopped up from the chair with ease. "Wow! Thanks! Look, I think it's better now!" Before he could protest or even register surprise, she grabbed her duffel and headed in the direction indicated by the sign for ARRIVALS. So much for her would-be suitor.

She discarded the glasses in a trashcan and whipped off the bonnet, letting her braids clack around her shoulders as their beaded ends were set free.

She wondered exactly what the clue would be. JFK was huge, and even as specific a location as the arrivals area of a single terminal provided hundreds if not thousands of places to conceal a clue.

Then again, she wondered just how hidden the clue could possibly be. Airports had incredible security, after all. So whoever had hidden the clue couldn't assume it would stay hidden. So maybe the clue wasn't something left behind— maybe it was a part of the terminal itself, something that was *always* there....

Bring cash, the voice had said. So she needed money to access the clue.

She stood in the center of the arrivals area, feeling enormously conspicuous as she turned a slow, mincing circle, taking in everything within her range of vision. At the same time, she tried to prepare a cover story in case some security official approached her. *I'm looking for my dad. My boyfriend. My ride. I've never been to New York before; just taking it in.* They all sounded lame and she wasn't sure she could sell any of them.

Excuses fluttered out of her mind when her eye caught the sign that said BAGGAGE STORAGE.

Bring cash....

She approached the Baggage Storage desk slowly, feeling as though she were being watched. Then she felt ridiculous. Of course she was being watched. It was an airport. There were probably three video cameras and a bunch of security guys watching her right now. *Everyone* was being watched.

There were two people working the desk and both of them were harried—the lines were long and unruly. Terminal four was international flights, Connie realized, and in addition to

Baggage Storage, this same desk also seemed to offer a variety of services—hotel bookings, currency exchange, and more. The customers were a patchwork of races and ethnicities and accents.

"I need to pick up a bag," Connie said, taking a wild guess.

"Ticket?" asked the East Asian woman behind the counter.

Crap. "I lost it," Connie said.

The woman grimaced and her eyes flicked to the long and impatient line behind Connie.

Connie saw her chance. Jazz called it "social hacking," like breaking into a computer, only with people. Channeling a vapid cheerleader, willing herself to look young, harmless, and cutely stupid, she moaned, "I'm soooo sorry. My dad will just *kill* me, y'know?" She yearned for some bubble gum to pop.

"What's the name?" The woman sighed.

"Conscience Hall." Gambling that Auto-Tune had left whatever it was under her own name.

The woman typed on her keyboard, grunted once, then said, "One bag?"

"Yes."

"Left here when?"

Another gamble. Connie put on her most focused, concentrated, "I'm not that bright" face. "Gosh...I guess it would have been...gee...like, earlier today, you know?" Hoping Auto-Tune had brought it here after talking to her on the phone. "A couple of hours?" She whooshed out a breath, as if all the thinking made her tired. "I've just been wandering around the city and I totally lost track of time." She smiled. "And my ticket." *Throw in a* tee-hee? *No, too much.*

"So you told me." The woman gritted her teeth. From behind, Connie heard people grumbling, and the woman's coworker—a tall, older man, also East Asian—looked over. "What's the holdup?"

Before the woman could explain, Connie jumped in, pumping up the cute lost girl crap to the max for the benefit of the older man.

"She knows when it was dropped off? She has the right name?" The man's expression clearly said, *How many people named "Conscience" could there be?* "No ticket, but do you have ID?"

Connie dutifully hauled out her driver's license.

"Give it to her," the guy said.

The woman sighed with relief. "Four dollars."

Connie gave her a five, took her change, and waited as the woman brought out a smallish black laptop bag. It was smaller and evidently lighter than the duffel Connie carried over her shoulder, and the woman regarded her with suspicion for a moment. Connie cranked up the wattage of her smile and made herself as guileless and as empty as possible, hoping that she looked dumb enough to have checked her lighter bag instead of the heavier one.

"Here you go." Handing over the bag.

Inside, Connie experienced a heart-thrumming trill, which she suppressed outwardly. She took the bag into the ladies' room. Catching a glimpse of her mottled face in the mirror, she took a moment to wash off the white lady's makeup, then ducked into a stall, waiting until the room was empty before opening the laptop bag. If it was a bomb or anthrax or a plague toxin in there, she didn't want to hurt anyone else if she could avoid it.

Fortunately, she didn't have to wait long until she was alone. She examined the outside of the bag—nothing exceptional about it. Just a generic laptop bag. There was a mesh outer pocket for a water bottle, but otherwise just the one top zipper, which she unzipped with her breath caught in her throat and her bottom lip between her teeth.

Nothing happened.

She pried open the bag. It was a single pocket within, padded, of course.

The first thing she saw was the gun.

Her heart jumped a beat into the future, even as her hand—as though remote-controlled—reached in to pull out the gun. It was a pistol—a revolver, to be precise—and as soon as she touched it, her entire body relaxed. It was plastic. An old, scuffed toy pistol, she saw, withdrawing it.

Ha, ha. Very funny. What am I supposed to make of this?

There was something else in the bag—an envelope. More family photos?

She opened the envelope and withdrew and unfolded a piece of paper. A second piece of paper fell out and into the bag, but she was focused on the one she held, which was typed with a generic font:

```
Connie:

Congratulations on making it this far.
Well done.
```

I wrote this letter when you first agreed to play my little game. In truth, it's not much of a game, and I apologize for that. You're a late player, and I haven't had time to prepare something adequate to your stature. I hope you'll forgive this oversight on my part.

As a way of making it up to you, I have included not one but two clues to my identity in this bag, as well as a pointer to the next clue. If you are smart and talented enough to have snared young Jasper, then I believe you will possess perspicacity enough to deduce both.

I look forward to seeing you soon.

It was, of course, unsigned.

It doesn't sound *like something Billy Dent would write. And come to think of it, Mr. Auto-Tune didn't really sound like him, either. Not the words he used. Not the way he talked. Is this Hat-Dog? Could that really be it?*

Two clues, the letter said. There was the gun, of course. Add that to the bell and it meant absolutely nothing.

The second piece of paper in the bag was a clipping from a magazine of some sort—a picture of the actor Kevin Costner.

What. The. Hell.

She had a bell, a gun...and Kevin Costner? This was supposed to help her somehow? These were clues to Mr. Auto-Tune's identity?

Is Kevin Costner a serial killer? Yeah, right.

She inspected the bag, even turned it inside out, but found nothing else. Nothing but the note and the gun and the clipping. Remembering how the bell clue had actually been a part of the lockbox, she scrutinized the bag for markings of any sort, but found nothing out of the ordinary.

What about the note itself, though? She thought of the note that the Impressionist had carried in his pocket, how there had been a simple acrostic *UGLY J* encoded into it. She studied the note, but found nothing of the sort. The opening letters of each paragraph, of each word, of each sentence, spelled nothing sensical. Which wasn't to say that there wasn't *some* sort of clue embedded in the note itself, only that she couldn't figure it out. But didn't the FBI have, like, a whole division of people who did stuff like this? Codebreaking? Deciphering experts? Cryptographers?

Maybe she could get Jazz to give the note to the FBI agent he knew. Maybe...

She sighed and stuffed the gun and the note and the clipping back into the bag, then left JFK, following signs that directed her to a taxi stand. The driver, a Sikh with a Bluetooth earpiece, nodded and smiled at her, shrugging with one shoulder when she said, "Brooklyn," and the address of Jazz's hotel.

"How you want me to go?" he asked.

Connie had no idea. She didn't think he would appreciate if she said, "Maybe with a car? On the road?"

"Whatever's fastest," she said.

"BQE?" he asked.

"Sure."

The cab took off. Connie laid her head back, letting lamp-post light wash over her in staccato waves as they pulled away from JFK and onto a highway.

It started to rain, a cold, ugly rain that made Connie shiver just from the sound of it on the roof of the cab, the silver slash of it in the headlights.

Connie thought that she couldn't have summoned by most ancient witchcraft a more perfect and more hideous night for what she had to do.

CHAPTER 53

Before they went any deeper into the storage facility, Morales popped the trunk of her car and hauled out a bulletproof vest. She strapped it on and then pulled her blazer on over it. She looked almost comically top heavy and squarish.

"I have another one," she said, indicating the trunk. "It's a little small, but it'll probably fit you."

"These guys don't shoot people," Jazz said.

Morales shrugged. "Protocol."

I like how it's so important to you to follow protocol while breaking the law with me, Jazz thought, but did not say.

With Jazz in the lead to scout out the cameras and guide Morales—now suited up and armed again—around them, they made their way to unit 83F. It was deep within a maze of tight, narrow corridors lit sporadically by overhead fluorescent tubes that seemed to spasm on and off of their own accord. The unit was on the second floor of what seemed to be a ten-story building, a concrete-and-metal bunker housing endless identical doors, differentiated only by the varying locks and the fading numbers etched onto their faces.

As they rounded a corner that would reveal 83F to them, Morales paused to draw her backup weapon. Her poise with the smaller Glock 26 was plenty intimidating—Jazz could only imagine how she would look with the bigger 22 in her grasp.

"What are you doing?" Jazz asked.

"You should have bought bolt-cutters at the damn hardware store. Now I'm gonna have to shoot off the lock," she said. "This ought to do it."

Jazz groaned. "Put that thing away," he said. "I can pick the lock."

"What if it's a combination lock, smart-ass?"

"I'm not bad with them, either."

Moot point.

As they came within sight, they saw that the lock was already unfastened, hanging loose in the open hasp of the door to unit 83F.

CHAPTER 54

Howie stood at the front door to the Dent house. The stars still hid beyond the blanket of clouds. He tried not to take that as an ill omen, but it wasn't easy.

Just go on and do it, he told himself. *And who knows? Maybe a hundred years from now, some dumb futuristic hemophiliac kid's dumb futuristic parents will be all like, "Buck up! Did you know that the famous* Howie Gersten *also had hemophilia?" Beats the living hell out of Genghis Khan, right?*

He had a key, of course, so he let himself in. The house was quiet. *Too* quiet, some idiot in a movie would say, then go in anyway.

Howie shrugged and went in anyway. He knew something that random movie idiots didn't know—where the shotgun was. He recovered it from behind the big grandfather clock. The barrels were plugged and Jazz had removed the firing pins, but Sam and Gramma didn't know that.

I'm going to cut the knot and figure this out one way or

the other, he thought. And then, resolute, he stepped into the living room, where Sam lay on the sofa, watching TV.

"Howie?" she asked, startled. "What are you—" She broke off as she realized he was pointing the gun at her. "Howie!" Her voice cracked. "What the hell? Are you *nuts*?"

"That's *exactly* what I was gonna ask you!" he said, astonished. "Wow. We're totally on the same wavelength. Please don't be a crazy serial-killer person."

"What are you talking about?" She drew her legs up onto the sofa, hugging her knees as though she could shrink into a space where a shotgun blast couldn't find her. "What are you *doing*? Point that thing somewhere else."

"In a sec. I need to know if you're a crazy serial killer like Billy. Are you Ugly J?"

"What's Ugly J? Put that gun down!" Her voice went high and panicked. Too panicked to be fake, Howie thought. Would a serial killer be afraid of harmless Howie, even packing heat? He didn't think so. The terror in Sam's eyes seemed real. Howie didn't think Billy had ever been afraid of anything in his life.

"Playtime!" a voice said from behind him. "Friends are here!" it singsonged, and Howie turned without thinking. Gramma had pranced in from the hallway, clapping her hands, but when she saw the shotgun pointed at her, she screamed.

"Whoa. Calm—"

"KILLER!" she yelled. "KILLER IN THE HOUSE!" So loud he thought her vocal cords would have to explode.

"It's okay!" he told her, but she screamed again—this scream high and wordless, a nonsense syllable of terror—and clenched tight, old fists.

From behind him, he heard Sam cry out, and then she was on him from behind, tackling him, and he thought, *That's gonna leave a bruise*, as he involuntarily pulled both triggers to the shotgun.

Boom. Not the sound of gunfire. No, the shotgun made only twin dry clicks as the hammers fell on empty space instead of firing pins. The *boom* rattled in Howie's skull as he crashed to the floor, Sam on top of him, screaming, and then a new sound, a cry of fear, and Howie looked up in time to see Gramma, hands grasping at her own throat as she choked out a hollow gasp and collapsed to the floor, her head cracking solidly on the hardwood right in front of Howie.

"Oh, Jesus!" he blurted out, not sure if he meant for Mrs. Dent or for himself and the damage done to his body by his own fall. Maybe both.

Sam clambered off him, snatching the shotgun from his now-nerveless fingers. She tore skin away and Howie went swoony at the too-familiar sight of his own bright blood spurting onto the floor.

"Mom!" Sam was up, pushing past him, the shotgun cradled expertly in her arms. Howie tried to push off the floor; his palm slipped on his own blood. Sam caught his movement out of the corner of her eye and scowled murder at him, hoisting the gun threateningly. It couldn't fire, but beating Howie to death would be the easiest thing in the world.

"I didn't mean—" Howie started, and Sam dropped to her knees next to her mother.

She shook her.

Gramma Dent lay silent and loose, a skeleton in a bag of skin.

Sam spun around, now wielding the shotgun like a club, a crazed glint in her eye. And despite that, Howie suddenly was worried not for himself at all. He could only think:

Oh, no. Oh, God. I just killed Jazz's grandmother.

CHAPTER 55

Jazz and Morales exchanged a quick look. And then Jazz knew the meaning of telepathy because in that instant, he knew exactly what Morales was thinking. She was thinking the exact same thing *he* was thinking, the thought stretched and shared between them like taffy:

Doggy needs a bone. But first, Doggy needs to play with his toys.

Belsamo. One half of the Hat-Dog Killer. He was in unit 83F right now. Gathering his tools for his next murder. They had thought they would beat him here, but he'd managed to get here first.

Before Jazz could say anything or signal, Morales single-handed her gun—good thing she was using the backup, Jazz thought—then grabbed the handle of the door down near the floor and flung it up. It rumbled and stuttered, but rolled almost entirely into the ceiling, revealing a ten-by-ten space within, lit by a portable battery-powered lantern.

Morales shifted her grip to two hands, her feet planted.

"Freeze!" she shouted. "Don't even *twitch*!"

The room was divided into halves by a strip of bright tape that ran down the center of the floor. Both sides had what looked like a makeshift workbench, each piled high with tools and boxes. On the right-hand side, Jazz noticed a bottle of clear liquid with a pair of eyes floating in it.

On the other side, the workbench held multiple small jars, filled with cloudy liquid and tight, curled shadows that Jazz knew would turn out to be five excised penises.

Oliver Belsamo stood in front of the left-hand workbench, half-turned to Morales, his expression one of complete shock. He had a small laptop shoulder bag on the workbench before him, partly filled from the look of it.

In his hand, now frozen, he held a wicked-looking scalpel, halfway to the bag.

"Drop the knife," Morales said, teeth clenched. "Drop it now or I drop you."

Jazz wondered if she would actually shoot him. Dog was her best—only—pathway to Billy. Would she really kill him?

"You…" Belsamo's voice. It was Jazz's first time hearing it since the interrogation room, when he'd cawed and played madman. It still had that off-kilter timbre to it, that lunatic's cadence. Belsamo was a man only marginally in control of himself.

His apartment. All the hoarding and OCD crap. That's how he tries to stay in control of himself. By complete control of his environment.

"You went into my *house*!" Belsamo whined, gripping the scalpel more tightly. He didn't even look at Morales—he

478

seemed to have eyes only for Jazz. "You took my *phone!*" As if that crime somehow outweighed all his own.

"You do *not* want to mess with me!" Morales yelled. "Put! It! Down!"

She probably wouldn't kill him. But he could easily see her shooting him in the leg.

"Better listen to her," Jazz said. He took a step toward Belsamo. "Drop the scalpel and step away from the workbench and you'll live, man. That's what it's all about, right?"

Above all else, serial killers did not want to die. They cherished their lives more than anything else.

Because you can't kill people if you're dead.

"Drop it!"

"Really, man. Drop it," Jazz said, and took another step. The strong, overwhelming scents of formaldehyde and bleach and metal from the storage unit curled his nose hairs and made his nostrils want to slam shut. "Dude, it's not worth dying."

"Get back," Morales said tightly. "Get out of there, Jasper. Now."

Jazz looked down. He hadn't realized it, but he had stepped into 83F. He had started to back up when he caught— out of the corner of his eye—Belsamo moving. His heart thrummed a quick, panicked beat.

But it was just Dog dropping the scalpel. It hit the workbench with a clatter.

"Good boy," Morales said in a voice loaded with irony and relief.

And then Jazz jerked as though awakened by a nightmare

as a flat cracking sound echoed in the claustrophobic confines of the storage hallway, followed by another one before the first could fade away.

In the time it took to blink, the entire world spun and shifted away from him, a dizzying amusement park ride gone horribly awry. For some reason he couldn't understand, he was suddenly staring up at the ceiling of unit 83F, and his heartbeat roared loud in his ears, drowning out everything else. In that single, nigh-imperceptible instant, something—and everything—had changed.

It took only another moment for him to realize what and how. In the space of that new moment, the pain hit him. The pain and the dampness of his own blood soaking through his clothes.

She shot me, he thought. *Morales shot me.*

CHAPTER 56

Connie's cabbie said nothing until they pulled onto the highway.

"Good thing not a little colder," he said abruptly. "All this be snow." He gestured through the windshield.

Connie nodded. That would suck. Being stuck out here by the airport, waiting for plows. Ugh.

She vaguely remembered that when Hughes had driven them to Brooklyn, it had taken almost an hour, so she knew she had some time. She dug into the laptop bag and produced the Costner picture, staring at it. Costner wore a three-piece suit and pointed a gun right at her. Was that the clue? A gun in the bag and then another gun in a picture...? Both fake guns, of course... Was the Costner picture because Mr. Auto-Tune knew that Connie wanted to be an actor? And if so, what was the message? This whole scavenger hunt seemed hand-crafted specifically for her, so what did two fake guns and a picture of an actor mean?

Two guns...

When in doubt, check the Internet. She Googled *two guns*, but got nothing helpful. Some kind of band, an Old West feature in Arizona, and a comic book character called "The Two-Gun Kid." Really helpful.

Then she punched *Costner* into Google. She tapped on some of the links, skimmed his Wikipedia entry. Then, for the hell of it, she tried *Costner serial killer.*

A movie called *Mr. Brooks* came up. Connie's eyes widened as she read the description. In the movie, Costner played a sociopath. A Billy Dent type, who went around killing people and even mentored a wannabe serial killer.

That makes some kind of sense. Is Mr. Auto-Tune the Hat-Dog Killer? Is it Billy's new protégé?

But according to Jazz, Billy had always said that *Jazz* was his protégé.

Wait. Maybe it's not Costner. Maybe it's the role *he's playing in this picture.* She compared the image on her phone for *Mr. Brooks* to the clipping. Costner looked much younger in the clipping, at least ten or twenty years, so she went back to Wikipedia and started looking at older movies.

"Okay to take Atlantic?" the cabbie asked suddenly.

She looked up. They were stuck in traffic and had barely moved since the last time she'd paid attention, almost a half hour ago. At this rate, she would get to the hotel sometime tomorrow morning.

"Yeah, yeah, sure," Connie said, returning her attention

to her phone. And then she found it. The clipping of Costner had been cut from a printout of the poster for the movie *The Untouchables*.

Kevin Costner had played an FBI agent. Eliot Ness.

This was it. It had to be. It was a clue with multiple levels, designed to lead Connie to this moment, to this name. Eliot Ness. First, the image of Costner led her to Mr. Brooks, assuring her that she was on the right path. Then to Eliot Ness. Was there a further step? Was there something in Ness's history? Or was Ness himself the clue?

She switched over to Google Maps and punched in *Ness*. Maybe it was a street name in New York or—

A pin dropped onto the map, spearing an intersection in Brooklyn. *Ness Paper Manufacturing*, it said.

Connie slid the map around and realized that the glowing blue dot representing her position wasn't far from the Ness Paper pin. "Hey!" she said to the cabbie. "Can you take me to..." She glanced back down at the phone and read off the intersection.

The cabbie did another one-shoulder shrug and blurted something in Hindi. Probably telling whoever was at the other end of the Bluetooth headset that the crazy girl was changing her mind.

Shortly, the cab pulled up to the intersection. "Where?" the driver asked, and Connie realized he wanted to know which corner to drop her off at.

"Doesn't matter. Here is fine." She shoved some money through the little slot in the plastic shield between her and the driver, then hauled her bags out into the cold, relentless rain. Gross.

"Hey, can you stick around for, like, two minutes?" she asked, but the driver—with that inscrutable single-shoulder shrug—just took off into the night. "Oh, terrific."

Some people milled about under umbrellas, but the streets were almost completely empty. Connie held the laptop bag over her head and stared up at the façade of the Ness Paper building. It looked like every other random building. Nothing exotic or strange about it. There were two large truck bays, closed off with corrugated garage doors, and a flight of steps leading up to a single door illuminated by a bright cone of light from a security lamp. The place was clearly closed.

"Good job, Conscience," she muttered. The rain chilled down to her bones and then dug deeper.

She turned, looking up and down both streets at the intersection. Cars whizzed by, but no cabs that she could see. She was just about to dig out her phone and look for the nearest subway station when she noticed it, right across the street from the Ness building.

It was just another Brooklyn tenement, notable only due to its severely ramshackle appearance. It was the sort of building they showed in movies to communicate to the audience that you were in a bad part of town, though as near as Connie could tell, this part of Brooklyn wasn't particularly scary. The building was almost out of place here, its face scarred and pitted, then made up garishly with layers of graffiti.

Only one graffito had caught her attention, though. New,

she could tell, or at least new*er* than the rest because it over-
laid them:

HELLO, CONSCIENCE

Almost as though she couldn't help herself, Connie stepped
off the curb and walked across the street, stepping carefully
over a puddle as she went.

CHAPTER 57

Jazz couldn't move. Harsh static buzzed in his ears. A lake of blood spread along his left flank, and that entire side of his body flamed with pain. He couldn't even tell where he'd been shot—it could have been anywhere inside the creeping red stain that stretched from his waist to mid-thigh.

Why? he asked no one in the confines of his head. *Why?*

And then another of the flat cracks dragged Jazz's attention away from his own pain. Morales was down on the floor, still. A man crouched over her, slightly winded, and Jazz realized—they'd struggled. For the gun. The man had come up behind them. Morales hadn't shot him. Not on purpose, at least.

"Good," said Belsamo. "Nicely done."

"Shut up!" the other man said, pointing Morales's gun at him. "Shut your mouth!"

Now Dog looked just as confused as Jazz felt. The scene swam before Jazz's vision, watery, indistinct. He wondered if he was going to pass out and was surprised by how cleanly and clinically he could examine himself right now. Pulse racing. Skin a little cold and clammy. *Am I going into shock? Don't go into shock, Jazz. You're no good to anyone then.*

Thank God Morales had had her backup weapon out. It was a light caliber—a nine-millimeter—not the full .40-caliber load her service weapon held. He knew he had a decent chance at surviving this gunshot wound without too much permanent damage. In most shootings, the victim did himself as much harm as the bullet, if not more: Thrashing around when shot only made you bleed more. And the shock of being shot often sent victims into cardiac arrest or caused further bleeding from an accelerated heart rate.

So when you get shot, Jazz, just fall down, nice and calm. Just keep cool.

Yeah, right.

He forced himself to draw in a long breath and then let it out slowly. Connie had once tried to teach him yoga breathing, which he'd found annoying and unnatural, but right about now, he was up for whatever would keep him alive.

Morales wasn't moving. There was a hole in her blazer, but no blood that Jazz could see. He was pretty sure the FBI vest could stop such a small caliber even at such close range. She would have had the wind knocked out of her and would have a hell of a bruise. He'd heard of people going into cardiac arrest just from the impact, though, even with a bulletproof vest on, but Morales seemed to be breathing normally. Knocked out when she hit the floor?

A surging wave of agony suddenly crashed upward from his leg and Jazz hissed in a breath. Forget Morales for now. He was *shot*.

He tuned back into the rest of the world for a moment and realized that Belsamo and the newcomer were arguing, going back and forth as though there weren't two wounded people and a growing puddle of blood on the floor between them. Dog's voice was flat and affectless, as though everything outside of his own skin was merely a curiosity. The newcomer spoke with heat, anger. Passion.

"You're not supposed to be here," Belsamo said with an almost autistic precision. "The rules clearly state that unless told to, we are not to be here at the same—"

"Shut up!" the other man shouted. "Just shut up about the rules! Do you have any idea what's happening here? Do you? You just had to be sloppy, didn't you? Had to leave your tributes to Ugly J everywhere. Idiot."

Jazz's vision began to clear, just a bit. He was almost directly between the two men, still inside unit 83F. Morales was inside, too, having been knocked into it during her tussle.

Her gun. That hand-cannon in her shoulder rig. If I can get to it...

It was no more than a few feet to her, but right now it looked like a marathon.

Just then, the overhead light in the hallway flickered to life for the space of two or three seconds and Jazz could see the face of the man with the gun. His gut turned in on itself, writhing and twisting. He knew this man.

Duncan Hershey. The very first man the task force had interviewed based on the FBI profile. Jazz had a potent flash of watching the interrogation, of watching him drink a cup of water and surrender that same cup.

Of course. He didn't care if we had his DNA because he knew it wouldn't match Dog's. Dog's Get out of Jail Free might as well have been Hat's, too.

"You're the other one," Jazz said, unable to help himself. "You're Hat. We *had* you."

Hershey snarled and didn't even bother to look in Jazz's direction as he spoke. "You had nothing. A ghost, a vapor. Nothing more. Quite possibly much less. And by the by, I'm not Hat. Not anymore. That was just my name in the game." His lips quirked into something Jazz imagined was supposed to approximate a grin, but was more of a leer. "The game is over now. I won."

"The game isn't *over*," Belsamo said again in that peculiarly emotionless voice. Still, Jazz could tell Dog was worried. "It's still my move. I still—"

"This has nothing to *do* with you!" Hat snapped. "Don't you get it? You were never in contention. Not really. You were just there to temper me. Anvil to my blade. Nothing more. A tool. Used. Used up. Discarded. Do you really not understand this?"

Jazz swallowed, his throat barely working. The pain from his leg—it was definitely his leg that had been hit, he knew now; all the pain radiated from his thigh—had cranked up, as if it wanted to remind him of something. The thought of moving at all terrified him.

But the gun terrified him more.

You got lucky once. Don't push it.

You have to push it. You have to. They're not gonna talk forever.

Hissing in a breath, he dragged himself along the floor, careful to go on his right side. Every time he moved, he jostled his left leg and it screamed at him in protest, but he bit down on his lip and refused to cry out.

Pain turns Hat on. He's the one who liked hurting women. He likes it when people are hurt. Dog doesn't think other people are real. They're just toys to him. But if Hat sees I'm in pain, that'll just get him off even more.

The pain doused his eyes with tears and his left side with napalm.

It also brought him a little closer—just a little—to Morales.

He blinked several times to clear his vision, which had gone watery again. Morales *was* breathing. He could tell. Hat had knocked her out in the struggle, was all. She was so close. Without a bullet in him, it would be nothing to dive for that gun and—

"What do you think you're doing?" Hershey had finally turned his attention back to Jazz.

"I'm just going to check on her," Jazz said, strong-arming his voice into a non-shaking, confident tone. Fighting the urge to whimper, to beg. "She's FBI. You don't want a fed's death on your rap sheet, man. Trust me. Even Billy was never stupid enough to—"

"Oh." Hershey blinked. "She's still alive?" He moved the gun a bit, pulled the trigger before Jazz could even shout.

Small-caliber bullet. Back of the head. It made a perfectly tiny entry wound and Jazz could swear he heard it ricocheting inside her skull, making a hash of her brain. One eye—her right—popped open as though in surprise. It filled with blood startlingly fast.

Morales thrashed only once, then lay perfectly still.

You're gonna be the death of that FBI agent, Jasper, I promise you that. You'll watch her die.

Oh. God.

Look at all these bodies, Jasper. Look at all these bodies pilin' up around you. You still think your hands are clean?

"You didn't have to do that," Jazz whispered. "You didn't have to. Even Billy—"

"Stop talking about Billy Dent," Hershey said in a tone of boredom. "I don't *care* about Billy Dent. I'm going to out-murder and out-terrorize Billy Dent. I'm going to kill my way up and down this country and from coast to coast, until my name is written in blood on the Statue of Liberty as a warning to anyone who dares come here. I'm going to fill the Grand Canyon with carcasses and blood. I'll be the greatest Crow ever."

Crows again. If Hat didn't worship Billy, Jazz knew his life was very much in danger. He thought back to the techniques he'd taught Connie for surviving a serial killer. All he could do now was try to keep Hat and Dog talking and maybe get his hands on Morales's gun.

"A Crow," Jazz said. "Is that what you guys call yourselves?" He gestured to Belsamo. "We called you Hat and Dog, but—"

Dog took a step back, but—and this impressed Jazz—kept talking. "You're ruining the game," he said. "They'll catch us now. *Both* of us."

"No. I'm not ruining anything. And they don't even suspect me."

And he pulled the trigger before even finishing the sentence. Belsamo gasped and grabbed at his chest as though he could snatch the bullet out before it could do any damage, but Hershey pulled the trigger again and this time a bright disc of red blossomed on Belsamo's left cheek.

An instant later—*less* than an instant later—blood and what appeared to be teeth gouted out of Belsamo's mouth. Dog collapsed to the floor, one hand pawing at his chest, the other grasping at his ruined face.

Jazz thought maybe he'd passed out for a second. Just a second. A wave of giddiness passed over him. The expression on Belsamo's face was priceless—shock and horror intermingled with a kind of guileless reproach, as though he'd just been slapped at a fancy dinner party.

The Dog Killer heaved out one last, heavy breath and went still, propped up against the workbench.

One down, Jazz thought, giggling inside. *One down and one to go!*

Get a grip, Jasper Francis. It was suddenly G. William's voice in his head, after so many years of Billy. *Think fast, kiddo, and figure out what you can tell this prick that'll make him let you go. You got a pretty little girlfriend back home and a best friend and some folks in the sheriff's department who'll miss you if it all ends here.*

492

He minced along the concrete floor. Another inch closer to Morales... and he couldn't help it. The pain was too much. A squeak of agony popped from his lips like a bubble.

Hershey turned to him, aiming the gun. "Really—do you think I'm stupid? Stop moving toward her gun. I will shoot you in the face and eat your eyeballs one at a time while you die."

Right. Got it. Keep him talking, Jazz. If he's talking, he's not killing.

"The game's over, right? So what did you win? What will Ugly J give you?"

A stab in the dark. But he was hoping to get a reaction like the Impressionist's. Instead, he got a shrug. "I've been training for this my whole life," Hershey said, without a hint of braggadocio or self-satisfaction. It was just a statement of fact.

"Me, too," Jazz said. *See, man, we're like brothers. Don't shoot me again.*

Hat cracked the smallest of smiles. "But my life is longer than yours."

He took the eyes. He's the one who wanted the eyes.

And then Hershey knelt down by Morales.

"Don't you want her eyes?" Jazz heard himself say. "Aren't you going to take them?" He tried to make it sound as appetizing, as sensual as possible, but somewhere between the subtle manipulation in his head and the actual words coming out, they became desperate and frightened. He couldn't help it. For the first time in his life, he was absolutely terrified. All he could do was try to manipulate this freak into mutilating Morales's body. That was his only chance. Because then the guy would put down the gun. And then maybe Jazz could—

"There are a lot of eyeballs in the world," Hershey said. "*Everyone* has them."

I just want to live. Please. I just want to live. I don't know if that makes me normal or if that makes me as bad as these guys, but either way, that's what I want.

Hershey patted down Morales quickly, keeping the small gun aimed at Jazz. His other hand seemed to want to linger on her, but evidently found no pleasure in the flat planes of her bulletproof vest.

To Jazz's terror and anguish, Hershey soon came up with Morales's service weapon.

Keep him talking. Jazz blinked rapidly, clearing his eyes again. They kept clouding over. He couldn't afford to sink into unconsciousness. He had to stay awake. Couldn't let shock claim him. He would keep *himself* talking, even if Hershey shot his foot off next.

"If the game is over," Jazz said, now beginning to shiver, "then where do you go to be crowned as winner?" He was guessing wildly now, kicking under the covers in the throes of a nightmare, hoping to knock away one of the dread dream beasties threatening him. He threw out another guess: "The Crow King. Billy's the Crow King, right?"

Hat sighed, relaxing a bit for the first time. "Billy? No. The Crow King is much, much worse than Billy."

Another desperate gamble: "What about Ugly J? What will Ugly J think of all this?"

Hat favored him with a mildly baffled expression. "Ugly J will be happy that the game is over, I suppose." He flicked the end of the gun at Dog, and Jazz tensed. But the gun pointed back at him right away; no chance to dive at Hat. "This one was poor competition. And a pervert, to boot. Can you imagine cutting off a man's special part? And *keeping* it?"

Yeah, that's over the line. Raping women and taking their eyeballs is completely normal, though.

"He was so sloppy," Hat went on. "Leaving his little 'homages' to Ugly J here and there...that's why he had to go. That's why he couldn't win the game. That's why there was never any chance he could *ever* win the game. It's one thing to...We had to send pictures, you understand. To prove we'd done it. But that was all. Actually marking his territory like that...he *was* a dog. A mongrel. It was always destined to be me."

"He tempered you," Jazz said. "Like you said before. He upped the ante and you had to respond in kind. It was a test, to see if you could keep up. He cuts off a penis, you have to cut off a penis."

Hat shuddered, but the gun remained steady. "It disgusted me, having to touch them *there*. But such are the rules of the game. Well, *were* the rules. This time."

Jazz perked up. "This time?" It spilled out before he could help himself.

Hat's expression changed for the first time, into an almost beatific smile. "The game is ancient. The game goes on forever. I would explain further, but you have no need for hearing."

He's gonna shoot me. He's totally gonna shoot me. Jazz tensed, ready to roll to one side. Anything to give himself an advantage. "But I want to learn!" he protested, buying time. "I want to hear more!"

"Enough talk," Hat said. "It's time for me to go. To claim my reward and move on." He stepped into the unit and took the battery-powered lantern. If Jazz hadn't been shot, he could have run like hell or tackled the guy. But right now all he could do was stare at the...

At the ceiling...

Looking straight up, he realized that he might be seeing his salvation. Maybe.

He had to time it just right.

Still shivering, his body definitely sinking into shock, Jazz forced himself into a sitting position.

Hershey walked past with the lantern, the only source of light in the storage unit. He was going to kill Jazz and leave the bodies here, and who knew when they would be found?

With an agonized shriek of pain, Jazz levered himself up from the floor, pushing off with his hands. He tried to keep weight off his left side, but it was impossible, and a fresh wave of hell erupted along that side of his body as he reached out for the rope he'd noticed hanging from the ceiling. Hershey, distracted for a moment, almost dropped the lantern. Raised the gun.

Pulled the trigger.

Just an instant too late.

Jazz had grabbed the rope and pulled with all his might, collapsing to the floor again to add his body weight to the tug he hoped would save his life. The corrugated steel door to unit 83F came crashing down between him and Hershey lightning-fast. It was so loud that Jazz didn't hear the sound of the gun going off again, but in the last instant of light before the door slammed down, he saw tiny dimples erupt in its steelhide.

Despite the pain plastered to his side like lava, Jazz found the strength to throw himself at the door. There was a metal lip inside the unit where the door met the floor and Jazz pressed down on it and leaned into it. Outside, Hershey cursed and pulled at the door, trying to raise it again, but Jazz refused to budge, holding it down.

No way. No way in hell. You are not *getting in here. Not a chance. At least now there's a door between that gun and me.*

Cold comfort, as the blackness surged around him.

Finally, Hershey stopped tugging at the door. Even though every muscle and nerve in his body begged Jazz to relax, he couldn't. He knew that it would be a trick, that as soon as he let up, Hershey would fling the door back up and open fire.

Still, the silence on the other side of the door was maddening. Was Hershey even still out there? Had he left?

That's what he wants you to think. And then you open up the door and the last thing you see is the barrel of Morales's gun.

Another wave of pain slammed at Jazz, bringing with it nausea. He realized someone was laughing and then realized that that person was him.

"There's nothing funny about your situation," Hershey said from outside.

Jazz agreed, but couldn't stop giggling for some reason. "Do you know who I am?" he asked. "Do you have any idea what my father—"

"I know exactly who you are. You're Jasper Dent. Crowson. And I don't care. You're not a part of the game. The dog creature was. Now he's lost. The whoreslut was because all whoresluts are."

Jazz closed his eyes. There was no light in the unit, so there was nothing to see, anyway. Then he forced them back open. *Keep them open. Keep looking. You're alive as long as you're looking.*

It was a standoff. For now. Jazz couldn't get out and Hershey couldn't get in. How long would that last? How long before Hershey decided to switch guns and just perforate the whole door—and Jazz—with the bigger-caliber gun? How long before—

Just then, he heard something scratching at the door.

What is—

And a tiny *click!*

No more standoff. He suddenly knew exactly what Hat planned to do to him.

Oh, hell *no. This guy is* not *going to Cask of Amontillado me. No way.*

"What are you doing?" He tried to keep the panic out of his voice, but he didn't do a very good job. The pain, the shock—they wrecked all his control, all his skills built up over a lifetime.

"I'll be back when you're more compliant," Hershey said through the door. "Or maybe I'll just come back when you're dead. Or maybe I'll just leave you here forever. Whichever. It no longer matters."

Jazz pounded at the door. It rattled and shook, but stayed in place. Hershey had locked him in. Locked him in the darkness with nothing but two corpses for company and a bullet wound that was slowly bleeding the life from him.

"Maybe we can make some kind of deal—" Jazz began, though what kind eluded him.

"No deals," Hershey said. "You die. I live. Simple as that."

"You left the message for me!" Jazz cried. "You were the one who welcomed me to the game! That was a Hat kill. You can't just—"

"I was *told* to do that. I was just following the rules."

A killer who followed the rules. Now Jazz had heard everything. He reached down to probe his leg, carefully feeling along as the pain increased.

He found a hole in his jeans.

And one in his thigh.

Still bleeding. Of course. All this moving around. Stupid.

Grimacing, he stuck his thumb in the bullet hole.

The sudden, new variety of pain jolted him like lightning. And in the same instant, his mind cleared and inspiration struck. The second workbench! This unit was divided in two—Hat and Dog shared it. A common space for their tools and trophies. He remembered the night—almost five years ago now—when Billy had realized that G. William was onto him, that the police would be at the Dent house within the hour.

Get into the rumpus room, he'd shouted to Jazz. *Gather up my trophies and run to Gramma's house. Do it now!*

Jazz thought of that second bench. That second set of pristine murder tools. And that jar of eyeballs.

"You wouldn't leave without your"—*Come on! What does he call them? Tools or toys? Trophies or mementos?*—"things, would you?"

In the silence that followed, he thought maybe he'd done it. He'd found Hershey's psychological weak spot, his most crucial vulnerability, and had gained valuable leverage.

But then Hershey just laughed. It was the most terrifying thing Jazz could imagine in that moment.

"There's always more out there," Hershey said. "It's time to clear the decks. Time to start over. You can have my old toys. There's a world full of new ones waiting for me."

"The new ones are never as good! You'll miss these!" Jazz cried desperately. "You'll think back to one of them and you'll wish you had..."

He drifted off. Out of breath, for one thing. For another...

He'd expected a last word from Hershey. Something insane or unintelligible. But as he put an ear to the door he heard only footfalls.

Receding.

Silence greeted him, silence stretched out to long moments. Silence and darkness.

He thought it possible that he'd passed out again. He felt into his pocket for his cell phone. He would call Hughes. Hughes would come get him. And then...and then they could chase down Duncan Hershey. The task force already had a nice, thick dossier on him. There were only so many places for him to run to.

The cell phone screen read NO SIGNAL.

Of course. He was in a massive structure of concrete and steel and aluminum, with eight stories above him. If his cell wouldn't work in a subway, it definitely wouldn't work here, either.

Jazz didn't panic, but he did allow himself to scream and pound on the door and hollow for help. He did it for roughly a minute, which is a long time to scream at the top of your lungs and beat your hands against a metal door, especially when shot.

He slumped against the door, sweat-drenched. He'd used up way too much energy on that temper tantrum.

No one came.

No one would *be* coming. Jazz did some quick math. His most conservative estimate was that there were close to three thousand storage units in this building alone. And given the twisty, narrow corridors, with their sound-killing corners, someone would probably have to come to one of the four or five units in this stretch of hallway in order to hear him.

Odds of five out of three thousand. Not the worst odds in the world, but when would someone come to their storage unit? Jazz didn't know what it was like in New York, but in Lobo's Nod, people only got storage units for stuff they didn't really need, but couldn't be bothered to get rid of. Stuff they might someday want, but didn't really think about all that often.

Maybe a security guard—

Yeah. Right. Jazz thought of the man he'd gulled to get in

in the first place. He could picture that fat-ass taking the elevator to each floor, poking his head out, saying "Good enough," and calling it a night.

He wondered when the smell of Dog's body and Morales's and his own rotting corpse would finally permeate into some part of the building where someone would notice it.

He wondered if he would bleed to death first...or freeze to death in an unheated storage unit in the middle of winter?

At least whoever Dog planned on killing tonight is safe, he thought.

And then: *And Connie. At least Connie is safe.*

CHAPTER 58

Someone had propped open the front door to the building tagged with her name, so Connie was able to go right in.

She had three clues to Mr. Auto-Tune already. She had a bell. A gun. She had Eliot Ness.

Somewhere in this building, there were more clues. There had to be.

Out of the cold rain, she paused for a moment to shake off the chill. A dim overhead light barely illuminated the entryway.

Now, before you go chasing waterfalls, do something smart.

She composed a quick text to Howie, sending him the address of the building. As an afterthought, she also included *bell, guns, Eliot Ness?* just in case it meant anything to him. She resisted the urge to send the same text to Jazz. With any luck, she would tell him all of this and more in person soon enough.

Exploring for any sort of hint as to what to do next, she

noticed that there was a missing mailbox on the wall—between the little doors for 2A and 2C, there was a gap. The mailbox door had been ripped off, the space filled with trash.

No mailbox meant no one living in that apartment. Right? And what better place to hide the next clue than in an abandoned apartment.

She heaved her duffel up a flight of stairs that smelled of urine and stale beer. Something crunched underfoot at one point and it took all her willpower *not* to look down. She didn't want to see. Fortunately, the lighting in the stairwell was so bad that she wouldn't have been able to tell what it was, anyway.

The second floor was just as poorly lit. Her pounding heart warned her away, but she told herself she'd come this far. She could check out 2B and then get the hell out of here.

TV shows echoed in the hall from 2A as she walked past.

The door to 2B was closed. She turned the knob and it moved freely. Then she jerked away, thinking twice. She should knock first. Just in case.

But there could be squatters in there. Homeless people. Drug dealers.

She knocked anyway.

To her surprise, the door opened right away, and Connie's breath fled from her.

"Well now," Billy Dent drawled, "ain't you just the sweetest piece of chocolate I ever seen."

Connie didn't even have time to gasp, much less scream.

Part Five

Game Over

CHAPTER 59

Jazz kicked off his shoes and stuck the tongue of one of them in his mouth. He needed something to bite down on as he peeled off his jeans.

His blood had matted around the wound, so pulling off his pants tugged the flesh, stretching it around the wound and causing more blood to well up. Red spots danced and capered before his eyes; he bit down hard, groaning into his own clenched teeth.

After a wave of dizziness and nausea passed—and then another...and another—he used the bright screen of his phone to examine his leg in the dark.

The bullet hole itself was almost comically small and nearly perfectly round. *Let's hear it for small calibers*, he thought.

There was nothing small about the pain, though. Or the blood.

He examined his thigh carefully, probing with his fingers where he couldn't see.

No exit wound.

The bullet was still in there.

I have to be ready....Hat could come back. He could come back and unlock the door and shoot me dead this time....

He stripped off his shirt and tied it tightly around his thigh, covering the wound. It would have to do as a bandage for now.

Have to be ready...

He leaned against the door and managed to work himself to a standing position. He found that he could hold the slightest bit of weight on his left leg if he only used his heel, so he limped around that way, gasping a little each time that left foot touched the ground.

Hat wasn't an idiot. For all his disinterest in Billy (and Jazz had never imagined the day when he would meet a serial killer who wasn't afraid of Billy—what did it mean?), Hat had allowed Billy to control him for purposes of the game. And Billy had done so, willingly. Billy didn't truck with morons. Thus and so: Hat wasn't stupid.

Which meant that there would be absolutely nothing on Hat's or Dog's workbench that could help Jazz escape or signal for rescue. Hat wouldn't have locked him in here if he'd thought for a moment that Jazz could get out. Still...

Gotta make the effort. What else am I going to go? Put my head down for a nap and just die of apathy?

"That's not how a Crow dies," Jazz said for no particular reason.

He used the phone's light to make his way to Hat's workbench. The eyeballs in the jar stared at him, bobbing gently.

Hat's workbench also had every sort of cutting, gouging, and slicing implement known to man. It had different varieties of tape. It had ropes, and cloth for gags. A grapefruit spoon (*I knew it*). It had—in a drawer—a collection of pins, buttons, and bits of cloth that Jazz knew had come from Hat's victims.

His trophies. Stuff that wouldn't necessarily be missed. Or that could be explained away.

Billy would have...not *liked* but rather *approved of* Hat. Jazz realized now that his father had sent Hat here specifically to kill Dog. Kill him in the storage unit and leave him here. It would take months if not years for someone to find him, along with the evidence tying Belsamo and Belsamo alone to the Hat-Dog murders. The gunshot was tough to explain, of course, but he was sure that hadn't been intended. Hat's original plan had probably involved knocking Dog out and injecting him with something that would simulate a heart attack. Then leave him with the evidence. When he'd shot Morales, though, the plan had changed. And Hat—for all his bluster and claims to filling the Grand Canyon with the dead—didn't have the creativity to roll with the punches.

Or maybe he just didn't care in this instance. Billy certainly saw something in Hat, and that was enough to spike Jazz's concern and respect for Duncan Hershey.

Billy played favorites. Or maybe he just got bored of the game. Either one makes sense.

Jazz moved slowly to the other workbench. Dog's tools were lined up neatly and precisely. His murders may have been, as Hat put it, sloppy, but his workspace, like his apartment, was pristine.

The two benches were nearly identical. Of course. In Monopoly, each player begins with the same amount of money. So Billy ruled on what tools and toys each player got at the beginning. And it guaranteed that the cops would believe it was one guy, since the brand of tape, the type of rope, the kind of blade would always be the same. Diabolical and almost admirable. In that oh-so-special sociopathic way Billy had.

A job worth doin's a job worth doin' well, Jasper.

There were bottles of detergent, bleach, and filtered water stacked in a corner. Jazz figured the water would keep him alive for a couple of weeks, but after that, starvation would kill him quite handily.

Assuming Hat doesn't come back. Assuming I don't die of blood loss. Or some kind of infection.

Leaning against the bench, Jazz winced and gasped at a new bolt of pain from his leg. He thought he might be able to get the bullet out. There was a chance. The fact that he was still thinking was a good sign. The fact that he could still breathe on his own. He wasn't in shock after all. He was just stunned by what had happened, ramped up on insane amounts of adrenaline. And now he was coming down.

Which, oddly, made him want to sleep.

No. Don't sleep. Right now, sleep equals death.

And if I don't want to let it get to that point...there's

always the bleach. Drink it down and end it all on my terms.

Stop being so defeatist!

Defeatist? Try realistic. There's nothing in here that will help me get out. No way to get through that door. No way to get through the walls. Sure as hell no way to open that lock from the inside.

You're contemplating suicide already? You've been in here all of ten minutes.

He decided that the colloquy in his mind was not a good idea, so he quashed it.

Of course, these two freaks didn't have a single narcotic or Band-Aid between them. They didn't even have antibacterial soap. Just water and detergent and bleach.

And plenty of knives.

All right, let's get this going.

He gathered a few things, then slid back to a sitting position at Dog's bench, right next to the killer's body. The angle of Dog's shoulder made a perfect place to put his cell phone so that the light stayed pointed at his left leg, jutting stiffly out in front of him.

Let's see what we've got here...blood flow is consistent, but not spurting....

Now when you go cuttin' up legs, Billy said from somewhere in the past, *you watch out for that there femoral artery up in the thigh. He's a big sumbitch, and you so much as nick him, you'll know it.*

Thanks, Dear Old Dad. The anatomy lessons are helpful.

The fact that the blood was dark, not bright, plus the fact

that it wasn't gushing told him that the bullet had avoided the femoral and most of its bigger branches. Which was a damn good thing. The fact that he was able to move the leg at all told him that the femur was probably still intact. The bullet hadn't shattered or cracked his bones; it was lodged somewhere in the meat of his leg.

He spilled a little bleach on the small knife he'd borrowed from Dog's workbench. It had a vaguely medical air about it, sort of scalpel-ish, and Jazz knew that Dog had used it to make the preliminary incisions when gutting his victims. Well, if it was possible to redeem a medical instrument, he was about to try.

He hoped the bleach would kill any random germs floating around on the knife. He poured some water on his leg to clear the field of operation for himself. More blood immediately welled up from the bullet hole, but he had a better view of it now.

Okay. Okay. You can do this, Jazz. You can do this. You've seen this on TV. You make a—what's it called—you make a lateral cut. You just cut right across the hole. Open things up a little 'cause you need a hole bigger than the bullet in order to find the bullet. Then you dig out the slug and you're done. Piece of cake, right?

But first...bleach. Right on the wound. To clean it. Just to be safe.

A burst of excruciating pain that was solar in its heat and scope burst from his leg and he actually screamed out loud, "Oh, Jesus Christ!" at the top of his lungs, and wept uncontrollably. He shook, the knife vibrating in his hand, and he had to grab his left leg with his hand to keep it from jittering out of control. The pain roared through him and he sobbed without self-consciousness, cried like a little boy as the bright, hot rage of agony slowly—over an infinity, it seemed—dulled to a throbbing ache.

He wiped his eyes and used the edge of his bloody shirt to blow the snot from his nose. In the dim light of the cell phone, his leg looked grayish, with splotches of blood and what appeared to be fizzing bubbles of bleach. He splashed a little water to clear the field again, and then—before he could think about it any further—he brought the knife down on his leg and he

cutting through

Oh, no.

See, Jasper, Billy said, guiding his hand in the past, *it's just like*

No. No.

His hand jerked and new pain lanced up his leg. Blood welled up in the trench he'd carved. But he was lost in his own memory, in his own past.

a knife in the sink and then

And then in my hand.

just like cutting chicken—

And it was. It was, he realized. Billy had been right, all those years ago.

knife in the sink, knife in your hand

Cutting his own flesh. Felt just like the dream and felt just like cutting chicken and

No no no no no no no

With a cry, he flung the knife away from himself; it landed in a dark corner, a ghostly clatter of chains in the haunted house the storage unit had become.

He couldn't do it.

He couldn't complete the cut.

Not while Billy echoed in him, laughing, encouraging.

I cut someone. As a kid. It's not just a dream. It was never just a dream. He actually made me do it. Who? Who did I cut? What did he make me do?

He stared at his leg. Fortunately, the cut he'd made was shallow. Especially compared to the hole the bullet had punched into him.

Snap out of it, Jazz. You didn't go into shock before. Don't do it now.

He ripped the sleeve off his shirt and wrapped it around the bullet hole. Then, to be safe, he twined a length of duct tape over it, then again. A crude bandage, but better than nothing.

He would just have to hope that it would be good enough. That it would stem the blood loss. That infection wouldn't set in from the bullet. That he wouldn't lose the leg.

You're assuming you'll still be alive to miss it, Jasper.

Dog's laptop bag lay on the floor next to him. Jazz went through it, finding another small knife, some rags, latex gloves... and a big butcher knife.

Come to Papa, he thought, hefting it. It felt good in his hands. If Hat came back, Jazz would at least give him a scar for his troubles.

There was no longer blood streaming down his leg, but his

thigh still throbbed and complained. Jazz had checked the entire unit, but hadn't found any sort of painkiller. He had watched Morales get ready for this little excursion into hell—he knew she didn't have anything on her that would help. Her purse—probably stocked with all kinds of goodies—was out in the car. Might as well be on the moon.

Was there anything he'd missed? Anything in the unit that he hadn't explored? *Yeah. Yeah, there's one thing.*

Jazz turned to Dog's body. He wasn't squeamish about touching a dead body. He'd touched plenty of them, many in worse shape than Dog's. Hat's shots had left small holes in Dog's body. Blood glistened in the light from the cell phone, no longer pumping and flowing, now tracery rivulets staining Dog's coat and shirt. Jazz spent a moment gazing into Dog's vacant eyes and didn't bother closing them.

Dog had collapsed against the workbench and still leaned partly upright. Jazz eased the body onto its back on the floor. Rigor mortis hadn't started yet—and even when it did in ten or fifteen minutes, it would start with the small muscles—so the body was still pliant and easy to maneuver. A slick of blood welled out from an exit wound, pumped along by the motion of the body. Jazz wrinkled his nose. It bothered him more for the mess than anything else.

Hat knew there was nothing in here that could help me escape, but he couldn't know if Dog brought anything new in. At this point, all I'm hoping for is a friggin' aspirin.

He frisked the body, then went pocket-diving.

Come on, Oliver. Tell me you get migraines and you carry a bottle of Advil everywhere you go.

No wallet or ID, of course. *Never carry any of that non-sense when you're prospecting*, Billy had told him. *You can always claim you lost it or got mugged, if you have to.*

A key ring, including—Jazz surmised—the key to the padlock that locked unit 83F. Nice to have. Even nicer if he had a way to reach the lock.

Some scraps of paper, covered in illegible scrawl. No doubt Dog's prospecting notes, scribbled down while stalking his next victim.

Really? No aspirin? Nothing? The crazy people talking in your head never give you a headache?

Last thing he found: a cell phone.

A phone with as much signal strength as Jazz's, which was to say none.

Jazz sat on the cold concrete floor, his back against Dog's workbench. He propped his leg up on Dog's corpse, keeping it elevated in an effort to prevent further blood loss.

There was nothing here and no way out and no way to stop the insistent, persistent ache from his leg, the pain that reminded him that he could die of infection, that he could end up an amputee, that—

Stay calm. You have water. You have two cell phones now. You just doubled your time to find a signal.

Oh, let's throw a party, then! You bring the water; I'll bring the bleach.

He opened Dog's cheap, disposable cell. Yeah, no signal.

But there was a little envelope icon. A message. *Must have come through before Dog came inside and lost his signal.*

Jazz opened the message. It was a photo.

Why are you here? he had asked Billy. *Who did you come to New York to find?*

Oh. My. God.

And Billy had said, *I'm gonna tell ol' Doggy. I'm gonna let him in on the secret. And then you can ask him.*

And Billy *had* told Dog. Had told him with a thousand words, with one photo that screamed at Jazz's eyeballs.

It had to be a trick of the light. Or, rather, of the darkness. Or his vision, gone bleary and illusionary from pain.

I've already passed out. I'm dreaming. This is all a dream as I lay dying.

He deliberately squeezed his leg just below the bullet wound and the pain jolted him into full wakefulness.

If there had been any doubt, the pain sluiced it away. He was awake. Conscious. Fully aware.

And he knew this woman. She was older, but he knew her.

On Dog's phone, a photo sent—Jazz knew—by Billy.

A photo of his mother.

She was *alive*.

Acknowledgments

Per usual, I have to start by thanking everyone at Little, Brown for making *Game* happen: Alvina Ling (editor extraordinaire), Bethany Strout (her thoroughly desensitized assistant), Megan Tingley, Victoria Stapleton, Melanie Chang, Jessica Bromberg, Andrew Smith, Zoe Luderitz, JoAnna Kremer, Barbara Bakowski, Alison Impey, Amy Habayeb, Kristin Dulaney, and those whose names I have unforgivably neglected to mention here. Thank you, one and all!

Then there is my agent, Kathy Anderson, and everyone at Anderson Literary, as well as the fine folks at Jody Hotchkiss and Associates.

I also have to thank my early readers: Morgan Baden, the uncanny Libba Bray, and Eric Lyga (who also bought me a Monopoly set—thanks, bro). Special thanks, too, to Darryl Aiken-Afam.

And now...the experts! Dr. Deborah Mogelof once again rode to my rescue with medical advice, promptly and clinically given, no matter how weird or distasteful the question.

Detective Paul Grudzinski of the NYPD was instrumental in matters pertaining to the police in Brooklyn, and Philip Edney and Special Agent Joseph Lewis of the FBI were invaluable in helping me figure out aspects of the Bureau. As always, when it comes to medical and legal matters, anything I got right is thanks to them; anything I got wrong is my own damn fault.